Praise for *White Heat*

"She weaves a strong strand of whodunit into a broader story about life in a twenty-first-century community on Canada's Ellesmere Island. The plot is wholly satisfying, and McGrath's portrait of a culture that uneasily blends yesterday and today is engrossing on its own merits. The Arctic is a big place—big enough, one hopes, for Edie Kiglatuk to find another mystery that needs solving between warm bowls of seal blood soup fresh from the microwave."
—Associated Press

"This debut novel encompasses the hard, otherworldly beauty of the far north and the rapaciousness of energy moguls determined to exploit the area's natural resources. . . . [McGrath] skillfully describes the destabilizing effects of global warming on both the landscape and the lives of the people settled there."
—*The New Yorker*

"Author McGrath's sense of location is spot on; her characters are believable, sympathetic, and complex. No surprise for an author of her caliber: In an earlier incarnation (as Melanie McGrath) she won the John Llewellyn Rhys Prize for best British writer under thirty-five."
—*BookPage*

"*White Heat* is a blazing star of a thriller: vivid, tightly sprung, and satisfying on all levels. Encountering Edie Kiglatuk, the toughest, smartest Arctic heroine since Miss Smilla, left me with that rare feeling of privilege you get on meeting extraordinary people in real life. A huge achievement."
—Liz Jensen, author of *The Rapture*

"Award-winning British journalist McGrath shares a wealth of knowledge about life in the High Arctic that is central to her story. Well written and researched, her excellent adventure murder mystery will hold readers' attention until the last page."
—*Library Journal*

"A solid thriller . . . A picture soon emerges that includes a fight for precious natural resources and secrets that stretch back generations. McGrath captures the frigid landscape beautifully, and her heroine personifies the tension between the Inuit and qalunaat ways of life."
—*Publishers Weekly*

"M. J. McGrath's *White Heat* pulls you along like a steel cable, inexorably welding you to the characters and a place that you'll never forget."
—Craig Johnson, *New York Times* bestselling author of *The Cold Dish* and *Hell Is Empty*

"A gripping crime novel in which the main character never runs (sweating leads to hypothermia), chews fermented walrus gut, and builds an emergency snowhouse with the right kind of three-layered snow in a matter of hours . . . [A] deft story of family loyalty and clashing cultures . . . charging forward to an unexpected, satisfying, and chilling conclusion." —*New York Journal of Books*

"McGrath has written a mystery . . . reminiscent of Tony Hillerman's culture-clash novels. The language is beautiful, especially the descriptions of the Inuit people, living in 'a place littered with bones, with spirits, with reminders of the past . . . surrounded by our stories.' Detailed in her knowledge of setting, McGrath vividly invokes the frozen land, and her portrayals of the rugged people who cherish its beauty and bounty, especially Edie and Derek, ring true. A promising first installment in an upcoming series of arctic adventures." —*Kirkus Reviews*

"M. J. McGrath's *White Heat* is a tour de force, a book with a stunning grip on all the elements that make a mystery story great. The characters are unique and profoundly human, the plot wonderfully labyrinthine, and the sense of place beautifully—chillingly—evoked. I challenge any reader to pick up this marvelous novel and not be completely mesmerized." —William Kent Kreuger, author of *Vermilion Drift*

"With a poet's confidence McGrath makes an unforgiving Arctic landscape and then gives us a smart and strong yet vulnerable survivor in Edie Kiglatuk. You root for Edie. You can't do otherwise. In her risk-all pursuit of truth resides the best in all of us."
—Kirk Russell, author of *Redback*

"Once in a blue moon a book comes along that exposes the world to us in a new light, makes us question everything: who we are, what we think we know, our beliefs and values, even the nature and purpose of our existence. *White Heat* is such a book. Seek it out and bask in it."
—James Thompson, author of *Lucifer's Tears*

A PENGUIN MYSTERY

WHITE HEAT

M. J. McGrath is an award-winning journalist and the author of *The Long Exile: A Tale of Inuit Betrayal*. She was awarded the Mail on Sunday/John Llewellyn Rhys Prize for best British writer under thirty-five and currently lives in London. Her second novel featuring Edie Kiglatuk, *The Boy in the Snow*, will be published by Viking in November 2012.

M. J. McGrath

White Heat

PENGUIN BOOKS

PENGUIN BOOKS
Published by the Penguin Group
Penguin Group (USA) Inc., 375 Hudson Street, New York, New York 10014, U.S.A.
Penguin Group (Canada), 90 Eglinton Avenue East, Suite 700, Toronto,
Ontario, Canada M4P 2Y3 (a division of Pearson Penguin Canada Inc.)
Penguin Books Ltd, 80 Strand, London WC2R 0RL, England
Penguin Ireland, 25 St. Stephen's Green, Dublin 2, Ireland (a division of Penguin Books Ltd)
Penguin Books Australia Ltd, 250 Camberwell Road, Camberwell,
Victoria 3124, Australia (a division of Pearson Australia Group Pty Ltd)
Penguin Books India Pvt Ltd, 11 Community Centre, Panchsheel Park, New Delhi – 110 017, India
Penguin Group (NZ), 67 Apollo Drive, Rosedale, Auckland 0632,
New Zealand (a division of Pearson New Zealand Ltd)
Penguin Books (South Africa) (Pty) Ltd, 24 Sturdee Avenue,
Rosebank, Johannesburg 2196, South Africa

Penguin Books Ltd, Registered Offices:
80 Strand, London WC2R 0RL, England

First published in Great Britain by Mantle, an imprint of Pan Macmillan 2011
First published in the United States of America by Viking Penguin,
a member of Penguin Group (USA) Inc. 2011
Published in Penguin Books 2012

3 5 7 9 10 8 6 4 2

Publisher's Note
This is a work of fiction. Names, characters, places, and incidents either are the product of the author's imagination or are used fictitiously, and any resemblance to actual persons, living or dead, business establishments, events, or locales is entirely coincidental.

THE LIBRARY OF CONGRESS HAS CATALOGED THE HARDCOVER EDITION AS FOLLOWS:
McGrath, M. J.
White heat : a novel / M.J. McGrath.
p. cm.
ISBN 978-0-670-02248-9 (hc.)
ISBN 978-0-14-312096-4 (pbk.)
1. Arctic regions—Fiction. 2. Canada, Northern—Fiction. 3. Inuit—Canada—Fiction.
4. Women hunting guides—Fiction. 5. Murder—Investigation—Fiction. 6. Natural resources—Arctic regions—Fiction. 7. Arctic regions—Foreign relations—Fiction. I. Title.
PR6113.C4775W55 2011
823'.92—dc22
2011013208

Printed in the United States of America

For Simon Booker

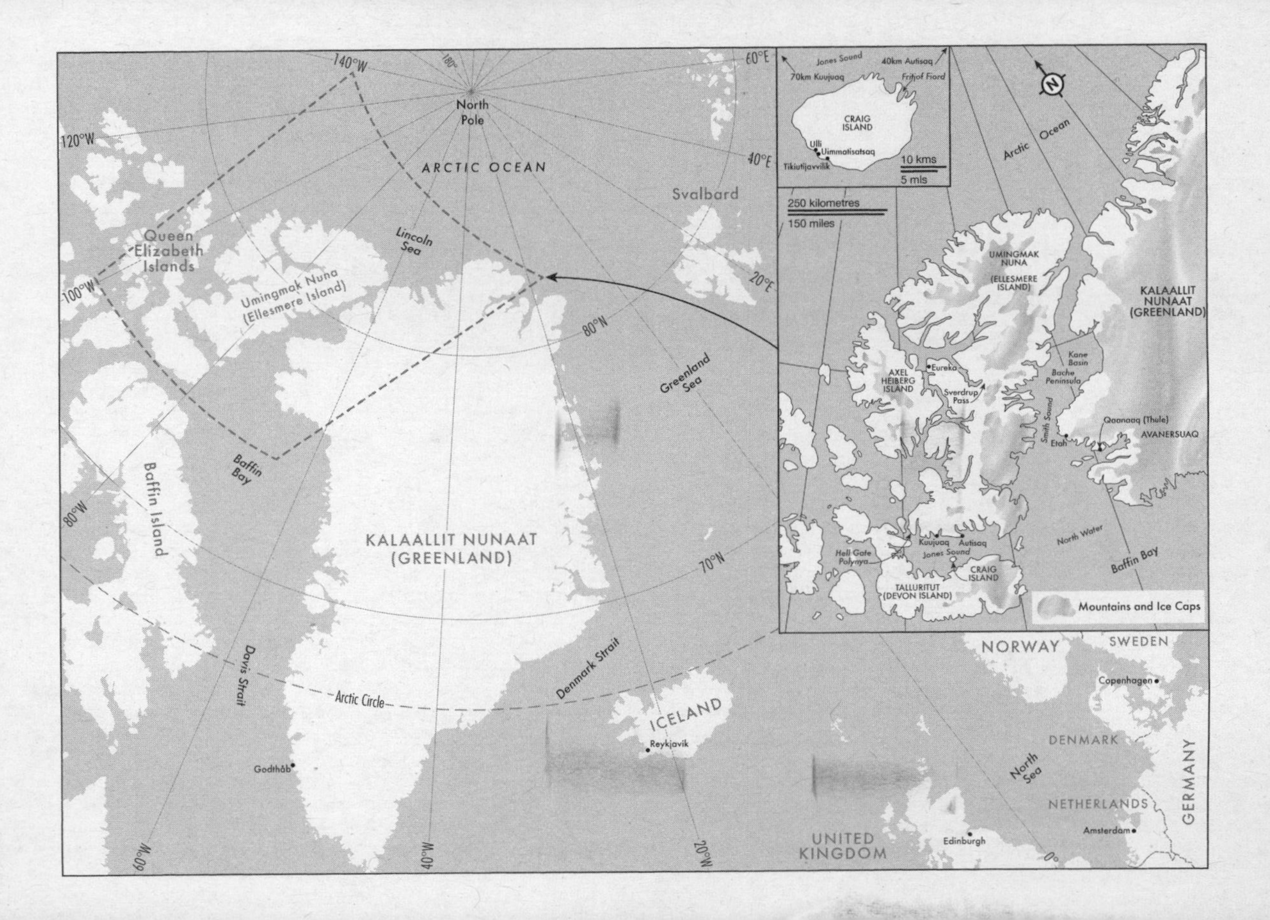

140°W
180°
North Pole
60°E
120°W
ARCTIC OCEAN
40°E
Svalbard
Queen Elizabeth Islands
Lincoln Sea
100°W
Umingmak Nuna (Ellesmere Island)
20°E
80°N
Greenland Sea
Baffin Bay
Baffin Island
80°W
KALAALLIT NUNAAT (GREENLAND)
70°N
Davis Strait
Denmark Strait
Arctic Circle
ICELAND
Reykjavik
Godthåb
60°W
40°W
20°W
UNITED KINGDOM
Edinburgh
North Sea
0°
NORWAY
SWEDEN
Copenhagen
DENMARK
NETHERLANDS
Amsterdam
GERMANY
Jones Sound
40km Autisaq
70km Kuujuaq
Fritjof Fiord
CRAIG ISLAND
Ulli
Uimmatisatsaq
Tikiutijavvilik
10 kms
5 mls
250 kilometres
150 miles
Arctic Ocean
UMINGMAK NUNA (ELLESMERE ISLAND)
KALAALLIT NUNAAT (GREENLAND)
Kane Basin
Bache Peninsula
AXEL HEIBERG ISLAND
Eureka
Sverdrup Pass
Smith Sound
Qaanaaq (Thule)
AVANERSUAQ
Etah
North Water
Baffin Bay
Hell Gate Polynya
Kuujuaq
Autisaq
Jones Sound
CRAIG ISLAND
TALLURITUT (DEVON ISLAND)
Mountains and Ice Caps

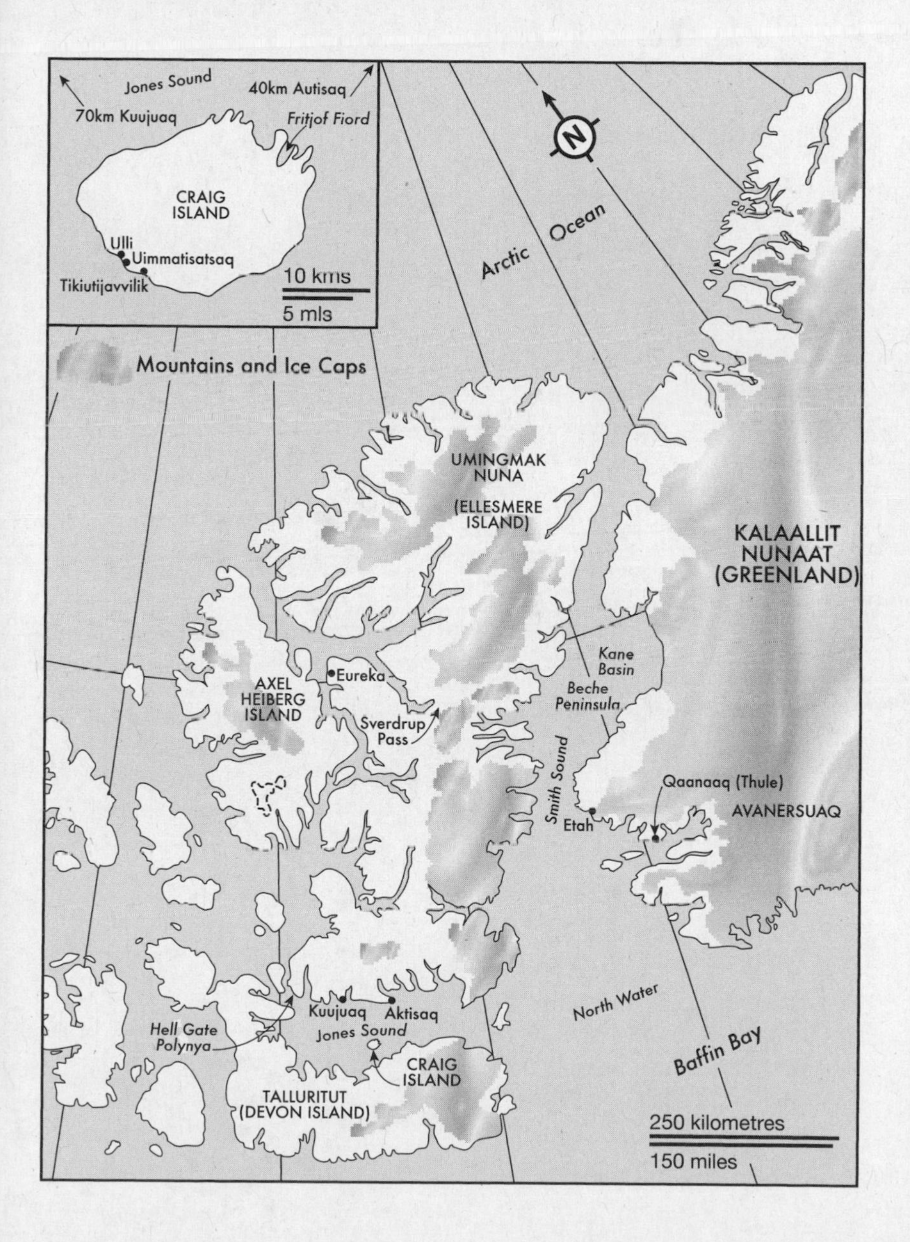

Jones Sound
70km Kuujuaq
40km Autisaq
Fritjof Fiord
CRAIG ISLAND
Ulli
Uimmatisatsaq
Tikiutijavvilik
10 kms
5 mls
Arctic Ocean
Mountains and Ice Caps
UMINGMAK NUNA (ELLESMERE ISLAND)
KALAALLIT NUNAAT (GREENLAND)
Kane Basin
Beche Peninsula
Eureka
AXEL HEIBERG ISLAND
Sverdrup Pass
Smith Sound
Qaanaaq (Thule)
AVANERSUAQ
Etah
North Water
Baffin Bay
Kuujuaq
Aktisaq
Hell Gate Polynya
Jones Sound
CRAIG ISLAND
TALLURITUT (DEVON ISLAND)
250 kilometres
150 miles

White Heat

1

As she set a chip of iceberg on the stove for tea, Edie Kiglatuk mulled over why it was that the hunting expedition she was leading had been so spectacularly unsuccessful. For one thing, the two men she was guiding were lousy shots. For another, Felix Wagner and his sidekick Andy Taylor hadn't seemed to care if they made a kill nor not. Over the past couple of days they'd spent half their time gazing at maps and writing in notebooks. Maybe it was just the romance of the High Arctic they were after, the promise of living authentically in the wild with the Eskimo, like the expedition brochure promised. Still, she thought, they wouldn't be living long if they couldn't bring down something to eat.

She poured the boiling berg water into a thermos containing *qungik*, which white people called Labrador tea, and set aside the rest for herself. You had to travel more than three thousand kilometres south from *Umingmak Nuna*, Ellesmere Island, where they were now, to find *qungik* growing on the tundra, but for some reason southerners thought Labrador tea was more authentic, so it was what she always served to her hunting clients. For herself, she preferred Soma brand English Breakfast, brewed with iceberg water, sweetened with plenty of sugar and enriched with a knob of seal blubber. A client once told her that in the south, the water had been through the bowels of dinosaurs before it reached the faucet, whereas berg water had lain frozen and untouched by animal or human being pretty much since time began. Just one of the reasons, Edie guessed, that southerners were prepared to pay tens of thousands of dollars to come up this far north. In the case of Wagner and Taylor, it certainly wasn't for the hunting.

Sometime soon these two were about to get a deal more High Arctic authenticity than they'd bargained for. Not that they knew it yet. While Edie had been fixing tea, the wind had changed; squally easterlies were now sweeping in from the Greenlandic ice cap, suggesting a blizzard was on its way. Not imminently, but soon. There was still plenty time enough to fill the flasks with tea and get back to the gravel beach where Edie had left the two men sorting out their camp.

She threw another chip of berg into the can and while the water was heating she reached into her pack for her wedge of *igunaq* and cut off a few slices of the fermented walrus gut. The chewing of *igunaq* took some time, which was part of the point, and as Edie worked the stuff between her teeth she allowed her thoughts to return to the subject of money and from there to her stepson, Joe Inukpuk, who was the chief reason she was out here in the company of two men who couldn't shoot. Guiding paid better than the teaching that took up the remainder of her time, and Joe needed money if he was to get his nurse's qualification. He couldn't expect to get any help from Sammy, his father and Edie's ex, or from his mother Minnie. Edie didn't spook easily – it took a lot to frighten an ex-polar bear hunter – but it scared her just how badly she wanted Joe to be able to go ahead with his nursing training. The Arctic was full of *qalunaat* professionals, white doctors, white nurses, lawyers and engineers, and there was nothing wrong with most of them, but it was time Inuit produced their own professional class. Joe was certainly smart enough and he seemed committed. If she was thrifty and lucky with clients, Edie thought she could probably save enough this coming summer to put him through the first year of school. Guiding hunting expeditions was no big deal, like going out on the land with a couple of toddlers in tow. She knew every last glacier, fiord or esker for five hundred miles around. And no one knew better than Edie how to hunt.

The chip of berg had melted and she was unscrewing the top of the first thermos when a sharp, whipping crack cut through the gloom and so startled her that she dropped the flask. The hot liquid instantly vaporized into a plume of ice crystals, which trembled ever so slightly in the disrupted air. The hunter in her knew that sound, the precise, particular pop of 7mm ammunition fired from a hunting rifle, something not unlike the Remington 700s her clients were carrying.

She squinted across the sea ice, hoping for a clue as to what had happened, but her view of the beach was obscured by the iceberg. Up ahead, to the east of the beach, the tundra stared blankly back, immense and uncompromising. A gust of wind whipped frost smoke off the icepack. She felt a surge of irritation. What the hell did the *qalunaat* think they were doing when they were supposed to be setting up camp? Firing at game? Given their lack of enthusiasm for the shoot, that seemed unlikely. Maybe a bear had come too close and they were letting off a warning shot, though if that were the case, it was odd that her bear dog, Bonehead, hadn't picked up the scent and started barking. A dog as sensitive as Bonehead could scent a bear a couple of kilometres away. There was nothing for it but to investigate. Until they got back to the settlement at Autisaq, the men were officially her responsibility and these days Edie Kiglatuk took her responsibilities seriously.

She retrieved the flask, impatient with herself for having

dropped it and spilled the water, then, checking her rifle, began lunging at her usual, steady pace through deep drift towards the snowmobile. As she approached, Bonehead, who was tethered to the trailer, lifted his head and flapped his tail; if he'd picked up so much as a hint of bear, he'd have been going crazy by now. Edie gave the dog a pat and tied in her cooking equipment. Just as she was packing the flasks under the tarp, a sharp, breathless cry flew past and echoed out over the sea ice. Bonehead began to bark. In an instant, Edie felt her neck stiffen and a thudding started up in her chest. Until that moment, it hadn't occurred to her that someone might be hurt.

A voice began shouting for help. Whichever damned fool it was had already forgotten the advice she'd given them to stay quiet when they were out on the land. Up here, shouting could bring down a wall of ice or an avalanche of powder snow. It could alert a passing bear. She considered calling out to the idiot to stop him hollering, but she was downwind from the hunters and knew her voice wouldn't carry.

Hissing to Bonehead to shut up, to herself she said: '*Ikuliaq!*' Stay calm!

One of the men must have had an accident. It wasn't uncommon. In the twelve years she'd been guiding southern hunters, Edie had seen more of those than there are char in a spawn pond: puffed up egos, in the Arctic for the first time, laden down with self-importance and high-tech kit, thinking it was going to be just like the duck shoot in Iowa they went on last Thanksgiving or the New Year's deer cull in Wyoming. Then they got out on the sea ice and things didn't seem quite so easy. If the bears didn't spook them, then the blistering cold, the scouring winds, the ferocious sun and the roar of the ice pack usually did the job. They'd stave off their fear with casual bravado and booze and that was when the accidents happened.

She set the snowbie going and made her way around the iceberg and through a ridge of *tuniq*, slabby pressure ice. The wind was up now and blowing ice crystals into the skin around her eyes. When she pulled on her snow goggles, the crystals migrated to the sensitive skin around her mouth. So long as no one had been seriously wounded, she told herself, they could all just sit out the storm and wait for help to arrive once the weather had calmed. She'd put up a snowhouse to keep them cosy and she had a first-aid kit and enough knowledge to be able to use it.

Her thoughts turned, briefly, to what the elders would make of what was happening. All but Sammy didn't much approve of a woman guiding men. They were always looking for an excuse to unseat her. So far, they hadn't been able to come up with one. They knew that she was the best damned guide in the High Arctic. She'd never yet lost a client.

The snowbie bumped over an area of candle ice and brought her to her senses. Like Grandfather Eliah used to say: speculation is a white disease. But then, she was half-white herself, so maybe she couldn't help it. In any case, it wouldn't do now. The key to getting everyone out of the situation, whatever the situation turned out to be, was to focus on the present. The High Arctic only ever made room for now.

On the other side of the pressure ridge, a human shape emerged from the gloom, the skinny guy, Wagner's assistant. Edie struggled momentarily to recall his name. In her mind he'd become Stan Laurel, without the charm. Andy, that was it, Andy Taylor. He was waving frantically. As she approached the gravel beach, he ran back to where the body of his boss lay splayed on his back. Edie brought the snowbie to a halt on the ice foot and made her way across the snow-covered shale. Taylor was gesticulating, trying to get her to speed up, the asshole. She carried on at the same pace. Running equalled sweating equalled hypothermia.

Closing in, she could see things were more serious than she'd allowed herself to imagine and suddenly she understood something of Taylor's panic. The injured man was not moving. A large pool of blood had gathered under his right arm, melting the surrounding snow, freezing into a purplish sorbet. A tiny skein of steam rose from the spot.

'What happened?'

'I was over the other side,' Taylor muttered. 'I heard the sound, I ran.' He pointed to some tracks, rapidly being erased by the wind. 'Look, look, see, see?'

Think, woman. Despite the company – or maybe precisely *because* of the company – she felt resolutely alone. The first thing to do was to call and speak to Robert Patma or Joe on the sat phone. Darling Joe, who had been volunteering in Patma's clinic for a year now and seemed to have accumulated almost as much expertise as the nurse himself. She glanced over at the injured man. No, on second thoughts, the *very* first thing would be to stop the bleeding.

She went back to the snowbie, took out the first aid kit, and bustled back up the beach towards the wounded man. Taylor was on his knees beside Felix Wagner now, a look of terror on his face, his hands scuttling across Wagner's body, loosening the fabric of the wounded man's parka. She fell to the ground beside him, gesturing Taylor out of the way.

'I swear, the shot came out of nowhere.' Taylor's voice was querulous and high-pitched. Something flickered across his face, a momentary despair, and, as if sensing the implausibility of his observation, he repeated it. 'Nowhere.'

Edie had never seen a man so wounded before; foam bubbled from his lips, he was panting and his eyes were darting blindly in their sockets. His face was the colour of limestone. A smell of urine drifted upwards, but Edie didn't know either man's scent well enough to tell which of them had pissed himself. She pulled aside Wagner's parka and inspected the wound through his polar fleece. It looked as though the bullet had penetrated his sternum, just above the heart. The wound was oozing, not fountaining, which she took to mean that the bullet had missed a major artery; the most immediate danger to Wagner's life would be if the lung collapsed. She turned briefly to Taylor.

'You didn't see anything, anyone?'

'I didn't fucking do it, if that's what you think.' Taylor's voice faltered and he held both palms out, as if surrendering. 'I told you, I was over there, taking a leak.' She met the fellow's eye, remembering that she hadn't liked him when he'd stepped off the plane two days ago. Nothing he'd done in the last couple of minutes had made her change her mind.

'Chrissakes, this has *nothing* to do with me.'

'Wrong,' she said, turning her attention to the wounded man. 'This has plenty to do with us both.'

Wagner's pulse was rapid and weak and he was sweating profusely. Edie had seen animals like this. Shock. Even if his lung held, it would be hard for Wagner to pull out of it. The immediate priority was to stem the blood flow and keep him warm. Given the position of the wound it seemed extremely unlikely that Wagner had shot himself accidentally but her instincts told her Taylor wasn't lying either. She glanced over at him: no discharge stains on his gloves. Unless she was very mistaken, the skinny one wasn't the shooter. Closing in on the wound site she picked a couple of bone fragments from the flesh and beckoned Taylor nearer. Wagner panted a little then calmed.

'Press on the wound and keep up the pressure. I'm going to call for help.'

For a moment Taylor looked like he was going to faint.

'Press? With what?'

'Palm of your hand, who cares?' *Use your dick if you have to*. She pulled the scarf from round her neck to give him something to press into the wound. Taylor reached for it with his left hand and did as he was told.

'What if the shooter comes back?'

She gave him a long, hard look. 'You're a hunter, aren't you?'

The sat phone was sitting in its insulated cover at the bottom of the pannier where she'd packed it. It was Autisaq council of Elders policy that all local guides leading foreigners carried one; otherwise she didn't bother with them. The cold made the batteries unreliable and the line was often scrambled. In any case, she'd never had cause to use one until now.

Sammy's voice came on the line. Edie took a deep breath. Today of all days, her ex-husband was on duty in the comms office. She checked her watch. Another southern habit, Sammy would say. It was 2p.m.

'We've got a hunting accident.' Keeping it simple for now. 'It's pretty bad. Chest wound. If we're lucky it won't bleed out, but the guy looks like he might go into shock. We need Robert Patma and a plane.'

'Where you at?'

'On Craig. At Uimmatisatsaq. Patma knows it. Joe took him fishing there one time.'

Sammy sucked on his teeth. She could tell from the way the sound of his breath moved that he was shaking his head.

'Hold while I check the plane schedule and the forecast.'

Waiting, Edie dug around in her pannier, drew out a sheet of polyurethane, took out her knife and hacked off a rough square.

The phone crackled and for a moment she could hear the faint intimations of another call, two voices speaking in some language she didn't understand, then Sammy's voice tinkled through the handset.

'Edie, there's a blizzard coming.'

'Yeah.' Holy walrus, the man could be irritating. 'Looks like one of those spring blow-overs.'

'We can't send a plane until it's gone through.'

'Air ambulance from Iqaluit?'

'I checked already. They're weathered out.'

Edie scrolled through the options. 'We get a medic here we might be OK. Robert Patma could make it on a snowbie.'

Silence on the phone, then another voice:

'Kigga.' It was Joe. Edie felt her body give a little.

Kiggavituinnaaq, falcon, his nickname for her. He always said she lived in her own world up in the air somewhere. Strictly speaking she wasn't his stepmother any more, not officially anyway. Still Kigga though.

'Robert Patma left for the south yesterday. His mother was killed in a crash, dad's in hospital. They said they'd send a temporary nurse but no one's shown up.'

Edie groaned. 'They' as in feds, held to be responsible for everything and nothing, as in, 'The spirits were angry with my sister so they made sure the feds didn't get her treated for her TB in time.'

'That gets out, Autisaq can forget its guiding business.' She was angry, not with Robert, but with a system that left them all so vulnerable.

Joe said: 'Right.' He sounded impatient with her for focusing on such a thing, even for a moment. 'But your fellow's breathing, right?'

'Just about. If we can stabilize him and stop the bleeding . . .'

'You got any plastic?'

'I already cut a piece.'

Some energy passed between them. Love, admiration, maybe a mixture of the two.

'Gonna pack the clinic's snowbie and come myself,' Joe said. 'Meantime, if the blizzard blows over, they'll send the plane. Keep doing what you're doing and don't give him anything by mouth.' His voice softened. 'Kigga, nothing you can do's gonna make it worse.'

'Joe . . .' She was about to tell her stepson to be careful, when she realized he'd already hung up.

Edie went back to the two men, pulled out the bivvy from Taylor's trailer and in a few minutes had it up and over the injured man. It had started snowing. In a couple of hours the blizzard would be upon them. Pushing Taylor back, she leaned over Wagner's face, fingered his neck for a pulse and temperature, took the square of polyurethane from her pocket, opened up his fleece with her knife and tamped the plastic over the wound. A small thought scudded across her mind. Only three days ago this stout little man thought he was setting out on a grand adventure, something to boast about at the clubhouse bar back in Wichita. The odds on Felix Wagner ever seeing the clubhouse again had just lengthened considerably. She turned to Taylor.

'Do everything you can to make sure no air gets into the wound or the lung could collapse. I'm going to get a snow shelter up. The blizzard goes big, this bivvy won't hold. Anything changes, call me, OK?'

Taylor said: 'You're not going to look for whoever did this?'

Edie bit back her irritation. One thing she couldn't abide was a whiner.

'Look, do you want to play detective or do you want your friend to live?'

Taylor sighed. She watched him disappear into the bivvy, then drove the snowbie to the old drifts at the back of the beach beside the cliff and followed the shingle up the slope to the high point, looking for footprints and shell discards. She wasn't going to give Taylor the satisfaction of knowing that was what she was doing. All the same, she wanted to be clear in her own mind that the shooter wasn't still around. Up on the high ground, the wind was already blowing the snow hard. If there had been any prints, they were gone now. She turned the snowbie back and was passing beside a rocky outcrop when she spotted something on the ground. She squeezed on the brakes, jumped off and went back to check. There it was, the remnant of a single footprint, which had been protected from the worst of the wind by a small boulder. She inspected it more closely, bringing to mind Taylor's footprints from earlier. This was different. A man's and recent. Wagner's perhaps. If not, most likely the shooter's. For a moment or two she stood and took it in, memorising the zig-zag pattern with what looked like the outline of an ice bear at its centre, as bit by bit the wind blew snow over its surface. Up on her feet, now, she could just make out the rapidly filling indentations where the trail of prints had once been, heading away out onto the tundra. If it was the shooter, he was long gone.

She made her way back to the beach and focused her energies on finding the right kind of building snow. Too hard and you'd never get the blocks to caulk together, too soft and the whole structure would be in danger of collapsing. A textbook she'd once read at the school listed the perfect building snow as having a density of 0.3–0.35gm/cm^3 and a hardness of between 150–200gm/cm^3. She'd remembered the numbers because they'd seemed so abstract and absurd. Out on the land, you had to do your own calculations.

As luck would have it, she found precisely the right kind of three-layered snow in a drift at the northern edge of the beach. For a while she worked, sawing the walrus-ivory snowknife to and fro to form rectangular bricks the size of breezeblocks, stacking them on top of the trailer and moving them in batches out from under the cliff to where the bivvy currently stood. The job took her a while, because she moved slowly to avoid breaking into a sweat. Bricks cut, she dived back inside the bivvy to check on Wagner. The wounded man was quiet now, his breathing shallow. She checked his boots. No ice bear.

'He still bleeding?'

Taylor shook his head.

'That case, you need to come help.'

She showed him how to place the bricks, then caulk between, and as he worked, she dug out the ice floor and levelled it off. Finally they built the little entrance tunnel, sloping down to prevent warm air escaping. It was crude, but it would do. Together they heaved Wagner inside and laid him on a small pile of caribou skins. Edie emptied his pockets of a white plastic ballpoint pen, a pocket knife and a few coins and tossed them in her bag, then went back outside to collect her things and untie Bonehead. The wind chill was formidable now, –45 maybe, the air foamy with ice frost. She built a crude little annexe on the side of the house, lowered Bonehead into it and bricked him in. The snow would keep him cosy. Then she went inside, poured what remained of the hot tea from the thermos and, handing a mug to Andy Taylor, raised hers in a toast:

'Here's to another fine mess,' she said.

Andy looked up from his tea, eyes glaring. Incomprehension, maybe. Contempt, more like.

'Laurel and Hardy.'

'*I know who it is.*' Andy Taylor shook his head, clucking like an indignant duck whose nest has been disturbed. 'Jeez, have you any idea how *inappropriate* that is?'

Edie wrinkled her nose and stared at her hands. It was as much as she could do not to punch him. If he'd been Inuk, she wouldn't have held off. Situation like this, you told stories, you drank hot tea, and you joked about. Only things keeping you sane. Fifteen minutes passed in silence. The blizzard was a way off still. It was going to be a long wait.

After a while, she said: 'We should eat.' It had been several hours since their last meal and she and Andy had expended a good deal of energy building the snow shelter. Hungry people made poor judgements. She poured more hot tea, then pulled a drawstring bag from her pack and went at its contents with her pocketknife, handing a slice off the block to Andy Taylor. Taylor took what was offered, eyeing it suspiciously.

She cut another slice for herself and began chewing, throwing Taylor a thumbs-up sign. 'Good.'

Taylor took a bite. Slowly, his jaw began to move. Pretty soon, a rictus of disgust spread across his face. He spat the meat onto his glove.

'What the fuck?'

'*Igunaq*. Fermented walrus gut. Very good for you. Keep you warm.'

The wind screamed. Edie chewed. Taylor sat in silence. Hail thumped up against the snowhouse walls like distant thunder. Taylor gave off anxious vibes.

'This man who's supposed to be coming,' he blurted. 'Does he know what he's doing?' He had to shout to make his voice heard above all the racket of the weather. 'How do we know he'll actually get here?'

It seemed like an odd question, a southerner's question. Why would Joe set off if he wasn't as sure as he could be that he'd reach his destination? 'It's not all that bad,' she said.

Taylor gave her a look of exasperation. 'It sure sounds bad. And if it's not bad, then why the fuck hasn't someone sent the plane?'

'The wind's coming in from the east.'

Taylor wiped his glove over his face. His voice was tainted with aggression, or, perhaps, frustration, Edie thought. Then again, she might be wrong. Southerners were difficult to read. She explained that the winds would gather through the gaps in the mountain passes, becoming fiercer, more localized and katabatic, like mini-tornadoes. The plane would have to fly right through those winds, which could prove incredibly dangerous, but at ground level, things would be a little easier. It would be rough travelling – too rough for them with Felix Wagner in the trailer, but Joe was very experienced at travelling in difficult conditions and he was bringing proper medical kit and more expertise than she could muster alone.

Edie sliced off another piece of *igunaq* and began chewing. She noticed Taylor back off slightly.

'You know I didn't have anything to do with this, right?'

'You ask me, I don't think you did.' She considered telling him about the footprint, then decided that right now, he didn't deserve to know. 'But it'll be hard to prove.'

A gust of wind blustered over the snow shelter, sending a patch of caulking falling onto Wagner, who began to groan again.

'What if your friend can't find us?'

Edie sliced off another piece of *igunaq*.

'You really should eat,' she said.

'For fuck's sake, we got an injured man here!'

Edie peered over at Wagner. 'I don't think he's hungry.'

Taylor pulled off his hat and rubbed his hair. 'Does *anything* rattle you?'

Edie thought about this for a moment. It wasn't the most interesting question, but it was the only one he'd asked that helped the conversation along, so they were making progress. 'There's this scene in *Feet First* . . .' she began.

'Scene?' His voice had risen to the timbre of a sexed-up fox. Despite the difficult circumstances, Edie realized she was quite enjoying herself.

'Yeah, in the Harold Lloyd picture. Anyway, there's this

scene, where Harold Lloyd is swinging from a scaffold on the side of this huge skyscraper, it's like he's just clinging onto the edge of a cliff and the wind is shaking it.'

Andy Taylor looked as her as though she was some crazy person.

'What the hell? A *movie*?'

People were always making this mistake. Edie was always having to put them right. 'Sure it's a *movie*, but Harold Lloyd did all his own stunt work.'

Taylor laughed, though probably not in a good way.

'Straight up,' she said. 'No doubles, no stuntmen, no camera tricks, nothing.'

The skinny *qalunaat* wiped his forehead and shook his head. After that he didn't say anything for a while. Time passed. The wind got up to a terrible pitch. Unsettled, Taylor began to fidget.

'Don't you people tell stories at times like these, about the animals and the ancestors, all that?' *You people*. That's rich, thought Edie. One of us sitting here is *paying* to be 'you people', and it isn't me.

'I just did,' she said.

'No, no, I meant like real stories, Eskimo shit.'

'Uh huh.' A familiar throb rose in Edie's right eye, a ringing in her ears. When she was a little girl, her grandfather used to say these feelings were the ancestors moving through her body. 'Listen,' he would whisper. 'One of your ancestors wants to tell his story.' She closed her eyes, those coal-black discs Sammy used to say reminded him of the eclipse of the sun, the perfect arch of her eyebrows rising like the curve of the earth above her broad, flat forehead. She thought about her grandmother, Anna, coming all the way here from Quebec, meeting Eliah out on a hunting trip, Eliah moving all the way from Etah in Greenland to be with her. Her thoughts ran to Eliah's great-grandfather, Welatok, who guided white men and journeyed all the way from Baffin Island and settled, finally, in Etah. Then she thought of Maggie, her mother, flying down to Iqaluit to look for her man, not finding him because he'd deceived her and wasn't there.

'How's about an ancestor story?' she said. 'Why don't you start?'

'What?' Taylor had a bewildered look on his face.

'Tell me about your ancestors.'

'My what?' Taylor sounded flustered, then his face seemed to bunch up, like he was trying to squeeze the juice from it. 'Hell, I don't know.' He waved a hand. 'My grandfather on my mother's side came over from Ireland. We didn't go in for that family history stuff.'

The vehemence of his response, the contempt in the tone took her back. 'How can you live like that, not knowing where you came from?'

'Pretty well. Pretty fucking well.'

'My great-great-great-grandfather guided *qalunaat* explorers.'

'Oh, that's just terrific,' he said, with some sarcasm. 'Nice family business you got here, generations of experience in leaving people to die in the middle of fucking nowhere.'

'His name was Welatok,' she said, ignoring the man's tone. 'He guided a man called Fairfax.'

Andy Taylor started. 'Right.' Going into his pocket, he drew out a hip flask, looking calmer suddenly. He took a few sips from it and waved it in the air.

'Think old Felix here could use some?'

'He's sleeping.'

Taylor put the flask back in his pocket. She knew why he didn't offer it to her. Inuit, drink: a match made in hell. She would have said no anyway. Her drinking days were long behind her.

'Old Felix here, he knows a thing or two about those

old-time Arctic explorers, all the heroes: Peary, Stefansson, Scott, Fairfax, Frobisher. Pretty interesting stuff,' Taylor said.

'He ever mention Welatok?' she asked.

Taylor shrugged.

'I guess not,' she said. 'We never did get much credit.'

Beside them, Wagner began making small moaning sounds. Edie thought of Joe, now struggling across the sea ice to reach them, and about what kind of future he would have in whatever was left of the Arctic once the developers and prospectors and explorers had swept through it. It was greed, she knew, though she'd never felt it. Well, greed for love maybe, for sex even, but for stuff, never. With Edie, same as with most Inuit, you owned enough, you hunted enough, you ate enough and you left enough behind so your children and their children would respect you. It wasn't about surplus. It was about sufficiency.

Some time later, Edie sensed Bonehead begin to stir and scrape about inside his ice kennel. Andy Taylor had fallen asleep. Wagner was still, though breathing. Throwing on her sealskin parka, she clambered through the entrance tunnel. Outside the air was alive with darting crystals and ice smoke, the wind roaring like a wounded bear. Edie edged her way around the snow shelter, took out her snow-knife and cut a hole in Bonehead's kennel. The dog burst from his confinement in a spray of snowflakes, greeted her briefly, then rushed off into the gloom to meet Joe.

Clambering back inside the snow shelter she woke Taylor to tell him that Joe was on his way. Neither of them heard his snowbie until it was already very close. Shortly afterwards Joe himself appeared at the entrance to the shelter.

'What happened?' Before anyone could answer, Joe crawled over to the wounded man. Removing his gloves, he pressed the index and middle finger of his right hand to

Wagner's neck, counting the pulse in the carotid artery. He took out a blue clinicians' notebook from his daypack and wrote something down.

Edie raised her hand in a thumbs-up but Joe only shrugged. She watched him inspecting the wound and felt the familiar surge of pride in her boy.

'How much blood has he lost?'

'A lot, maybe more than a litre.'

Joe turned to his daypack, pulled out some antibacterial wipes and began washing his hands. Five minutes later Felix Wagner was on a saline drip with codeine for the pain. The situation was pretty grave, Joe explained. The injured man was now in full hypovolemic shock. His chances of survival depended on the severity of the shock and that could not be established until he was properly hospitalized. If the shock was severe enough, kidney failure would set in and gradually, one by one, the organs would begin to shut down. It might take a few hours or as long as a week, but, unless Wagner was extraordinarily lucky, the outcome would be the same.

'We need that plane, Sammy.' Edie was on the sat phone again.

'We're still being pummelled over here.'

'Can you get Thule out?' It was a big ask. The US airbase across the water in Greenland had bigger planes, built better to withstand Arctic conditions than Autisaq's Twin Otters. They were usually unwilling to intervene in what they saw as Canadian problems, except in the case of an outbreak of TB or measles or some other some infectious illness, but Wagner was one of *them*, an American.

When the response came moments later, she could barely hear it and asked Sammy to repeat, then abruptly lost the signal. After a few minutes' wait the phone rang back. This time the signal was poor but Edie could just about hear a man's voice through the crackle, something about visibility.

'Sammy, listen.' She had to shout above the shriek of the wind. 'What about Thule?' But the phone had already gone dead.

'They flying?' Joe looked hopeful.

Taylor opened his mouth to speak.

'Don't.' Edie held up a hand. 'Just don't.'

They finished up the tea in the flasks and waited. It was rough still, but the wind moved across to the north-west and began to ease off. A little while later, Bonehead began scratching about and barking, Edie put her ear to the ground and detected an engine vibration. Martie. It had to be. No one except her aunt would be crazy enough to fly through the tail-end of a blizzard.

In no time, they were loading the patient, the snowmobiles and equipment on board Martie Kiglatuk's Otter. Martie was large, at least by Inuit standards, with skin the colour of an heirloom suitcase and a voice like a cartoon train wreck. She also happened to be Edie's best friend.

The plane hugged the shore-fast ice of South Cape and turned west along the Ellesmere coast. Before long, it had cleared sufficiently for Edie to be able to watch the land sail by. She was struck, always, on her rare flights, by how much the Arctic was shrinking back into itself, floe by floe, glacier by glacier. Witnessing it was like watching a beloved and aged parent gradually and inexorably come apart. Every year a little more death and dying and a little less life. In thirteen years' time, when Joe was her age now, she wondered if anything would be left at all.

The crags softened then gradually fell away to flat shoreline and the northern hamlet of Autisaq rose into view like a set of ancient teeth, jagged with age and wear, clinging on uneasily to the bony foreshore. Behind her, Joe whooped.

Martie said: 'Seatbelts on, folks, we're coming in.'

Edie felt a familiar ear-pop as they began to descend and then, muffled, but unmistakeable, the sound of Joe's voice again, only this time alarmed, and when she looked back over her shoulder she could see Felix Wagner foaming at the mouth, his eyes rolling back, his whole body quaking and jerking and Joe frantically signalling Andy Taylor to hold the wounded man steady while he filled a hypodermic. Time warped and bent. Edie was aware of the plane's steep descent and a bunch of fractured shouts and barked instructions. She tried to loosen her seatbelt to help but could not get a grip on it. Behind her, Joe was pumping at the man's heart, blowing into his mouth, and the plane was pitching and diving towards the landing strip. Suddenly, Martie was shouting; 'Seatbelts on *now*, people. *Tuarvirit!* Quick!' and the two men fell away from Felix Wagner like old petals.

Moments later, the familiar skid and grind of the tyres on gravel signalled their arrival and as Edie swung round she saw Felix Wagner's arm escape from underneath the blanket.

Martie taxied to the end of the strip, shut down the engine.

'What we got?'

Joe said: 'Trouble.' He was out of his seat, kneeling beside the body of Felix Wagner, looking crushed. 'The *qalunaat* just died.'

'*Iquq*, shit.' Martie glanced out of the window at the welcome party of Sammy Inukpuk and Sammy's brother, Simeonie, Autisaq's mayor, heading towards them.

'I guess I'd better go spread the good news.'

The pilot's door opened and Martie climbed down onto

the strip. A moment of discussion followed, Martie signalled for someone to open the main door and let down the steps and Sammy and Simeonie came on board.

Simeonie, slyer and more calculating than his brother, turned to Edie:

'Does the skinny *qalunaat* understand Inuktitut?'

Andy Taylor did not respond.

'I guess there's your answer,' Edie said. She didn't like Simeonie. Never had, even when he was her brother-in-law.

'Did he have anything to do with this?'

Edie could see the man's mind already at work, cooking the story, working the facts into whatever version of the truth best served Simeonie Inukpuk.

She went through it all in her head. Andy Taylor had two rifles with him, a Remington Model 700 and a Weatherby Magnum. Felix Wagner had insisted on three: a Remington, a 30-60 Springfield and a Winchester, most likely a 308. Both men had discharged their Remingtons in the morning during an abortive hare hunt, but not since. She briefly considered the possibility that Felix Wagner had shot himself, but from the position of the wound it seemed so unlikely it was hardly worth the expenditure of energy in the thought. Then there was the zig-zag footprint with the ice bear at its centre. A theory suddenly came together.

Edie said, in Inuktitut: 'The way I see it, someone out hunting mistook Wagner for game and took a shot at him.' The hunter was probably on his way back to Autisaq or one of the other hamlets right now. Most likely he'd lie low for a few days, then fess up. It had happened before; the *qalunaat* had signed a release form, absolving the community of responsibility in the event of an accident. It was unfortunate, but not catastrophic. The elders would shrug *ayaynuaq*, it couldn't be helped, there would be a generous insurance payout to Wagner's family and the whole episode would be forgotten. The Arctic was full of dangers. She'd made sure Felix Wagner had understood that.

Simeonie coughed, glanced at Taylor to make sure the man wasn't following, then, drawing himself up to his full height, said:

'Speculation is a white man's disease. Take the other *qalunaat* back to the hotel, make sure he's got whatever he needs.'

She nodded.

'One thing, he hasn't got a sat phone, has he?'

Edie shook her head

'Good, then don't let him make any calls.' He turned to Andy Taylor: 'We're very sorry about this accident, Mr Taylor. We have to ask you not to leave until we've made some investigations. Small stuff, just details really.'

Andy Taylor blinked his understanding.

Joe leaned forward and spoke in a low voice: 'Uncle, none of this is Edie's fault.'

Inukpuk ignored him, reverting to Inuktitut:

'There'll be a council of Elders meeting tomorrow to decide what steps to take next,' he said, stepping out of the plane and back onto the landing strip, something threatening in his tone.

Joe shook his head. '*Aitiathlimaqtsi arit*.' Fuck you too.

Back at the hotel, Andy Taylor showed no interest in making phone calls. He only wanted to have a shower and get some rest. A man not used to death, Edie thought, watching him heave his pack along the corridor to his room at the rear of the building. It occurred to her that she ought to go home and wait for Joe. She'd been bothered by a sense of foreboding, the feeling that she and Joe were somehow being drawn into something. It was nothing she could put her finger on yet, but she didn't like the way Simeonie Inukpuk had spoken. Never trusted the man much, even when he was kin. Trusted him even less now.

She waited downstairs in the hotel until she could hear the sound of Taylor's snores, then went home. The moment she reached the steps up to the snow-porch door, she knew Joe was already inside waiting for her. In the same way that a frozen ptarmigan would gradually revive when put beside the radiator, it was as if the house gradually came to life when Joe was there. She pulled the door open, peeled off her boots and outerwear in the snow porch and went in.

Joe was sitting on the sofa staring at a DVD. Charlie Chaplin was playing table ballet with two forks stuck into two bread rolls. She plunked herself down beside her stepson and stroked his hair.

'I can't help thinking this is my fault, Kigga.'

'Are you crazy? No one's going to blame you, Joe, not for a minute. And if they do, they'll have me to answer to.' On the TV Charlie Chaplin continued to twirl the bread rolls into pirouettes and *pas de bourées*. 'This was an accident. Someone from Autisaq, or maybe one of the other settlements. Maybe he couldn't see, maybe he'd had a bit to drink. It happens.'

Joe said: 'You think?'

'Sure,' she said. 'It'll blow over, you'll see.'

The bread roll ballerina took her bow and Edie flipped off the player. A moment of regret drifted between them.

Joe said: 'Only thing is, a man's dead, Kigga.'

She looked at him, ashamed at her own momentary lapse of principle. She was her best self when she was with him, he made sure of it.

2

'Bee El You Bee Bee Ee Ar.' Edie drew the letters on the whiteboard as she went. She'd hadn't slept well and was finding it hard to focus, thinking about Wagner's death and the council of Elders meeting where she was going to have to account for her actions.

Pauloosie Allakarialak put up his hand.

Edie underlined the word with her finger. 'Blubber.'

Pauloosie's arm started waving. 'Miss, did someone kill that *qalunaat*?'

Edie rubbed her hand across her face. Shit, if Pauloosie knew, then everyone knew.

Edie pointed to the word on the whiteboard. 'You know what this says?'

The boy looked blank. Poor kid. Sometimes Edie had to wonder what she was doing, spending her days drumming into Autisaq's youth words they would almost certainly never use in English – 'baleen', 'scree', 'glacial', 'blubber', words so much more subtly expressed in Inuktitut, and prettier, too, written in script. Of course, the hope of the federal government in Ottawa was that some of them would go on to graduate from high school and even take degrees in southern universities, just as Joe planned to do, but it was a rare kind of Inuk who harboured such ambitions. Going south meant leaving family, friends, everything familiar for a city where the streets were flustered with buildings and cars crowded in on one another like char in a shrinking summer pond and where, for at least six months of the year, it was intolerably hot. Why put yourself through that in the hope that you might finally land the kind of job back home that had, for decades, only gone to *qalunaat*?

No, the fact of the matter was that most of the faces before Edie now would be married with kids by the time they were old enough to vote. Most would be lucky to get as far as Iqaluit, the provincial capital, let alone to the south, and the vast majority would never once have occasion to have to spell 'blubber' in English. And the irony of this was that, all the time they were sitting in rows learning how to spell 'baleen' in English, they could be out on the land, learning traditional skills, discovering how to be Inuit.

The recess bell rang. On her way to the staff room, an idea sprang into Edie's mind. It was something the headmaster, John Tisdale, would no doubt call 'unorthodox pedagogy', a disciplinary offence, if he found out about it. Not that Edie cared. She'd been up before him so many times for flouting the rules – his rules, *southern* rules – that she'd come to expect it. In any case, she suspected Tisdale secretly approved of her methods, even as he was rapping her over the knuckles for them. The man had come a long way. A few years ago, when he'd first arrived with a brief to 'broaden education in the Arctic', she'd asked him what exactly he thought they were educating Autisaq's children *for*.

'To take their place in the world,' he'd replied. He really had been a pompous ass back then.

She'd waited until the look of self-satisfaction had faded a little from his face then said: 'Maybe you don't realize, *this* is their world right here.'

Tisdale had marked her down as a troublemaker but Edie hadn't been bothered by his condescension. She knew it wouldn't last. Pretty soon he'd begin to find himself out of his depth, then he'd come looking for her with his tail between his legs.

It happened sooner than even she had anticipated, after a sermon he gave Autisaq's parents on the dangers of violent computer games. What a blast! Everyone had laughed at him. Hadn't he noticed where he was? Up here, violence was embedded in almost everything: in the unblinking ferocity of the sun, in the blistering winds, the pull and push of the ice.

In any case, most Autisaq kids had neither the time nor the money for computer games; their leisure hours were taken up with snaring ptarmigan and trapping hare or fox, or helping their fathers hunt seal. They spent most of the time they weren't at school being violent.

The day after the talk, the headmaster found a dead fox hanging across his snow porch, but instead of heading south on the next plane, as many in his position would have done, he'd knocked first on Edie's door then on others, asking where he'd gone wrong. He'd stuck it out until, over the years, he'd come to realize that 'broadening education in the Arctic' included him.

He'd pretend to disapprove of today's 'unorthodox pedagogy', but it was all a sop to his masters back in Ottawa. Head down, so she wouldn't have to make conversation with anyone on the street, Edie trudged through dry and squealing snow to the meat store at the back of her house, picked out a small harp seal she'd hunted a few weeks earlier, attached a rope to its head and dragged it back along the ice to the school building. She waited until no one was around then smuggled the dead animal into the school through the side entrance.

The moment the kids returned from recess and caught sight of the creature, their faces, sensing an end to the abstractions of language lessons, lit like lanterns. Edie got two of the oldest boys to help her lift the animal onto the table. Then she handed over two hunting knives and left the kids to get on with the business of butchering, instructing the older children to show the others how to handle the knives, and to write down the name of everything they touched *and* the verbs to describe their actions in English and Inuktitut on the whiteboard.

It worked. Before long, the seal lay in a number of neat pieces on the table and the kids were encouraging one another to dig deeper and cut more finely, jostling to be the first to the front to write 'spleen' or 'whiskers' or 'flense'. Butchering the animal and noting its parts had become a gleeful and very Inuit kind of a game. Even Pauloosie Allakarialak was joining in. He'd forgotten the white man's death and the fact that he didn't know how to spell 'blubber'.

At lunchtime, Edie trudged across to the Northern Store, thinking to buy some Saran Wrap and plastic sacks she could use to package the chopped seal before it thawed and became difficult to handle. Swinging open the door into the store's snow porch, she banged her boots against the boot-scraper, glanced out of habit at the announcements board (nothing about Wagner) and went inside.

The Northern Store was officially a co-operative, owned by the inhabitants of Autisaq, every one of whom had a right to a share of the profits, if ever there were any. It was managed by Mike and Etok Nungaq.

Mike was an affable, steady sort of guy. He had an interest in geology, which he cultivated whenever geologists from the south came into town. As a thankyou for some favour, an American geologist had left him a laptop a couple of summers back and Mike was now the person anyone came to when they had computer problems. Not that many did. Some of the younger generation had games consoles, but few in the community had bothered with computers and there were only three in public use connected to the internet: one in the mayor's office, one in the nursing station and one in the library at the school.

When he wasn't digging out rocks and fiddling with computers, Mike Nungaq lived for gossip, though rarely the malicious kind. Mike just liked to know who was doing what, with whom, and when. There was something in his makeup that meant he couldn't help himself. If you needed to know what was really going on in town, you just had to ask Mike.

Mike's wife, Etok, disapproved of her husband's chattering. Around Autisaq, Etok was known as *Uismuitissaliaqungak*, the Person with Crooked Teeth who is as Scary as a Mother Bear. People watched themselves around her. She looked harmless enough but at the slightest hint of gossip, Etok's eyes would freeze over and she'd bare a set of fangs that wouldn't have disgraced a walrus. But despite her best efforts to quash them, rumour and innuendo persisted, fanning out through the aisles of the Northern Store to the farthest reaches of the settlement, often transforming in the process from harmless titbit to outrageous slander and loathsome smear.

It was Edie's habit to pass by the cash till to say hi to Mike before she began her shopping, but today she knew he'd want to know about the Wagner affair and she didn't feel like talking about it, so she took herself directly to the third aisle at the back of the store where the plastics were kept, between the cleaning products and the snowmobile maintenance section. They didn't have the extra-wide Saran Wrap Edie had seen advertised, so she picked up a packet of the regular stuff plus some plastic sacks and was walking back up the aisle when Pauloosie Allakarialak's mother,

Nancy, appeared. Nancy Allakarialak was a cheerful woman, regretful at having brought her son into the world with foetal alcohol syndrome, and keen to make amends. She took a great interest in Pauloosie's education and was usually eager to discuss his progress with Edie. Today, though, she only smiled faintly and edged her way past down the aisle.

It was a bad sign. Word had obviously already got around that a *qalunaat* had died on Edie's watch.

Edie slapped the roll of plastic bags and the Saran Wrap on the cash desk. Etok was standing with her back to the desk, sorting the mail. She looked around, registered Edie then slipped through the door at the back to the store. Mike Nungaq watched his wife go then sidled along the desk to the till.

'Hey, Edie. Nice day out.' He met her eyes and smiled. As he handed over her change, his fingers lingered over her hand.

'I'm shunned already.'

'Oh no,' Mike said. 'That thing yesterday? Folks a bit unsettled by it is all. Once the council of Elders have met, everything'll settle right down.'

She nodded and smiled back, appreciative of his attempt to reassure her. She wondered if the council of Elders would see things the same way. They had the right to revoke her guiding licence and Simeonie, at least, had the motivation to do it. He'd been running for re-election as mayor when the business of Ida and Samwillie Brown blew up.

Until Edie got involved, everyone in Autisaq had been quite prepared to put Samwillie's death down to an accident. He was unpopular and a known wife-beater. Edie's intervention in the case – 'meddling', Simeonie Inukpuk called it – had led to Ida's conviction for her husband's murder. It was widely believed that Simeonie had lost the election on account of the bad publicity and the affair had cast such a shadow over his political ambitions that it was another four years before he finally managed to get re-elected. Edie often wondered if it was Simeonie who had been responsible for the death threat she'd received not long after Ida's trial began.

Her ex-brother-in-law had other reasons to hate her, too. He blamed her for the breakup with Sammy. Too caught up in women's rights, he'd said at the time. What about a man's right to have his woman stand by him? No matter to Simeonie that, by the time she left, she and Sammy were drinking one another into the ground. Most likely they'd both be dead by now if they hadn't split. Maybe Simeonie Inukpuk would have preferred it that way. He was casual with his family. Sammy had always been loyal to him, but Simeonie had never returned the favour.

Edie knew she had a lot to lose. It wasn't the investigation itself she was afraid of. Joe was right. A man had died a long way from home and it was only fair to his family that they get to the bottom of it. What she dreaded was that Simeonie would use Wagner's death as an excuse to persuade the elders into rescinding her guiding licence. None of the elders except Sammy thought anything of women guides; some of them had probably been looking for an excuse to get rid of her for years. In any case, most of them would be glad to see her go.

For herself, she didn't much care. The years of drinking had taken away what pride she might once have had. But without her guiding fees, there was no way Edie would be able to help Joe fund his nursing training. Part-time teaching barely covered her living expenses. He wouldn't be able to turn to Sammy and Minnie. His mother drank away her welfare and his father had an old-fashioned idea of what constituted a real Inuk man, and it wasn't studying to be a nurse. Besides, Sammy didn't want his son doing anything that might involve him having to leave Autisaq. Over the years, Sammy had let a lot of things slip by him: a few good jobs, a couple of wives and a whole lot of money. Along with booze and American cop shows, his boys were one of the few comforts remaining to him.

After school, Edie walked back home past the store and the little church she last visited on the day of her mother's funeral. Sammy's shitkickers were lying inside the snow porch and his blue government parka was hanging on the peg. Two years after she'd kicked him out, Sammy still regularly treated Edie's house as home. At first she'd discouraged it, then she'd given in, mostly because when Sammy was at her house, Joe spent more time there too.

The smell of beer drifted in from the living room, along with some other, more chemical, aroma. Edie prised off her boots and hung up her hat, scarves and parka, then opened the door into the house. Sammy and Joe were sitting on the sofa watching TV.

Edie said: 'Hey, *allummiipaa*, darling.' The remark was directed at Joe but Sammy looked up with a hopeful smile on his face. Edie didn't miss the days she'd called her ex darling, but Sammy did. If Sammy had his way they'd still be married and she'd still be a drunk.

'I put my stuff in my room, Kigga,' Joe said. The boy went to and fro these days – a few nights at Sammy's, a week or two with Minnie – but right now he was spending more time with his stepmother than usual, and she couldn't help liking it.

'You break up with Lisa, Sammy?' The past couple of years, Sammy had gone through women like water. Lisa was just the latest. For some reason whenever one or other finished with him, he came to Edie's house to lick his wounds. He gave a little shrug, looked away.

'Sorry,' she said. She wasn't consciously mean to him but sometimes a little bubble of meanness popped out. She guessed that somewhere, somehow, she was still angry about the situation, which probably meant that somewhere, somehow, she still had feelings for Sammy and was doing her best to ignore them.

'My TV bust,' Sammy said.

Edie took a piece of seal out of her pack and put it on the surface in the kitchen then switched on the kettle for some tea.

'Plus I broke up with Lisa.'

They laughed. Sammy raised his eyes to heaven. Even he'd come to think of his love life as a bit of a joke. So long as he was the one to say it.

'Get together with anyone else yet?'

Sammy nodded, sheepish.

'Who?' asked Edie, a little too quickly.

'Nancy.'

'Nancy Allakarialak? Pauloosie's mum?'

'Uh huh.'

For an instant all three made eye contact, then just as quickly looked away. It was odd how sometimes they felt like a family again. Odd and unsettling. Then Joe got up to go to his room.

'Call me when we need to leave?' Not his deal, this old stuff between her and Sammy.

After he'd disappeared into his room there was a pause.

'I didn't get a chance to say thanks for helping out with Felix Wagner,' Edie said, wanting to change the subject.

Sammy took a swig of the beer at his side and said nothing.

Edie said: 'You spoke to Andy Taylor?'

'Simeonie just left him. Seems pretty keen to forget the whole thing and get back down south.'

'I guess there'll have to be a police inquiry, right?' Edie said. 'They'll want to call in Derek Palliser.'

Sammy cleared his throat and made a study of his feet.

'That's not what I'm hearing,' he said in a way that indicated he knew something and was keeping it back. Edie gave him a long, hard stare.

'Listen,' he said defensively. 'I don't control the council of Elders.'

Everyone knew who did control the council of Elders: Sammy's older brother, Simeonie. Sammy had always stood in his brother's shadow and he wasn't about to get out of it now. Anything involving confrontation, particularly to do with his brother, Sammy usually ran a mile. He rattled his beer can to make sure he'd polished off the contents and stood to go.

'Edie, stay out of trouble. Try to toe the line, for once.'

When he'd gone, Edie put on her best parka and oiled her pigtails, then called Joe from his room. They walked up to the mayor's office together. The elders had asked them to the meeting on the understanding that they were there to give their version of events, and would have no say in the outcome. For this reason alone, Edie had a bad feeling about what was about to happen. It was typically screwed up Autisaq politics. The elders paid lip service to inclusiveness but when it came down to it, they huddled together like a group of harried musk ox.

They opened the door into the council chamber and went in. Sammy was already there, beside him on one side Pauloosie's grandfather Samuelie and on the other, Sammy's cousin, Otok. Three or four others Edie knew by name, but not well personally. The driftwood and sealskin chair at the head of the table that had once been taken by Edie's grandfather, Eliah, was now occupied by Simeonie

Inukpuk, who pointed Edie and Joe to a couple of office chairs brought in specially and motioned for quiet. The only other woman in the room, Simeonie's assistant, Sheila Silliq, was taking notes.

Simeonie began by thanking them for coming. The council simply wanted to hear from each of them their version of events, he said. Perhaps, since Edie was present when Felix Wagner had his *accident*, she might begin.

Out of the corner of her eye, Edie saw Sammy glaring at her.

'Sure,' she said, 'the *event*.' Thinking, *toe the line*.

Till the moment the shot echoed out across the sea ice, the day had in fact been pretty *un*eventful. In the morning, the party had gone after hare, unsuccessfully as it turned out. They'd had lunch and in the early afternoon, a couple of hours before it happened, she had left the two hunters on the leeward side of the esker at Uimmatisatsaq on Craig Island, within sight of the char pool. The men said they wanted to try their hands at ice fishing and promised to start putting up camp. Since the party was low on drinking water and Edie knew of a nearby berg, she left them to go and fetch freshwater ice. Both men were carrying rifles, she hadn't seen any bear tracks en route and when she left them the weather was clear, so she wasn't worried for their safety. She took her bear dog, Bonehead, with her and, in any case, she reckoned she'd be gone no longer than an hour or so.

Edie paused momentarily to check the expressions on the faces of the men sitting round the table but Inuit were brought up to be good at hiding their feelings – you had to be, living in such small communities, where each was so dependent on the others – and no one was giving anything away. She took a steadying breath and carried on.

Afterwards, Simeonie congratulated her on her recall. She sat back, expecting questions, and was bewildered when the mayor merely summarized her account, added in a couple of editing notes for Sheila Silliq then moved on to Joe. Already, then, she sensed the outcome. Nothing she or Joe could say would make any difference; the elders were just going through the motions.

Joe began to run through his version of the day. He had been in the mayor's office picking up a consignment of Arctic condoms that had come in on the supply plane a few days before. The condoms were wrapped in cute packets made to look like seal or musk ox or walrus, some well-meaning but patronizing southern initiative to encourage Inuit in the eastern Arctic to have safe sex, as though everyone didn't already know that the only way to make sex safe in the region would be to decommission the air-force bases.

Sometime in the early afternoon, Sammy had called him through to the comms office. He'd found his father standing by the radio and doing his best not to look anxious. Sammy outlined what had happened on Craig, or the bare bones of it. While he went to check the weather forecast, Joe skimmed down the planned flights log book to see if any planes were likely to be in the area and could pick up the party, but there were no flights listed. In any case, when he met Sammy again briefly in the corridor and exchanged information, it became clear that the weather was going to make flying out to Craig impossible. That was when Joe first suggested he head out to the scene by snowmobile.

The journey out to Craig had been tough because the winds were gusting and every so often a blast caught the snowbie and threw it off balance, but the new snow was at least dry and Joe had ridden the route only last week so he knew where most of the drifts and open leads were likely to be. When he got near, his stepmother's dog met him and led him directly to the camp. Edie was calm and purposeful, clearly in control of the situation. By contrast, Andy Taylor seemed withdrawn and shaky. Joe described Wagner's condition in some detail. He was keen to emphasize that Edie had already taken appropriate action, stemming the flow of blood and covering the wound with plastic to prevent air filling the thoracic cavity and collapsing the lungs. The bullet had shattered part of Wagner's collarbone and shredded the flesh beneath and there was what looked like an exit wound through the scapula. His pulse was racy and weak and it was clear that he had lost a great deal of blood. More worrying still, he was showing all the signs of advanced hypovolemic shock. He reckoned at the time that Wagner's chances of survival were small but he hadn't said so for fear of discouraging Edie and Andy Taylor, as well as Felix Wagner himself. He knew it was important that everyone was agreed they were on a mission to save a man's life.

Simeonie wanted to know if waiting for the plane had affected Wagner's chances. Joe was sure it hadn't helped, but to what degree the wait for the plane had affected the outcome he couldn't say. It was possible Felix Wagner would have died anyway.

The elders listened to the remainder of Joe's testimony without comment. When he finished, Sammy Inukpuk asked Edie and Joe to step outside and wait in the administration office.

To pass the time, Edie went into the office kitchen and made tea. While Joe sat at one of the workstations picking at his nails, Edie sat cradling a hot mug. Neither felt relaxed enough to talk. Why were they there? As witnesses? Suspects? Defendants? Edie thought about Derek Palliser. She'd been thinking about Derek a good deal over the past twenty-four hours, assuming there would have to be a police investigation into Wagner's death. Now she wasn't so sure. The mayor usually handled any small community disturbances – drunkenness, domestic squabbles, petty theft

– but this was bigger than that. Any unexpected death, Derek was automatically called in, wasn't he? She tried to recall the number of times in the past few years. Only twice, she thought. The first time was after Johnnie Audlaluk beat his little stepson to death, which must have been eight or nine years ago. The elders had wanted to deal with the situation internally, but news of the boy's death reached a relative in Yellowknife and she had called the Yellowknife police who had in turn alerted Derek Palliser. Audlaluk was held for psychiatric assessment, later tried and found guilty of manslaughter. He was still lingering in some secure psychiatric unit somewhere.

His case illustrated precisely why the elders preferred not to involve police unless they had to. Almost everyone in Autisaq, including Johnnie's own parents, thought it would have been more humane to deal with him the Inuit way; take him up to the mountains and, when he was least expecting it, push him off a cliff. No one said this to the then Constable Palliser, of course, but he'd picked it up anyway. His insistence on bringing the case to trial had made him enemies.

Though Edie had disagreed with Derek's actions, she had a lingering respect for the man, which was probably why she had helped him out in the Brown case five years ago. Everyone else had been in favour of burying that one too. At the end of a particularly harsh winter a passing hunter had found Samwillie Brown's dead body out on the land. The foxes had made a meal of him. The council of Elders had put the death down to an accident or natural causes and the whole thing would have been buried along with the remains of Samwillie Brown had it not been for the fact that the arrival of Brown's body back in Autisaq happened to coincide with one of Derek's routine patrols. The policeman had made himself extremely unpopular by insisting on another investigation. Samwillie Brown had been a cheat and a bully and most people were glad to see the back of him. The only person who seemed genuinely upset by his death was his wife, Ida, who was also the one person most frequently at the business end of Samwillie's fist. But that was how it was sometimes. No doubt some southern shrink would label it co-dependency. Up here in Autisaq it was known as loyalty. Ida had asked Edie to accompany her to the formal identification of the body. They were friends of a sort. Ida had stayed over at Edie's house a few times when Samwillie was drunk enough to be dangerous.

The moment Edie saw what remained of the dead man, she was struck by the parchment-coloured sheen on the skin. After Ida left, she stayed on at the morgue on the pretence of using the bathroom, returned to the body and lifted the one remaining eyelid. The eye looked like a lunar eclipse of the sun, the greyish jelly rimmed by tiny yellow flames, the classic symptoms of vitaminosis. She went directly from the morgue to Derek's room in the police office to tell him that, in her opinion, Samwillie Brown had died of an overdose of vitamin A, which in the Arctic could only mean one thing: the man had eaten polar-bear liver.

Derek listened, then shrugged the information off, pointing out that Samwillie Brown was a drunk and looked jaundiced most of the time. Edie had been startled by his casual indifference. Until that moment, she'd had Derek Palliser down as the old-fashioned type – dedicated, something of an outsider, perhaps, but a by-the-book kind of man. But now he seemed to be quite determined to abnegate responsibility. She wondered if something had rattled him, if he'd become temporarily unhinged. Inuit often said that was what happened when you spent more time in an office than out on the land; one by one you lost your senses. After that, you lost your mind.

Eventually they went back to the morgue together, Edie lifted Samwillie's one good eye and Derek Palliser agreed: the flames did seem to indicate vitamin A poisoning.

A couple of days later Derek flew in a pathologist who ran tests which confirmed that Samwillie Brown had died of hypervitaminosis, the deadly overdose of vitamin A that comes from eating bear liver. Knowing no Inuit, even a drunk one, would ever be so stupid as to eat bear liver voluntarily, Derek went back to the house Samwillie and Ida shared, taking Edie's bear dog with him. She tried to recall which Bonehead it had been. She thought back to the date. Bonehead the Second most like.

In any case, when Derek Palliser insisted on defrosting some hamburger he found at the back of the meat store, Bonehead Two went crazy at the smell of fresh bear meat. Not long after that, Ida confessed. What else could she do? The circumstantial and forensic evidence meshed up. Unable to tolerate Samwillie's violent and brutish behaviour any more, she'd started feeding her husband raw hamburger tainted with bear liver. No one seemed to notice him getting sicker because no one liked him enough to care. Derek Palliser had been promoted to sergeant for 'an outstanding investigation', but he and Edie realized they'd both been naïve. Autisaq didn't exactly thank Derek Palliser for what he had done but, with the exception of a few hardliners who hadn't forgiven him for progressing the Johnnie Audlaluk case, the inhabitants grudgingly accepted he was just doing his job. They weren't so understanding of Edie.

Edie and Joe finished their tea in silence. Pauloosie Allakarialak came skating by the building, followed by Mike and Etok Nungaq, fresh from closing up the store. Joe began chewing his nails again. Edie tried not to pull on her pigtails. The clock swung round to 9 p.m. The sun continued to burn. They could hear muffled voices coming from the council chamber but couldn't make out any words. After what seemed like an age, the door to the chamber swung open and Sammy Inukpuk's weathered face appeared, looking grim. There was something sly or perhaps evasive, Edie thought, in the speed with which he withdrew back into the room, as though he were signalling that his loyalties were to the men inside.

Edie and Joe followed him in. The elders watched them in silence as they sat. No one smiled. After a moment Simeonie Inukpuk began to speak in oddly formal tones, the kind Edie associated with the feds and do-gooders from down south.

'The council of Elders has considered the circumstances surrounding the death of the hunter, Felix Wagner,' Simeonie began, 'and has determined his death was caused by a bullet fired by him from his own rifle ricocheting off a boulder and hitting him in the collarbone. There were two witnesses to the accident, Edie Kiglatuk and the white man, Andrew Taylor, who will confirm this.'

For a moment, Edie and Joe sat in astonished silence, then Edie heard Joe gasp, stiffen, and open his mouth to speak. She elbowed him under the table and shook her head minutely. Whatever he had to say now would make no difference.

'The dead man's family will be informed immediately of the accident. As a matter of form, Sergeant Palliser will be sent a written report from the council. Given that the two witnesses to the event are happy to sign an affidavit to the effect that Felix Wagner's death was caused by a self-inflicted wound, we do not consider it necessary to ask the police to investigate the matter further.'

Simeonie held Edie's gaze. Now was the time for her to speak up. She drew breath then, for an instant, caught Sammy's eye, and thought she saw him give her a tiny, almost imperceptible nod.

'Since the hunter's death was a rare and unfortunate accident,' Simeonie continued, 'the council of Elders has concluded that there will be no need to revoke Edie Kiglatuk's guiding licence.'

So there it was. The deal she had just wordlessly struck to give credence to the lie and keep her job. She bit her lip and reminded herself that she was doing this for Joe.

Sammy accompanied Edie and Joe back to Edie's house. Nobody spoke on the way. Edie sensed her ex-husband had insisted on stringing along because he was gofering for Simeonie. Maybe the mayor had asked him to make sure they didn't call Derek Palliser until a formal announcement had been made. She couldn't blame Sammy. She knew when she married him that he would always live in his brother's shadow. Now she understood why Simeonie had gone to speak to Taylor at the hotel. He'd struck some kind of deal with him too. You had to take your hat off to the fellow. He was slick.

At the house, Joe made directly for his room, saying he was tired and would skip supper, but the real reason, Edie was sure, was that he was disgusted: with the process, with the council of Elders, and even, or maybe especially, with her and Sammy. She heated seal soup while Sammy flicked through the TV channels until he found an old episode of *NYPD Blue*. They ate their food on the sofa in awkward silence. She wasn't going to open old wounds by tackling him about what had just happened. He still thought her leaving him was an act of betrayal, not, as she saw it, a means of survival. He would see what had just happened as a bit of truth-tinkering for greater ends. And maybe that's exactly what it was.

3

Derek Palliser bent down in the gravel to get a better look at Jono Toolik's graffitied sealskins.

'What did I tell you?' said Jono Toolik, in triumphant tone. 'Vandalism.'

There was no arguing with the evidence. Someone had branded the word *iquq*, shit, in middle of the skin where there would be no disguising it. And there was more – two *iquqs*, three *itiqs*, asshole and, towards the bottom of the pile, a *qitiqthlimaqtisi arit*, fuck you, or more accurately, fock you, since whoever had created it couldn't spell.

'Listen,' Derek sighed, 'why don't you just store your skins under lock and key for a while?' Jesus Jones. Small-town politics. He felt in need of a cigarette and reached into his pocket for his Lucky Strikes.

'Oh no.' Jono Toolik wasn't going to let him off so easily. He jabbed a finger at the skin branded *qitiqthlimaqtisi*, pulled it out and swung it in front of Derek's face like a pendulum. 'This is a threat to my livelihood, I know who did it and I want him arrested.'

Derek knew who did it too, and in an hour from now, when news of the incident had done the rounds in Kuujuaq, everyone else would: Tom Silliq. The Tooliks and the Silliqs had been mortal enemies for about four hundred and fifty years. When they weren't busy pissing one another off, they were recounting tales of the historical injustices perpetrated upon them centuries before by the scumbags on the other side.

Derek took a cigarette from his pack, lit it and waited for Jono Toolik to kick off. Whatever he was about to say, Derek had heard it before. He'd um and ah to give an impression of attentiveness and use the time to take a smoke and think about lemmings.

He was probably thinking too much about lemmings. People were beginning to tease him about it, but thinking about lemmings stopped him dwelling on how Misha Ludnova had ruined his life. For three summers she had burrowed into his heart and now she was gone there was nothing left but a hole. Initially, she'd come up to help lead a bunch of summer camps for kids. She'd been hopeless at it, of course, forever complaining about the conditions at camp and the squandering of her artistic talents on children who were more interested in killing caribou than painting them. Despite all this, perhaps in some perverse way because of it, within the first week of her arrival, Derek had fallen hopelessly in love. Her looks had only added to his feelings for her: her long, slender limbs, spring sky eyes and hair the colour of cotton grass in the fall. Even though she'd shown no interest whatsoever in him that first summer, he'd nurtured the hope that she'd change her mind when she returned the next year, as indeed she did. It was during that second summer that Maria Kunuk's boy had nearly drowned while in Misha's care – or, rather, lack of it; there had been an outcry in the village and a call for her to be let go. But he'd stood up for her, pointing out that Kuujuaq was a dangerous place to live and that what had happened had nothing to do with Misha and everything to do with the Arctic. The Kuujuaq council of Elders had imposed a fine, and it was not long after Derek paid it that Misha began to take an interest in him. By the time she left at the end of that summer, she'd made him giddy, like a man half his thirty-nine years and he'd been fool enough – or vain enough – to suppose she loved him.

The third summer she came up to be with Derek and to paint. Her real vocation, she said, was as an artist, and she'd persuaded some foundation or other to sponsor her to work on a project 'negotiating the interface between global warming and the disappearance of selfhood', whatever that meant. Turned out the sponsorship was more in the way of an honour than any financial award, so Derek had invited her to move in with him. They'd spent what Derek had thought was a blissful summer together, after which Misha had gone back to Yellowknife and refused to return his calls.

The most painful part of all this was not that he had been used; it was the fact that knowing he'd been used made no difference to his feelings. *There is no getting around it, when it comes to that woman I'm a sap.* Even now, months since she'd left, he could still see no future for himself that did not involve some continuation of his saphood. Though he was embarrassed to admit this, even to himself, he'd spent far too much of the winter thinking long and hard about how he might win her back and concluded that he had two options. The first was to crack some high profile crime that would get his name in the papers and result in a promotion. He might even be able to persuade his bosses to grant him a secondment to Yellowknife. Being one of only two police on an island the size of Great Britain and a population of a couple of hundred gave you a lot of freedom but it stopped you from plugging into anything bigger than the small-time hustle going on around your ears. No one in Kuujuaq or any of the other tiny settlements making up the population of Ellesmere Island and the surrounding areas had done anything worth investigating. There was that event in Autisaq a few weeks back, the death of the *qalunaat* hunter – what was his name – Wagoner? – but the case didn't have any of the right ingredients to qualify as high-profile. It wasn't as though Wagoner had been a movie star or some big-time politician. Besides, the council of Elders had made it clear that they wouldn't welcome him opening up the case. He'd read the report and knew perfectly well that the chances of a man being killed by his own bullet ricocheting off a rock were about as slim as a slice of ice in a hot kettle, but he also knew how dependent Autisaq was on its hunting and guiding business and he'd taken the decision not to interfere. A fudging of the facts only became a cover-up when someone challenged it, and no one had.

The only guaranteed way to get himself back on Misha's radar in the foreseeable future was to follow the second option and persuade the editor of one of the big scientific journals, *Nature*, maybe, to publish his lemming research. To do that, he needed to be wasting less of his time mediating centuries old feuds and more of it in the field.

Derek Palliser finished his cigarette. The time had come to assert himself. He let himself be pushed around too often. He'd been too passive, too keen not to ruffle any feathers. Now was his chance to change all that. The place to start was right here, right now, by putting a stop to this ridiculous fight between the Toolik and Silliq clans. Drawing himself up to his full height, which was considerably higher than Jono Toolik, he expressed regret about the sealskins but explained that next time he expected the Tooliks and the Silliqs to resolve their petty disputes themselves, without involving the police.

Stunned by this new, less pliant, Palliser, Toolik took a pace back and blinked. His mouth pumped like a beached fish. For a moment Derek thought the man was going to punch him out. But he'd expended so much energy over the years playing along with small town politics, to absolve himself now felt nothing short of revelatory. The two men eyed one another for a minute or two, Jono Toolik's face a smear of disgust. Then, spitting on the ice path beside him, the hunter turned and went back into his house, banging the door to the snow porch behind him.

Derek shoved his hands in his pockets and trudged back to his little office in the prefabricated A frame that served as the Kuujuaq detachment. It was at times like these that he wished he'd taken up that job offer he'd had from a visiting Russian geologist, cleaning oil derricks in Novosibirsk. 'Plenty money for a man who don't mind the cold!' the geologist had said.

Grabbing a mug of tea, he slumped down in his chair and stared into the middle distance. He was not quick to anger, but the midget-sized problems of small-town life seemed intolerable all of a sudden. He felt horribly stuck. Picking up his mug he downed the last of the tea and rehearsed in his mind his resolve to act. At that moment the door yawned open and Constable Stevie Killik burst in, bringing with him a savage blast of icy air.

'That Toolik fellow is a walrus dick,' Stevie said, stamping the cold out of his feet. Derek's sidekick was by nature a mild-mannered man. If he called anyone a walrus dick it was because they were.

'Let me guess, Tom Silliq's had a word with you.'

'Right.' Stevie pulled off his glove liners and went to put the kettle on. 'Want some tea?'

Derek stared into his mug. The emptiness unsettled him. 'Sure thing,' he said finally.

While they waited for the water to boil, the two men swapped stories. Tom Silliq had approached Stevie on the ice road by the cemetery, in a very agitated state, claiming Jono Toolik had sent two of his half-starved huskies to raid his meat store. The dogs had gnawed through most of a haunch of caribou and several seals, torn open sacks of the dog biscuits Silliq kept for his own dogs, and pissed up against a stack of walrus heads, ruining hundreds of dollars' worth of meat and dog chow. When Stevie had asked whether Silliq had actually seen the dogs himself, he said he'd dreamed about them.

'So you told him there was a principle in law called burden of proof.'

'Sure.'

'And?'

'He called me something unrepeatable.' Stevie shook his head. 'Sometimes I don't know why I do this job,'

'Maybe it has something to do with the fact that there aren't any other jobs for about a thousand kilometres in any direction?'

'Not true, D.' Stevie perked up. The two of them spent many happy hours fantasizing about jobs they might have had in some parallel universe in the south. 'They're always needing someone to drive the night-honey truck.'

'Oh, how could I forget the opportunity to wade around knee-deep in Tom Silliq's shit.'

'We both got the experience, boss.'

Stevie disappeared into the kitchenette.

Derek went over to the fax machine and flipped through the pile of faxes. The High Arctic Police Service was the smallest of several indigenous forces, independent of the RCMP, but licensed to use certain centralized RCMP services like supplies and police labs. Once a quarter the Royal Canadian Mounted Police headquarters in Ottawa sent out routine faxes requesting various administrative forms and reports, which the Kuujuaq detachment routinely ignored. The current pile dated back three years. No one at RCMP HQ seemed to notice. From time to time Derek went through them to make sure he hadn't missed anything urgent. The act of flipping and scanning the pages gave him thinking time.

Whoever's dogs had broken into Tom Silliq's shed, the complaint called for action. In his new, more forthright guise, Derek felt motivated to take some. Make a stand. People couldn't be allowed to leave their sled dogs untethered at night. The animals weren't house pets. On more than one occasion huskies had got out and mauled young children. Derek was damned if that was going to happen on his watch.

When Stevie reappeared with the tea, he instructed his constable to post a couple of notices at the mayor's office and at the store pointing out that, with immediate effect, all dogs allowed to roam free in the community at night would be mistaken for wolves and shot.

Stevie nodded and switched on his computer. Moments later he looked up. 'Hey, boss, remind me how to create a new file?'

Derek raised his eyes to heaven and went over. After years of petitioning he had finally persuaded the RCMP supply centre to send up a couple of computers. He'd immediately fallen in love with them because they cut the time he spent doing administration in half, which gave him more time for his beloved wildlife patrols. After Misha left, he'd set up a satellite internet connection and discovered a world of lemming research at his fingertips: Finnish surveys of population cycles, a paper from Norway on snowy-owl predation, some US stuff on the implications of global warming on subniveal wintering. That was when he'd realized that his interest in lemmings wasn't simply a personal quirk. There were plenty of others interested in them too, proper scientists, people with more qualifications than he'd ever have. Aside from being fascinating in themselves, the hardy little rodents were a barometer of climate change. People could snicker, but lemming research was on the cutting edge.

Derek had tried to encourage Stevie to share in his new love for technology, but, despite being younger than Derek, Stevie had never really got it. In his view, computers were basically sinister, like the spirits of rogue ancestors. Constable Killik understood they were part of the police landscape now, but it wasn't a part he was keen to frequent.

Derek brought up a blank page and returned to his desk.

'By the way,' he said, 'what *did* Tom Silliq call you?'

'You won't like it.'

Derek gave him a look that said, go on, amaze me.

'He said I allow myself to be bossed about by an Indian lemming fart.'

Derek laughed bleakly. For a small minority in Kuujuaq, he'd always been an object of derision on account of his mongrel blood: part *qalunaat*, part Inuit and, almost unforgivably, part Cree, the Inuit's natural enemy. He'd grown up with the idea that he was someone who probably didn't belong anywhere, but that didn't mean he liked being reminded of the fact. He drew out his carton of cigarettes then, thinking better of it, got up from his desk and went into the radio room to make his usual morning calls. He didn't want Stevie to see he was rattled.

Since the cutbacks the Kuujuaq detachment had been given the communities of Hell Gate, Jakeman Fiord and the scientific station on Devon Island to police, in addition to the original beat of Kuujuaq, Eureka and Autisaq. There wasn't much at Hell Gate or Jakeman Fiord – a couple of tiny weather stations, a few hunting camps open mostly in the summer, and, at Jakeman, a small geologic survey, but he was expected to make contact with someone from each community at least once every other day and to be prepared to fly out at short notice should anything untoward happen.

Other than the death of Felix Wagner, nothing untoward had happened in quite some time and Derek's calls had taken on a slightly desperate air. It was not that he was willing anything bad to befall any of the five Arctic settlements and the science station under his wing, it was just that the lack of an event calling for his intervention or assistance fed the feelings of impotence and redundancy that had already been brought on by Misha's departure.

To amuse himself, he'd invented a series of rubrics to determine in which order to make the calls: alphabetical one day, then the next in reverse order of the number of vowels in the name. Today, he decided to go for a simple reverse alphabetical, which meant starting with Jakeman and working his way to Autisaq.

He sat down in the caribou-leather radio chair and donned the headphones.

'Hey, Derek,' a voice crackled through the static from Jakeman, 'you're wasting your time again.'

He made his way through the list, taking a break for a cigarette at Eureka. Nothing happening anywhere. His final call was to Autisaq. A familiar voice answered.

'Joe Inukpuk. Haven't heard you on radio in a while.' Derek smiled to himself. He'd always liked that boy. They bonded over their support for Jordin Tootoo, the first Inuit pro ice-hockey player, who played for the Nashville Predators. On a trip south one time, Derek had bought Joe a Predators thermos and hat with the sabre-tooth tiger logo. The boy had worn the hat until it fell apart.

'I've been busy at the nursing station, sir.'

'Aha,' Palliser said. Word had got around that Joe was hoping to go into nursing training. Unusual for an Inuk. Still, he was to be admired for his ambition, not just for himself, but for his community. It was time the territory of Nunavut started training Inuit professionals instead of relying on southerners working short-term contracts.

'See the Predators game?'

'Oh man, it was a smash,' Joe said.

'Tootoo, what a star!'

'Too, too much.' It was their little joke, one Joe had first alighted on gleefully at the age of fourteen. They'd been telling it regularly in the six years since.

'Everything OK where you are?' Derek remembered this was supposed to be an official call.

A pause on the line. 'Sure.'

Derek heard voices in the background. The boy didn't sound sure. 'Really?'

'Just one thing, sir.' There was a hissing on the airwaves, interference probably, either that or Joe was whispering.

'My stepmom, Edie Kiglatuk? She'd like a word.'

'Go ahead and put her on,' Derek said. He always enjoyed talking to Edie and he was conscious, after the Samwillie Brown case, that he owed her.

'Can she call you at the end of the day?' Interference again. Some technical problem at the Autisaq end was jigging the connection; it was getting hard to hear the kid.

Derek said: 'But everything's OK, right?'

Joe said: 'Business as usual.'

They signed off and Derek Palliser went back to his paperwork. Something about the conversation with Joe began to gnaw at him. He had an idea that Edie was going to bring up the Wagoner affair. Why else would she contact him?

The remainder of the morning passed uneventfully. At lunchtime, Derek went to the store, bought three packs of instant ramen noodles and sat at his desk eating them while Stevie went back home for lunch with his family. Afterwards, Palliser made coffee and checked briefly on his lemmings. The weather had perked up since the early morning; the sun now blazed through thin, high cirrus and it was a balmy –25C, perfect for a trip out on the land.

He'd see if he could finish his paperwork in time to go for an evening ride to the polynya at Inuushuck cove. A pod of beluga had holed up, taking advantage of the clear water to rest before carrying on their travels. He'd seen bear tracks there and was curious to know if the animal had returned.

As he was thinking, the door to the snow porch swung open and Derek could hear the sound of boots being stamped to rid them of ice. A few moments later, Stevie appeared.

'Good lunch, D?' He spotted the empty ramen packets and tried to change the subject. 'Turning out to be a great day.' He walked across the office and peered behind the Venetian blinds. 'I thought, with the weather being so soft and all, we'd set up the barbecue for supper. The kids would love it if you came too.'

'Thanks.' It was so obviously a mercy call. Stevie meant well, but being pitied by your own constable, that sucked. 'I'm real busy with this research, though. Next time, eh?'

'Oh sure, D.'

They passed the afternoon in administrative duties. At five, Stevie rose from his desk and said he was going round to post the notices about wandering dogs and knock on a few doors to spread the word. After he'd gone, Palliser went back to his quarters on the southern side of the constabulary building, took off his uniform, heaved on his Polartec all-in-one, pulled his sealskin suit over the top, threw on a few pairs of mittens and some hats and made his way out to his snowmobile.

It was one of those beautiful, crystal-clear Arctic evenings where everything seemed picked out in its own spotlight. The sky was an unimpeachable blue and before him stretched a fury of tiny ice peaks, unblemished by leads. In the distance the dome-shaped berg, which had bedded into the surrounding pack for the winter, glowed furiously turquoise.

Derek took his vehicle through the path he had cleared back in January when the ice had finally settled. As he picked up speed, he felt first the freezing of his eyelashes, then the hairs in his nose. Even with his snow goggles on, tiny ice boulders began to accrete in the corners of his eyes. He enjoyed the feeling of encroachment, of being willingly and haplessly besieged by nature. A raven flew across his sight line and for the first time that day he felt content, even happy. Out on the land he forgot the radio conversation he'd had with Joe Inukpuk, the small-town stir-ups. He forgot Stevie Killik's well-meaning but humiliating pity, forgot Misha and best of all, he forgot he was a cur, a mixed blood, someone fashioned at the borders out of the scraps no one else wanted.

He reached the edge of the floe that marked the start of the open water of the polynya. Here the ice began to feel wetter, not quite yet unreliable, but deserving of caution and, leaving his snowbie, he proceeded on foot across patchy floe running between leads. It was dangerous ground, but Derek had enough experience to know when to take particular care. The conditions required his total concentration and he thought of nothing more until he reached the edge of the ice, where it gave out to clear, moving water, the restlessness of the currents beneath ensuring that it stayed ice-free all year round and, as a result, attracted zooplankton, then char, seal, orca and beluga, all the way up the food chain to polar bear. He wanted just to take a look at the beluga.

Derek hadn't hunted whale himself in a very long time. There was a good reason for that. Some years back he'd set up camp on the beach at Jakeman Fiord. Exploring the immediate area, he'd come upon a stretch of temporarily opened water at the foot of a fiord. Mistaking the water for a polynya, where the water was open all year round, a pod of young, inexperienced beluga had gathered. As the water had begun to solidify, they had taken it in turns to swim about and edge away the ice with their noses. As the ice crept further and further in, so their attempts to clear it became more frantic. The splashing eventually attracted a large male bear. Each time the beluga rose from the water to breathe, the bear harried them with his paws. By the time the bear had managed to drag a young beluga out onto the ice, the others, wounded and weak, were completely trapped as all around them the water turned to bloody ice.

Derek had never been able to see beluga again after that without something in him reaching out to them. It was this feeling of protectiveness that had brought him out to the polynya today, though the likelihood of this lot sharing the fate of those others was small, because the polynya opened out to deep-sea waters way out from the shoreline. Not so long ago, bears would have followed their prey out that far, part swimming, part jumping from floe to floe, but in the past four or five years the breakup had come so early that the great white hunters could no longer rely on their old ice routes and were wary of getting themselves stranded out in the open ocean. In the short term this was good for whales, bad for bears. In the long term, it was just bad.

Derek reached the edge of the water and waited a while but nothing stirred on the surface and it was with a sense of relief that he realized the belugas had moved on. Returning to Kuujuaq he was overcome with a feeling of melancholy. Not for the first time in his life, he wished he'd had the opportunity to go to college and study some aspect of Arctic zoology. He would have been happier as a naturalist than he was as a policeman, he thought, as he stuck the kettle on.

He looked around the little apartment and thought about Stevie's invitation. Next time he'd go.

After supper of canned beef stew, Derek went back to his office computer to work on his lemming project. The conventional wisdom in the scientific community was that the four-year lemming population cycle was somehow independent of the chief lemming predators, the fox, the snowy owl and the stoat, but, from his own observations in the field, Derek had begun to suspect that the predator population actually drove the cycle. It was a whole new angle on the relationship between predator and prey and he knew he'd have to be extremely careful to get his facts right before approaching anyone with a view to publishing his findings. His email popped up. He scanned the messages, saw none from Misha and buried his feeling of disappointment by getting up and making himself a cup of tea. He sat down and typed 'Arctic fox population' into Google, then, on a sudden, sickening impulse, deleted it and tapped in Misha's name instead. He'd done this so many times, hating himself, but unable to stop. Some people got addicted to internet gaming or porn, but with Derek it was Googling Misha. The only comfort to be had was the fact that the intervals between each trawl had grown longer. It had been three or four months since he'd last Googled his ex.

A familiar batch of thumbnails began to collect themselves together on the screen. He scrolled through until he reached one he hadn't seen before. Misha standing next to a man; they looked to have their arms around one another. Some overwhelming impulse drove Derek to click on the 'enlarge' command and he found himself staring directly into the eyes of a tall, blue-eyed, well-built *qalunaat* man with tremendous cheek bones. From the man's stance and Misha's defiantly happy gaze there could be no doubting they were a couple.

Derek felt his stomach turn and his head grow light, as though he'd just been launched from a rocket. Beneath the image he read: 'Tomas and Misha in Copenhagen'.

Derek reached out and pressed the off button on the computer. The screen froze then went dark, leaving the image of the couple burned on his retina. For a moment, he wanted nothing more than to smash something. He stood up, went back into the apartment and forced himself to lie on his bed until he felt more composed.

He was woken from his reverie by the sound of the detachment door bursting open and a man's voice shouting: 'Palliser? Come out, you *uhuupimanga*.'

The reek of cheap vodka followed the sound of the voice. Derek had been called a lump of sperm before, but never on his own turf. He opened the door into the office. In the light still streaming through the closed Venetian blinds he saw Tom Silliq and Jono Toolik standing none too straight.

'I hope this is some kind of emergency.'

'Emergency, eh?' Tom shouted and, tottering forward, threw a poorly aimed punch. 'It will be.' The man was cataclysmically drunk.

'Now then, fellas, go home,' Derek said, scouring the room to make sure neither he nor Stevie had left a weapon on view.

Silliq and Toolik looked at one another. Silliq began to giggle. Taking advantage of this momentary distraction, Toolik took another swipe at Derek but he managed to dodge it.

Figuring it was probably safer to be outside, he headed for the door, only to be grabbed on his way out by Silliq. As Derek pushed him away, Silliq swung his fist randomly and, as luck would have it, it slammed into Derek's left eye. Shocked as much as hurt, Derek felt himself stumble as

Toolik took another punch of his own, socking the policeman in the nose. Blood from the nose wound sprayed onto Silliq's parka, and for a moment or two everyone froze, uncertain what was supposed to happen next.

Dimly recalling snatches of the morning's grievances, Toolik opened his mouth and said, approximately: 'Stay out of our business.'

Then, whirling about, he headed unsteadily for the door, belched and, with the blustering dignity of the paralytic, made his way outside. Tom Silliq stood a little while in the constabulary office, as if awaiting instructions, before staggering silently after his neighbour.

Derek rushed for the door and locked it behind them. They'd be back sometime in the morning, red-faced, semi-sober and deeply apologetic. He wiped his nose with the back of his hand and was surprised at the amount of blood. His eye hurt too, he realized, and since he couldn't see out of it he assumed it had closed up.

He made his way to the bathroom in the apartment and was busy washing away the ooze from his face when he heard a buzzing coming from the office. At first he imagined Silliq and Toolik were back. Then, with some relief, he remembered that Edie was supposed to be calling on the radio. He quickly washed his hands of blood, picked up a hand towel and made his way into the comms room.

'Edie?'

'Hey, Derek. How are you?'

Derek opened his good eye wide and stretched his mouth a few times to make sure he could talk.

'Just dandy.' He didn't ask why she had chosen to call so late. He reckoned she had her reasons.

'Is this a bad time?'

Derek pressed the towel against his eye and felt something pop.

'Couldn't be better.'

There was a pause, which Derek felt incumbent upon himself to fill.

'This isn't about the hunter fellow, the one who died, is it?'

There was an awkward kind of a sigh. Derek's head throbbed and his mouth felt dry, his tongue brittle. He felt his brain sinking back.

'You're not sick, are you, Derek?'

'No,' he said. 'Not sick.' He liked it that she'd asked.

'I'm sorry,' Edie said. Her voice grew serious. 'I know this isn't exactly going to make your day.'

'Oh, don't you worry about that, Edie,' Derek said. He raised his fingers to his right eye. It was already swelling. 'I'm having a super time. Any case, you might have noticed, the day ended a while back.'

'The business with Felix Wagner,' Edie went on. 'Truth is, Derek, I shouldn't have signed that council of Elders' report.' She sounded tired and defensive. 'A week ago I went back to where it happened. I walked around the spot, kind of recreating the moment.'

'Edie, it's late,' he said, 'and you *did* sign, remember?' He was hoping to shame her into going away, but she didn't take the bait.

'The bullet entered Felix Wagner from the front, at an angle from above. At the time I found a footprint on the bluff above the beach, where the shooter must have been standing. Zig-zag with an ice bear in the middle. I told the council but it didn't make it into their report. Point is, Derek, there's no way Felix Wagner was killed by his own bullet.'

Derek prodded his eye very gently.

'No one's complained about the council of Elders' report. Ask me, the matter's closed.' The moment the words left his lips, he felt a bit ashamed.

'Come on, Derek.' She had this way of appealing to his better side, to his conscience, maybe. No one else was able to tweak away at him the way she did.

'Edie, listen to me,' he said, in a last ditch attempt to justify his inaction. 'This isn't Samwillie Brown. This Wagner fellow and his sidekick, they aren't our people.'

'With respect, Derek, you're missing the point. Felix Wagner is dead. No one really buys the story about the ricocheting bullet and the only other person we know was at the scene didn't do it. You know how it is. No one comes or goes in or out of these settlements without everybody knowing.'

He did know that. By God he did. You couldn't take a piss without someone having an opinion on it. One of the many ironies of northern living. The tundra had to be the only place in the world where there was everywhere and nowhere to hide.

'So . . .' Edie continued, 'whoever killed Felix Wagner is still here in Autisaq, or somewhere nearby, most likely in one of the settlements or maybe out on the land.'

Derek suddenly felt exhausted. He and Edie had stirred up a lot of bad will going after Ida Brown. The elders had washed their hands of this one. You had to ask, was it worth it?

'Edie, you're forgetting something.'

'What?'

Derek took a long breath.

'Nobody. Gives. A. Shit. You have nothing to gain by going over this and you have a lot to lose.' He felt a twinge of self-loathing as he said it, but he carried on all the same. 'You'll stir up a load of politics and it won't go anywhere. No one will co-operate.'

There was a short silence, then Edie came back on and in a low, resigned voice, added: 'Including you, it seems.' The radio fizzled out.

Derek listened to the white noise for a while. She hadn't sounded angry, he thought, only disappointed, which was worse. In any other world she'd be right, but this was the Arctic and up here, however much he and the High Arctic Police and all the other government agencies and NGOs and the do-gooders wanted to imagine otherwise, the only rules that mattered a damn were the ones the land imposed on those struggling to carve a living from it.

He went back into the apartment and stared at his eye in the bathroom mirror. It was puffed and purple, the lid now completely obscuring the eyeball. Damn Edie, he thought, she didn't even have anything real to go on. Even if what she said was true, and Wagner hadn't been killed either by Andy Taylor or by his own bullet, some Inuk hunter out on his own probably mistook Wagner for a caribou or a bear and took a shot. When he realized what he'd done he'd panicked and scarpered.

Derek climbed into bed and pulled up the covers but his eye was hurting and the conversation with Edie had rattled him, so he got up, pulled on his Polartec and insulated trousers, three pairs of socks, two scarves, two hats and his mukluks and went out into the annexe which once served as a coal shed but was now home to his lemmings. He flipped on the low-level lighting. The creatures were asleep in the tank he'd kitted out to simulate the subnivean space where they spent their winters in the wild. The last few years had been tough on the little critters, the snow under which they usually passed the winter, not hibernating exactly, rather sleeping and keeping warm, was beginning to rot too early. It was collapsing inwards and crushing them in their burrows. This lot would have died if Piecrust hadn't scented them out. For a few moments he just sat there, watching them sleeping, so peaceful they could almost be dead.

4

Edie sat on her own in front of the TV, trying to cheer herself up with her favourite supper of *maktaq* and sea urchins. The *maktaq*, thick, chewy whale skin underscored with a layer of creamy, slightly sour fat, put her in mind of the scent of the sea in summertime. She couldn't remember the last time she'd eaten it.

All the Arctic settlements were being warned off marine mammal fat, but she was in the kind of mood where she didn't care about PCB – polychlorinated biphenyl – contamination. You couldn't see, touch or smell PCB and no one seemed able to agree where it was coming from – theories varied from Russian nuclear plants, through wartime radar stations to US naval submarines – and the warnings felt abstract and nebulous. She didn't doubt that PCB caused the birth deformities scientists claimed and she commended Robert Patma's efforts to get women of childbearing age to restrict themselves to eating fish and caribou, flesh that wasn't so contaminated, but there was nothing like *maktaq* to make you feel at peace with the world and, in any case, Edie wasn't planning on having any kids. She'd drunk her way through her most fertile years and now that she was thirty-three and ready, at least in theory, to start a family, there was no one to start one with. She wasn't bitter about it. She'd been a stepmother to Willa and Joe for seven years and was as close to Joe as any human being could be. She just wished she felt as attached to Willa, but somehow it hadn't worked out that way.

The conversation with Derek Palliser had unsettled her. She knew she'd become overly insistent with him, displaying too much *ihuma*, the fieriness and ego that had once made her such a good hunter and later, Sammy would say, a difficult wife. The more rational part of her knew he was right. For once in her life, she should just learn to toe the line. What did it *matter* exactly how Felix Wagner had died? On the other hand, Joe had set some dark energy roiling in her belly and she knew she would not be content without the answer. Perhaps being sober had made her more protective of a reality she'd spent so many years avoiding. So here she was eating *maktaq*, despite knowing it wasn't good for her. Pursuing this Wagner business wasn't good for her either and yet, still she felt compelled to discover the truth.

The door to the snow porch opened and Sammy Inukpuk poked his head round. Not wanting to give him an excuse to stay, she turned off the DVD.

He said: 'Hey, Edie,' and noting the debris on her plate, 'any left?'

'You're out of luck.' She motioned him to the seat on the other side of the TV, but he sat down beside her anyway. 'TV packed in?'

'Ah, nope, not exactly.'

He hovered. 'A beer'd be good.' Then, adopting a cheery tone, 'Hey, did you see the job Joe did on his snowbie? Looks like new. Phwooee. Must have cost something. Where'd the boy get the money?'

Edie shot him a look. Her ex knew well enough where Joe had got the money. She had given Joe an advance on what she'd been owed for the Wagner trip. After Wagner died, the wife had refused to pay up, and she hadn't felt like asking Joe for the money back. Sammy wanted her to know that he was aware she was broke, which could only mean one thing: he had some kind of money-making proposition up his sleeve.

'About that beer?'

'Sammy Inukpuk, whatever you got to say, say it sober.'

He put on a hangdog look.

'Aw, Edie, it's been a hard day.' He had a way of making her feel bad and it played on her that he knew it.

She went into the kitchen and set the kettle on. While it heated up, she fetched the key to the cupboard where she kept her booze. Getting the key was a palaver. She intended it to be that way. Whenever people asked, which they rarely did, she told them that she kept the booze for visitors and guests. In fact its perpetual presence was a test she'd set herself. She knew she wasn't yet strong enough to keep the cupboard unlocked but that was her goal. Only then, when there was booze around that no longer tempted her, would she know she was truly free of it. She plucked out a can of Bud, locked the cupboard back up and made herself a mug of sugary tea. Sammy popped the can and took a long slug.

'I got you a guiding job.'

This was good news, and unexpected. Sammy's propositions weren't usually so substantial. Edie felt a twinge of guilt at harbouring ungenerous thoughts towards her ex. Somehow when the two of them were together it always resulted in her feeling bad.

'Fellow called Bill Fairfax, descendant of that old-time *qalunaat* explorer, what's his name?'

'Sir James Fairfax? Is this the fella who was up here before?'

Someone purporting to be Sir James's descendant had been up on Ellesmere several years back with a film crew, making a documentary following the explorer's penultimate voyage. She couldn't remember much about it. Happened during her lost years.

'Yeah, that one. He wants to locate his ancestor's body. Reckons it could be on Craig. Bringing an assistant, just the two of them. Think they might be able to get some TV company interested.'

On the surface, this sounded like the perfect gig. Small party, presumably with some knowledge of local conditions, no hunting involved and she knew Craig Island as well as anyone. It seemed unlikely they'd find Sir James Fairfax's body, she thought, but you could never tell. Under all that snow and ice, the tundra was one great open-air charnel house: bones, antlers, skeletons scattered all over. Nothing ever rotted or even stayed buried long. There was no deep archaeology, no layering of history here.

Southerners often marvelled at the way the recent and ancient past were equally present, as though there had only ever been one yesterday and everything in the past had happened on that single day. Only a couple of years ago a group of anthropologists from the University of Alberta had located the first mate from some old-time expedition. His comrades had buried him under rocks but decades of wind and weather had moved the body out from under them and he was found lying out on the ice, in more or less pristine condition.

All the same, it was kind of a weird time to look for a man, the ice and snow not yet melted off, and Edie said so.

'I told them that,' Sammy said. 'But it didn't seem to bother them.'

'So long as they know we're unlikely to find anything.' *Qalunaat* ventured north for all kinds of reasons, often not the ones they supposed.

'Maybe the body was left in some cave or something, I dunno much about it.'

'They're paying?'

Sammy nodded. 'The usual.'

'Why aren't you doing it then?' She narrowed her eyes, waiting for the catch.

Her ex looked at his feet. 'I got council of Elders business.' He drained his beer and belched. 'Any case, you always get first dibs on Craig, Edie.' This was true, though he was only saying it to soften her up.

Edie thought about the money. 'Sure.'

She was still waiting for the catch.

'They're arriving on the supply plane tomorrow.' He hesitated. 'There's just one thing.'

Edie wrinkled her nose. Right. The same old Sammy; slippery, never giving you the whole picture, the Sammy she divorced. *First dibs on Craig, my ass.*

'All it is, Bill Fairfax's assistant . . .' He dropped the ring pull into his empty can and rattled it around a little. '. . . it's that Andy Taylor fellow.'

The name came at Edie like an unexpected gust of cold wind. What the hell was Andy Taylor doing back in Autisaq? Just when she'd squared it with herself to leave the whole Felix Wagner business alone. Now it was coming right back at her.

'You know how I feel about that guy. Can't you do this, I'll do the next one?' A dark slick of anger seeped over her.

'Like I said, Edie, I got business.' Sammy twirled the ring pull round inside the can some more.

She didn't want anything more to do with Andy Taylor. On the other hand, if she turned this down, she'd have to go to the back of the line for the next gig. She needed the money and Sammy knew it. He'd backed her into a corner.

'Don't worry, I fixed it so you won't have to guide him. You'll be working with the other one.'

'Why? Taylor staying in the settlement?'

'Not exactly,' Sammy said. 'He and this Fairfax fellow want go out in two separate parties, one to the west by Uimmatisatsaq, near where you were before, the other around Fritjof Fiord in the east. I told them you would take Fairfax to Fritjof. Joe already agreed to take Taylor.'

Edie felt startled. All this time Sammy had been cooking this up and now he'd somehow cajoled Joe into agreeing to it, without even asking for her opinion.

'Wait up just one second, Sammy Inukpuk,' she said. 'You're not letting your son out with that man. Andy Taylor's a panicker, he's inexperienced, unreliable.' The look on Sammy's face darkened.

'You don't get to tell me how I should treat my son. *You* abandoned *us*, remember?' He stood up and swept to the door.

She'd seen this before, Sammy trying to take the moral high ground. It was as though, in his eyes, that was all she had become, some kind of flaky, no good bolter. She made a grab for her pigtails and saw him bite his lip. At least he knew how much the A-word hurt her.

'Three days, six max,' he said, shaking his head at her.

She went after him, reached the internal door to the porch and yanked it open. The cold felt like a bad dream. 'Sammy?'

He looked up from tying his bootlace.

'This goes wrong, I won't forgive you.'

He finished his lace, stood up and waved her away. 'I'm not asking you to trust me, Edie, not any more, but try to have some faith in your stepson.'

She felt herself blush, a sense of shame needling her belly. Sammy was right. Joe was a highly competent guide and he knew Craig almost as well as she did. It wasn't as though Andy Taylor was a bad man. He was just high maintenance was all.

'Sure,' she said, in a chastened tone. He winked at her and smiled. She waited while he opened the door and stepped out into the cold.

'Sammy?'

'Yeah?'

'You owe me a beer.'

The following morning, Edie drove the snowbie along the shoreline then took the ice road up beside the school towards the landing strip. As she bumped along the ice, she turned over the details of the trip. It was late enough in the spring season for the ice to be just beginning to destabilize but it hadn't begun to rot in earnest yet. That wouldn't happen for another three months. Some leads would have opened up in the shore-fast ice but so long as she and Joe were careful, the routes should be pretty unproblematic. Taylor and Fairfax were expecting to be out on the land for three days. That might stretch to five if they got weathered out, but at this time of the year blizzards were short-lived.

Before long, she caught the sound of the plane humming in the far distance but the sky was a drab blanket patched with low and clumpy clouds and she couldn't see it yet. It would be bumpy up at fifteen hundred metres today. She hoped Andy Taylor and Bill Fairfax were good flyers.

She passed the lonely little cemetery thinking about the bodies of Sir James Fairfax and his crew, lying out on the tundra somewhere, far, far from home. Like her great-great-great-grandfather, Welatok, buried out near Etah in Greenland, a different country, his spirit rootless and unreachable.

Here in Autisaq, the tombstones were completely obscured by snow, but relatives had stuck plastic flowers in the ground and the cemetery looked like some weird, otherworldly art project. When the time came, she wanted to be buried in the proper Inuit way, under a pile of stones out on the tundra, with an *inukshuk* or a low stone cairn marking her place.

It struck her then that those of his crew who had survived him might have erected some kind of marker for Sir James. If there *was* a marker, it was odd she hadn't seen it. Then again, perhaps she didn't know Craig Island as well as she thought.

The Twin Otter nudged out from behind clouds. Edie had checked the manifest the night before and knew that Aunt Martie was at the controls. When she wasn't drinking, there was no finer bush pilot across the High Arctic. Martie was one of only a handful of Inuit pilots, and the only woman. She'd had to be twice as good as any of the men just to get her licence. Sure, she was eccentric, a bit of a loner even, but she'd handed a lifeline to Edie so many times she'd lost count and, despite her own struggles with booze, she'd always tried to keep her niece away from drink. Edie respected and loved her all the more for that.

Martie was bringing in the plane from behind the mountains so she wouldn't get caught up in a patch of turbulent wind. Banking into a sharp turn, she swooped back and brought the Otter in level. For an instant it seemed to hover above the surface of the landing strip before coming into a long, controlled skid along the gravel. The plane stopped right outside the tiny prefab that served as a terminal. Moments later, the door opened and a tall, slender man emerged down the steps, visibly stiffening in the cold. Behind him followed Andy Taylor, looking shaken. The instant Taylor hit the gravel, he doubled over and was violently sick. Bill Fairfax turned momentarily, wrinkled his nose in disgust and walked on towards the terminal building. So, thought Edie, the relationship between the two men was strictly business.

Fairfax was an elegant, chiselled man in his fifties. He

was wearing traditional caribou mukluk boots, a sure sign of a man in the grip of Arctic nostalgia. As he walked, the nap on his sealskin parka caught the light and lent him the appearance of something radiant and mystical. The gossips who hung around the back of the Northern Store would be having fun over that outfit for weeks.

Edie went over, introduced herself and apologized for Joe's absence, explaining that he was busy assisting Robert Patma in the nursing station. At close quarters her charge bore a remarkable resemblance to his ancestor, whose portrait Edie was so familiar with from the school history book. The match was exact enough to be unsettling, as though an old spirit had appeared in modern guise to sort out some unfinished business.

'Taylor said you were a bear hunter.' Bill Fairfax spoke in precise, clipped English. Sammy hadn't said where he was from, but Edie guessed England. Elizabetland, the locals called it.

She said: 'Once. Not in a long, long while.'

'Ah well.' He sounded disappointed.

An awkward moment followed as they tried not to watch Taylor out on the strip, kicking gravel over the mess he'd made.

'But you're quite the landswoman, I hear,' Bill Fairfax continued, returning to the subject of bear hunting.

Edie wondered for a moment if he was expressing a lack of confidence in her, then realized that it was just the opposite. Even though she was herself half *qalunaat*, she quite often found it was hard to read southerners.

'That hunting trip sounded *terrible*,' Fairfax went on.

Edie felt a lurch. Surely Taylor hadn't been stupid enough to have confided in Fairfax about the Wagner affair?

'Just bad luck,' she said, hedging.

'You're too modest. Taylor told me all about it, throwing

up that snowhouse. Nasty blizzard you two got caught up in.'

'Oh, that.' Edie felt herself relax. She guessed Taylor was lying for the same reason that she would go along with his lies: they both needed the work. Maybe he wasn't so stupid after all.

After she'd settled the two men in the hotel, Edie went across to the clinic to let Joe know she'd arranged a briefing meeting at the mayor's office and was met at the door by Robert Patma. Joe was busy talking to Minnie Toluuq, Robert explained, but he'd be free very shortly.

In the three years Robert Patma had been in the community, Edie had found herself growing increasingly fond of him. Like most *qalunaat*, he'd come up on a two-year contract, but, unlike almost all, he'd stayed. He was a hardy, uncomplaining type and although on the surface very cynical about his reasons for remaining in Autisaq – citing northern hardship money and long leave entitlements as chief among them – he'd often gone above and beyond what was called for under the terms of his contract. For example, he hadn't been under any obligation to allow Joe to volunteer at the nursing station but he'd showed a great deal of generosity and commitment to him and over the months the two men had become good friends. Joe often went round to Robert's apartment after work and the two would listen to music together and eat the curries the nurse liked to cook.

She made a point of following him into the kitchen where he was making tea and asking after his father.

'He's OK,' he said. 'Sugar?'

'Sure,' she said. She watched Robert drop a single cube into the mug. 'I'm sorry your mother didn't make it.'

He blinked. 'I don't really like to talk about it much.'

She reached for some more sugar, but he pushed the mug towards her as it was.

'You want to watch that,' he said. 'Diabetes. Arctic epidemic.'

'Another one.'

Robert smiled bleakly.

Just then Joe emerged from the consultation room at the back. He and Robert had a brief discussion about various things that needed doing then Joe put on his coat and boots and he and Edie walked down the ice road towards the mayor's office.

Edie said: 'Sweetheart, if you don't want to take this Andy Taylor fellow, you don't have to. You know that, don't you? You don't have to do anything just because your father says.'

He looked at her with affection and shrugged. 'It'll be different when I'm qualified.'

'You'll stay here in Autisaq, right?'

He shook his head. 'Yellowknife, Iqaluit maybe, somewhere bigger.' Then, tapping her on the nose, he said, 'You'll come too, Kigga?'

'Sure,' she said. 'Sure I will.' She meant it.

The heat in the mayor's office was stifling. Fairfax had complained about the cold, so Sammy had turned up the furnace. Edie glanced at the thermostat. Sixteen degrees. A hot house. Taylor was sitting in his Polartec, wiping away the sweat around his collar, looking ill at ease. Fairfax spread out in a chair beside him, giving off an air of entitlement.

After the success of the first TV documentary, Fairfax had been approached by the TV company about another idea, a search for the body of his ancestor.

'I guess you know the rumours?'

Sammy, Joe and Edie nodded. Everyone knew the

rumours. When Sir James's final expedition got into trouble, some Inuit had passed by the camp and seen what they took to be human meat hung out to dry. As the story was passed on to various white traders who came into and out of the area it was embroidered and elaborated upon. By the time it reached London it had become quite a scandal, casting a shadow over the explorer's reputation. It was on account of this that Sir James's backers had refused to send out a rescue party to try to locate the explorer and his crew. Probably it would have made no difference anyway. Fairfax's ship, the *Courageous*, was found drifting and abandoned by an American whaler just north of Cumberland Sound. None of the bodies had ever been recovered.

As Bill went on, Joe caught Edie's eye, looking for some kind of steer. He often thought of her as a bridge between his world and that other, unknowable place to the south. She signalled back with a reassuring smile; they'd talk it over later. She'd read enough about the old white explorers to know that the prospect of cannibalism hung over them like some malevolent spectre. To the Inuit, eating human flesh was merely the survival tool of last resort. The most dishonourable thing an Inuk man with a family could do was to take the easy way out, to give up the struggle to provide for his loved ones, lie down and die. That way he condemned his present and future family and brought shame on his ancestors. In the *qalunaat* world, the opposite was true. Dishonour had become attached to Sir James Fairfax's name precisely because he'd done everything he could, right down to eating his own kind, in order to survive.

Sir James's last known diary had recently surfaced among the effects of Bill's great-aunt, he continued. The explorer had been a punctilious diarist, keeping meticulous notes of weather conditions, navigational decisions as well as lists of supplies and a day-to-day account of happenings among the crew. His diaries from his first two Arctic expeditions, in 1840 and 1843, had long been part of the collection at the Scott Polar Institute at Cambridge University. It was always assumed that the diary of the penultimate voyage of 1847 was somewhere among the family papers, but it hadn't turned up until Bill himself had discovered it in an old port box filled with bits and pieces which his great-aunt had left him in her will. Bill doubted that his great-aunt had known the contents of the box; she'd left him several dozen, and most had contained nothing more interesting than old copies of accounts. But this was quite a prize. The diary was of particular interest because it contained a detailed plan of Sir James's proposed next voyage, the one during which, as it turned out, he and his crew disappeared.

Bill Fairfax hesitated. The newly recovered diary revealed that Sir James had planned to stay at Craig Island during the migration of beluga whale which passed close by during September on their way south. He hoped to kill enough whale to provide meat through the winter months, and had scouted out suitable campsites on a previous expedition, one of which was near the present-day Uimmatisatsaq, the other on the east of the island at Fritjof Fiord. Bill Fairfax spread his maps on the table, pointing out the two spots for Edie and Joe to examine.

No one knew what went wrong, he said, whether the beluga travelled by another route that autumn or the crew were struck down by disease but Bill Fairfax had a hunch that his ancestor made it to Fritjof. In any case, if he could find Sir James's body, he was convinced that recent advances in forensic testing would reveal the real cause of his death to have been scurvy or vitaminosis and not the starvation that might have led him to resort to the unspeakable.

The room fell silent for a moment, then Edie spoke up:

'Even with all these maps and the diary, unless there are

some pretty big grave markers, you may as well be trying to find a snowflake trapped inside an iceberg. It would make your job easier to come back in the summer, when the ground is partly exposed.'

Fairfax coughed. 'It's a little awkward,' he said. 'But I'm under some pressure to sell the diary and when I do, the information will become public. We're hoping to get enough material together to interest the TV people. Then we'll come up again with a film crew in the summer, you see.'

So it's about money and ego, Edie thought. Not that she cared. This wouldn't be the first ego trip she'd guided – she thought back to the French property tycoon who'd been determined to prove that the Gauls discovered Baffin a thousand years before the Vikings and the American movie star who'd wanted to live in a snowhouse to explore 'ice in the soul' – and she was pretty sure it wouldn't be the last.

She said: 'So long as you understand the likelihood is we won't find anything.'

Bill, leaning over to shake her hand: 'Perfectly understood.'

Much later that evening, after she'd finished checking her snowbie and packed for the morning, Edie finally sat down to watch *The General*. Of all the great comic movies of the silent screen, this was her favourite. There was something life-affirming in Buster Keaton's daring, the way he cheerfully launched himself off skyscrapers, dodged oncoming trains and ran into the path of runaway horses, brushing death off over and over again as though it had no more power over him than a light spring shower. Edie found that however many times she watched it, her pleasurable anticipation of the scenes ahead never dimmed.

Time bypassed her altogether, so she had no idea how

long she had been watching when there was a knock on the door. She knew at once that it must be one or other of the *qalunaat* – Inuit considered knocking an insult, an acknowledgement that the visit might not be wholly welcome – and shouted for whoever it was to come right in. An instant later, Andy Taylor's face appeared around the snow porch door, smelling of whisky, a can of Budweiser in his hand.

'A word?'

'Sure,' she said, keeping her eye on the screen, hoping that he'd pick up the message. 'Come in.'

He stood before her, lank and anxious-seeming, a diamond stud twinkling in his right ear. He'd come to make his peace and wasn't sure how he'd be received.

'You probably didn't expect to see me.'

'No,' she said. She felt a little disgusted by him.

'What are you after?' she asked.

He took a long gulp of his beer and put the can down on the table. He seemed a little unsteady on his feet.

'Like the man said, a documentary.'

'Musk-ox shit.'

'Fact is, I'm broke.' He shrugged his shoulders apologetically. 'Wagner's widow, that bitch, she refused to pay me.' Edie noticed that his fingernails were bitten to the nub. He seemed keyed, like a hunted thing. 'You think I'm a whore, I get it, but there's no high ground here, lady. Look at you, playing at being an authentic Eskimo. You and me, we're both in the same game.'

'Maybe,' Edie said. 'I don't care what your motivation is, but you behave with Joe out on the land the way you behaved with me a few weeks back, and you can be sure your career, or whatever it is you're doing here, is over.'

'Three days,' he said, 'then I'm out of your hair.'

She got to her feet and went to the door.

'See you in the morning.'

He took the hint, smiled as he passed her and went into the porch to put on his snow boots.

When he'd gone, she picked up the can of Budweiser and shook it. The base of the can felt heavy and its contents swooshed softly, a sweet, hoppy swoosh. She went to the kitchen and poured the remains down the sink. At that moment she heard the door swing open and Joe came in. She hastily threw the empty can in the trash and covered it over before he could see it.

'Been with your father?'

Joe came through to the kitchen and opened the fridge. 'Uh huh. We checked over the snowbies, sorted the equipment out. I lent Andy one of my leisters so he can get some proper ice fishing in.'

For the first time since the Felix Wagner affair, he seemed relaxed and happy. He didn't ask about the boot tracks leading up to the door and she didn't tell him. He needs this, she thought, a good, simple trip, no one dying on his watch.

'Eat already?'

'I guess,' he said. It was what he always said when he'd filled up on junk food at his father's house.

'Listen,' she said. 'That skinny *qalunaat*? Be careful with him. He's slippery.'

'Kigga,' he said, touching her nose with his finger. 'I'm all grown up now.'

The next day the party left early and took the snowmobiles across the shore-fast ice ridge and the rim of ice heaves to the flat expanse of the year ice. By mid-morning the few thin ladders of low cloud had burned off, leaving the air clear and dry, perfect travelling weather.

By mid-morning the travellers had split into two parties, Joe leading the way towards the west coast of Craig and

Edie following the well worn hunting paths across the ice dunes towards Fritjof in the east. Twice they stopped briefly to eat and drink hot tea, before setting out once more across the ice desert. Visibility remained superb throughout the afternoon and into the evening, illuminating the long, craggy outline of Taluritut, which southerners called Devon Island, to the south. As they travelled, Edie could hear Fairfax behind her, whooping like a child.

In the sparkling light of the late High Arctic spring evening, they set up camp on the shore-fast ice, feasting on duck stew and oatcakes. For a while they watched the sun circling the horizon, exhausted.

'Tell me something, Edie,' Fairfax began.

'About what?'

'Oh, I don't know, something about the Arctic.'

Edie thought for a moment: how to begin? She flipped through her mental file of Arctic facts. 'Arctic rainbows are circles.'

'That so?' Fairfax laughed, a great, relaxed, wide laugh, a different man from the one she met at the airstrip yesterday. 'I guess there's no pot of gold at the end, then.'

'I guess not.'

A pair of eiders flew by, lost maybe or just very early. All the migratory birds were coming in earlier now. Edie followed them with her eye until they disappeared in the faint gloaming that served both for twilight and dawn at this time of year.

'Before I came up here the first time, I never understood why in God's name my great-great-grandfather kept returning to the north; the frostbite, snowblindness, living on frozen whale blood and ship's biscuit.'

Edie half-listened to the white man, but her thoughts were with Joe. He and Taylor would have set camp on Craig by now. She imagined Joe fixing the white man's supper.

Perhaps she'd overstated her case a little to Taylor last night, but that's how she was when it came to her stepson: a mother bear protecting her cub. Everything about Taylor told her not to trust him. On the other hand, Sammy and Joe were both right: it was time she put more trust in her boy. It seemed no time since she was helping him with his schoolwork but she had to accept he was twenty years old now. Plenty old enough to look after himself.

'I guess you've read your ancestor's diaries, you know he was guided by Welatok.'

'Sure, but they fell out. Sir James mentioned that in the penultimate diary, said if he was going to come again, he'd probably have to find another guide.'

'Yes,' Edie said. 'I know.'

'You do?' Fairfax looked puzzled.

'Welatok was my great-great-great-grandfather.'

'Ha, that right? Hey, we could include you in the doc,' Fairfax beamed. 'The descendant of Sir James Fairfax's guide, guiding the great-great-grandson of the great man himself.'

Edie shook her head.

Fairfax looked whipped. 'There'd be a fee in it for you.'

Edie smiled blankly. *Qalunaat* just didn't get it. Wasn't it enough that she sold herself? What, she should sell her ancestors now, too?

Fairfax sucked his teeth. 'Simeonie told me all you folk got moved up here by the Canadian government in the fifties from Quebec?'

'Uh huh,' she said.

The episode was still too painful to talk about much. It had happened because the Americans were sniffing around the area after the war and the government wanted Canadians on the land. Only people they figured might survive up there were Inuit, so they'd persuaded nineteen families to make the twelve-hundred-mile trip by telling them they'd be able to hunt whatever they liked and come back home when they were done. It was only after they'd arrived, seen the barren rock and had to find a way to survive through the first winter in twenty-four-hour darkness and with temperatures hitting –50C that they realized they'd been had. Most of them never got to see the families they'd left behind again. Lot of people said the problems they had with alcohol, the suicides, you could trace them right back to this one traumatic event.

Edie explained that her own grandmother on her mother's side, Anna, had been one of the original exiles, but her grandfather was a descendant of Welatok. He'd been born in Greenland and had come across to Ellesmere to trade with the new arrivals there.

The following morning they set off and reached Fritjof Fiord around lunchtime. The fiord was still very iced up and they were forced to hack out a path through some new pressure ridges with picks. After an hour, they made their way through onto the other side.

'My God,' Fairfax sighed, carried away by the sight before them.

It *was* astonishing. The interior of the fiord stretched into the far distance: windless, white and magical. Layer upon layer of snow had fallen over the course of the long winter and lay packed into dense, creamy undulations, interrupted here and there by bear, musk ox or human tracks.

The spot Fairfax had marked, the place he reckoned most coincided with the place his great-great-grandfather had marked out for overwintering, was a wide gravel beach huddling beneath granite cliffs half a kilometre into the fiord, away from the worst of the tide and sheltered by the rocks behind it. Here Edie started the work of setting up camp while Fairfax went off to survey the surrounding area on foot, returning several hours later with photographs and measurements.

'You were right about the body.' This over a supper of caribou steaks. 'Perfect excuse to come back in the summer with a film crew.'

They passed the remainder of the evening in their separate tents, Edie turning stories over in her mind while Fairfax sat in his sleeping bag a few feet away, frantically scribbling in his notebook.

The following morning, after a breakfast of seal-meat porridge, they broke camp and headed back towards Autisaq. The journey was uneventful and they reached the settlement late that evening. While Bill went back to the hotel to change out of his travelling clothes, Edie took off home for a hot shower then drove round to Sammy's house to ask after Joe's expedition. She'd been hoping to see her stepson's snowbie parked outside her house but it wasn't there and there were no tracks to indicate anyone had come by that way. On the way to Sammy's she passed by Minnie's house just in case he'd decided to stay with her, but his snowbie wasn't there either. Sammy's place smelled of the usual blend of stale booze and junk food.

'See Joe yet?'

'Nope,' he said. He was sitting on the sofa watching an episode of *Columbo* and didn't look up. 'Don't expect to, least not for a day or two.'

'They get bad weather?'

Sammy nodded. He didn't seem too bothered.

'How bad?' Her voice sounded calm. She reminded herself to keep it that way.

'Bad enough we can't reach them on the sat phone.'

'A spotter plane go out yet?'

'Maybe,' Sammy said in a vague tone, his eye still half on the cop show. 'Poor visibility over there today but it'll clear, always does in Craig this time of year. Don't worry so much.'

Edie envied Sammy his cool-headedness. Inuit men were brought up that way, to save the worrying for the things they could actually do something about. Everything else stayed buried under the surface. Joe was the same. She didn't know why she worried so much – perhaps it was the *qalunaat* in her, perhaps it was just part of being a woman.

She went across to the hotel to check on Fairfax and give him the news, and found him in the communal area, drinking a large mug of hot chocolate and making notes in a fancy-looking hardbound book. He was immersed in his own discoveries and, she thought, didn't seem particularly concerned about the situation, except in so far as it might delay his return home. He had family business to attend to. If Taylor was delayed too long, he would have to leave without him.

'It was his idea anyway.'

Edie raised her eyebrows.

'You thought I put up the money?'

'Actually, yes.'

Fairfax shook his head. 'Andy contacted me, said he had interest from some TV outfit, but their schedules meant we'd have to go up on a recce right away.'

She recalled what Taylor had said about being broke. Maybe he was just the hustler for the TV company.

'No offence, why did he need you?'

Fairfax looked up, a little offended all the same. 'The name,' he said. 'I'm the name.'

Sleep eluded Edie that night. She passed the long hours touring the list of rational explanations for Joe's absence.

Trips got weathered out all the time. The ice shifted, some large leads unexpectedly opened up, the wind started gusting badly, the air whited out. It was nothing – nothing – to be two, three, even four days late on even the shortest trip. All these things she told herself, over and over, until by the time the morning came she felt exhausted by them.

It was hard to concentrate on her teaching that day and the children sensed it. As a result, the lessons went badly; the class was bored and played up. Edie felt rotten for letting them down but didn't seem able to pull herself together. The moment the final bell rang, she yanked on her outdoor boots and went to the mayor's office. No further news of the Craig Island expedition.

At four the supply plane came in, unloaded its cargo, loaded up the mail and a few bits and pieces of electrical plant being sent away for repair. Fairfax took his seat beside the pilot and was gone.

On her way home, Edie was taken with a sudden impulse to search Andy Taylor's room in the hotel. It was unethical, but right now she didn't care. Padding upstairs and along the corridor, she nosed through the doors to the rooms until she found the only one currently inhabited. There was a lock, but the key had long since been lost and no one had bothered to replace it. Aside from what he'd taken to Craig, Taylor didn't have much with him: a couple of magazines, an empty notebook, a tape recorder and an iPod. Edie picked up the headphones, caught a snatch of a Guns N' Roses track, then replaced the player on the table. In a leather pouch she found a spare pair of glasses and, wrapped in foil, presumably to fox the drug dogs, a thumbnail-sized piece of dope. A half-empty whisky bottle sat on the chest of drawers.

Something about the bleakness of the hotel room gave her new purpose but she knew that if she went back to Sammy, or to the mayor's office, she'd be told to stop worrying. She didn't want to hear any of that now. Sure, Joe was only twenty-four hours late, but in Edie's mind that was twenty-four hours too long. From the hotel she walked directly to Minnie and Willa's house and found Willa in front of the TV playing Grand Theft Auto.

'I need you to come out to Craig with me tomorrow and look for Joe.'

Willa glanced up sufficiently to register her presence but did not otherwise respond. He was like that with her now, sullen and unco-operative. She strode over to him and grabbed the joystick.

'Not a request, Willa.'

Willa reached for the joystick, but she held it out of his reach. For a moment they were locked in a humiliating game of snatch.

'Look, Joe got weathered out. Big fucking deal.' His voice was petulant and full of resentment. 'Why do you always treat him like he's still a kid? *Your* kid? He's not, OK? He's Minnie and Sammy's kid and, by the way, he's not a kid any more.'

She handed him the joystick back. The tinny sound of cars colliding emanated from the machine.

'Why don't you pay for *my* training?'

Edie took a breath. This was all so familiar, so painfully hopeless. Edie had taught Willa for a while at high school. He'd been an indolent student, playing up to his friends and acting as though it was all too much hassle. He didn't graduate.

'*Huvamiaq*,' he said finally. Whatever. 'But I'm doing this for my brother, not for you. Now get off my back.'

'Early start.' Her voice softened. 'Make sure you look your snowbie over.'

The remainder of the evening passed in a blur of indecision and self-doubt. Edie lay in bed, alone and sleepless, in the bright light of the spring night. At some point she must have drifted off because she was woken in the middle of a dream by Sammy's voice.

'Hey, Edie. Get up. Up!' He was standing in the room in his outdoor gear. Joe had returned. He was at the nursing station.

She pushed off the cover and sprang from the bed, aware of being naked but not caring, pulling on her clothes.

As they marched up towards the medical building, Sammy explained that Joe had pitched up at his house an hour earlier. He'd lost Taylor in the blizzard then his snow-bie had broken down, so he'd skied all the way back from Craig. The journey had taken him two days and a night. He was weak and distressed and hypothermia had set in, so he wasn't making a great deal of sense.

From what Sammy could make out he and Taylor had gone to investigate separate cairns. He was up on the high tundra there when the blizzard came down. Taylor was on lower ground. Joe managed to make his way through the whiteout back to the beach where he and Taylor had agreed to rendezvous, but by then the visibility was terrible and he couldn't see any signs of his companion. His own tracks were being covered with new snow almost instantly, so he knew it was pointless trying to look for footprints. He'd tried to call home but he couldn't get the sat phone to work.

He was rambling, repeating himself, Sammy explained. He said he'd seen his ancestor, Welatok, walking through the snow towards him but when he got closer, Welatok became a bear and ran away. At one point, Joe said, the cloud had lifted and he'd spotted a green plane. He waved and shouted, and the plane dropped height and came in close but then just as suddenly it seemed to veer away. He went back inside the makeshift shelter he'd built, convinced that the plane would make a second pass, looking for somewhere to land, but when he next went out he realized what he'd thought was a plane was actually a rocky overhang on the cliffs opposite and he figured that the engine he thought he'd heard must have been the roar of the wind. Sensing himself gradually becoming less rational, he decided to get back to Autisaq for help before the hypothermia rendered him completely crazy. It was then he discovered his snowbie wouldn't start. The journey on skis had taken him so long that he was worried that Taylor would be dead.

They reached the clinic and clattered up the stairs. Robert Patma was waiting for them just inside the door.

'I just went over to wake the mayor,' he said. 'Simeonie's already spoken with Sergeant Palliser. He's going to get an S&R plane out.'

'Let me see him,' was all Edie said.

Joe was lying asleep on a gurney in the nursing station under a fluorescent light with his black hair flipped across his forehead, his mouth slightly open. His nose was greyish from frostbite, but not alarmingly so.

'I guess Sammy told you we couldn't get much sense out of him.' Robert turned to Edie. 'He'll be OK. I've given him something to help him sleep. We'll put him in one of the obs rooms.'

Edie suddenly felt very calm. 'No. I want him to wake up in his own bed. In my house.'

Sammy and Robert exchanged looks. Sammy shrugged.

The nurse raised his eyebrows. 'I don't think that's a good idea. He needs to be monitored.'

Edie gave the nurse a pleading look and said nothing. She had to teach in the morning but she could be back to look after him by the early afternoon.

'It's OK,' Sammy said finally. 'I'll stay with him while his stepmother's at school.'

Edie flashed him a thankyou.

Robert put on a frail smile and said, 'Well, OK, then, if you really must.'

It was only when she'd completed the school register later that morning Edie realized she hadn't marked anyone present. At lunchtime she considered returning home to check on Joe then decided to leave it till after the end of the school day. If Joe was asleep she wouldn't want to wake him and if he was awake, she wouldn't want him to see how torn up she was. Their first encounter was going to be difficult, she knew. He'd be blaming himself for losing Taylor and she'd be blaming herself for letting the two of them go out on the land together.

The afternoon dragged and by the time the bell finally rang to signal the end of the school day the events of the previous twelve hours already seemed murky and a little unreal. Edie went to her locker, packed her things in her daypack and walked up to the store, thinking to take Joe some of the caribou hamburger he particularly liked and a packet of his favourite tangerine Tang.

Reaching the snow porch she called out softly, but got no reply. She took off her shitkickers, wondering whether she should have spent a few dollars more and bought ribs instead of hamburger.

There were some empty cans lying on the floor beside the sofa. The air was thick and unnaturally still. She felt a small nip of irritation that Sammy had left the house.

The door to Joe's room was shut; he was probably still sleeping. She listened and heard nothing except the creak of the plastic cladding at the front of the house where the sun was heating it, and the rustle of her fingers around the bag of hamburger meat.

She put the shopping down on the worktop in the kitchen then noticed that there was a residual smell of blood in the air so she grabbed the hamburger, put it in the fridge and returned to the living room. The smell followed her. In that instant, she felt a raw thump, a terrifying wrench. The smell of blood wasn't coming from the kitchen at all. It was coming from Joe's room.

The door gave way under the pressure of her hand. Inside the curtains were drawn and it took her a few seconds to adjust to the poor light. Joe's Xbox was lying on the floor and beside it there was a half-empty can of Dr Pepper. Out of habit, she picked up the can, intending to leave it on the bedside table so that Joe wouldn't knock it over when he got up, but at the same time she knew: something was terribly wrong.

Joe Inukpuk was lying in bed, his legs slightly bent at the knees, his face obscured by the comforter. As she walked towards him she felt something underfoot. She put the can down on the bedside table, lifted her right leg and plucked the remains of a pill from the sole of her sock. Lifting her gaze, she reached out to put the fragments on the bedside table. Time peeled away.

She looked at the figure lying in the bed and knew there must be no more excuses. Taking a breath, she threw the eiderdown aside.

Joe's eyes were closed and his mouth hung slightly open. She might have mistaken him for being asleep were it not for the fact that there was blood thickening on his lips and chin and, where the skin was in contact with the pillow, his face was already beginning to blacken.

5

Derek Palliser was doing his best to ignore his creeping nausea. He was never at ease on a plane; small planes in particular got to him. Whenever he was flying, as he was now, he couldn't help recalling the fate of his old friend, Lott Palmer. In twenty-three years' experience piloting Twin Otters above the 60th parallel Palmer had come down twice and both times lived to tell the tale. The third time, he was cruising just beneath the cloud line off the coast of Cornwallis Island, when a freak katabatic wind reached down, picked up the plane and tossed it a thousand metres through the clouds towards the ice. Lott managed to wrest enough control of the thing to land it in one piece. He radioed for help and a ski plane was dispatched from Resolute. The plane arrived at the scene just in time to see a spear of lightning swoop out from the cloud and punch Lott Palmer and his plane to kingdom come. When the rescuers landed they found nothing but a small ball of blackened tin burning a hole in the ice.

If he didn't have pressing business when he reached his destination, Derek liked to pop a Xanax to help him cope with the chopping and bumping that went with flying tiny planes through blowy, unpredictable Arctic conditions. But today he was flying clean. He'd been woken some time after seven by a radio call from Simeonie Inukpuk. An unexpected blizzard had swept across Craig Island and a man was missing. A *qalunaat*. The missing man had been travelling with Joe Inukpuk when they'd been separated in a whiteout. With the only available plane in Autisaq grounded on account of the pilot, Martie Kiglatuk, being too drunk to fly, Simeonie needed Derek to conduct a search and rescue from Kuujuaq. He and the police pilot, Pol Tilluq, were to fly over Craig looking for signs of the missing man. It was just possible that he'd managed to find somewhere to shelter and was still alive.

It had taken Pol a couple of hours to ready the plane and check the forecast but by nine thirty that morning they were in the air and heading east towards the target area. Pol Tilluq was among the most competent pilots in the region: visibility was good and, despite his fear of flying, Derek knew he was in capable hands.

Simeonie had faxed over the expedition questionnaire Joe and Edie had completed before taking their parties out on the land. It was mostly a box-ticking exercise that all guides on Ellesmere were required to fill out, giving details of the proposed route, the equipment taken, the number of days the expedition was expected to last. Derek took it out now. Reading made his nausea worse, but he pressed on all the same, knowing that the more he understood about the expedition, the more likely it was that he and Pol would find the missing man. The trip looked like a pretty routine entry-level tourist caper. To anyone experienced in High Arctic travel, like Joe Inukpuk, Craig Island was relatively unchallenging. Guides often took visitors out there. The routes across the ice pan were well-established and the terrain was pretty soft; no glaciers, sheer cliffs or moraine slips. To someone unfamiliar with High Arctic conditions, though, Craig would be extremely forbidding. The advice the guides gave in the event their clients got separated was always to stay put and wait for help. Their best hope was that Taylor had holed up somewhere safe and was doing just that. If he'd been stupid enough to try to get himself off the island, he'd almost certainly be dead by now, and the odds on finding his body would be about the same as discovering leprechauns living in the lemming shed.

They flew over Cape Storm and continued east towards South Cape. Before long the roads and buildings of Autisaq appeared, tiny pixels on an otherwise blank screen. They'd offered to pick up Robert Patma and take him with them in case they found Taylor in need of urgent medical attention, but the weather forecast was predicting low cloud and the mayor thought it best not to waste time while conditions were still clear. If they found Taylor, it would be easy enough to fly directly back to Autisaq and get him looked at there.

Pol turned the plane south towards the low coast of Cape Sparbo. Ahead, across the solid ice field of Jones Sound, loomed the purple ellipse of Craig Island. At this height, it looked like nothing so much as a plum in a bowl of cream, but in reality it was two banks of sloped cliffs divided by an icy plateau about twenty kilometres wide. The west coast was lower and quieter, the east rockier, bifurcated with finger fiords in the north and in the south, small glaciers that tongued out into the sea. The coasts had very distinct weather patterns. It could be blowing a blizzard in the east and still be perfectly sunny in the west. The region of fiords in the northeast was different still, which was how it was that, while Joe and Taylor were being battered by two-hundred-kilometre-an-hour winds, Edie and Fairfax had been able to snowmobile back to Autisaq in almost perfect conditions.

The two men had planned to make their way systematically across the island, flying east–west until they reached the southern fringe. They had already agreed that, if they spotted any sign of life on Craig, Pol would try to make a landing on the ice-covered plateau above the cliffs and Derek would go out on the land and investigate. They were carrying a snowbie, a sled and a first-aid kit and Derek had brought the police-issue sat phone.

For over an hour they flew in long lines across the terrain at an altitude of five hundred metres but they saw only a few birds and, once, on the western coast, a bear moving over the shore-fast ice. There was no sign of the man or of the two snowmobiles. They had covered most of the island when the low cloud predicted by the weather forecast suddenly came over, blocking the view. Pol shook his head.

'No way we'll get under that, D,' he said.

Until the cloud cleared there was no point carrying on. Reluctantly, Derek radioed in to Autisaq and let them know they were temporarily calling off the S&R and instructed Pol to head south for Taluritut. The policeman's plan was to drop in on the Devon Island Science Station while they waited for the cloud on Craig to clear.

For a number of years a team from NASA and an eccentric not-for-profit outfit known as Space Intelligences Research had, among other things, been actively testing prototype landing vehicles for future expeditions to Mars at the science station on Taluritut's north coast. As the most senior member of the two-man Ellesmere native police, Derek had jurisdiction in the area and it was his job to keep a friendly but nonetheless watchful eye on them. The team usually flew in during March and Derek tried to make a habit of calling in on them within the first couple of weeks of their arrival, but this year he'd been too busy. He figured on chatting to the station director, Professor Jim DeSouza, a while, checking out some cool space buggies and grabbing a bite to eat before taking off for Craig once more.

DeSouza himself came out to the landing strip to greet

them. A genial, fiercely intelligent and, Palliser suspected, ambitious man, DeSouza had taken over the running of the station a couple of years ago. Though Derek hadn't had much to do with him, he liked what he'd seen so far. He was less standoffish than most of the *qalunaat* posted up here and seemed particularly keen to understand the perspectives of local people. At the same time he never overcompensated by pretending to hang on your every word, the way that some bleeding-heart *qalunaat* did. He was confident, easy in his skin.

The professor checked his watch.

'Don't think I don't notice you two always arrive at mealtimes,' DeSouza said, clapping Derek and Pol on the back.

They sat inside a cosy modular unit and ate burgers and French fries. DeSouza seemed strained, less his usual avuncular self, Derek thought, but it wasn't until dessert came that he understood why. A stream of funding had just dried up, DeSouza explained, and the station had been warned to prepare itself to undergo a NASA review, which was often a polite precursor to the axe.

'These days the focus is off pure exploration and much more on resource acquisition and bio-sustainability,' he explained. 'We're all out of a job unless we can come up with some new direction.'

'By bio-sustainability you mean life, right?' Derek asked. He saw in DeSouza an ally for his scientific research.

DeSouza nodded. 'They want us to find them a planet we can escape to once this one's all burned up. You gotta love those guys.' He gave a laugh that was as sharp as a scalpel.

'That so crazy?' Derek said.

DeSouza pushed aside the remains of his dessert. 'Not necessarily,' he said. 'But you're missing the point.'

'We got a few distractions going on,' Derek said. It wasn't like the professor to be so spiky.

DeSouza checked himself and offered to fetch some coffee. Derek asked for tea.

'Oh, I forgot,' DeSouza said. 'The Brits really got to you people.' He shook his head, raised a pinkie. 'Tea,' he said, in a British accent.

He returned with the drinks and put them down on the table.

'You guys are police, so you do police work, right?'

Derek and Pol glanced at one another. The professor really was a little off-kilter.

'When they let us,' Derek said.

DeSouza's eyes lit up. 'That's just it, see, that's exactly it. I'm a scientist. I'm a damned good scientist. If I'd wanted to be a politician or some kind of policy goon I woulda been. All my life, from being a small kid, I just wanted to do science. But the fucking politicians, the funding agencies, the think tanks, all those fucking wastes of space out there, they make it impossible. The things we could do, the things we'd know, if they only left us alone.'

'I hear that,' Derek nodded. He flashed Pol a look that said, *Let's get the hell out of here*.

Less than an hour and a half after they'd touched down, they were back in the air and heading for Craig, but the island was still shrouded in low cloud and Derek decided there was nothing for it but to carry on to Autisaq and wait for it to clear. Upbringing and experience had taught him not to feel frustrated by the vagaries of the weather; it was what it was. In any case, no one had seen Taylor alive in three days and the likelihood was that he was gone. An hour or a month wouldn't make much difference.

As they were beginning their descent into the settlement, Derek's gaze happened to land on graffiti someone had scratched in one corner of the passenger window glass. He hadn't noticed it before.

D Palacer is a dick-sucking prick.

He tried not to let it bother him. Every policeman had enemies. Among a certain crowd he was still seen as some kind of collaborator. And there were plenty of folk up here who didn't see the need for a legal system at all, considered it just another southern import. They didn't want to know that more often than not Derek kept the southern legal system off their backs.

He licked his finger and rubbed it across the engraving. The dampened letters faded momentarily, gradually resuming their previous form as they dried. He reached in his pocket for his Leatherman, glanced over at Pol to make sure he wasn't being watched, flipped open the hoof pick attachment, made a few adjustments to the lettering, scratched out the middle section and read the sentence back to himself.

D's Palace is brick.

After that, he put away the Leatherman, closed his eyes and braced himself for landing.

Simeonie Inukpuk was waiting for them in the tiny terminal building, looking like a hare who's just realized he's gone down a fox hole by mistake. Derek met the expectant shine in his eyes with a shake of his head. He took out his pack of Lucky Strikes and offered the mayor a cigarette.

Derek said: 'We got round most of the island before the cloud came down, but there were no tracks, nothing. Till that cloud clears it's impossible.'

'*Ajurnamat*, that really is too bad,' Simeonie grumbled. He sucked on his cigarette.

Derek said: 'I'd like to talk to Joe; maybe he can give us a better idea of where he last saw Taylor.'

Simeonie grunted. 'We'd all like to talk to Joe.'

The news of the young man's death hit Derek like a musk-ox charge to the spleen. For a while he just stood rooted to the spot, shaking his head, mumbling 'Ah no, ah Jesus, no,' helpless in the maw of some terrible stupefaction. Of all the young men. Joe Inukpuk was a beacon of hope in what was otherwise a fog of drink, boredom, unwanted pregnancies, low expectation and educational underachievement. He took out another cigarette, lit it, sucked up the smoke and tried to gather his thoughts.

'How's the family holding up?'

Simeonie shrugged as if to say, *How do you think?*

'The body's at the nursing station.'

Derek crushed the remains of his smoke under his boot and told Pol to radio Kuujuaq detachment and update Stevie. Then he followed Simeonie to the nursing station.

He was aware that the number of suicides in Nunavut and Nunavik, the two principal Inuit districts of Eastern Canada, had doubled in the last decade. Inuit were now eleven times more likely to kill themselves than their fellow Canadians living in the south. Eighty-three per cent of suicides were of young people under thirty and eighty-five per cent of them male. Down in the south, it was often assumed that the majority of suicides north of the 60th happened when the suicide was drunk, but this was just another way in which the south absolved itself from responsibility for the fate of its northern peoples. Sure, the Arctic had its share of boozers, but the connection with suicide was much looser than the sociologists, politicians, health advisors and policy makers imagined. Take Joe. Derek knew the boy well enough to know he barely drank: he'd seen what drink had done to his parents.

He followed Simeonie up the steps to the station, hauled off his snow boots, and swung open the inner door. As he went in he saw Edie Kiglatuk sitting at one end of the waiting room. She looked up and acknowledged him but without her customary smile. On the opposite side of the waiting room sat the boy's blood family. Joe's mother Minnie had fallen asleep with her head resting on Willa's shoulder. Derek went over to offer his condolences. As he drew near he could see that Minnie was sleeping off the results of a heavy drinking spree and Sammy had a glazed look on his face. The smell of weed drifted up from the bench on which they all were sitting. Derek said how sorry he was.

'I was sitting with him.' Sammy's voice was subdued but there was something hysterical lurking just below the surface. 'I was sitting with him but then I went to tell his mother he was safe. Safe! Can you believe? When I left he was sleeping, you know? I had no idea he was going to do anything, no idea at all.' His body lurched forward and his voice broke.

Derek left a pause before turning to Willa, but Joe's brother continued to stare at his feet. Shock or simple misery, Derek didn't know. Either way, it was clear there was nothing Derek could do for him.

Next, he went over to Edie and just sat beside her. At one point he noticed she was shaking.

Then Robert Patma directed him to the body. The young man was lying in a bag on the morgue slab. Robert slid the zipper down far enough for Derek to be able to see Joe's face.

'Who found him?'

'Edie. She's pretty cut up. I just checked the pharmacy,' Robert said. 'One hundred and fifty Vicodin missing, fifteen blister packs. He must have taken them while Sammy and I were in the other room.' The nurse sucked his teeth. 'He had the keys to the pharmaceutical cabinets. Shit, maybe I shouldn't have given them to him, but he helped me out round here, you know? I can't tell you how bad I feel.'

Derek acknowledged the nurse's feelings with a nod. 'You took some samples?'

Patma gestured towards some specimen bags and bottles lying on the counter.

Derek said: 'I'll get them down to the police lab in Ottawa.'

He signalled the OK for Patma to zip up the body bag.

'Any chance of finding the other guy alive? Andy Taylor?'

'Not much chance of finding him, period. If he's dead or dying, we would have expected to see some wolves in the area, maybe foxes. If he's alive then he's keeping very quiet about it. Either way, no clues.' Derek looked towards the door to check it was closed and, seeing that it was, continued. 'You knew Joe well, right?'

'Pretty well.'

'Anything different, suspicious?'

Patma handed over a bag of labelled samples and asked Derek to sign for them. 'Joe usually kept his feelings to himself but he was pretty shaken up about the death of that hunter guy, Wagner, was it? This latest thing just made it worse. When he got back here yesterday, he was a mess: hypothermic, confused, out of his mind. He kept saying he'd left the guy to die.'

'You think something happened out on Craig, the two men got into some kind of argument and it got out of control?'

Patma met Derek's eye. 'No, no, that's crazy . . .' He looked at the body bag, considering, then checked there was no one standing at the door. 'Well, it's possible, I suppose,' he said. 'And there is something else. I didn't like to say anything to the family. A couple of days ago I was on the computer. Joe's the only one who ever used it, except me. I found a website in the history, seems Joe had been there a lot, so I clicked on it, just out of curiosity, and some virtual poker thing came up. It asked for a password and I couldn't get in. Joe was always really keen to help me out with the admin and I just used to leave him to it . . .'

Suddenly a great deal of shouting came from the waiting room. Derek strode to the door, swung it open and saw Edie standing near the exit. Sammy was beside her. From what Derek could see, he was trying to restrain Minnie, who was screaming at Edie and swinging fists at her.

'Keep her away from me,' Edie was saying.

Minnie lunged again and was held back by Sammy. Derek looked around for Willa and saw him still sitting in his seat, a look of contempt on his face.

'That bitch took my husband and now she's taken my son,' Minnie shrieked. She staggered for a moment then collapsed into Sammy's arms.

'Damn, Sammy, keep your crazy ex-wife off me,' Edie spat.

Derek made to stand between them. 'C'mon,' addressing himself to Edie. 'I'll take you home.'

They reached the front door to Edie's house in silence and took off their outerwear.

Derek said: 'You want some tea?'

'Uh nuh.'

'Listen, Edie, I need to look in Joe's room,' Derek said. 'You don't mind staying out here?'

'Actually, Derek, I do.'

He didn't have the heart to argue with her. So long as she remained in the doorway, she could look, he said. He stepped inside the room, a typical young man's bedroom, full of the flotsam and jetsam of a life beginning to be explored. It broke his heart to think that, of all the young men he knew, Joe Inukpuk was the one to decide he had nothing to live for. He noticed that someone had taken the bedcovers.

'Sammy,' Edie explained. 'They were stained. He took them away.'

'I'm sorry,' Derek said. 'This must be very tough.'

Edie didn't reply. He had the sense she was trying to hold herself in.

'Did you find any foils, from the tablets?'

'I didn't think to look,' she said quietly.

He moved towards the bed and pulled open the little drawer in the bedside cabinet. There, wedged between a notebook and the edge of the drawer, were fifteen blister packs, stamped with the Vicodin trademark, all empty and neatly piled in criss-cross formation. He drew out a pair of vinyl gloves, took out the notebook and flicked through it, hoping to find some explanatory note, but it just seemed full of nursing details, technicalities about dressings and saline drips.

'Think you can face talking about it?' he asked.

They sat on the sofa cradling mugs of hot tea.

'I'm wondering, did he say anything yesterday? Any clue as to how he was feeling?'

Edie was quiet for a moment, running the question though her head, he imagined. He noticed that her hair had come unbraided, as though she'd been picking at it. For some reason it moved him. He felt slightly agitated, aroused maybe, and had to tell himself to shape up.

'Not really. I mean, by the time I saw him he'd taken a Xanax. Me and Sammy had to help him walk back here from the nursing station. He was kind of out of it. When Sammy and I . . . when we were together, Joe and Willa had bunk beds in that room. They practically grew up in there.' Edie stared ahead, trying to gather her feelings, the tears streaming down her face like meltwater. 'Now it just looks like an empty box.'

'Robert said Joe was pretty cut up about losing that Wagner guy.'

'What he was sore about was that no one . . .' She glared at Derek. '. . . no one wanted to investigate it.' Edie punched her chest with a tiny fist. 'Goddammit.' She held her hand over her mouth and nose as though hoping to stifle her breath. 'You know, this was my fault,' she said. 'I shouldn't ever have left Joe with that asshole.' Derek waited for her sobbing to die down.

'Edie, you know anything about gambling?'

'What, Joe?' She snorted. 'Ridiculous.' Her voice became sharp, wary. 'Who said that?'

'He belonged to some online site.'

'That's crazy, he was saving for school.' She looked exhausted. 'No, no, I can't believe that.'

He thought about asking whether Joe and Andy Taylor could have got into a fight but, conscious of the pain he would cause, held back. In any case, it was a futile question. Until Taylor had been found everything was just speculation.

'Have you eaten?'

She waved him away. 'Not hungry.'

'You should eat.'

He went over to the kitchen and looked in the fridge.

But by the time he had gathered together a few crackers, she was asleep on the sofa. He picked her up and put her to bed. It was late now and he didn't want to leave her to wake up on her own, so he lay on the sofa and closed his eyes. After an hour or so, with sleep still eluding him, he sat up, switched on the lamp and looked around the room for something to occupy his mind. Eventually his eyes alighted on a DVD sitting beside the TV. He picked it up and turned the cover over. Charlie Chaplin in *The Gold Rush*. He slotted the disc into the player and sat back. In a while he heard a soft sound coming from behind and Edie appeared and came and sat with him on the sofa. He took her hands in his. Without saying anything, she leaned her head on his shoulder. They sat like that, in silence, for what seemed like the longest time, watching Charlie in the log cabin as it pendulumed from the cliff side to the abyss.

By eight the next morning he and Pol were back out flying over Craig but after a few hours the low cloud reappeared and they still had nothing.

Back in Autisaq Derek paid visits to Joe's family and took formal statements from everyone who had seen him on his return from Craig. Early evening, with one final statement to do, he dropped in on Edie and found her staring at a bowl of caribou liver soup.

'I feel like I'm trapped under the ice,' she said. 'I can *see* out, but I can't *get* out.' She pushed away the soup. 'It's just so difficult to take in.'

Derek took her hand and squeezed it. When Misha had left him, he'd found a website listing Kübler-Ross's five stages of grief: denial and isolation, anger, bargaining, depression and acceptance. Since Misha had gone, he'd worked through the first three and found himself stuck in the depressive phase. Edie had only just started out. He felt for her. It would be a long journey.

By nine that evening, he was at the terminal building beside the airstrip with Pol. The mayor was seeing them off.

'You'll be reporting the *qalunaat* missing, presumed dead,' he said to Derek. 'Lost in the blizzard.'

'Unless any evidence emerges to the contrary.'

'He should never have gone off like that on his own.'

Derek tried not to look surprised. 'Are we sure that's what happened?'

Simeonie gave a little snort, as though he found the

question absurd. 'You know, kids like Joe, young Inuit men and women, they deserve a shot at proper employment.' His voice had taken on a chummy, avuncular tone Derek found sickening. 'If this whole tragedy tells us anything it's that Autisaq needs to be brought into the twenty-first century. Jobs, technology, enterprise. We need our young people to aspire to more than massaging the egos of *qalunaat*.'

They flew low over Derek and Misha's old house and turned towards the landing strip. Pol put on his headphones, spoke briefly to whoever was on shift in the control room, took out his gum and stuck it above the altimeter, ready for the next flight. The settlement lights sparkled like ice crystals caught in a flashlight beam.

Pol said: 'No place like home.'

Derek said: 'No place at all.'

The plane bump-landed onto the strip and they slid across the gravel, coming to a halt beside the control and cargo building. They filled in the necessary flight papers in the terminal building and made for their snowbies. Derek didn't notice Pol waving him off until the pilot was half way down the path leading away from the strip towards the mayor's office. He tipped Pol a loose salute in return.

'See you tomorrow evening?'

Derek gave an exaggerated shrug.

'The party at Joadamie Allak's?

Derek hesitated, trying to recall when he had been invited, then realized he hadn't. He made as if to remember and gave the thumbs-up, watched the pilot's shrinking back for a moment, then set off in the opposite direction.

As he reached the spur leading to the police detachment he spotted a husky sniffing around under the school building, coat blank and featureless, ribs like lead pipes. No way to know whose it was. An instant later he saw another, trotting blithely along the path to the garbage dump, past the telegraph pole and the sign about keeping dogs tied at all times. A sudden flare of anxiety rose up from his gut. He'd been in Kuujuaq ten minutes and already he felt like a lab monkey strapped to an electric chair.

Derek took off his snow boots, pushed open the door to the detachment office and went to his apartment at the back. He made himself a cup of instant ramen noodles and went to bed.

When he appeared the following morning, Stevie was already sitting at his desk. The familiar bleeps and pips of World of Warcraft sailed over. Seeing Derek, he flipped out of the game into a boss screen.

'Tea, D?' Stevie said, adopting a perky air.

Derek decided to let last night's dog business, as well as the game, drop for the moment. Right now there were more important things to attend to. He intended to spend the rest of the day writing a preliminary report into Taylor's disappearance and Joe's apparent suicide. The samples from Joe's room would have to go off to the path lab and it was also his job to call Ottawa to try to trace Taylor's next of kin.

Simeonie Inukpuk had agreed to send out another search and recovery team but until they found a body, Andy Taylor would have to remain on the official missing list. He emailed a quick update to Ottawa, then started to work on his report.

There was no doubt in his mind that Joe had killed himself. Derek knew better than most how such impulses were sown then slowly cultivated. He'd developed his understanding as a teen at residential school in the south, where they'd kept him on a diet of potatoes and gravy and beaten first the Cree and then the Inuktitut out of him. Looking back, he realized only a very healthy investment in masturbation had prevented him from tying his sheets together, sneaking out to the football pitch at night and stringing himself up from the goal post. He knew other kids, less well-versed in the pleasure principle, who had gone down like catapulted dovekies. Three over one particularly dark summer: Ben Fleetfoot, found floating in the lake, pockets full of ice-hockey pucks he'd stolen from the gym; Holbrook Brown, who'd had to be pulled from the bathtub with the red water pouring from his body like summer melt, and Katryn Great Elk, who'd raided the sick bay and swallowed as many pills as she could find.

What was less certain was why. Derek flipped a packet of Lucky Strikes from his shirt pocket, turned over the perky 'Welcome to This No-Smoking Office' sign hanging on the door, lit a cigarette and tried to put himself in Joe's shoes. Looked at one way, everything in the boy's background and circumstances had him down as a suicide waiting to happen: the guilt he was carrying about not being able to save Felix Wagner, compounded by the loss of Andy Taylor; the tangle of loyalties he felt towards the various factions of his family; and what seemed to be a gambling habit. A mixture of shame, guilt and hypothermia coupled with easy access to drugs could well have amounted to an insurmountable force in the boy's mind, propelling him in a moment of confusion into taking his own life.

Still, there were a number of oddities to the story, the first of which was Taylor himself. Why did he return so quickly after the Wagner business? Edie said he needed the money and maybe he did, but why then had he seemed so nervy? Edie mentioned he'd been drinking the night before they went out. Then there was the fact that Joe had skied all the way from Craig to fetch help. Usually an Inuk would wait out a storm, even if there *was* someone missing. If Joe had killed Taylor, accidentally or otherwise, would he have gone for help? Except as a cover, perhaps?

Maybe Joe had buried the body under rocks? That might explain why they hadn't found any trace of Taylor. On the other hand, Robert Patma had said Joe had been rambling and incoherent. Surely, in his confusion, he would have given himself away.

Derek's train of thought was interrupted by the phone ringing. He didn't feel like talking but he picked up anyway. It was the mayor.

'Hey, Derek. Flight back OK?'

Derek shifted the papers on his desk around. 'I'm guessing you didn't find the body already.'

There was a noisy pause and what could either have been interference on the line, very common up at these latitudes, or a cough of irritation.

'Martie and Sammy will be flying out to Craig just as soon as the weather improves.'

Simeonie had a way of making you feel you were the sled dog and he held the tracing.

'You tell the family yet?' he said.

'Not yet. I'm waiting for confirmation on next of kin.'

'Be sure you don't get their hopes up.' That little cough again, held back just enough to communicate the effort Simeonie was making to seem reasonable. 'Best all round we just be honest, eh? It's four days now since the man went missing. *Qalunaat* couldn't take a piss on his own without assistance. He's *inuviniq*, a dead man. It might be more helpful to the family to know that we'd seen the body from the air but couldn't land to retrieve it. That way family gets closure and we don't have a missing person on our hands.'

So that was what the call was all about. Simeonie had a point: finding Taylor alive was about as likely as a branch of Prada opening up in Kuujuaq. Whether there was a body or not, Simeonie wanted Andy Taylor buried. Missing persons made longer headlines than dead ones. Any uncertainty might send a flush of southerners up to Autisaq asking awkward questions. All the same, in the law's eyes Andy Taylor wasn't officially dead until a body had been found or a lot more time had passed.

The line crackled and all Derek could hear was the wailing of some Chinese opera. Then Simeonie's thin, insistent voice returned. The mayor was in the middle of saying something about his nephew.

'There's money for this kind of thing. Suicide prevention. One of the things I'm thinking, it might help the initiative to have more of a police presence. Build a brand-new detachment right here in Autisaq, expand on the existing facility, install all the latest equipment, budget for travel. Set up a cadet force, boys' club kind of thing, roll it out across the region, nail this suicide stuff.'

'Strictly speaking,' Derek said, 'we should fly in a pathologist, examine Joe Inukpuk's body directly.'

The mayor barked instructions to someone in the office then he came back on the line.

'Look, the kid was my nephew.' A bleeding-heart tone now. 'I just want to make sure other families don't have to go through this and I think, with the right funding, you could be at the heart of that.'

The mayor was trying to bulldoze his way back to normality.

Derek had to hand it to him. He was good.

The sound of distant voices came on the line. 'I have to go,' Simeonie said suddenly. 'Development consultants. Derek, we're on the same page here. Write your report: an accidental death and a suicide. Do the right thing. Let Joe's family bury his body.'

The line went dead. Derek swung violently on his chair. He wanted to punch someone. Instead, he lit a cigarette. He'd hardly taken his first drag when the phone rang again.

'Let me speak to the other fellow,' Derek recognized the voice immediately. Tom Silliq.

'Fuck off.' Derek sent the phone clattering back into its cradle. The graffito sprang to mind. Asshole.

Stevie left it a few minutes before calling across: 'Like a brew, D?'

A while later, the computer pinged to announce the arrival of an email. The research office in Ottawa hadn't found any close living relatives for Andy Taylor. No record that he was ever married or had any kids. His next of kin seemed to be a forty-six-year old man in British Columbia, a third cousin. Derek dialled the number. A woman answered and said the cousin had moved on and no, she didn't have any of his contact details.

Derek punched in the number for the mayor's office in Autisaq, then thought better of it, and looked up the number for Mike Nungaq in the Northern Store instead. Mike answered after the first ring.

The voice on the end of the line sounded spacey. Derek chewed his lip. His gut told him not to start anything public that could be misconstrued as an investigation. He summoned a tone of casual professionalism. 'Can you get a message to Edie to call me? I'm working on the report into Joe's death. Just need to check a couple of things.'

A long time later, the phone rang in Derek's office. It was Edie.

'How are you doing?' Derek said, then kicked himself. The woman had just lost her stepson. How did he suppose she was doing?

She hesitated for a long moment. 'I'm guessing this isn't a social call.'

Derek picked a cigarette butt out of the ashtray and

began turning it around in his fingers. He felt slightly affronted by Edie's tone.

'Edie, can you tell me what you know about Andy Taylor?'

'What, like, he was *nutaraqpaluktuq*, bad-tempered, hysterical?'

'I was hoping for something more specific. He tell you where he came from? Ever mention a girlfriend, family?'

'Nope and nope. Guns N' Roses fan's about all I know. Can't you get this stuff from some police database?'

'Maybe. Listen, do you think that Fairfax fella might know a bit more about him?'

'I have his number somewhere, you want to give him a call.' She sounded pleased that he was investigating. Evidently, it hadn't occurred to her that her stepson might be implicated in Taylor's death. He heard her rooting around somewhere. Moments later she came back to the phone and rattled off a strange configuration of numbers.

'That Canadian?'

'Uh nuh . . . Overseas. London, I think.' Edie hesitated. 'Derek, you really think Joe killed himself?' He felt her willing him to be on her side.

He paused. 'I guess so,' he said. 'Yeah.'

'I have to go,' she said stiffly. Evidently she was having a hard time accepting what had happened. He didn't blame her for that. He wasn't finding it so easy himself.

Derek spent the remainder of the afternoon trying to draft his preliminary report, but over and over again his mind wandered back to the conversation with Simeonie. It was a pretty good offer. Put the whole Joe and Andy Taylor thing to bed with the minimum of fuss and be rewarded with a brand-new detachment building and some proper back-up. Most likely Taylor's body would never be found and even if it was, animals or snow would have made sure it was impossible to determine the cause of death anyway.

Later, after Stevie had left for the day, he took himself for a walk to help chew things over. As he turned out onto the street the bony dog he'd seen earlier appeared, this time in the company of another, larger husky with a brown patch over one eye and notched ears marking fights the animal itself had long since forgotten. The two were bent low, hackles up, smiling ugly smiles, locked in some kind of peripatetic confrontation. The large one lunged and caught the other in the tenderness of the neck. A fully fledged fight started up.

Derek reached for his gun then hesitated. Thirty years ago a bunch of Mounties had shot every last sled dog in Kuujuaq after a rogue animal mauled a kid to death. The act had caused a world of pain, revenge attacks, families pitted against one another. It was this more than anything that led to the setting up of the High Arctic indigenous police force. The sergeant reholstered his weapon, moved into the fray, grabbed the smaller of the two dogs by its ruff and hauled it off.

For a while he walked along the edge of the shoreline then, returning, set his usual supper of noodles and tinned steak on the table and, while it was cooling sufficiently to eat, he pulled on his shitkickers and went out to the lemming shed. He was bothered how much the conversation with Edie had unsettled him but he couldn't quite put his finger on why. Being with the lemmings sometimes shifted his thinking. Almost always made him feel better anyhow.

He reached the door and found it slightly ajar. This was odd. There had been no reason for anyone to go into the shed while he was away. He entered. It was dim inside but there was light enough to see the bodies of a dozen lemmings scattered about the floor in grotesque formation.

Ignoring his cooling supper, he grabbed his dog catcher from the snow porch and went back out into the night.

Kuujuaq's three streets were empty. Those who were going out hunting after work had already gone. People were inside eating or else watching TV. Gradually, one by one, he rounded up the huskies. It took him four hours, at the end of which, he had twelve huskies in the pound. He went to his equipment shed, fetched some dog chow and threw enough into the cages to keep the dogs quiet until morning. Then, his anger sated a little by sheer exhaustion, he took on the dismal business of cleaning up the lemming shed.

This was just the first act, he thought. It was his own fault, for being so passive. Unless he found some way to reassert his authority Silliq and Toolik would go on and on exacting revenge on him until he was eventually driven out. He thought about Simeonie's offer again. What the mayor was asking him to do was wrong. It was his duty to investigate all the possibilities surrounding Andy Taylor's fate. Right now, though, the prospect of a move to Autisaq had never looked more attractive.

He reheated the noodles in the microwave then took a long, hot shower. By the time he was done, it was half past two and brilliant sunshine. Knowing he wouldn't sleep, there seemed no point in going to bed. Instead he went back into the office, made some tea, switched on his computer and keyed in Misha's name. He waited for what seemed like an age for the page of search results to load, then reached down and switched off the CPU.

For a few moments he leaned back in his chair, feeling his self-respect return. By now it was nearly three, not far off eight o'clock in the morning London time. Taking a deep breath he dialled Bill Fairfax's number. A voice answered.

Derek Palliser ran through in his mind just what an investigation into Andy Taylor's fate might achieve. Then he replaced the phone in the cradle, tore up the number and threw it in the trash.

6

The tests on Joe Inukpuk's body confirming his death from an overdose of Vicodin had been back a week when his family took his body out to Craig Island and laid it under a cairn on the cliffs overlooking Jones Sound.

The burial had created the usual battles between tradition and modernity; Minnie had wanted Joe buried in the cemetery by the airstrip, Christian-style, but Sammy had overruled her: his son's body would be left out on the land in the old-time way. Edie was pleased about that. She'd often spoken with Joe about his beliefs and though there were elements of the Christian story that appealed to him, like her, he'd never been wholly convinced by it.

Joe had believed in what he saw all around him: nature, spirits and the land. It tended to be the older generation, the ones who'd been born on the east coast of Hudson Bay, nearly three thousand kilometres to the south, and forcibly removed in the 1950s to populate Ellesmere, who clung most fervently to Christianity. It was no wonder, Edie thought, that these new settlers found particular comfort in the old biblical stories of banishment and exile; they had been through many of the same things. Joe, on the other hand, belonged to a generation of High Arctic Inuit who saw themselves as Ellesmere Islanders, natives of Umingmak Nuna, or Musk-Ox Land, as they preferred to call it. Stories of expulsion and promised lands had no real hold on him. For Joe, Ellesmere Island *was* the promised land. It was incredible that he should have killed himself in the place he so loved.

The men of the family went to Craig together to build the cairn and settle the body, leaving the women to content themselves with a church service after the event. On the morning of the service the weather was undecided, the sun taking refuge in a sky patched with high cirrus. By the time the opening tune of the breakfast show crackled through the radio, Edie had been up hours already. She'd showered, then oiled and plaited her hair, tying the plaits at the back with rick-rack and a ribbon sewn from Arctic hare. Though she had no appetite, she made herself eat a breakfast of tea and seal blubber, then she donned her best outfit, a dress of embroidered knitted musk ox, her sealskin parka and kamiks, stood back and looked in the mirror. The wind had weathered her face – she didn't look twenty-five any more – and the events of the past weeks showed in her eyes if you looked hard enough, but she passed muster. In her traditional garb you wouldn't even know she had a *qalunaat* for a father. The small, slightly fierce woman staring back at her looked one hundred per cent Inuit and she liked it that way.

Mid-morning she walked up to the church alone. Neither Minnie nor Willa wanted her there, but she'd decided to go anyway and stand somewhere at the back where she wouldn't be noticed. They couldn't deny her that.

A big crowd of familiar faces had already gathered. Most of the aunts, uncles and cousins returned her greeting. A few held back. There was still a feeling among some that if Edie hadn't sent Joe out with Andy Taylor he'd still be alive. She understood the feeling, shared it almost. People had forgotten it was Sammy who had first put Joe and Andy Taylor together and Sammy obviously hadn't seen fit to remind them. Not that it would have made much difference.

He now stood with Minnie and Willa, each doing their best to put on the united front they had spectacularly failed to achieve when Joe was alive. Although when it came to family solidarity, Edie could hardly claim the high moral ground. Hadn't she abandoned Joe and Willa when she'd left Sammy? Willa certainly thought so.

The vicar waffled on. Land of Snow, blah blah. He'd arrived in Ellesmere from Iqaluit three years ago and hadn't yet noticed that above the 76th parallel snow didn't count for much. Up here, it was all about ice. Locals often said the difference between Inuit and southerners was that southerners thought of ice as frozen water, whereas Inuit knew that water was merely melted ice. Edie resolved to have a chat with the man about it sometime.

She waited until the sermon was in full flow then slipped away. Starting back home, she'd reached the steps up to her house when an idea suddenly came to mind and she turned and made her way back towards the Town Hall. Inside, the offices were deserted. Everyone had been given the morning off to attend the church service. She used Joe's old keys to open the comms room, radioed the police detachment at Kuujuaq and was acknowledged by a weary-sounding voice.

'Oh, Edie, it's you.' Derek seemed cheered. 'Simeonie let you use the radio?'

'Joe worked the comms room's rota, remember? I put his keys on my key ring. For a rainy day. Derek, I was wondering, did you speak to Fairfax?'

She heard Derek take a deep breath and shift about in his chair.

'Man didn't have anything to add.' He sounded evasive. She wondered if he was lying and, if so, why.

'Did you ask him about Felix Wagner?'

'Why would Fairfax know the other guy?'

'Wagner. I don't know. It's just a feeling.'

'The lab results on Joe were pretty conclusive. The mayor wants a line drawn under the whole business as quickly as possible.'

'In good time for the start of his re-election campaign.'

Derek sighed. She'd got him on the defensive. 'Look, we flew right across Craig twice. If Taylor had been alive, we'd have seen him from the air.'

The weary sound had crept back into Derek Palliser's voice. Sometimes she wished she could just shake the man. Banish the degree of his cynicism, his indifference to the world, to himself.

'What's your interest in this guy anyway?' he said. 'I thought you hated him.'

Edie ignored the jibe. 'You mean you didn't land?'

'There was no need.'

'I thought you said a band of low cloud came down?'

Did he imagine she'd forgotten the conversation they'd had the night after Joe died? He was underestimating her, which was unlike him, and it bugged her all the more for it.

'Man, you have a nerve, Edie, you know that? In any case, Simeonie sent Martie out after, remember?'

For an instant, her hackles rose, then a little burr of shame blossomed on her face and tears begin to run hot down her cheeks. She bit her lip hard so he wouldn't know she was crying. Ever since she'd found Joe on the bed, she'd had a hard time keeping control of her emotions.

'Edie, I know you're upset,' he said. His voice was emollient, soft. 'Isn't it best for everyone if we just put all this behind us, get back to normal?'

She hooted with what she hoped was the right amount of impatience. 'Oh yeah, I forgot, let's celebrate our marvellous community and pretend it's not full of fuck-ups and drunks and high school drop-outs.' She took a deep breath and gathered herself. 'Derek, you ever consider where your lemming brain might be driving you?' They cut off the call.

Too agitated to settle, she took herself to the stretch of shore-fast ice where she kept her dogs tied, quietened them down, clipped on their tracings and set the komatik running, with Bonehead trotting along freestyle by her side. Like most people, she still kept a dog team for those trips, especially across the mountains and into the interior, where the going was too rough for snowbies or just for when she wanted to feel closer to the land.

Plus this way, she could sneak out without anyone hearing her.

She had a feeling of wrongness, nothing she could put a finger on, but unsettling all the same; something told her that from now on she had to be careful. It wasn't just the way the deaths of the *qalunaat* had been hastily swept away, it was the ease with which everyone seemed prepared to accept Joe's suicide. She felt in her bones that there was some kind of connection she didn't understand yet between the death of Felix Wagner, the disappearance of Andy Taylor and Joe's suicide. It was just all too much of a coincidence. Simeonie sensed that too, she thought. That was why he was so keen to keep a lid on the thing.

The day had decided to clear now and the sun had hauled itself as high as it was going to in the southern sky: perfect mirage weather. Edie tied up the dogs, made a note to herself to watch out on the return trip, and walked over to the snow porch of Martie's cabin.

The woman had never been able to settle in the new government prefabs. If she'd wanted central heating, she said, she'd have gone to live in a volcano. She'd built the cabin herself one summer from a pile of two-by-fours a construction team working on the mayor's office left behind. She'd double-walled it and Edie had helped stuff the cavity with a mixture of moss and musk-ox hair. A primus sat in one corner, an old coal-fire stove, a hangover from the fur time, in the other. Caribou skins lined the floor and walls and made the place cosy. Very unusually for an Inuk, Martie lived alone.

A thick stench of cheap whisky filled the tiny living area and there were mugs lying on the table that were too clean inside to have been used for tea. Edie called out and Martie appeared from behind the curtain marking off her sleeping room, looking like a musk ox in a bad mood.

'Oh, it's only you, you crazy little bear.' She waved her favourite niece to a seat and shuffled to the kitchenette. 'Shit, I could use a brew,' she said, lighting the primus and sticking a pan of water over the flame. 'What are you doing here anyway? Aren't you missing Joe's service?'

Martie hadn't shown up at the church, which wasn't much of a surprise since she didn't wholly approve of Christianity, one of the many things she and Edie had in common. Growing up, Edie had taken comfort in Martie's reassurances that to be different was OK.

The water in the pan began to boil. Martie picked up the two mugs on the table and, reaching up to a shelf, she pulled down a large bottle of Canadian Mist. As she watched her aunt pouring a large slug into one of the mugs, Edie found herself hit by a terrible and familiar need. Not a drop of booze had passed her lips in two years, but not a day had gone by when she didn't miss it. Sitting here, now, with her aunt, she was suddenly struck by an absolute conviction that she could not go on a moment longer without a little taste. Martie noticed the direction of her gaze.

'Aw, shit, Edie.'

'Martie, they're burying Joe.'

Her aunt gave her a look, then poured a shot of Mist into the second mug.

'I wanted to ask you about the S&R over in Craig.' As

Derek had reminded her, Simeonie had sent Martie out a couple of days after his own recce.

'We didn't see zip.' Martie lit a cigarette. 'I was all for landing, but we had instructions.'

Edie looked up in surprise. Martie caught her expression.

'What? Simeonie's instructions: fly-over only.'

Edie took a big gulp of boozy tea. The whisky felt good, warm and homely, like a cuddle, only simpler and purer. Two years of sobriety gone in an instant. Right now she didn't regret it.

'Martie, see how bizarre that is? You're sent out to look for someone who could have been sheltering in an ice cave or fallen down a crevasse. How you going to find that person without even landing the plane?'

Martie shrugged and offered her niece a top-up.

'Listen, Little Bear, I just do my job.'

Edie recalled the time, many years before, when she'd done just this, turned up without warning at Martie's door, though for other reasons. She and Sammy had been drinking all day, all evening. Willa and Joe were in bed. A fight had broken out, she could no longer remember what it was about, except that it was about what it was always about – the booze. It had got pretty nasty. At one point she'd picked up her gun and Sammy had picked up his. They'd stood staring at one another, guns in hand. It was ridiculous, looking back on it, like a scene from a Buster Keaton movie. Just as she was wondering what to do next, the boys' door creaked open and Joe's face peered out, Willa behind him. It still pained her to think about what those boys had witnessed. Edie had grabbed her parka then and fled out here, to her aunt's cabin. Martie had made her a large flask of tea and some caribou soup, locked her in the cabin and left her there for three days to sober up and cool down.

Now, Edie drank her refill down with what even she recognized was unseemly haste. This time the whisky just felt normal.

The return journey to Autisaq went smoothly and Edie got back for her three o'clock class. She decided to give a lesson about the Time of the Kidnappings. She liked to capitalize the name, give it an authority it didn't possess in any of the history textbooks.

The first *qalunaat* to kidnap Inuit had been the British adventurer, Martin Frobisher, who brought one unfortunate Inuk back with him to London in 1571. The Inuk man died shortly after, but this didn't dissuade other *qalunaat* explorers from following suit, dragging numberless Inuit back first to Europe, then to North America, for exhibition or to be given away as gifts to expedition sponsors and other notables. The Inuit almost always died from western diseases within months of arrival and the families they left behind often starved. It got so bad that several European states felt obliged to ban the practice. When she'd finished speaking, Pauloosie Allakarialak piped up:

'Why did they take people from their families?'

'What's your view?'

Pauloosie hesitated before venturing, 'Because they could?'

She smiled. Eight years he'd been at the school and she was finally getting through to him.

After school, she swung by the Northern Store looking for something good to eat. She'd lost her appetite since Joe's death. Perhaps it was the booze, but she felt something in her had changed since returning from Martie's. For the first time in weeks, she no longer felt guilty and defeated. On the contrary, she was angry.

At the counter waiting to pay she ran into Sammy. Their

eyes met briefly, awkwardly. He clocked the contents of her basket and a frail smile of recognition spread across his face. It was odd that two people could predict what the other would buy in the supermarket and yet be in so many other ways incompatible. She wondered if he had seen the bottle of Canadian Mist she thought she had hidden carefully under a rack of ribs and a jar of peanut butter. She hoped he hadn't.

'Need company?'

She considered how good it would be to feel him beside her on the sofa then, later, in bed, and she knew he was thinking the same thing. For an instant they stood like that, together, as though they were right back at the beginning and all of the rocky surfaces, the sharp, brittle stones, that had come between them over the years had dissolved. But then there would be the morning. There was always the morning.

'Another night,' she said, reaching out and squeezing his shoulder.

A pained look flitted across his face and he backed away a little, just enough so that her arm fell from him.

'Sure, Edie.' His voice was tinny with fake bonhomie. 'Sure thing.'

She left it until she felt quite drunk before approaching the door to Joe's room. For a while she stood before it, this simple door, leading to the simple, rectangular room. Since his death the house, her home, had become this door and what lay inside. She turned the handle and went in, heart thudding. For a moment she thought she could smell that heartstopping smell, the peculiar spicy stench of dead flesh, but it was only a memory. Closing the door behind her, she stepped into the room and sat down in the chair beside the bedstead.

'Joe, *allummiipaa*, darling?' The sound of her voice surprised her.

She waited a while but the silence, the sucking airlessness of the room, left her dizzy. Whatever she had expected to find, dreaded, or perhaps longed for, it wasn't there.

She threw the groceries in the trash, then she sat and waited for the night wind to come down from the mountains. She waited for it to begin its yelling and raging and she went out into it.

The following Sunday she decided to pay a visit to Minnie and Willa. Edie had largely managed to avoid her stepson's mother and brother. It was only now she realized that she had been angry with them for blaming her in some measure for Joe's death and angry with herself, too, because there was a part of her that thought they had a point. But who was really responsible for Joe's suicide? Was it her fault for allowing Sammy to send him out on his own with a neurotic, incompetent and manipulative jerk? Or did Andy Taylor somehow get Joe involved in something, wrapped him up so tight he couldn't see any way of loosening himself that didn't involve taking his own life? What it came down to was, she needed their forgiveness and she needed to know she was worth forgiving.

Minnie was on the sofa, watching TV, a bottle wrapped in brown paper beside her. So it had got that bad, Edie thought, too urgent to wait for a glass. She knew what that felt like.

Minnie took her in momentarily then returned her gaze to the screen.

'Just what we need.' She hawked up and spat on the green speckled linoleum tiles. 'A royal visit.'

Edie bit back her irritation and took a deep breath. Sure, Minnie was angry. So what? It was easy to be angry, she was angry herself, but no one seemed to be able to agree who to be angry with. Perhaps there *was* no one and the rage that roared in after Joe's suicide, after any suicide, was like an avalanche tumbling from a glacier; all you could do was to bear witness to its terrible energy and hope you would still be alive at the end of it.

'Minnie,' Edie said simply. 'I'm sorry.'

In that moment she didn't know what she was sorry for. Everything maybe. Minnie gave Edie a look so thick with hatred that it felt like a punch to the face.

'You wanna talk to him, Willa's in there,' pointing at the door to Willa's room, then spitting into her hand and rubbing the palm across her face. 'You're wasting your time with me.'

Edie found Willa sitting on his bed beside the open window, smoking dope.

'Your mother's mad at me.'

He shook his head. 'No, she just hates you.'

'Any idea why, aside from the usual?'

Willa took a long toke with his eyes closed. He said: 'Where to begin?'

Silence.

Edie started again. 'Do you remember that time out on Craig when we went spear-fishing? You, me and Joe.' Trying to bring him back to her. 'What are you now, twenty-two, right? So it must have been, what, about seven, eight years ago?'

She'd taken them char fishing. There was an area of deep water just off the coast of Craig. It was a particularly good year, the fish came in so close to the coast you could wade out a hundred metres clear of the beach and almost lift them from the water.

Willa and Joe were just kids, then, of course. Joe went in the water first. Joe was such an enthusiast about almost everything, but he loved spear-fishing in particular and he'd practised till he'd got good at it. As usual, Willa hung back. He never wanted to put the work in, but resented his little brother for his superior competence. She remembered Joe whooping as he brought his harpoon down and called excitedly to his brother to come and keep the fish from escaping while he went for a net. With Willa pinning the fish, Joe kicked his way back to the beach in a fury of excitement, shaping the size of the fish with his hands. She saw Willa lift the spear and bring the creature pinned at its end out of the water. Joe was right. It was huge, a beauty, more than enough to provide supper for all three of them. Then something unexpected happened. As Joe bent over to pick up the net, his back to the sea, Edie watched Willa bring up his free hand and with one great swipe, push the fish from its anchor and plunge the empty harpoon back into the water. Just then Joe turned and leapt back into the sea, the water unfurling into white rags about him, shouting, 'Keep it fast, Willa!' It was only when Joe reached into the sea to grab the harpoon he realized there was no longer any fish to net. He stood up, a look of devastation on his face. It was as if the sea had snatched his whole world. For an instant Joe just looked at Willa and in that instant Edie could see that Joe knew what his brother had done and decided to forgive him anyway.

'I don't remember any fishing trip,' Willa said now. There was defiance in his voice. 'Look, Edie, it was you insisted Joe went out with that *qalunaat* and I guess you'll just have to live with that.'

Edie saw now she had been stupid to imagine the Inukpuks would forgive her. Neither Minnie nor Willa were ever going to want to understand why Joe had died, because they had already decided that Edie was to blame. Sammy had spun a version of the story and the Inukpuks had bought it. Anyone else, she'd think of it as a betrayal. But Sammy wasn't bad, he was just weak. She'd known it when she'd married him and nothing had changed. Some day Willa might find out the truth, but she wasn't going to be the one to tell him.

She turned and picked up her outerwear, then she walked out of the house and went back home. She spent the early part of the evening watching Buster Keaton punch, bludgeon and flee his way out of trouble in *The Frozen North*, feeling by turns numb and unhinged. Eventually she got up and, fetching the steps from the utility room, clambered up to the high kitchen cupboard and took out the bottle of Canadian Mist.

The Frozen North was on its fourth or maybe fifth loop, and Edie was on her third double when Sammy's face peered around the door.

'Edie, you OK?' He came over and sat beside her.

'You know what day it is?' she said.

Sammy looked puzzled. 'Sunday?'

'A month.'

Sammy helped himself to a glass of whisky. Some kind of dark energy came over the room. Neither of them said anything. A thought burst into her mind, a horrible, pricking thought, but one that she couldn't altogether dismiss.

'Sammy,' she said, 'you don't think Willa could have have held something over Joe?'

Sammy instantly flung down his glass, stood up and went to the door.

His voice was cracked and tremulous: 'You know what, Edie? Sometimes I'm amazed I ever loved you.'

A few hours later, when she could not sleep, she found herself at Sammy's door. The light was still on, and she went inside.

He was sitting on his cheap sofa, the one that smelled of old beer and rancid seal fat, maudlin with drink. Beside him sat several empty cans of Coors and a half-bottle of Wild Turkey. She went over and for a while they held one another in silence. Then he poured a shot of whisky into a grimy glass sitting on the table and pushed it towards her. She lifted the glass to her lips; the booze burned its way into her stomach. Beside her, her ex-husband sat watching intently.

'I'm sorry,' she said.

He waved her apology away, as though everything had returned to how it had always been and by the simple act of sharing a drink, they had achieved a perfect understanding.

'I came round to tell you something before,' he said. 'About Andy Taylor.'

The evening before the trip, Taylor had asked to go to the mayor's office to make an urgent phone call.

'You know where to?'

'Uh nuh. Family situation, he said. It'll be on the record, though.'

Edie took him in. Even now he was a puzzle to her.

'Sammy,' she said, 'why are you telling me this?'

He smiled thinly. 'I'm not brave, Edie. I know you'd like me to be, but I'm not. Not like you.'

Someone had left a desk light on inside the Town Hall offices and its light cast faint stripes across the empty desks and office chairs. She passed by the conference room where, what now seemed like a hundred years ago, the council of Elders had agreed not to investigate Felix Wagner's death while she and Joe waited outside like scolded school kids.

At the comms room she turned right down a side corridor and headed towards the large grey door at the end, which led into the mayor's office. The office itself was locked. For a moment she sat at the desk of the mayor's personal assistant, Sheila Silliq, just outside Simeonie's office door. Sheila was one of those women who'd willingly given up their sense of being Inuit for a cosy office job and a twice-yearly trip down south to the bright lights of Ottawa. Polite, efficient, and with just the smallest air of superiority.

Beside her desk was a metal shelf and on it sat a number of box files, neatly labelled. Edie found the one marked 'phone log', and scrolled through the sheets to April. Almost no one made calls to anywhere other than the surrounding area, Iqaluit and, occasionally, to Ottawa. The US area code stood out a mile. She scribbled down the number, closed up the records and was putting them back in the cabinet just as the door to the main entrance swung open and Sheila appeared in the corridor, bustling towards her, rosy from the wind outside.

The only thing for it was to go on the offensive. 'Couldn't sleep,' Edie said, trying to appear as though her presence at a desk not hers in the middle of the night was nothing out of the ordinary. 'What's your excuse?'

Sheila stared at her, open-mouthed, an expression of bewilderment on her face. 'I left my flask.'

It wasn't until she got back home from the school the following day that Edie allowed herself to look at the number Andy Taylor had called. The area code wasn't one she recognized: nowhere in Nunavut, Ottawa or Toronto. Taylor had told Sammy he wanted to make a private call to his family but, as Derek had discovered, the skinny *qalunaat* didn't have any close family.

Pulling on her outerwear, Edie hurried to the Northern Store and asked Mike if she could make a long-distance call from the phone in his office. The number picked up on the second ring and a voice in a drawling accent said, 'Zemmer?'

The name sounded familiar, but for now she couldn't put her finger on where she'd come across it before.

'Is Andy Taylor there?'

A pause on the line. 'We don't have an Andy Taylor.' The voice sounded wary. 'Who is this speaking?'

'I'm sorry,' she said. 'Maybe I got the wrong number. Is this the computer place in . . .' She searched her mind, '. . . Washington, DC?'

'No, ma'am, this is pizza delivery in Houston, Texas.'

Edie ended the call and went back into the store.

'No one in?' Mike put on a sympathetic smile.

Edie shook her head. You had something to hide, it was best to act mute. Something she'd learned from silent movies.

She'd just stumbled on something whose significance she didn't yet understand, but she knew it was significant all right. Not even Andy Taylor was crazed enough to call for takeout from some pizza joint six thousand kilometres away.

7

A week later, during a break from school, Edie gathered her gear and provisions and walked down to the beach to where her komatik sat. With the exception of the quick trip to Aunt Martie's cabin, Edie hadn't been out in it since Joe's death and it would need some routine maintenance before it was safe to take it out in what was by now still compacted, but ever so slightly softening, late May ice.

Most people used plastic runners these days but to Edie they had the effect of separating her, somehow, from the ground, a feeling she found distracting and unpleasant. The old liver-and-mud paste on the komatik's walrus-ivory runners would need chipping off and a new lot spread on. She preferred to sled old-style.

While the runner paste was freezing and hardening, she'd re-knot the slats with sealskin rope and check over the dog harnesses.

She told herself she was going fishing under the ice at Craig. This was true, but it wasn't the whole truth and she knew that too. Had she really only been interested in ice fishing, there were closer and better spots.

There had been no news of the whereabouts of Andy Taylor since the second and final S&R and Joe's family, Simeonie and even Derek Palliser had seemed almost indecently keen to put both Taylor's disappearance and Joe's suicide behind them. If she had any sense she'd do the same, but Joe's death had stirred in her some compulsion which she was unable to ignore. Call it a hunter's sense, intuition, mother love, whatever, she didn't care. All she felt sure of was that the two deaths and Taylor's disappearance were somehow connected. If Joe hadn't died maybe she *would* have done as Sammy suggested, toed the line and shut up, but now she felt sure the fates of the two *qalunaat* offered the key to understanding what had happened to her stepson. Openly challenging Simeonie's authority would make her life extremely difficult, if not impossible, which was why she had kept her intentions so secret that she could hardly even admit them to herself. But she knew that if she didn't get to the bottom of Joe's death, there would be no point in her going on.

When she'd finished on the komatik, she pulled it along the sea ice to where she kept the dogs chained. She'd already fed the animals the morning before, and wouldn't now feed them again until she pitched camp that night. It was important to keep the team just on the edge of hunger. If they were sated they wouldn't run.

For the past few seasons, her lead dog had been a dusty grey bitch she'd called Takurnqiunagtuq, Happiness. The name seemed ironic now. Joe had always teased her for her sentimental attachment to her sled dogs. She was thinking about it now, as she went among them, squeezing their ribs to gauge the strength of their chests and checking their feet for abrasions that might cause trouble on the trail. Paws and lungs were often the first to go. Candle ice could cut the pads to pieces and when it got really cold some of the weaker dogs would cough blood. She'd had dogs in the past whose lungs had burst like blown bags. But for the most part they were a hardy lot, bred from the fierce, lean Nunavik animals brought up by her grandparents and the larger, more placid Greenlandic dog with its tremendous coat and tiny ears that prevented it losing too much heat.

She picked out fourteen and tied them to the fan harness, leaving two to run alongside as backup. Giving her clothes and gear a final check, she tied a pile of caribou skins tightly over the komatik, called Bonehead to heel and mushed on the sledders with a *Ha! Ha!*

It was perfect sledding weather. High cloud had kept the temperature at a pleasant –20C, cold enough for the ice to remain hard but not so cold that the sled runners would bounce, and the wind was gusting softly enough not to raise the snow into frost clouds.

As the komatik bumped along on the shore-fast ice towards the bank of pressure ridges signalling the start of the floating pack, a scene from *The Frozen North* came unbidden into her mind and she heard herself chuckle. It seemed so long since she had laughed at anything. There, in her head, was Buster Keaton desperately trying to mush together his team of teeny nonsense dogs.

Up ahead, a great jumble of pressure ice brought her back into the present. This was one of the things she loved most about sea-ice travel, the way that, if you let it, your progress across the land could become your thought universe, pushing all other thoughts to one side until everything seemed embedded in the journey and movement itself seemed like the only thing that had ever mattered. Was it wiser to travel on the pack or along the ice foot? From what direction was the spindrift coming? Were they entering bear country? Were the tides high enough to break up the ice?

At the first ridge she stopped the dogs, pushed the anchor into the ice then went ahead to look for a route through the jumbled ice steeples and towers onto the pack beyond. Returning, she led Takurnqiunagtuq slowly through, running back to balance the komatik each time it threatened to overturn. It was strenuous work and by the time Edie reached the smooth floating pack on the other side, she was ready for a rest. She threw down the anchor, commanded the dogs to lie down, then kicked a few steps into a nearby iceberg and clambered up for a view.

In the far distance the cliffs of Taluritut rose from the sea ice. The Inuktitut name meant 'tattoo', after the ridged and folded cliffs which looked from a distance like the tattooed whiskers Inuit women used to wear on their chins. So much more expressive than the *qalunaat* name, Devon. A few kilometres to the north, its windswept edges glowing bruise-mauve in the sea ice, sat Craig Island.

Edie took off her snow goggles, closed her eyes and set her face towards the sun, feeling the first intimations of warmth. How beautiful it was. All over Craig now, under vast hills of blown snow, mother bears would be stirring with their cubs and in a few weeks the eiders would appear, followed by dovekies and walrus. Turnstones, snow geese, knots, snow buntings, and kittiwakes would show up and all at once it would be summer.

On his thirteenth birthday, Edie had presented Joe with a second-hand komatik and a pile of pups. Over the next couple of years the boy put a great deal of his energy into raising and training those pups and by the age of fifteen, he could hold his own against the most experienced mushers in Autisaq. Joe used to race her out here. As late as early July, just before the breakup, he would beg her to harness her dogs and they would take themselves off to the edge of the pack, where the bears hung out waiting for seal. Often, he'd go on ahead of his team and she'd watch him, testing the ice, often just leaping from floe to floe. It was incredibly dangerous but he had a knack of knowing exactly when the floes would merge or split apart, of how to place his body, when to open a stride, how far to jump and when to hold back. He used to tease her that he'd learned his timing from the 'greats', by which he meant Lloyd and Chaplin, Keaton and Laurel and Hardy.

She started up again. It was eerily calm now, the wind nothing more than a faint stirring, the sun bouncing from the sea ice and sending up a heat haze. If you weren't careful in all this dazzle, you could be snow blind in thirty minutes. The blindness itself wouldn't kill you but with no sight you'd be reliant on your dogs to get you home safely. Edie could name four or five hunters who would not be alive today were it not for their dogs. Just another reason why, wherever possible, when Edie went out on the land alone for any extended period, she preferred to travel in the traditional way.

In any case, in good conditions, the journey to Craig wasn't all that arduous. Once you'd got over the pressure ridge you were on flat sea ice all the way. The distance from the beach at Autisaq to Tikiutijavvilik on Craig couldn't be more than fifty kilometres. But in difficult conditions, it was a whole other story. Looking out across the huge and largely featureless expanse now, she was struck by what a miracle it had been for Joe to have made it back in the middle of a whiteout, hypothermic, frostbitten and confused. A rush of anger came then. On that fateful trip out with Fairfax and Taylor she and Joe had both wanted to take their dog teams. They figured it would be easier to pick up signs of old cairns or burial mounds that way, but Taylor had insisted on taking the machines. He'd used them in Alaska and was absolutely convinced of their superiority over dogs. Edie had pointed out that Alaska was as far south from Ellesmere as California was from Alaska but this didn't seem to impress him. He'd been in such a hurry.

Too many thoughts. Edie mushed on the dogs and tried to focus once more on the route.

A couple of kilometres from the coast of Craig she saw something stirring on the horizon, a *puikaktuq*, a mirage, in Inuktitut literally 'rising above the sea'. At first a shining silver cloud, the *puikaktuq* began to quiver then slowly to coalesce and, as it did so, Edie realized to her amazement that a figure was forming from the cloud. Slowly, slowly, the cloud billowed and shrank, gathering an outline, until there was no question in her mind that the outline was that of a young man and, more specifically still, from the way it moved, that what she was looking at was a *puikaktuq* of Joe: not the Joe of the bones and meat, interred beneath rocks on the muskeg, but the Joe of the spirit world, the *atiq* Joe, a soft, surrounding presence. There he was, a great Northern Light shimmering on the horizon. The dogs, too, seemed to have sensed something because they set up a furious howling and began pulling excitedly forward. As the komatik raced across the pan, Edie felt the ice crystals forming little boulders in the corners of her eyes, the moisture between her lips freezing, the hairs in her nose pulling at the snot as it froze inside her nostrils until she could sense him all around her, little particles of Joe, tumbling across the sea ice.

Then, just as suddenly as he had come, the *puikaktuq* disintegrated, the dogs slowed and standing on the shorefast ice not far away, the figure of a man appeared, and beside him, resolving in the dazzling sun, a small komatik and six dogs. Edie realized that it was this man, not the *puikaktuq*, who had been the reason for her team's excitement.

Waving and calling, she made her way towards the figure, but got no response. As she neared, she could just make out the shape of Old Man Koperkuj. He was fishing through the ice. He'd clearly been there some time, because there were six fat char lying beside his fishing hole.

'You sent the fish away,' he grumbled, as she anchored her dogs and walked up to him.

Edie apologized. He was quite right to be upset. Had she been observing proper custom, she'd have pulled her dogs up some way off and awaited his signal to approach. The incident with the *puikaktuq* had made her forget her manners and now she had probably cost him some fish.

Though she'd known Saomik Koperkuj all her life, she'd never had very much to do with him. He lived in a cabin not far from Martie and came into town only to pick up his welfare or trade a pile of furs. One of the original Nunavik exiles and a bit of a drinker, it was said. Rumour had it that he and Martie had something going for a while, but even if that was true, Edie regarded it as nobody's business but their own. All the same, he was an ill-tempered old musk ox, been on his own so long he had forgotten how to be in company. All that snorting and showing his horns. She couldn't understand what her aunt had seen in him.

'You coming to visit the boy, I suppose,' he grunted.

Edie was startled. For a moment she thought he'd seen the *puikaktuq* too, but then she realized he'd meant the grave.

'Shame about the boy,' he mumbled. 'No call for it.'

Koperkuj invited Edie to squat beside him. 'I was fond of him, he had good *ihuma*. You don't find that so often these days. When your ancestor, Welatok, was around, maybe, but now, not so often.'

'No,' she said, glad that, unlike almost everyone else, Koperkuj clearly hadn't seen Joe as the unstable kind.

He motioned to the pile of char lying beside his fishing hole, the leister beside them. He'd been hunting hare, too. Two males and a female lay slung over the bars of his komatik.

'You hungry?'

Edie nodded. Until then she hadn't realized how much.

She watched while Koperkuj expertly sliced open a char and sorted the guts, laying the edible ones on the ice and putting aside the lower digestive tract, no doubt to take home and wash out. Char gut made good patching for sock linings. As he worked, he passed her the choicest morsels, shining and bloody, and she tucked in appreciatively, relishing the taste of the sea still on the flesh.

The old man had already set up a primus and the fish was followed by hot sweet tea. Edie fetched her thermos of Canadian Mist from the komatik and added a splash to each, the old man nodding encouragement to her to keep pouring.

When the first fish was all eaten up, Koperkuj instructed Edie to go fetch another and as she went to the ice hole, her eye was drawn to the fishing leister sitting beside it, which was marked with a blue stripe and a sticker of a sabre-tooth tiger. It was familiar to her. She gave the leister a closer look. The sticker was the marque of the Nashville Predators ice-hockey team. Joe and Derek Palliser were supporters. The leister was Joe's old one, the one he'd been given a few years back by his father. What was Old Man Koperkuj doing with it? Then she remembered. Hadn't Joe said he was taking the spare out for Andy Taylor? Wanted to show him how the experts did ice fishing. The leister had been in Andy Taylor's gear, which could only mean that Koperkuj had come across it on Craig. She stood up, and, without betraying the turmoil in her mind, calmly walked back with the char.

She said: 'You been ice fishing before this spring?'

'Once, back in April.' Koperkuj wiped his mouth and gave her a wary look, the kind of look a starving fox will give you if you hold out meat for it.

'Good catch?'

He shrugged: 'The usual.'

She passed him the whisky and encouraged him to take a few slugs. He let out a satisfied little chuckle. She knew him well enough to recognize, any direct question about anything, he'd clam up. For a while they swapped hunting stories while she plied him with more booze. She'd have to come in on this one slowly, obliquely, so he wouldn't even notice he was caught.

'Good-looking hares you got there,' she said, cutting her glance to the corpses hanging on the sled bar.

'Oh sure,' he said. 'Round here, hare's easy.' He turned and pointed back to a headland to the south. 'I got those near Tikiutijavvilik. But any of the spots south of there are pretty good. You know, where the wind blows the snow off the ground cover.' He named a few places, giving their descriptions in Inuktitut.

'Mind if I take a look?' She went over, ostensibly to admire the pelts, her eyes scoping along the length of the sled.

At the back, balanced on the slats, he'd left a hunting rifle, a Remington 700, pretty new. Identical, in fact, to the one Andy Taylor was carrying when she'd taken him and Felix Wagner out birding.

'You get these hares with that 700?' she said.

He nodded, loose now.

'Sweet,' she said.

Inside, she felt winded. No way an old man like Koperkuj could afford a new Remington. Had Koperkuj come across Andy Taylor's abandoned snowbie? It was possible, but it seemed unlikely. Even the skinny *qalunaat* wasn't so stupid as to leave his vehicle without taking his rifle. She decided to go off-tack while she gathered her thoughts, get back to the topic subtly once the old man had a few more slugs of whisky.

'Get any big game recently?'

He swayed and reached for the flask. 'Got a wolf a while back. Not on Craig though. The crazy thing is, when I cut him open I found this inside the stomach.'

He drew out a gold chain on which hung a mottled stone the size of a raven's skull and offered it to her. Edie picked up the stone, weighed it in her hand, then let it fall back onto the old man's parka. The rock was weirdly heavy, unlike any she'd come across before.

The old man giggled. 'They're hungry enough, wolves eat anything.'

'Amazing.' Edie did her best to look impressed.

Koperkuj chuckled approvingly. The old musk ox was so pickled now he didn't even cop the fact that he'd just told the world's most unconvincing lie. No wolf would get so hungry it would eat a stone. In which case, how'd the old man come across a gold necklace? Could the stone have belonged to Andy Taylor? Edie ran a theory over in her mind. Did Koperkuj kill Taylor? Not likely. The fellow was an opportunist but he wasn't a murderer. What *did* look increasingly likely though was that Koperkuj had got up close and personal to the *qalunaat* and rehomed some of his things. Not that she was going to get any kind of confession out of the old ox. He was drunk, but he wasn't a fool.

A thin wailing started up: Koperkuj was trying some of the old-time songs, beating out a rhythm on a nearby rock, voice like a vixen on heat. A plan hatched in her mind. She plucked her flask from the gravel, flashed Koperkuj a polite smile, then thanking him for his hospitality and wishing him good travelling, returned to her team.

She made land at Ulli, the crescent-shaped shingle beach where once she, Joe and Willa had gone collecting eider duck eggs, tied in the dogs and fed them some pemmican.

Then she scrambled up the scree to the cliff top where the *inukshuk* for Joe looked out across the ice of Jones Sound and made her way on wind-blown, compacted snow, to the slight dip in the plateau where Joe's body lay under a cairn of small boulders. At some distance, from the safety of a rocky outcrop, a raven watched.

She said: 'Joe, it's Kigga.'

A wind blew up and the raven took off on it. For a while, Edie squatted by the cairn trying to conjure the places Joe might have taken Andy Taylor, the hideaway little nooks he and Edie explored when he was a boy, places the old man might know about too. If Koperkuj had run into Taylor's body it was likely that he would have come across it in one of his regular haunts.

She decided to make camp a few miles to the north of Tikiutijavvilik near Uimmatisatsaq. The beach there was shallow and the tide relatively small, protected somewhat from northwesterly winds. It was on this western coastal fringe that Bill Fairfax and Andy Taylor thought they might find evidence of Sir James Fairfax's camp. It was also the first of Koperkuj's hare-hunting grounds. After that, she'd head south and make a search of all the hideouts she and Joe had explored together. It was possible that Joe had pointed them out to Taylor or even that the *qalunaat* had found one of them himself. It was a real long shot, but right now, long shots were the business she was in.

Once she pitched camp, Edie pulled out her thermos and drank tea, while the light spun from south to north and the bright stare of the midnight sun shed its shadows from her spot around the fire. The swell of land above the beach at Tikiutijavvilik, low though it was, looked out across a stretch of relatively flatter coastline before the land rose up at Uimmatisatsaq and the cliffs proper began at Ulli. From that spot, using binoculars, Edie had a view of the customary landings all the way to the northern tip of the island.

Already the snow was becoming soft and wet in places, impossible for a snowbie to negotiate and difficult enough even with a dog team. Ten years ago, Edie wouldn't have needed to think about that, but breakup started earlier now and the ice was so much less predictable. In a couple of weeks from now, she supposed, the melt would begin in earnest and she wouldn't be able to travel on the land. Then, in late July, leads would start opening up in the sea ice and any travel across large distances, such as that between Ellesmere and Craig, would become very dangerous until breakup proper in late August or early September, when the sea became navigable by boat. So if Edie couldn't find traces of Andy Taylor now, she would have to wait three months for another opportunity.

She gave the dogs cooled weak tea and carved off pieces of the frozen seal she'd brought, then settled into her sleeping bag. For a while the clatter of guillemots and dovekies kept her awake, but not for long. When she woke, the southern sun was beating through the canvas, heating the air in the tent. She went out onto the snow and stretched in the fragile warmth of late spring. Over a breakfast of the fish she'd traded with Koperkuj for dog pemmican and more sweet tea, she decided to explore the area directly around Tikiutijavvilik then head south where the land rose up to cliffs, shaggy with greenish talus cones, whose placid, iced feet protected the shore-fast ice from tide cracks and where there was good travelling ice. There were no maps for this kind of a search. If Andy Taylor was to be found, it would not be at a set of co-ordinates. It would be on the land.

It was very late when Edie finally called it quits. It had been a frustrating search. Some time in the afternoon Bonehead had started signalling the proximity of bear. Edie thought it odd, since by this time of year the bears were usually to be found up on the east coast of Ellesmere, taking advantage of the rich supply of seal and beluga at the *sina*, the floe edge where the ice pack met the North Water, or west at Hell Gate, but in recent years, as the ice began to break up earlier, their routes had become less predictable. For several hours she'd had to slow the dogs right down and scan the horizon with her binoculars just in case.

Eventually, when neither bear nor tracks appeared, Edie mushed on the team but the delay meant that by the end of the day they had covered less ground than she'd hoped, and hadn't come across a single clue to the whereabouts either of Andy Taylor or his snowmobile. The incident *had* made her think though. If there were bear in the area, it was possible that Taylor had been killed and eaten. Sitting in the lea made by the tent she mugged up a brew and made a note to herself to look out for bear tracks or for the tracks of foxes who often followed behind in the hope of some good scavenge.

She ate a supper of three guillemot eggs she had found in an abandoned nest, cracking the shells in the palm of her hand and throwing the contents into her mouth raw, then wrapped herself in her caribou sleeping bag and set her internal alarm clock to wake her early. Sometime in the night she dreamed of the *puikaktuq* again, but by the time she woke she was conscious only of its shadow on her mind.

Before the seabirds had even risen from their roosts, Edie started out south along the coast through early morning coastal fog. Usually at this time of year, the fog gave way to low-lying cloud signalling drizzle, but this morning the sun burned it off and the day soon became bright with patches of high cirrus.

They had rounded the headland just south of Uimmatisatsaq when Edie decided to move down onto the beach itself. This was where Joe and Andy Taylor had most likely spent at least part of their time and she wanted to make sure she didn't miss anything.

She and the dogs were making their way along a sloping clamshell-rubbled beach when Edie's eye was drawn to an intense sparkle not fifty metres up ahead. Ice sparkled, snow sparkled, in the right conditions some rocks sparkled; fish skins sparkled, as did the hooves of musk oxen and caribou and the metallic parts of snowbies and komatiks, but nothing Edie could remember encountering before sparkled quite like this.

Bringing the dogs to a halt, she anchored them by the komatik and went ahead on foot. A thin, hard covering of compacted ice obscured the shelly beach in places and made it harder to locate the exact source of the sparkle. Wondering if she'd imagined it, she began an Inuit search, walking round in minutely expanding circles, eyes evenly scanning the small segment of ground immediately in front.

And, suddenly, there it was. A ray of sun had pierced the cloud cover in just the right spot and the sparkle had returned. Edie bent down and picked up a gold earring, plain but set with a brilliantly cut diamond, identical to the one Andy Taylor wore in his right ear. She clasped it in her hand – *thank you, sun* – and suddenly felt quite weightless, as though she might blow away. A thought brought her back to earth, one of those sudden, painful reminders of the life she had lost. Joe hated her habit of saying thank you. Gratitude is a *qalunaat* custom, he'd say. Inuit were entitled to help from each other. Gratitude didn't come into it.

She took off her kamiks, then the Gore-Tex socks she always wore, followed by her outer socks stitched from softened caribou leather so that finally she was left standing in nothing but her bare skin liners. Then she began to shuffle across the clamshells and the shale, moving in tight, slowly expanding circles, eyes fixed inside, mind and body focused absolutely on the sensations of the stones on her soft, sensitive feet.

Pretty soon she detected something other than stone, shell, shale or ice, possibly a remnant of cotton grass or a piece of dried lichen. Reaching down, she pushed aside the thin covering of ice around the spot. At first she didn't see anything, but Edie was hunter enough to be able to weigh the evidence of her various senses and to decide that, in this case, her feet were right and her eyes were wrong. She sank to her knees then lowered her body onto the shale to be nearer to whatever was lying there. She had felt it once and she would just have to try to feel it again. It was what she'd do if she were trying to detect the presence of a seal beneath the ice and she figured that this object was like the seal, something that did not wish to give itself up.

She removed her mittens, then her outer and inner gloves, finally the glove liners and began to probe around in the snowy shale, very delicately, so as not to force what she was looking for deeper into the layers of shell and stone. Despite the spring sun, it was still bitterly cold. Without gloves, the tiny, almost invisible hairs on her fingers froze and the moisture on her fingertips bedded in as ice. Then she put her thumb on it. Pulling it gently from the shale, she felt first the hard nub, then the crispy layer around. She had just unearthed a fragment of torn fabric, once most likely yellow, now bleached to a mottled tea colour, attached to what was once a shirt button. The button had cracked and only a thread now held the pieces. There was a stain on one corner, blood maybe. Jumping up, she began circling again, her heart beating out a satisfying thud. Here it was, the moment the paths of the hunter and the hunted first collide.

Not far from this first find, her feet detected something larger, a man's watch, the face so scratched by ice that Edie couldn't make out whether or not it was still working, though it hardly mattered: Inuit rarely wore watches and would never risk one out on the land where, in any case, they were redundant. This was the watch of a *qalunaat*.

Over the hours that followed, turning her circles, Edie gradually and meticulously accumulated the bits and pieces of a partial human skeleton, the flesh mostly torn off by animals, marking each piece in her mind as she went: a length of femur, a piece of skull, both metatarsals, three finger bones. When she was too cold to go on, she gathered her findings together and went into her tent to inspect them.

Edie had a familiarity with bones. If you were Inuit, you couldn't not. All her life, she'd been flensing them of their flesh, chopping them to get to the marrow, to make soup or to give to the dogs. When they'd been boiled and cleaned, she'd carved them into seals and birds, or whittled them into needles. Bones had been her drumsticks, boot jacks, ear picks and head scratchers. If you counted antlers, they'd been coat hooks too. And her experiences with bones hadn't been confined to animals. In the summer, as the snow retreated from the land, it left behind it the strewn remains of humans as well as creatures. Nothing on the tundra rotted much. After you buried a body under piles of rocks, the ice and the wind would eventually liberate it, if the foxes, wolves and bears hadn't already done so. The whole history of human settlement lay exposed there, out on the tundra, under that big northern sky. There was nowhere here for bones to hide.

Animals had been at these, which explained the pattern of their scattering. They seemed almost unnaturally clean, though Edie thought perhaps that was because April and May were hungry months and a number of scavengers had been over them. A few were splintered and on one or two of the larger bones there were teeth marks consistent with fox. She picked out a fragment of skull, from the top back of the head, she thought. In the midst of it was a small hole, about the size of a nickel, almost perfectly round. The unmistakeable entry wound of a bullet.

So here it was, proof all of a sudden that Andy Taylor hadn't simply got lost in the blizzard and died of hypothermia but that someone had killed him.

But who? She thought of Old Man Koperkuj but dismissed the idea. Koperkuj avoided people whenever he could. For the first time, the thought occurred to her that Joe and Taylor might have had some kind of falling out, but the instant it came into her mind, she chased it away, ashamed of herself. Joe was no more capable of shooting a man than Bonehead.

She picked out a piece of femur and turned it over in her hands. The first faint bloom of algal growth had already begun to appear over the surface. Though the growing season could not really be said to have started, the snow covering had insulated the bones from the worst of the cold, as it did lemmings and bear cubs, and all snow-buried things. The algae had grown a little more densely in the hairline cracks and indentations of the bone. The difference was very subtle but it had the effect of creating a faint frilling over the bone. Out of curiosity, she scraped at the markings with a finger. The algae concealed a tooth-like pattern. The marking had been scrubbed by weeks under the shifting snow, but to a hunter, it was absolutely unmistakeable. Someone had cut at the bone with a serrated hunting knife.

She could see now that the same pattern was picked out

very faintly in algae on some of the other fragments too. Edie sat back on her haunches, floored. The murderer must have dismembered the body before it had frozen solid and become more difficult to work. But why? The only reason she could think of was that this way, if the body was ever found, it would look as though Taylor had just died in the blizzard and his bones had been scattered by animals.

Edie pulled out her primus, put on a brew and tried to think the situation through. There was no question in her mind that she would have to hand at least some of the bones over to the authorities. Things could turn out very badly for her if someone came across some other fragments and it was subsequently discovered that she had said nothing. In any case, if she was careful, it might actually be in her interest to report her find before the snow cleared from the land and anyone else went looking for the body. Still, she needed to exercise caution. In Autisaq, the rumour mill had always been infinitely more powerful than the facts and if anyone got wind of the knife marks and the bullet hole, they would jump to conclusions. The one thing she didn't want was for this find to be used to implicate her stepson.

It made sense to hand over only those bones on which there was no evidence of bullet holes or knife cuts. The bones would be positively identified as belonging to Andy Taylor and it would be presumed that the *qalunaat* had died of exposure during the blizzard. Simeonie would ensure that no one went looking for the remainder of the skeleton and she would buy some time to discover who had killed Taylor, and from that learn something about Joe's state of mind as he stumbled back into Autisaq that day.

The next task was to find Taylor's snowmobile in case it carried clues and neutralize the evidence to fit in with the natural death story. It made sense that the vehicle would be somewhere not far distant from the body. It was harder to lose a snowbie than a body, so the fact that none of the S&R expeditions had located it suggested it had been hidden away somewhere or was sitting under a mound of wind-driven snow. Edie doubted the latter. There hadn't been a great deal of snow since April and the prevailing winds tended to drift it on the east-facing slopes.

In her mind she followed Craig's southern coastline from east to west, as though she were kayaking it, past rocky outcrops, beaches, cliffs and landings, alighting anywhere accessible to a snowbie. She was half way to Bone Beach, as she now thought of this spot, when she remembered the ice cave.

It was Joe who had found it, three or four years ago, a roof of *sikutuqaq*, multi-year ice, enclosing the two walls of a narrow passage between two cliffs, hard to spot from land and impossible from the air. Those who were not as familiar with Craig as Joe was wouldn't have any reason to know it was there. In the winter, the entrance was blocked off with snow, in the summer it tended to be obscured by outcroppings of willow and sedge; but Joe had started to use it as a shelter from bad weather. Edie fed the dogs and made herself another brew with extra sugar. She would snatch a little rest and get going again sometime after midnight when the sun was in the north, and the ice conditions were at their best. Three hours' sleep, then onwards.

The smell of metal at the cave's entrance made her pulse race. She switched on her flashlight. A snowy owl flew up towards her, then swished along and away. At the back of the cave something large glinted in the torchlight. It was Taylor's snowbie, the trunk open, the sides covered in owl guano where the animal had been preparing its nest. Beside it, scattered on the shale, were a tent, some waterproof waders and diving gear. Nothing had been torn or attacked, merely tossed aside. It looked as though someone had gone through Taylor's stuff in a hurry. Old Man Koperkuj maybe.

Above her, the old, grey ice squealed as it shifted against the rock walls. Already, the rime on the vehicle was beginning to melt near where the owl had been roosting. Edie flashed the light around the walls of the cave, searching for cracks, but it appeared to be sound for now.

She was about to direct her flashlight back towards the snowbie when her eye was drawn to a contrasting patch in the ice. Up close, she could see that there was an area of compacted snow pressed into the surface of the ice, the marks of fingers still on it.

She took out her *ulu*, the crescent-shaped knife carried by Inuit women, and prodded the spot until a few pieces of snow fell away. Working her way around it with the *ulu*, she uncovered a Styrofoam cup. Inside it was a plastic bag. She pulled out the bag and looked at the contents. Three sheets of paper had been fastened together with a paperclip that had rusted and bled. On each sheet, one edge was worn, the other razor sharp, as though it had been cut from a book. The paper itself was thick and ridged and each page was covered in tiny, precise handwriting in ink that had once been black but had faded brown. A combination of rust and damp had eaten away most of the words; with the flashlight, Edie could pick out only a few fragments, but nothing that made any sense. On top of the pages was a strip of what looked like ordinary notebook paper that someone had torn out. On it, written in another hand in ballpoint pen, Edie made out a single word in English: salt. She folded the paper and put it in her pocket, inspected the snowbie and decided then and there to head for home.

On the way back to Autisaq the *puikaktuq* appeared again. For a moment it was unmistakeably Joe. There was something about the expression on his face that shook her.

When she got back home she poured herself a stiff drink, then another. If Taylor had meant to shelter in the ice cave, why was his body so far from it? Had he known whoever shot him? Was he trying to hide the pages of old paper and the note reading 'salt'? The more she thought about it, the more she felt herself being sucked into something she hadn't bargained for and didn't understand.

The next day the *puikaktuq* invaded her dreams and she woke afraid, tears running down her cheeks.

By the time the school bell rang to signal the end of the day, she was seriously worried. She'd done nothing with what she'd found out at Craig and she felt as though she might be going crazy. She thought of going to Koperkuj, who had a reputation for being a shaman, but she didn't want to see him again just yet.

Two days passed, and on the morning of the third day she woke, still drunk, to find her sheets in such disarray she wondered if her spirit had been attacked in the night. She phoned in to school to say she would be late and took herself down to the nursing station. There were only a few people in line at the morning drop-in and she didn't have to wait long.

Robert Patma ushered her into his room. He seemed surprised to see her. She had never been a great one for doctors and had only called on him once during the three years he'd been in the post. He threw her a sympathetic look and asked what was wrong.

'I don't know,' she said. 'I can't sleep.'

'It's a big thing you've been through. You just need to let everything settle.'

'I'm seeing things.'

For a moment Robert looked taken aback. Then, gathering himself, he leaned forward, concern written across his face: 'What do you mean, you're seeing things?'

'*Puikaktuq*.' It sounded stupid and in the moments that followed she tried desperately to think of ways of taking the admission back.

She glanced behind her to make sure the door to the consulting room was closed. People would think a bad spirit had possessed her, or that she was going crazy. Her voice lowered to a whisper.

'I saw a mirage out on the land, then it followed me. Now it's with me all the time.'

Patma was lost in thought for a moment, then he said: 'This *puikaktuq*, did it look like Joe?'

She nodded, then corrected herself. 'Sometimes, then not.' She shivered. 'Am I sick?'

Patma shook his head. He didn't seem so great himself, she thought. He looked like he needed a sleep. 'Uh nuh, you're not sick and you're not going mad. I think what you're describing are probably bereavement hallucinations. They're very common.'

'Did you get them?' she asked.

Robert sat back.

'When your father died?' Was it his father? She couldn't remember. So much had happened since then.

He frowned. 'My mother,' he said.

'Yes, of course,' she said. 'I'm so sorry.'

He acknowledged her with a slight nod.

'You need to get some rest, Edie,' he said. 'All this, it's a big shock.' He considered for a moment. 'Look, I guess you know Joe had problems, Edie.' He looked up. 'I mean the gambling.'

The sudden change of subject floored her.

'It doesn't make any sense to me.'

'Me neither,' he said. 'We were pretty close.' He reached for her hand but didn't quite clasp it. 'But you know, Edie, sometimes you just gotta accept things. It happened, it was a tragedy and we're all just going to have to get used to it.'

She noticed his hand was shaking.

'Those hallucinations will move on just as soon as you do.'

All of a sudden she felt uncomfortable, wanting to be out of there. She stood up.

At the door he called her back and in a sterner tone, he said; 'I could give you something to help you sleep, but you'd have to quit the drinking.'

8

Derek Palliser had been watching lemmings stir for weeks and by the middle of June, what he'd seen had convinced him a swarm was gathering. None of the lemming experts had predicted it but, the way Derek saw things, that was because they'd got the business of population dynamics back to front.

It had started when he'd been out walking Piecrust one day at the beginning of May, very early in the year for lemmings to have roused themselves from their winter quarters underground, and detected fresh lemming droppings among the willows scraped clear of ice by caribou. Next time he went out on the land, he took a notebook and began writing down the position of the runways and nests, marked by sprigs of the dried grass the lemmings had used to insulate their winter quarters, and by tiny piles of fibrous droppings, and sometimes only by Piecrust's excitable barking.

It was still early in the breeding season and already the lemming population was showing signs of exploding. On the river banks he began to see more fox spoor than usual and twice, while walking along the cliffs on Simmons Peninsula, he'd spotted pile after pile of jaeger pellets consisting entirely of lemming fur and bones. Droppings littered those parts of the muskeg where the sun had cleared the ice and the willow buds had been nibbled to nubs.

In a few weeks from now he expected the pressure on food resources to be so extreme that the lemmings would begin to eat their young. After that, they'd begin gathering in great living sheets, hundreds of thousands of them, all pressing forward in the search for new terrain. As they began to swarm, the pressure of numbers would send those on the periphery cascading over cliffs and ledges, and the meltwater streams would become seething bridges of live and drowning rodents, each successive wave trampling over the other in their push for new ground.

In the world of his fantasy he had so often imagined this frantic exodus to new pastures, the mass tramplings, drownings, tumblings from cliffs and rocks, the frenzy of predators, that he felt he'd somehow brought the moment into being. He thought of himself as the brave and selfless reporter sending dispatches from the middle of the war zone, because, make no mistake, the lemming swarm was war, a Darwinian struggle for survival played out on a breathtaking scale.

More than at any other time in his life, Derek was conscious that he could not afford distractions. He would have to focus his every waking moment on the meticulous, systematic gathering of the evidence so that when he finally presented his findings – to *Nature*, perhaps, or to *Scientific American* – the whole package would be watertight. The thought that he alone might predict a lemming swarm when scientists with PhDs and grand reputations were saying the population wouldn't peak for another year was thrilling. He'd waited too long in the wings for this not to be the moment that changed everything.

Even though there had been no formal investigations, the dismal events of the spring had tied up a great deal of detachment time. In a normal year, he and Stevie would start out on their spring patrol at the end of April. This was their chance to survey the land, check on caches, conduct a few low-level experiments, complete their wildlife assessments for the year ahead and make a courtesy call on one or other of the more remote weather stations.

Now the snow had mostly cleared from the low-lying tundra, and though it lingered in drifts and in the lee of cliffs and eskers, it was too late to travel any distance on the land. On the other hand, the sea ice was still solid and it was light all the time now, so there was nothing to stop them travelling twelve, fifteen hours a day. More importantly, Derek would be able to gather more evidence of the impending lemming swarm and be ready to report on it on his return.

They would sleep 'upside down', travelling during the cooler hours after 10p.m. In good conditions they would average two hundred kilometres a day, though there were places where travel would be tougher, such as at the narrow strait where the Colin Archer Peninsula of northwest Devon Island reached up to the southwestern tip of Ellesmere. The strait was part-blocked by North Kent Island, which functioned like a cork in a bottle. Here the sea was open all year and huge ice boulders raced through violent and unpredictable currents. Derek reckoned on taking a couple of days to get around it.

He'd also factored in three research stops on the way. The first would be his own pet project, a count of lemmings on the Simmons Peninsula; the second was a Wildlife Service survey of wolves up on Bjorne Island. This was a trickier proposition altogether, because it was so hard to get anywhere near a Bjorne wolf. Then from Bjorne they'd head across Baumann Fiord into Eureka Sound and drop into the weather station there for the third and final stop, though most of the research up at Eureka would be of the strictly social kind.

They set off in light drizzle and, after a few hours of uneventful travel across the pack, made camp on the green beach at the tip of the Lindstrom Peninsula and clambered up onto the plateau. Thaw slumps had appeared since the last spring patrol. Stevie took pictures, making a note of the shrunken ice wedges in amongst the rocks and of the relative profusion of mountain sorrel caused by the retreating spillway. When that was done, they checked on the police cache they'd planted there a couple of years previously, in case they ever got into trouble.

The two men made such good time that they took the afternoon off to rest and fish at the ice edge beside Hell Gate and that evening feasted on char and bannock bread before starting their second night ride. It had stopped drizzling now and the air had taken on the electric smell of the dry west country.

They started out again around 10 p.m. and hadn't gone far when Derek remembered that neither of them had yet checked in with the detachment, which was being manned in their absence by Pol. One of the joys of the patrol was how quickly you lost all sense of clock time, particularly, as now, when it was light twenty-four hours a day. Now wasn't such a good time to stop. The tough conditions around North Kent Island lay ahead and Derek needed the petty distractions of small town life like a hole in the head. In any case, he figured, nothing significant ever happened in Kuujuaq while they were away. Getting in contact was a formality as much as anything, a way of registering that he and Stevie were doing OK. He made a note to himself to do it next time they made camp.

As it turned out, the ice foot was pretty smooth and still plenty wide enough to accommodate the snowbies riding side by side. By the end of the third night's travel they had already passed North Kent and were on the pack in Norwegian Bay.

Around 6a.m. they scouted the far corner of a beach

gouged by ice blocks, which gave a view out to the low coast of Graham Island. They'd camped here at least once a year for as long as Derek could recall. Just to the west of the beach there was a tidewater glacier surrounded by steep moraines from where it was always possible to chip out sweet water. In the winter, there was good ice fishing to be had here and in the summer, murres, kittiwakes and dovekies nested along the low, blunt cliffs, eiders bred among the finger willows and caribou came down to drink at the spillways.

It was the start of bear country. They were often to be found way out on the pan, hunting seals, though in recent years, the melting pan had forced them inland earlier, but the air was most often clear and the country was low with wide vistas so man and bear weren't likely to run into one another by accident. That said, you couldn't be too careful. A decade or so ago, he'd seen them regularly playing with the dog teams on the ice outside Kuujuaq but these days the bears were more likely to view the dogs as an easy meal. It was a hard time to be a bear.

When they'd finished erecting the tent, Stevie set up the primus and the two men mugged up and put on some bannock to heat. Neither was a big talker and while they waited for the bread to cook, they mostly sat in silence, speaking only when some question came to mind they couldn't answer for themselves.

'You read that piece in the *Circular*?' Stevie said. 'Hermaphrodite bears.'

'Uh huh.' A long pause. 'Actually, no. What the hell *is* a hermaphrodite bear?'

'One that's both male and female. That's what the *Circular* said.'

Another long pause, while both men chewed this proposition over, then Stevie said: 'Now, wouldn't *that* save a heck of a lot of trouble.'

Later, Derek lit a cigarette while Stevie cranked up the sat phone and made a brief call to his wife, who was just getting the kids off to school. Stevie signed off: 'I guess we should check on the detachment.'

Derek replied reluctantly: 'I guess so.'

Out on patrol was the one time Derek had the luxury of forgetting about the place.

A while later, Stevie came loping across the shale towards his boss.

'We got a problem.'

Derek said: 'Like what?'

'Like that hunter woman over in Autisaq, Edie Kiglatuk.'

She'd been on the radio three times, Pol said, always at strange times, saying she needed to talk to Sergeant Palliser urgently. 'Wouldn't tell Pol what it was all about, kept saying she'd only speak to you.'

What could Edie possibly need to talk to him about that was so urgent? If he was to get ahead of the game, Derek would need to submit an article to the *Circular* before the swarm actually began. His scientific paper could wait a little longer, but not too long. He didn't want a bunch of zoologists and environmental researchers pitching up in the High Arctic before he'd laid claim to the territory. But he needed some stats from the survey he was planning to carry out on Simmons. He imagined Misha reading about him or even – he hardly dared hope it – switching on the TV news.

Working through several options in his head, he decided that none of them involved going back to Kuujuaq to sort out Edie Kiglatuk. Any case, they'd be up at Eureka a week or so from now. Nothing was so urgent it couldn't wait a week.

He said: 'I'll call her from Eureka.'

Over the next few days he had no reason to regret his decision. The wolf survey was a bit of a fiasco but the lemmings were spectacular. All the way up the southeast coast he scoured the tundra for lemming trails and burrows. As each day passed, his notebooks and sample bags filled with the evidence that was going to change his life.

A week later, as the two police snowmobiles drew up to the main complex building at the Eureka High Arctic weather and research station, Derek Palliser was in state of some excitement. He parked his snowbie and dismounted. It had been a long ride up and his back was jarred from the hours spent in the saddle but all he could think about right now was getting warm enough to be able to tell the station chief, Howie O'Hara, an old ally, about his lemming findings. He didn't even wait for Stevie, just went right to the front entrance of the main building, reached for the door handle and pulled.

Derek found himself in a heavy-curtained snow porch, the sound of Hawaiian music throbbing through the walls. The door to the outside opened and Stevie appeared. Derek looked at his watch. He realized he'd lost all sense of time. It was 1a.m.

'Ten days to get here and they start the party before us?'

Fat hope of collaring Howie at this hour, he thought.

'Uh, maybe it's not our party, D.'

'You don't say?'

They pulled off their outer parkas, hats, gloves and boots, pushed open the door and took in the scene. Inside the mess hall, a couple of dozen men and women dressed in plastic grass skirts and leis were doing the conga. Beside them, on a long table, in what looked like specimen jars, sat a line of the biggest mai tais Derek had ever seen.

The two police continued to stand in the doorway. Stevie threw Derek a glance.

'Good luck, bud. It was nice knowing ya.'

Just then a flash of colour whizzed past Derek and he

felt a plastic lei lasso his neck. Next thing he knew, an oversized cocktail was being pressed into his right hand and someone in a plastic grass skirt was loading his cheek with wet kisses. Before he had time to gather himself, he was sucked into the conga from which there was now no escape.

'What's the celebration?'

The woman who'd dragged him into the dance line pointed to two men and a woman sitting at a table, a two-litre bottle of vodka in front of them.

'Our Russian friends.' The woman had to shout above the sound of the music, slurring her words. 'Back off to Vladivostok or wherever the hell they're from.'

She began jigging up and down out of time with the music. Palliser took a good look at her and realized he was eyeing a woman so caned it was a miracle she was still upright.

Later on, the Cossack dancing started up and Palliser found himself sitting at the table with one of the Russian men and the now-empty bottle of Stolichnaya.

'Back home tomorrow?'

The Russian smiled and shrugged.

'Only two week.' He held up three fingers. 'Scientist exchange.'

'I'm a scientist,' Derek said. He heard himself saying it and cringed, but he'd started now, so there was no choice but to go on.

The Russian laughed. 'You're policeman,' he said.

Derek was wagging his finger about in random fashion.

'Same thing,' he said. He tapped the finger to his nose. 'Investigation.'

The Russian man leaned in, still laughing.

'What you investigate, science police?'

Derek looked at the man. He was huge and red-faced.

Somehow it didn't seem the right time to tell him about lemmings.

'Crimes,' he said. 'Suspicious deaths.'

The Russian didn't believe him.

'Oh yeah? What death you investigate, science police?'

'Right now?' Everything in Derek's head seemed very fuzzy. He held up two fingers. At least he wasn't too drunk to count. 'Two deaths,' he said. 'Craig Island.'

'That so?' the Russian said.

Derek drew back and tapped his sergeant's stripes. The dancing Russian was calling his friend onto the floor. Derek tapped his nose again.

'Can't discuss it,' he said.

The Russian swayed a little. His eyes narrowed.

'But you can be sure of one thing,' Derek said. He knew he was ridiculous, but he couldn't stop himself. 'We'll leave no stone unturned.'

He lurched for his glass but when he turned around the Russian was gone.

When Derek woke up his head clanged, his back ached and his tongue had sunk like some dead and rotting seal into the foul maw that was his mouth. There was also a strange woman lying next to him.

'Hi there,' the woman said, slipping her hand under the covers and stroking the thin sprinkle of hair on his chest. Her eyes shifted about his face, looking for reassurance. She was *qalunaat*, brown-haired, around thirty-five. Other than that, he had no idea.

'You have a good time?'

'Super.'

For all he knew, it was true. He had almost no memory of the night before at all, let alone how he'd ended up in bed with this woman. He didn't even know her name.

He thought: *How am I going to get out of this?* Then Edie Kiglatuk sprung to mind.

'Aw shoot, I have to, uh, radio back home.'

'Now?' The woman sounded pissed off.

Derek shrugged and did his best to look mysterious. 'Urgent police work.' *What can I say?*

He staggered from the bed out into the corridor and made his way to the comms room, helping himself to some coffee from a thermos in the kitchenette just inside the door and sloshing it around his mouth to get rid of the rank taste of old cheap cocktails. The place was deserted. He realized that he felt rather sick, was probably still drunk. Last night remained a blank.

It occurred to him then that it would be good to let Howie or someone else on the permanent staff know he was intending to use the radio. Inside the overheated atmosphere of the station complex, people tended to be territorial about the smallest things. The place was a natural breeding ground for petty resentments. It wasn't as though there was anywhere you could go to cool off. Freeze, sure, but cool off, not so much.

He stepped outside, scanning the site for someone to ask, but the station seemed deserted. He checked his watch. It was 5.32a.m. and Derek Palliser felt like shit.

What to do? He could hardly go back to the complete stranger he'd woken up beside and ask if she would mind him sleeping off his hangover in her bed. Even if he could remember her name or how to get back to her room. Plus she'd looked rather expectant and he realized he'd been kind of rude and rejecting. Who in hell makes urgent radio calls at 5.30a.m. after a night on the tiles? It would be bad enough having to face her over the lunch table; he certainly couldn't go back there now.

He decided to find a chair to settle into in the comms

building, catch up on some sleep there, and was making his way back when he heard a pattering of paws and, turning, saw Piecrust come trotting after him. There was another thing he'd forgotten, the damned dog. In the kitchenette he came across a tin of baked cookies and slung a handful on the floor for Piecrust's breakfast.

Some hours later, he was woken with a shake. He opened his eyes. He was slumped in a chair by the radio with the dog draped over him, still fast asleep, its nose jammed in his ear. He lifted a hand to his cheek and scraped at the crust of dried dog drool.

'We mustn't keep meeting like this,' a voice said. It was the woman he had or hadn't slept with.

He smiled thinly, fishing around desperately for a name. Oh Jeez, now he remembered. In Hawaiian, she was Palakakika and he was Jamek, or something like it.

'The radio is password protected,' Palakakika said.

'Yeah,' he lied. 'So I discovered.'

'Which means you have to get the password from the chief comms officer.'

'Who is . . .?'

The woman stuck out a hand. 'Agent Palakakika.' She shot Derek a conspiratorial look. Shit, what sad little game had they been playing together? 'That gets out, I'll obviously have to have you killed,' she added.

'Agent Palakakika.' Derek felt suddenly very sick. 'Could I make a radio call?'

Night shift at Autisaq answered and was immediately interrupted, as so often at these latitudes, by a snatch of some other transmission, the guitar solo from Pink Floyd's 'Time', Derek thought.

The interruption gave him an instant to think. What was he doing? He couldn't just radio in and ask to speak to

Edie, not without everyone in Autisaq getting to hear about it. She wasn't the most popular person in the settlement right now. Being radioed by the police in the early hours wasn't likely to make her any more so. Besides, hadn't she said she wanted to talk to him privately? When the comms operator in Autisaq came back on he told him not to worry, it just a routine call and that he'd be back at his desk in Kuujuaq tomorrow. The voice copied the message and called off. Derek pushed back his chair and handed the headphones to Agent Palakakika, who noted the time and made an entry in a navy blue log book by the side of the radio.

'Funny how the word *urgent* means different things to different people,' she said, throwing him a hungry look. She reached into the zipper of his pants. 'You've shown me what you mean. How's about I show you what *I* mean?'

Nah, Derek thought. Approximately two-tenths of a millisecond later, he had a change of heart. He smiled at Agent Palakakika.

'The name's Bond,' he said. 'Jamek Bond.'

The following afternoon Pol showed up in the Twin Otter, as arranged. The trip back to Kuujuaq was short and alleviated, for Derek, by the dazing swill of sex hormones coursing around his body. From the airstrip, he went directly to the detachment building, threw up, then called Mike Nungaq's number in Autisaq. The shopkeeper greeted him with his usual cheer.

'Package coming in?'

As supervisor of the district's mail, Derek occasionally spoke with Mike about any unusual, valuable or dangerous packages, including game trophies and pelts expected to arrive or leave on the supply plane out of Autisaq.

'Not this time.'

Mike sounded disappointed. 'Only I thought it might be the election posters.' Mike explained that Simeonie Inukpuk had asked him to look out for a consignment of posters he was having printed and air-freighted up from Ottawa.

Derek said: 'I think I'm missing something here. We got kids taking drugs, we got kids killing themselves because they don't see any future. And Simeonie's making *posters*?'

Mike said: 'He didn't make them, he's having them shipped up.'

Derek realized this line of discussion wasn't going anywhere. There was a pause.

Mike said: 'But that's not what you called about, right?'

'No.'

Derek said he was signing off his report into Joe Inukpuk's suicide and needed to clarify a couple of things with the young man's stepmother.

'Just routine stuff. Only, between us, eh? I don't want to upset the blood family.'

Phone call over, Derek put on the kettle and checked his emails and the fax machine, but nothing whatsoever had happened in the period he'd been away. It was only when he was going back to the kitchen to make his brew that he noticed a piece of paper lying on the floor: a copy of his official report into Andy Taylor's disappearance. The coroner had signed it and faxed it back for filing with his English spelling mistakes corrected. He threw it on his desk, thinking the coroner ought to try out Inuktitut sometime.

Fetching his tea he went and sat in his office chair, letting his mind wander, leafing through the week's *Circular* and noting down the editorial number. Should he call them to suggest an interview or write a short news piece and fax it to them? Figuring he'd sit on it for a couple of days, until he'd got his breath back from patrol, he finished his tea, went outside and took Piecrust for a quick spin around

Kuujuaq, looking for, but not finding, any loose dogs. Then he made his way to the store and stocked up on groceries.

Back in his apartment he realized how exhausted he was and went directly to bed without bothering to get himself any supper. He was woken by the sound of knocking and, glancing over at his bedside clock, saw with a thump that it was mid-morning and he'd overslept by hours. The knocking continued. Whoever it was wouldn't go away. He felt a thin needle of irritation somewhere at the back of his head. Why wasn't Stevie on it? Then he remembered that he'd given his constable the day off.

Swinging himself out of bed, he pulled on his uniform, slapped cold water over his face and made a cursory attempt to smooth his hair, shouting for whoever it was to wait, and thinking it was almost certainly some busybody or other wanting to know why he hadn't opened up yet.

He loped across the office and unlocked the front porch. At first he thought he was experiencing some kind of flashback, a result, perhaps, of the recent surfeit of mai tais. But no, there she was, standing on the steps smiling at him.

Misha.

She was wearing a fox-trim parka with the zip partially open, revealing the supple curves of her breasts. For an instant he thought he might buckle or burst out crying or in some other way humiliate himself. In the year since he'd seen her, she'd grown more beautiful. Her face was like a spring sun halo, otherworldly in its perfection. There was only one word to describe her: astonishing.

'I catch you at a bad time?' Her voice, inflected with remnants of what always seemed to him to be a dozen accents, stole over him like a spring breeze full of ice crystals and he had to look away, instantly and hopelessly aroused.

For a second the whole awful, cringe-making business of Agent Palakakika flashed into his mind and he had to swallow hard to make it go away. Misha moved towards him and he held the door open as she walked through. For a moment they simply looked at one another. The strength of his feeling floored him. He knew he should be angry with her, but he didn't have it in him. He felt like a hopeless teenager.

When she offered a hand, he took it without thinking and as she pulled him into her he could feel her breath on his lips and his heart in his mouth. It was suddenly clear to him that the months of torturing himself over the Dane no longer mattered in the least. She was here, with him.

'You living in the apartment now?'

He nodded, feeling himself blush. The second summer they were together, they had moved out of the apartment into a more spacious house. Derek had retreated back to the apartment not long after Misha left.

Walking across the office to the apartment entrance, she said, 'You can bring my bag.'

And so, in the hours and days that followed Derek Palliser emptied himself of lemming swarms and suicides. He told Stevie to take the week off. He forgot the Dane and Copenhagen. He forgot Agent Whatever and the urgency of letting the *Arctic Circular* know about his research. He even forgot to ask himself whether the timing of Misha's arrival was purely coincidental. And three or four times, when the radio beeped, and the phone rang, he forgot that anyone was trying to reach him.

9

Edie went to her meat store to check Andy Taylor's bones were still in the two old pemmican tins where she'd put them and to chip off a couple of shards of iceberg. Then she went inside with the tin containing the cut marked bones and the ice and poured herself a large glass of Canadian Mist on the rocks. She took out the skull fragment and slid her pinky into the bullet hole. She poured herself another drink, picked up a pen lying on the table and pushed it through the hole. As she followed the angle of it upwards with her finger, a series of thoughts came into her mind. The fragment was from the bone around the crown which could only mean that the shot had come from above. The angle of the pen gave a degree nearly perpendicular to the skull itself. She thought back to the low-lying land around Bone Beach, as she now thought of the place, and turned the fragment of skull around in her hand, but she couldn't figure out how the shot could have hit the skull from such a wide angle. Was it possible that Andy Taylor had been shot from the air?

It was past midnight when she went back out to the meat store with Andy Taylor's bones, but it could have been any time; the sky never darkened now and the sun never set. A raven flew past. Edie idly followed its progress, wondering why Derek Palliser had not answered her radio calls. No particular reason for him to be avoiding her, except that he'd done it before, during the Ida Brown case. Something in the man resisted action until it was forced upon him. What was the animal they always said had its head in the sand? Ostrich, that was it. Derek Palliser was an ostrich.

She, on the other hand, had to resist the impulse to rush at everything. Once she went out with her father, Peter, and her mother, Maggie, for a few days' ice fishing. She must have been very young, four or five, but she could still remember it as though it had happened a week ago. The weather was calm, and the sun was shining, but it was so cold her tear ducts filled with ice pebbles. They caught three char, then her mother went inside the tent to lay out the sleeping skins. She didn't know where her father was. Maybe he'd gone to collect sweet water. She was playing on the ice when her eye was drawn to something shining. Driven, perhaps, by the smell of the char, a young jar seal had come up through the ice hole and was looking about, its chin resting on the surface of the ice, the water droplets in its fur catching the sun. Without a second thought, Edie picked up her father's harpoon and threw it, embedding the barb in the seal's side. The animal dived, pulling the weapon and its rope down with it. Edie remembered seeing the rope whip by her and grabbing for it. She clung on, spinning along the ice so fast she had no time even to cry out. Down she went, into the water under the ice. For a long time she seemed to be buried, then, blood humming in her head, her mother's screams reached her from somewhere distant.

'You're a good hunter,' her mother said, afterwards. 'But until you learn *anuqsusaarniq*, to wait patiently, you will never be a great one.'

Another raven landed on a drying rack and pecked at a sealskin. It made her think about the raven on the back of the twenty dollar bill, the Trickster Raven of the Haida Indian legend, sitting in the Haida canoe, his wing on the steering rudder. It was the Trickster Raven who was steering her back to her old, reckless, hard-drinking self. Where had that old version of Edie ever got her? By her mid-twenties, she'd already drunk away her hunting career and was well on the way to drinking away her life. It was Joe who'd saved her, Joe who had taken the rudder from the Raven and given it back to her. 'I hate it when you drink because you won't come out and hunt with me,' he'd said. Simple, true, like a spear to the heart. Not long after that, she'd stopped drinking.

Joe had given her back her life and she had given him what? Now she wondered if that death wish she had carried was infectious, some terrible, unintended legacy she'd passed on to her stepson.

The bird rose up from the drying rack and flapped off to the south. Edie went back inside and poured another double shot of Canadian Mist, flipped on the DVD and used the remote to skip to the scene in *Safety Last!* where Harold Lloyd climbs the outer wall of the department store. How many times had she sat through that scene since her father first put her in front of a movie projector? But still she got a kick out of it, Harold in his boater and his glasses ascending the sheer wall of rock, the world below him gradually shrinking away. It made you want to cry with the sheer fragile pleasure of being alive.

She poured herself another shot, and closed her eyes to make the feeling last. When she opened them, she thought she saw the *puikaktuq* staring in at the window.

When she woke on the sofa later that morning, Harold Lloyd was still climbing his walls. She reached out for the remote and shut the power. Her tongue felt like an angry walrus and her head thrummed. She took herself to the bathroom and threw up in the toilet.

At the end of the day, she took herself directly home

from school, mugged up and pulled down the blinds. From the meat store she took out the two cans containing Andy Taylor's bones and brought them inside.

If you've got something to tell me, she said to the bones, *now would be a good time*. She waited, but the bones remained silent. Those few facts she knew about the *qalunaat*'s death seemed like an ice pack in formation, fragmented, insubstantial and unable to bear any weight. But she remembered the lesson of the seal at the ice-fishing hole. *Anuqsusaarniq*. Patience.

The following day she struggled through her classes with a hangover, then went home, and was frying *tunusitaq*, caribou guts, for her supper when Sammy breezed in, blowing the ice crystals from his nose.

'Great smell.'

'You always did have good timing, Sammy Inukpuk.'

He chuckled. 'I brought a half-sack.' He'd come to make his peace with beer, as he always did.

They sat on the sofa watching TV and drinking, just like old times.

He said: 'The reason I came . . .'

'Oh,' she said, disappointed and not even trying to hide it. 'And here was me thinking you liked my company.'

He flashed her a look that said, *Stop right there, sister, you abandoned me, remember?*

He said, 'I wanted to tell you, so you didn't get it from someone else: I'm guiding a trip, a couple of *qalunaat*, tourists. They wanna go eider hunting.'

'You taking them down to Goose Fiord?' Best eider hunting on Ellesmere there.

'Maybe.' Sammy blushed and fixed his gaze on the TV. To his credit he'd always been a lousy liar.

'I get it,' she said. 'You're going to Craig.'

He nodded, a little shamefaced, and Edie felt a thickening in her throat. Now she understood why he'd come. The council of Elders usually divvied up the guiding jobs and in the past, it had always been understood that Edie would have first pick of any involving Craig Island. She and Joe knew the place better than anyone in Autisaq, with the exception perhaps of Old Man Koperkuj, but Simeonie had cut her out and given the job to her ex-husband. Sammy was here to get her blessing and, maybe, her forgiveness. She patted his thigh.

She said: 'Thanks for letting me know.' A pause. 'Why Craig though? This time of year, eider hunting's lousy there.'

He shrugged. 'That's where they wanted to go.'

Funny how popular the place had got with *qalunaat* all of a sudden.

The following morning, as she was walking to the store, a green Twin Otter flew overhead: the *qalunaat* tourists Sammy spoke about. The Otter's livery didn't belong to any of the charter companies operating out of Iqaluit or Resolute Bay. She wondered if someone new had set up and hoped they wouldn't kill off Martie's business.

Later, while she was teaching, she spotted the Inuk pilot out of the window, strolling along the path towards the store with two tall *qalunaat*, one of whom was skinny, like Taylor, the other with such light blond hair it looked like a clump of cotton grass growing on his head.

The plane came by again a couple of days later and took the tourists back down south. During the school lunch break Edie walked over to Sammy's to see how the trip had gone – she'd missed him, it was no fun drinking alone – but he'd already dumped his bags inside the house and gone out, so she left a note, inviting him for supper. She noticed he'd turned his Bible face inwards. That only ever meant one thing: he was drinking heavily again and didn't want God to see. Her heart went out to him then. What kind of god did he think he was being loyal to? One who would condemn a man who had lost his son from trying to find comfort where he could?

In her short absence from the school, someone had been in and put up posters in the corridors announcing Simeonie Inukpuk's candidacy for re-election as mayor. No one had ever held an election campaign like this. It was troubling and bizarre. Inuit didn't do business that way, pitting one candidate against another. Sure, there was a vote, but everyone knew the real decision emerged slowly from discussions in the community. Nothing got decided until a consensus had been reached which everybody could live with. Besides, if there was any money to spare, the last thing it should be spent on was election posters.

She made her way back to class, set an assignment, put Pauloosie in charge, marched directly to the head's office and swung open the door without knocking. John Tisdale looked up from his desk and raised his hands in surrender.

'Don't shoot!'

She didn't smile. His face fell. He knew exactly why she was there.

'Look, Edie, it's not my fault, it's just the way Simeonie wants things done from now on.'

Edie let out a snort: 'What Simeonie *wants* is for someone to do him the courtesy of letting him know what an asshole he's being.'

'He does?' Tisdale screwed up his face.

She turned on her heels and shut the door, a little too firmly. The posters had been stuck on with some kind of putty and came off easily, particularly once she got the class involved. When all the posters were down, she handed one to each of her pupils and explained what they were going to do and why they were going to do it. Protest, she called it. Civil disobedience.

Ten minutes later, twelve children were waiting outside the mayor's office with excited, expectant looks on their faces. At the secretarial desk, Sheila Silliq ummed and tutted.

'I know you have your own way of doing things, Edie, but I wish you'd left my two out of this.'

'It's what's known as a class action,' Edie said. She patted the two Silliq children on the head to reassure them. 'You should be proud.'

Simeonic Inukpuk poked his head around the door and raised his eyes to heaven.

'You got five minutes.' He held up one hand.

As Edie ushered the class towards the mayor's office, he palmed a stop sign. 'Uh nuh,' he said, pointing a finger at Edie. 'Just you.'

He closed the door behind her and took up his position behind the desk without inviting her to sit.

'You're a disgrace, using the kids to fight your battles.'

'*Me?*' she said. His hypocrisy was breathtaking. 'This isn't about Craig, if that's what you think, it's about using the school to play politics.'

'I don't care what it's "about". You're point-scoring.' He shook his head in a gesture of condescending disapproval that made her want to jump on his skull and tear out his hair. 'You always were a hothead, Edie Kiglatuk, and for some reason you've decided to become a troublemaker too.'

For a moment they stood facing one another off.

'*Ai*, brother-in-law,' she said, hoping that reminding him of their family connection might soften him a little. 'Election posters? This is Autisaq, Nunavut, not Atlanta, Georgia.'

Sheila's head appeared behind the door. Someone was on the phone from London, England.

Simeonie settled himself into his chair and adopted an expression of grand detachment.

'It's a lady selling the diary of one of those old explorer fellows.' Simeonie, who had been hoping for something more substantial, just shook his head and waved the call away.

'I'll talk to her,' Edie said. It was as good a way as any to call time on her audience with the mayor.

She picked up the phone on Sheila's desk and introduced herself. The woman on the other line had an accent, but Edie couldn't tell what it was. She explained she was a researcher at Sotheby's auction house. They were selling the diary of Sir James Fairfax's penultimate voyage and the researcher was after what she referred to as 'the native perspective'; an anecdote about the old times, maybe.

'If Fairfax had spent more time hunting and fishing like the locals and less time writing a diary, his explorer's career might have gone on longer,' Edie said. She felt vaguely pleased with herself. 'How's that for the "native perspective"?'

The woman coughed politely. Edie could tell from her voice she was young and probably not all that certain of herself.

'I'm sorry,' she said. 'I haven't really read the whole thing. It only came to us very recently and the owner . . .'

Edie interrupted. '. . . Bill Fairfax?'

'Mr Fairfax, yes. You know him?' She sounded taken aback.

Edie explained how she and Fairfax had met. The woman listened, then, lowering her voice, she said, 'He needs a quick sale.' She coughed again. 'We were hoping someone your end might be able to fill in a bit of the story. The diary isn't quite complete. When Mr Fairfax found it among his great-aunt's things, there seemed to be three pages missing. Our paper expert says the pages were excised not long ago but the great-aunt's dead so there's no knowing exactly when or why. If we could get hold . . .'

Three pages? Edie's brain cranked up a gear.

The girl continued. 'My boss said Inuits never forget anything.' A moment's hesitation. 'Actually, he said Eskimos, only I know you don't call yourselves that any more.'

Edie felt her pulse hum, her neurones zapping.

'Tell you what,' she said, 'why don't you Xerox a couple of pages of the diary just before the missing part and fax them over, jog our memories?'

'Really?' The girl brightened. 'That's brilliant.'

'Just send them right on over. I'll be standing by the fax machine.' She lowered her voice. 'Oh, and by the way, it's Inuit, not Inuits.'

As she waited for the fax to stammer through the feeder, Edie considered calling Fairfax, then thought better of it. She didn't know enough right now to be able to ask the right questions.

The first page slid into the keeper. Edie picked it up. The writing did look remarkably similar to the pages she'd recovered from the ice cave: long swirled upstrokes with cross lines thick at one end and thin at the other, like a musk-ox tail, the whole leaning to the east as though it had struggled against a prevailing wind.

The phone rang and Sheila picked it up.

'It's that woman. She wants to speak to you.'

Edie scooped up the pages and made her way to the door.

'I just left.'

Back home, she sat on the sofa with the pages she'd taken from the ice cave and a large glass of Canadian Mist. Though the paper was so damaged by frost and weather that the writing was almost illegible, she could immediately see by the shapes that it was a match for the diary. Edie made herself a brew, poured another slug of Mist in the mug and sat down to examine the pages more closely. Whatever was written there was important enough for someone – Fairfax himself, she presumed – to have brought it all the way up to Autisaq. And for Andy Taylor to have hidden it in an ice crevice. But why?

In the soft light by the sofa she could decipher virtually nothing. An idea came to her. She went to the laundry room where she kept her hunting equipment, picked up the telescopic sight, pulled on her waterproofs, kamiks, dog-skin hat and the pair of expensive snow goggles a *qalunaat* had given her as a tip and opened the door to the outer snow porch. Outside, the sun flared and in the distance to the south, a journey of two or three sleeps, the cliffs of Taluritut shone like baby teeth. The air was exceptionally dry and clear: a good day for discovering things.

She went over to the drying shed where she kept her sealskins, squatted down against the far side where she could not be seen from the Town Hall, the store or the school, pulled the paper from her pocket and unfolded it onto her lap. Then she drew out the telescopic lens and held it up to the paper. Though it was still hard to make out whole words, faint impressions of ink on the page began to resolve themselves. She returned to the sight, this time beginning, as a hunter would, at the centre and gradually circling around until she came to what she thought might be a 'g' or a 'q'. Going very slowly so as not to lose her place, she moved the sight slightly to the left and saw a ghostly but very definite 'u'. All that remained of the letter to the left of the smudge was a tiny, hovering point, the remnant, perhaps, of an 'l', 'lug' or 'luq'. She nudged the sight ever so slightly to the left once more and saw what must once have been an 'i', the line clearly broken, in contrast to what sat to its left, an 'l' for sure, and beside that another 'i'. The first letter was larger, a V, with a smear beside it. *Vililuq*. A word that meant nothing either in Inuktitut or English.

Returning to the paper, she tried to separate the first page from the second and in the process tore it slightly. Even without the tear, though, it was hopeless. The last and final page had remained separate, protected from damp by the presence of the two above it. There was only one paragraph on this page and, below it, a line drawing, or perhaps a map. It looked like no part of any land she knew, but then, she didn't really read *qalunaat* maps. Of the writing, she could make out only a few words in English, 'waited', 'told', 'dogs' and a single, small phrase: 'which I exchanged for a penknife'.

The pages described a trade of some sort. What had Sir James Fairfax received in return for his penknife, she wondered? She cast her eye along the paragraph. Dogs? That would make sense. She turned her attentions to the slip of paper to which the pages were attached. The handwriting on this was quite different from the rest. It looked newer and had been written in ballpoint pen, by Andy Taylor himself, she supposed. A single word. 'Salt'.

Edie went back inside the house. She realized she was a little drunk. Nothing made any sense. She needed to take better care of herself. Something to eat would help. She was delving about in the cupboards when Sammy appeared and sat himself down on the sofa. She thought about asking him to leave, then decided against it. The standoff with Simeonie made her feel in need of company.

'I got rye,' he said. She brought two glasses over, tossed back her glass and waited for the alcohol to hit her belly. Nothing felt warmer than whisky.

'Here's to *qalunaat*,' Sammy said. 'Those people *pay*.'

She said: 'They behave themselves?'

Sammy made a waving motion with his hand. 'A coupla pups. They just wanted to see Uimmatisatsaq.'

'And go eider hunting, right?'

'That's what they said, but when we got to Craig, they didn't seem too interested. They were, like, digging about in the shale, in the rocks. Rockhounds, I guess.' Sammy helped himself to another drink. 'Whatever.' He patted the sofa next to him. 'They paid and they're gone.' He grabbed Edie's waist and pulled her towards him. The smell of his breath was as good as love. 'Come on, woman,' he said, 'let's celebrate.'

It wasn't till a long while later, when they were in bed, that Edie became aware of the smell of burning food. She stumbled to the kitchen and took the pan off the heat. Sammy was up and in his thermals; he grabbed her from behind and gave her a good squeeze.

'I worked up an appetite in there,' he said. 'What you got?'

They sat on the sofa, ate leftovers, and played around some more. When they were finally exhausted from their efforts, Edie made a brew, stuck *The Gold Rush* on the DVD and they huddled together beneath a caribou blanket on the sofa in silence, watching Big Jim McKay and Black Larsen fight it out for Jim's gold strike, then Larsen tumble to his death leaving Big Jim, his memory lost in the fight, to stumble about the Frozen North trying to remember where he'd left his gold.

'I guess that's what they call a cautionary tale,' Edie said.

She looked over but Sammy was already fast asleep. Reaching across him, she shook the rye bottle, out of habit only, since there was nothing left inside it.

As she went to put it back on the table, she disturbed something under a pile of papers, and a white plastic ballpoint pen fell out. Recognizing it as the one she'd taken from Wagner's pocket a couple of months before, she picked it up and as she did so, she noticed the word 'Zemmer' written along its side in tasteful dark green lettering.

Her mind turned a somersault. The so-called pizza take-out place. Suddenly, she felt frighteningly sober. Whatever Zemmer really represented, it had to be the link between the two dead *qalunaat*.

She shook Sammy awake.

'You need to leave.'

He caught her expression and didn't protest. At the entrance to the snow porch, she went back inside, picked up his bottle of Canadian Mist and asked him to take it.

She watched him trudge down the pathway and felt a twinge of sadness but also, somehow, better.

The sky was hedged with high cloud and the sun came and went through the gaps. She bundled on her kamiks, dog-skin hat and outdoor parka and went to feed the dogs. On her way back into the house it struck her that whatever Sir James Fairfax had traded with Welatok in exchange for a penknife it couldn't have been dogs because Sir James, like most *qalunaat* explorers of the day, refused to use them.

Retrieving the pages, she grabbed her telescopic lens and went out into the deserted street. This time she found what she thought she was looking for at the very end of the second page, the lettering bunched up where Fairfax had been trying to conserve paper. There, phonetically written but correctly this time, was the word '*uyaraut*': a precious stone, and in the same sentence – she could hardly believe she hadn't seen it before – the word 'Craig'.

Just at that moment, she felt the sharp prick of an ice crystal on her face, then the welcome watery coolness. Another arrived, then another. One had landed in the middle of the top page and melted slightly, washing the smear around the V in the word '*Vililuq*' and clarifying what had before been an unreadable smudge. The word was fainter than before but there was no mistaking it. *Wilituq*. She sat back. Was it too far-fetched to suppose that Wilituq was Fairfax's version of Welatok?

Sir James Fairfax had traded a penknife with Welatok for what the Inuk described as a precious stone. All at once she thought back to her encounter with Saomik Koperkuj on Craig and to the jewellery he had claimed to have taken from a wolf: a gold chain on which had been suspended a strangely heavy stone.

The following evening, after school, she bought a half-sack of beer in the Northern Store, then packed a bag and took off along the ice foot east on her snowmobile. At the little cove where dovekies sometimes gathered, she left her snowbie and scrambled up the cliffs and along the short path across the plateau to Saomik Koperkuj's cabin.

She opened the door and peered in. No one at home. Advancing into the cabin, she spotted a hunting knife on the table and picked it up. Making her way to the curtain at the back where Koperkuj slept, she tweaked it open and peeped inside. Suddenly there was a creak from behind. She drew back, startled. The old man was standing inside the door with Andy Taylor's Remington in his hand.

He said: 'Get lost.'

For a moment, he didn't seem to know who she was, then recognizing her at last, he lowered the rifle. The expression on his face remained the same.

'Not in the mood for visitors, Saomik Koperkuj?' Edie dropped the hunting knife in her bag, reached in and pulled out the beer. She was relieved to see the necklace was still hanging around his neck. 'Maybe this'll help.'

The old man's face softened for an instant, then resumed its brittle expression.

'What are you after?'

She flipped the ring pull and handed him the can.

'I'm taking some *qalunaat* hare-hunting later in the summer,' she lied. He stared at her, his eyes narrowed. 'I thought you might be able to give me some tips.'

He nodded, seeming content with her explanation, and took a long drink. She pushed the remaining cans nearer.

'Look,' the old man said grudgingly, 'I got nothing against you personally, I just don't like people.'

They sat for a while in silence while Koperkuj made his way steadily through the can.

'Maybe I'll find a wolf and a necklace like yours,' she ventured.

The old man plucked the stone round his neck and held it up.

'This is a lucky necklace.' He helped himself to another beer, levering off the ring pull with his walrus snowknife. The booze had loosened the old man's tongue. 'I didn't actually get it from a wolf.'

'Oh, really?' Edie did her best to sound neutral.

Koperkuj chuckled. He was enjoying this. 'You think a wolf would really eat a stone? Women! Uh nuh. I found this at Craig, on the beach there, near Tikiutijavvilik.'

'You did?'

'I'm telling you,' he said. 'Right there on the beach.'

'Well, isn't it odd, the things that wash up there,' Edie said. 'I could use some luck, I should borrow it,' trying to look as though she was having the idea for the first time.

Koperkuj met her gaze.

She took out the little sealskin pouch she'd sewn and handed it over to him.

'I'll give you this for it.'

He looked at her.

'Open it.'

His old, arthritic fingers fussed around the tie. Finally he peered inside, turning the pouch upside down so Andy Taylor's diamond earring tumbled out on the palm of his hand. Edie watched for any sign of recognition, but there was none.

'What is it?'

'What does it look like?'

'*Uyaraut,*' he said.

'More than *uyaraut*,' she said. '*Qaksungaut*, diamond.'

The old man peered at the stone more closely. His eyes blazed.

'How do I know it's real?'

'Go ask Mike Nungaq.'

Mike was the community rockhound. In another world, in another life, he'd have been a geologist, but there was no call for Inuit geologists in Autisaq. Still, anyone find anything they thought they might be able to sell, they brought it to Mike. 'It turns out to be a fake, you can come get me and break my legs.'

Koperkuj fingered the stone. He was wavering.

'You can keep the gold chain,' she said.

'What's so special about this stone that you want it?' The old man was running it up and down the chain with his hand.

Edie shrugged. 'Nothing special. Just caught my eye is all. You know women, we always want something.'

The old man nodded at the truth of this. Eventually, he said:

'OK. As a favour to you. But I keep the chain and the *qaksungaut*.'

He pulled the stone from the chain and handed it to her. It was small, no larger than a fox's heart and more or less the same shape, a liverish colour embedded with tiny sparkles and unusually heavy. She'd never seen anything like it before but now that the stone was in her possession she felt both strangely powerful and a little afraid, as though, after months following old tracks, she'd finally come across something fresh and new. The object in her hand seemed less like a stone and more like a key.

She found Mike Nungaq bent over the cereals row at the far side of the Northern Store, pricing up a consignment of cherry Pop-Tarts. He greeted her and asked how she was, his expression clouding over as he realized she'd come into the store for more than just groceries.

'Etok's up at the airstrip with a cargo of resupply,' Mike said with a sigh. 'In case you're wondering.'

She wrinkled her nose, conscious that she was stretching the limits of their friendship. 'Can we talk?'

'I was hoping you wouldn't ask that,' Mike said. 'Come on then.'

He led the way past the stacks of special offers, flipped up the countertop and ushered Edie into the back. They sat down at a scruffy Formica table.

'This about the election posters?' Word got round fast. 'Or about Elijah running against Simeonie?' Edie blinked.

Mike's brother was a notorious deadbeat, as likely a mayoral candidate as Pauloosie Allakarialak.

The storekeeper blushed a little around the ears. 'You want to know, Simeonie talked him into it.'

Edie let out an involuntary snort. 'An unelectable rival. Smart.' She grimaced. 'Sorry.'

'The man's my brother.' Mike looked at his shoes and shrugged.

He got up and poured some tea from a thermos into two mugs, then spooned six heaped teaspoons of sugar into one of the mugs and returned to the table with a fragile smile. Edie sensed she was on probation. The thing with Elijah had rattled him and she'd been insensitive.

'I found a stone,' she said, pulling a package from her pocket. 'I could use your opinion on it.' She pushed the package across the table. He plucked the stone from its wrapping, weighed it in his hand and held it close to his face. Edie saw him register the hole where the gold chain had threaded through it then bite his lip, as if to hold back the next question.

'Heavy,' he said.

Getting up, he fiddled about in a chest of drawers at the other side of the room and came back with a magnifier, then he sat with it clamped in one eye, turning the stone over and over in the fingers of his right hand while Edie drank her tea and looked about the room. A bubble of order marked the place where Etok worked. There was a trestle table and above it a series of shelves, neatly stacked with box files. On the table itself sat a desktop computer and a filing stack, each section neatly labelled. Etok had pinned up a poster of a tropical sunset bearing the inspirational legend: 'For every door that closes, two more open.' On the far side was a peg on which she had hung a magnificent sealskin parka, trimmed in fox.

Mike replaced the stone on the table.

'You want an expert opinion or you want mine?'

'Yours will do for now,' Edie said.

'Did you notice how heavy it is? And this dark brown varnish?' Mike pointed to a small black patch on the stone. 'See here? This is a fusion crust. It's where the rock melted when it entered the atmosphere.' He looked pleased with himself. 'This is a meteorite, the only source of metal up here in the Arctic before the Europeans arrived.' He poked inside where the hole had been drilled. 'Look, this light, chalky interior matrix here?' He leaned in close to give Edie a better look. 'The best meteorites, from the Inuit point of view, were solid iron nickel, but those are rarer. Most of them are like this, stones with metal embedded.'

Rising from the table, he went over to the small kitchenette and pulled something from the fridge door. When he returned, Edie saw it was a fridge magnet of a palm-tree-lined beach with a woman dressed in a bikini kissing a man wearing some kind of tiny briefs. Mike looked slightly sheepish.

'One of Etok's friends in Iqaluit sent it to her. They went on a pilgrimage to the Holy Land.'

Mike touched the picture lightly to the stone and lifted it. The stone clung for a moment, before falling with a thump.

'Magnetic, see?' he said. 'Iron-nickel. The thing about them up here in the Arctic, because they're so rare, is that so long as you know something about the geology of the area, you can trace every meteorite back to where it fell from the sky almost exactly.'

'Like GPS.'

'Better than GPS. No LED screens to freeze up.'

Etok's voice floated in from outside. She had returned from the cargo hold at the strip and was giving instructions to someone about where to put the boxes.

'I got a friend I could send this to. He's a nut for space rocks. He could give you a value on it. Do it for free, too, I'll bet.'

'Value?'

'Sure, I mean, it's not like a diamond or anything, but space rocks are usually worth a coupla hundred loonies.'

Edie flicked a hand in the direction of Etok's voice. 'So long as it won't get you into trouble.'

Mike carefully wrapped the rock, pocketed it and winked. 'What the eye doesn't see.'

Edie said: 'It's a shame Etok hates me. You and I could be better friends.'

'That's exactly what she's trying to avoid,' Mike said.

At the door Edie turned back and pointed over at the sealskin parka, wanting to lighten the atmosphere.

'Hey. That's a beautiful piece of needlework.'

Mike said: 'Yeah.' He began to follow her out of the office. 'Minnie Inukpuk made it.' He lowered his voice. 'During one of her good spells. Never got paid for it though. That hunter guy, Wagner, he ordered it.' Mike shrugged. 'We're hoping one of the scientists up for the summer might buy it but Minnie made it to the fellow's specifications. Such a waste.'

Edie went over to the coat, ran a finger down the exquisite fur patchwork, then noticed the hand-written label pinned to it. Instantly she recognized the writing as the same as that on the note clipped to Fairfax's diary. So it was Wagner, not Taylor, who had written the word 'salt'. Then how had the pages got into Taylor's hands?

'Wagner wrote out his measurements, wanted it to be exact. Fussy fellow.'

'Mind if I take it?'

'The coat?' Mike looked confused. 'I don't know, Edie, that's a pretty valuable coat.'

She unpinned the label, held it up for him to see, then slipped it into her pocket, remembering as she did so Taylor's hands fumbling through Wagner's parka right after he got shot. Taylor could have taken the pages from his boss as he was dying. This was beginning to get interesting. It seemed more and more likely that it was something in the pages, the stone or both that got Wagner killed. Maybe Andy Taylor too.

Just then Etok appeared. Mike nodded reassuringly at his wife then lowered his voice. 'Edie, what are you up to?'

'Oh you know, the usual: trouble.' She smiled politely at Etok as she slunk past.

Mike raised his eyes.

Edie said: 'The Wagner fellow, he buy any salt from you?'

'Why would he buy salt?' Mike stared into the middle distance, thinking back. 'Uh nuh, don't think so. That would have been weird. Pretty weird question, come to that.'

Edie pressed a finger to her nose: *don't ask*. 'Mike, I owe you one. Election comes round, I'm voting Elijah.'

As she walked back to the house she saw John Tisdale waiting for her at the top of the steps and her heart suddenly felt as heavy as an old whalebone.

'Can I come in for a moment?'

'Sure,' she said, ushering him into the front room. She took a while unlacing her boots and taking off her parka. She was trying to imagine what Tisdale might want. He'd never come to her home before.

'A brew sound good?' she said, putting on a bright, brittle little smile.

He nodded. He seemed on edge, she thought.

A few moments later, when she came back with the tea, he was staring ahead, chewing on the cuticle of his right index finger. He thanked her rather too effusively.

He said: 'I've come with bad news.'

'I guess that's why you look like you've been trampled by a herd of stampeding caribou.'

He held up his hands. 'Edie, I think you're great.'

'But?'

'But we're having to make some budget cuts at the school and . . .' He tailed off. She sensed what was coming next. He was about to 'let her go'. She felt for him. He'd woken up to find himself in Simeonie's pocket. A lousy place for any man to be.

'You know,' he said, 'you don't do yourself any favours with the drinking.'

There didn't seem much point in telling him she'd decided to stop.

'I've always supported your wild ideas, well, I've turned a blind eye anyway, but taking the kids to protest outside the mayor's office?' He gave a little laugh. 'I mean. Are you *crazy*?'

She leaned over and put a hand on his arm.

'It's funny you should say that,' she said.

10

Derek Palliser shook himself awake, scanned the room and glanced at the clock. It was just after six and he was lying in a pool of his own rapidly cooling sweat. Normally he'd have been up by now sipping the first brew of the day before doing his early morning rounds, but he was sleeping later on account of having his nights disturbed by the heating in the room. When she'd first arrived, Misha complained about the cold, but the heat left him restless and feeling as though he'd barely slept.

Today of all days he needed to feel on top of his game. He was expecting a visit from Jim DeSouza over at the science station on Devon Island. It was a courtesy call, DeSouza said, though Derek didn't quite believe that. DeSouza wanted something. Still, Derek liked the fellow and felt he was someone he could work with. There was mutual respect there. In the three – or was it four? – years he'd been heading up the science station the professor had always been meticulous about consulting Derek on anything that might stray into police territory. And even though it was way out of his area of expertise, DeSouza had always been supportive of Derek's lemming research, promising to help him with media contacts if he ever needed them.

It was a matter of pride that the hamlet and the detachment were looking their best. In particular Derek was worried about loose dogs. The problem was better than it had been, but there remained one or two families who persistently failed to control their animals. He or Stevie would need to pay special visits to these folk.

He took one last look at Misha. It was as much as he could do not to get back between the sheets. There was something about that woman. He reached out for her long, honey-coloured hair.

'Derek, don't be annoying.' As she pushed his arm away with her hand, he felt at once aroused and abandoned.

He washed, shaved and dressed then slipped out of the apartment into the office. He put some coffee on to perk (Misha didn't like tea) and while it was brewing, took a quick turn around Kuujuaq.

When he returned to the office, Stevie was already poring nervously over the computer screen on his desk.

'Dog round?'

Derek blinked a yes.

'Get any?'

A no.

'Which reminds me, D, the kids are loving having the Pie stay. Come over for ribs one day this week, say hi to the old fellow.'

Derek acknowledged Stevie's offer with a flicker of a smile. After Misha had complained about his barking, Derek had sent Piecrust to live with his deputy. He told himself it was stupid, but he missed that dog like crazy. At the same time, he had no intention of paying the Pie a visit. Couldn't bring himself to watch his erstwhile Best Friend going through his hysterical welcome routine only to have to abandon him again. Still, it was good of Stevie to suggest it. Man had his heart in the right place.

He made his usual round of radio check-in calls. Nothing had happened to require his attention. It seemed that the events at Autisaq of a few months back weren't up for discussion. The path lab results had been signed off, the reports written, the forms filed. The official line had stuck. Wagner had died in a hunting accident, Taylor was lost in a blizzard and Joe Inukpuk had taken his own life while confused by hypothermia and distressed about the loss of the men in his charge.

Misha appeared at the door in a quilted top and tight jeans then sashayed past towards the kitchenette, reappearing a moment later with a mug of coffee in her hand. She smiled at Stevie. The constable cracked a grimace and returned to his screen. The hostility was mutual.

Just then the door to the outside burst open. The detachment wasn't yet officially open but Jono Toolik didn't care. He tore in, his face meaty with rage, his right arm swinging a plastic bag like a mace, and emptied the contents of the bag across Derek's desk. Several dozen condoms skittered across the woodwork, each one wrapped in a little cardboard envelope featuring the head of a musk ox. Derek picked up a pack, pretending to inspect it.

'Gee, Jono, I didn't know you cared.'

After the last confrontation, he had run out of reasons to be polite to Toolik and suspected him of allowing his dog to kill Derek's lemmings. He hadn't been able to prove it but he wasn't going to be adding Toolik to his Christmas card list any time soon.

Toolik's face twisted with anger. '*Aitiathlimaqtsi arit*, Palliser. Fuck you too. I'd sooner dip my stick in a beluga's ass. The point is, these don't work.'

Derek shrugged. 'Maybe musk ox is the wrong size for you.' He paused for effect. 'Have you tried ptarmigan?'

Toolik's hands balled and he would have thrown some punches had Misha not appeared and stood between the two men. Immediately, Toolik's stance softened. Misha approached Derek's desk and picked up a condom.

'Someone brought us present, how sweet,' sweeping her hand across the pile. 'But these won't even last us a week.'

Jono Toolik wheeled round, unsure how to proceed. Was this some kind of joke?

'I am needing some civilization,' Misha continued. 'You find me in my sculpture studio.' She walked across the room to the back door, turning momentarily to give a flirtatious little wave before letting herself out into the yard where Derek had made her a studio from what had once been his lemming shed.

The instant she was gone there was a tangible sense of relief in the room, as though a blizzard had begun to move off.

Jono Toolik was already backing towards the door with his hands in the surrender position. 'You know what? Just forget it.'

Not long after he left, the science station plane wheezed overhead and Derek grabbed his parka, pulled on his police baseball cap and went outside to the detachment All Terrain Vehicle, ATV, following the Otter's progress through low cloud towards the landing strip.

DeSouza beamed and greeted him like an old friend.

'Nice little settlement you got here.'

Derek nodded. He didn't think the professor meant to sound quite so patronizing.

'We aim to please,' he said.

DeSouza laughed.

Over a lunch of caribou steaks, in the detachment's little dining nook, DeSouza filled the two policemen in with the science station's plans for the summer season. As he talked, his mood grew sombre. The news was all budget cuts and cancelled programmes. Now that NASA had abandoned its plans to send a manned flight to Mars, he said, it would be much more difficult to secure funding in future.

'Years and years of hard work and when we're this close to some significant breakthroughs.' He drew the finger and thumb of his right hand into a pinch.

Stevie shot Derek a look that said: *this visit is less fun than I expected.*

They finished up lunch and Derek lit a cigarette.

'I guess you never found that hunter guy,' DeSouza said. It was part question, part statement.

Derek shook his head. 'Officially he's missing, presumed dead.'

'Any links to the other guy, Wagner, was it?'

'Andy Taylor worked for him for a while but if you're asking me if the deaths are connected, I'd have to say no, except in so far as the High Arctic's a dangerous place to be clueless.'

DeSouza flicked his head at the pack of cigarettes on the table.

'Mind if I have one?'

Derek pushed the carton across and held out a light. He had the feeling they were about to hear the real purpose behind the professor's visit.

DeSouza sucked in the smoke. 'Reason I came.'

Doing his best to sound casual, Derek replied, 'And there was me, thinking it was for the mental stimulation.'

DeSouza smiled and got back to business. 'No major crisis, nothing like that, only something we need to sort out. Between ourselves.'

Derek and Stevie exchanged glances. Derek took a last drag on his cigarette and stubbed it out. He wanted to look more serious, focused.

'It's the glasshouse.'

The house had been erected a few years back, before DeSouza's time, to investigate whether crops could be grown up beyond the 70th parallel using nothing but solar energy and a water recycling system. The experiment had been a failure and after a few years, the project had been abandoned, though it was still officially part of the station's programme.

'I guess it would have made sense to have taken it down. I thought about it but the logistics sucked.'

The glasshouse stood on an inaccessible bluff overlooking the Colin Archer Peninsula, looking like some freakish transplant from another world. It was miles from the main station complex. Someone must once have thought the bluff was a good place to put it, but no one was going to own up to that now.

'Thing's a bit of an eyesore, but it doesn't represent any significant kind of environmental contaminant, so I'm cool about it,' Derek said.

'When did you last visit?'

'Up on the peninsula there?' Derek thought back. It must have been years ago. 'A while,' he said.

'That explains a lot,' DeSouza said.

Derek wasn't following. 'Like?'

'Like why some loser was able to set up a weed factory in there.'

Derek tried not to look as stupid as he was feeling. He'd had no idea about any factory. Weed wasn't a huge problem on Ellesmere, in the sense that it didn't cause any public order problems, but it did keep young men stuck inside instead of going out on the land and for that alone Derek felt its use was to be discouraged.

DeSouza tipped his head. 'Hydroponics, the lot.'

For a moment Derek felt as though DeSouza might be questioning his competence, then he remembered that the glasshouse was officially the station's thing. This was on DeSouza as much as it was on him.

'Any idea who's responsible?'

DeSouza shrugged. 'Two of ours in it for sure. We did a spot search at the station. They've already been sent back down south, contracts cancelled. But they couldn't have got as far as they did without local help.' His lips pursed, projecting regret. 'We've cleared out the marijuana plants, the hydroponic equipment. It was all quite primitive. But I guess that's no surprise up here.'

'Anything to go on?' Derek asked.

DeSouza leaned into his daypack and drew out a large, tatty-looking metal flask. 'Found this among the plants. Someone's repaired the shoulder strap, used sealskin ties. Kind of a giveaway, don't you think?' He handed it across for inspection.

Derek turned the flask over in his hands and felt his heart take a break. There was no mistaking it. This was the Nashville Predators thermos he'd given Joe Inukpuk a few years back. Still, he wasn't about to tell DeSouza that. He liked the fellow, but he *was* still *qalunaat*.

'We'll see what we can do,' he said. 'The two employees, your guys, any police action down south?'

DeSouza shook his head. 'Counterproductive. Far as I'm concerned, it's been dealt with at our end. But one thing I want to be clear about, I won't have drugs around the station. They mess with motivation, everything. I won't allow it.'

Derek didn't much like the way DeSouza was today, telling him how to do his job. Not after the last time, and the professor's ill-tempered lecture about wanting to be left alone to work without interference. He put DeSouza's attitude down to stress. The fellow clearly had a lot on his plate.

'Uh huh,' he said non-committally. 'I got that.'

He waited for DeSouza to leave then went out on the land to give himself a chance to think. The visit had left him antsy and irritable. Chasing petty drug dealers wasn't what

Derek had in mind for himself. And he didn't appreciate any *qalunaat* telling him how to be native police. You couldn't just go around arresting people or sending them down south. It didn't work that way. Besides, he already had a pretty good idea who the culprit was and the kid wasn't about to cause any more trouble.

He decided to check on the build-up of moraine around the edges of the small outlet glacier that pushed into the sea just to the east of Kuujuaq. The snow had blown or melted off the land and the breakup was in full swing out on the sea ice. The glacier had shrunk so much that heaps of loose rock were left dangerously exposed on either side. Most Inuit would avoid going anywhere until the ice cleared in August; those who had a particular reason to go to the interior might be tempted to risk travelling on the glaciers until they reached one of the major ice fields or the two or three trans-island passes. This particular glacier, though, was a killer. But, for now, there was nothing Derek could do except to post some notices around town warning travellers to give the place a wide berth, at least until the moraine was more settled.

While he was out, Derek thought he would clamber up to the plateau to check what was happening with the lemming population. Misha's arrival had taken up so much of his time and energy that he'd had to put off the idea of writing the feature for one of the southern newspapers.

Over the past few weeks he had wondered whether he'd done the right thing, welcoming her back. He was beginning to come to the conclusion that during their period apart he had allowed himself to spin stories about their romance that didn't altogether fit the facts.

As he reached the top of the plateau, his eye alighted on movement in the willow. A handful of ptarmigan rose up and fanned out over the Sound. The willow itself appeared restive, in constant motion, and the ground beneath the twigs was littered with lemming droppings and the tell-tale fragments of sedge leaf where the rodents had been feeding. He could feel his interest in the swarm reviving and made a mental note not to allow himself to get so slack again. He needed to be ahead of the pack on this.

On the journey back across the muskeg to Kuujuaq, he made up his mind to take no further action in the matter of the glasshouse. It might have been Joe's flask on the scene but Joe wasn't the sort to have come up with the idea by himself. His brother, Willa, probably had some hand in the operation. But what did any of it matter now? Joe was dead, the glasshouse had been emptied and the distributors sent back where they came from. Next time he was in Autisaq he'd have a word with Willa, but that was all. In a week or so, he'd radio DeSouza and let him know he'd sorted the problem.

He swung open the door to the detachment to find Stevie peering into the back of his computer.

'Oh hey there, D. Damn machine's bust. You'd be doing me a favour to take a look.' As Derek paced across to the constable's desk he saw quite clearly what the problem was. During the course of Jono Toolik's visit, someone, probably Toolik himself, had inadvertently kicked the power cable and the plug was half-hanging out of the electrical socket.

'Go check for dogs, Stevie, I'll have a look at this while you're out.'

The constable got up and Derek sat down in his chair, pretending to inspect the computer. He waited until Stevie had left then nudged the plug back in the socket with his foot. The machine pinged awake and started rebooting. When Stevie returned not long afterwards Derek was back at his desk finishing his spring patrol report.

Stevie said: 'You got that sucker rumbling.' He gazed at the screen. 'Picture's even back.'

'It just needed a boot,' Derek said.

Stevie sat back down. 'Damn right it did. A jackboot.' A sudden thought came into his head. 'Oh, D, I forgot. While you were out, that strange woman came round.'

'Edie Kiglatuk?'

Stevie nodded. 'Yeah, that's the one.'

'What did she want?'

Stevie shrugged. 'She seemed to think we'd ignored her messages. She was pretty mad, said she would be doing some fishing down at Inuak for two sleeps and you'd better go visit or . . .' He tailed off.

'Or what?'

Stevie stared pointedly at the back door. Misha was back from her studio, a stormy expression on her face.

'Hey,' he said.

She said: 'Where have you been? I needed help with my sculpture. Now is ruined.' She sliced through the air with her hand.

Derek remembered that slicing motion from before. He also remembered he didn't like it much. He heard himself heave an involuntary sigh and felt his stomach clench. Stevie shot him a look of solidarity. Misha specialized in three-dimensional representations of clouds that she sculpted first in modelling clay then had forged in bronze. According to her, the work was a postmodern exploration of the terrible lightness of being, whatever that meant. Recently she'd experimented by modelling the clouds in fox fur stretched over wire, but this was a two-person job, requiring a helper, in this case, Derek, to hold the wire frame while Misha stretched the pelt.

'Well, I guess I'd better be getting on home,' Stevie said,

pulling his outerwear over his jacket. 'You two have a lovely evening.'

'Uh huh,' Derek said, forging a fragile smile.

It was not a lovely evening. Having been locked out of the apartment by Misha, Derek spent the night in his office chair and woke up early, stiff as frozen seal meat and about as lively. Rubbing the circulation back into his legs, he recalled first that Edie was expecting him at Inuak, then that she'd tried to contact him several times while he'd been out on patrol. In all the excitement of Misha's arrival he'd completely forgotten to get back to her. He guessed she'd found out about Joe's little horticultural business and wanted to make sure Derek didn't intend to stir anything up over it. In any case, it would be a relief to get away for a day or two.

He packed the police skiff with camping gear and emergency kit, poured hot tea into the Nashville Predators flask and set off west, leaving Stevie a note not to expect him back for a couple of days. Aside from answering Edie's call and having some time on his own, there was something else pushing him towards Inuak. The river there fed sedge meadows on either side, which were in turn protected from the prevailing easterlies by a rocky outcrop. These meadows were home to a large population of lemmings. If there was a swarm brewing it might well begin there.

He set off in the skiff in a gentle mist, feeling more purposeful than he had since returning from patrol. The mist reduced visibility to a few feet but Derek knew the Ellesmere coastline so intimately it slowed him only a little and once he was around the headland and into Jakeman, where the glacier cooled the air, the cloud disappeared completely and he jacked up his speed.

It didn't take him long to reach Inuak. Just to the east of the estuary, he spotted a white duck canvas tent glowing in a flash of sunlight and, on the cliff top, the tiny figure of Edie Kiglatuk. He waved. The figure stopped for a moment then waved back. A little burst of good feeling spread through him. It surprised him how glad he was to see her.

He'd reached the spot where the river bled into the sea. The freshwater ice was for the most part melted now, and the shoreline was a mess of sea-ice boulders bobbing in river runoff. He jumped into the shallows in his waders and began to head for the shore, pulling the skiff behind him. Edie Kiglatuk was making her way down the low cliff to greet him, striding along the naked slick rock as though it were some gentle alpine meadow. She looked good, Derek thought, the early summer air suited her.

'I was just about ready to give up on you and find someone more intelligent to talk to,' she said.

He palmed one hand in a gesture of surrender. There was no excuse, really, for ignoring her, least of all forgetfulness. He still owed her one, after all.

'I'm sorry, Edie, I've been real busy,' he began.

'You're here now,' she said simply. 'I was about to go for char, just upstream, where the river widens into a little lake, but now you've come we could go seal hunting.'

'Fishing would be cool,' he said, glad that she wasn't in any hurry. Right now, a spot of fishing sounded just the thing.

He followed her across the shale to where she'd set up camp. She handed him a cup of the sweetest hot tea he'd ever tasted.

'I just realized,' he said, 'I don't have a leister, or any jigs, come to that.'

She slipped inside the tent and came out with a well-worn leister and a jig made from what looked like an old coffee tin.

He took them. 'What will you use?'

'I thought I'd come along and look decorative,' she said.

He laughed and they set off up the low cliff. He had to increase his speed to keep up with her.

Before long they came up over the brow of a small incline. Before them the land stretched flat and wide, a carpet of tiny flowers and cotton-head grasses, striped here and there with low, wind-torn eskers. Human life hadn't penetrated the crust here, Derek thought. It was the antithesis of the south, where the harder and deeper you searched the more you uncovered. Down there, human stories lay buried under the weight of eons. Here, everything was so much simpler. You dug deep, all you found was ice.

He sighed and she turned and smiled at him.

'Quite something, isn't it?'

They reached the lake and walked around to the sunny side where the fish were most likely to be closer to the surface, feeding on zooplankton and the tiny invertebrates that collected in the warmer water. Derek went over to assess the likelihood of catching anything. After a while he returned to where Edie was sitting on a willow mat and announced his intention to begin jigging over by a large rock. The sun had heated the rock and the water directly below would be slightly warmer. The difference would be minimal, but it would not be lost on the fish. He returned to the place with the jig in his hand.

The world in which dope-smoking and zero tolerance mattered seemed as distant as the tiniest star, and in the passing of the hours Derek forgot that Edie had come wanting something from him. He had become, simply, a fisherman.

The fish in this part of the river were used to the attention of human beings, and wary as a result, but after he had no idea how much time, a large male char came up to the jig long enough for Derek to spear it. He pulled it out, killed it and placed its mouth next to the water, to let its soul go home. As he was clambering back to the spot where Edie was sitting, the fish dangling from her leister, it occurred to him that, for the first time in as long as he could recall, he was completely happy.

Back at the camp, they set up a fire with dry heather, and nibbled on walrus meat while they waited for the fish to cook, then they divided the head, the most delicious part, each sucking out an eye and crunching contentedly through the bones. When they were finally done, Edie said:

'Now I'll tell you what I've come to say.'

She related the story of finding Andy Taylor's bones, about the knife cuts, the bullet hole in the skull which seemed to suggest Taylor had been shot from above, about Felix Wagner and the pizza takeout place called Zemmer to which the two *qalunaat* were connected.

There was something on Craig, she said, something so valuable it was worth killing for. She didn't know what it was, yet, but the clue lay in three excised pages of Sir James Fairfax's diary and a small piece of meteorite, a stone Sir James had swapped with her great-great-great-grandfather for a penknife more than a century ago. She was pretty sure now that whatever was on Craig, Wagner and Taylor were after it and someone – or some corporation perhaps – didn't want them to have it. Whoever had taken a shot at Wagner couldn't have known then that Taylor had the same information, otherwise surely they would have shot him then too? In any case, she was beginning to think they had caught up with Taylor the second time he came looking. She recalled Joe saying that not long after losing Taylor he'd seen a plane, but by that time he was doubting the evidence of his senses. It wasn't beyond the bounds of possibility that Taylor had been shot from a plane and someone had cut up the body to make it look as though the *qalunaat* had died of hypothermia and foxes had got to the corpse.

Derek held up a hand. She was going far too fast for him. 'Edie, there was no visibility out there in that blizzard. How could anyone have landed a plane?'

'I know, I know,' she said. 'What I'm saying makes me sound crazy.'

Derek thought about Kuujuaq, and saw the prospects for his ever leaving it and moving into a brand-new detachment building in Autisaq diminishing by the second. This was incendiary stuff, stuff he wasn't going to be able to ignore, whatever Simeonie thought about it.

'I don't see what this has to do with Joe taking his life,' he said.

'Right now, Derek, nor do I. But supposing Joe saw something, supposing he saw whoever it was who shot Andy Taylor. Supposing, oh I don't know, he blamed himself, or maybe someone threatened him.'

'Edie, has it occurred to you that Joe might have shot Taylor himself?'

Her face froze, then she took a deep breath.

'I'm assuming you said that as police, Derek, not as a friend.'

What little remained of the heather spluttered among the stones.

'It's what *people* might say.'

It was as though she hadn't heard him. 'I want you to hold off on this.'

'Why tell me, then?'

Listening to Edie's story had felt like watching a hole opening up into the past. Compared with this, the glasshouse really was nothing. He didn't want to think about what it all might mean, for the police, for the settlements, for the families. He wished then that they were still out on the lake fishing.

She shrugged: 'I needed to tell someone.'

'Thanks,' he said drily.

Edie went inside the tent and began arranging bedding. She came out with a small square made of stitched hare pelts.

'Since you haven't set up your tent, I'm guessing you're planning on sharing mine.' She waved a cloth and a toothbrush at him. 'I'm going to the river to wash. If you're getting in with me, you will too.'

Later, he woke needing to pee, and went outside. The breeze was icy but the sun had some warmth to it. Feeling oddly protective of his modesty, he trudged across the muskeg to where the river bank sloped down and unzipped his waterproofs. He peed, shook himself and readjusted his trousers. When he looked up he saw a wolf bitch standing on the other side of the bank, watching him. Beside her was a single cub. For a while he didn't move and the wolf went down to the water's edge to drink, not once lifting her eyes from him. Gathering the cub to her side, she turned back up the bank and the pair loped away over the rocks.

When he returned Edie was already up and brewing tea. He walked back to his skiff, unhitched the tarp and took out Joe's thermos. She recognized it immediately and he saw by her expression that she didn't know anything about the glasshouse. He hesitated, unsure whether he was doing the right thing by telling her, then decided she had a right to know the truth.

Her face began to fall as he told her what he knew. By the time he was done, she seemed to have shrunk in size. He reached out and put his hand on her shoulder.

'Edie, your boy was in a whole world of trouble.'

The instant the words came out he regretted them. They weren't the consolation he'd hoped they might be. She shrugged him off and threw him a long look that made him feel like a whipped dog.

'You can say what you like,' she said. 'I already lost my kid and my job. I've got nothing left to lose. I'm a hunter, Derek, I intend to hunt this one down.'

'I'm sorry,' he said, 'about the job. About Joe, too, of course.'

They drank another mug of sweet tea in silence, then he offered to help her break camp. They worked through a light fug of hostility, their labours accompanied only by the sound of rushing wind and the crackle of shale underfoot. Derek tried to think of a way back to her, but she seemed obscured and remote. It wasn't all about his tactless remark, he thought. There was something still lingering from having spent the night together.

Once they were all packed up, they agreed to go to where the river snaked out from under the cliff to take water for a brew. After their exertions, they would cool quickly and would need hot tea to keep them warm on the journey home.

She brought Joe's old thermos. As she was bending to fill the container, she gave out a yelp, stood up straight and, rubbing her head, said:

'Yow, something fell on me.'

Derek said: 'A rock?' They both directed their gaze to the cliff, but there was nothing that might account for the object. Derek scanned the shingle around him but that, too, gave no clues.

'Must be,' Edie said. 'It was kind of soft though.'

Returning to the water, they filled their containers and screwed on the tops. The instant Derek went to make his way back to the campsite, he saw something sail through the air. At first he thought it was a ptarmigan, then something else arced over.

An unmistakeable sound reached them on the breeze, a

high-pitched chorus, a million little squeals, conflating into a single, pixellated buzz.

He fixed his gaze on the line of low cliff. This time he knew what he was looking for. Above them, on the plateau, the lemmings had started swarming.

He slung his water canister across his shoulders and raced for the rudimentary path that led up through the moraine, all his energies focused on reaching the high point, everything else forgotten. Below him Edie headed up the path. He felt his heart thrumming. This was the thing he had been waiting for, and the final few moments of anticipation were almost overwhelming. Reaching the top, breathing raw in his chest, he steadied himself. He closed his eyes and waited for the patina of light and dark to fade. Then he took a breath and opened them.

All around him, the muskeg was on the move for as far he could see; a mass of reddish grey pulsed and throbbed across the willow, south towards Jones Sound and west across the Inuak River, obscuring everything in its inexorable progress forward. He knew now that it was a lemming that had fallen onto Edie, another he had seen tumbling through the air. Here it was, the swarm. Not suicide, as the myth had for so long had it, but a great swell of life, the survival instinct in its purest form, thrilling in its intensity. From where he stood, Derek could see, in the frazzled water of the river, bodies swirling and kicking, struggling frantically to reach the other side.

Edie came up beside him, laughing, exhilarated by the swarm and they moved towards the pack, standing firm for a while to feel the rodents flowing over their feet like molten rock, the racket of squeals and the musky smell of lemming droppings overwhelming.

'Edie,' he shouted over the cacophony. 'I've thought about what we said last night. You're a hunter, I get that.

You want me to hold off, I'll do it. Not for ever, but for a while.'

He'd been prepared to let the deaths in Autisaq go. Now, he knew that, sooner or later, he would have to act. For her sake, he would make it later.

'We got a deal?' she said. She looked at him with those fierce button eyes of hers.

He nodded.

'Another fine mess, right?' she said, but she was smiling.

Hours afterwards, when he finally arrived back at the detachment, he found Misha waiting for him. He went to her and kissed her cheek.

'You're late,' she said.

He told her about the swarm.

'You're still late.'

He looked at her and suddenly felt incredibly clear. *I have no idea what I am doing with this woman.* The thought saddened him but he felt relieved of the burden of loving her, too. She seemed to sense the change in him. He saw her back away a little.

At last he said: 'I think you should leave.'

'Yes,' she said. Her voice was resigned, not at all vindictive as he might have imagined it would be. 'I was going anyway.'

'I don't know why you came.' The words sounded crueller than he had intended.

'Tomas split with me. I was on my own,' she said. 'I thought maybe I loved you.'

'But you didn't?'

She smiled ruefully. 'No.'

11

Edie found Willa at Sammy's house, watching TV with Sammy's new on-off girlfriend, Nancy. Beside them sat a bowl of popcorn and there was something heating in the microwave but no sign of Sammy.

'Hey,' she said, aware that she shouldn't mind seeing her ex-family reconstituted into something new, but minding anyway. Nancy looked up and smiled. Willa didn't.

'What do you want?' he said. 'I'm watching this.'

He was in one of his confrontational moods, but wasn't he always like that with her these days?

She said: 'Just a small thing.'

Nancy shifted awkwardly in her seat, then rose. 'I'll go fix some food.'

Edie waited for her to disappear into the kitchenette, and turned to Willa: 'We need to talk in the snow porch.'

'What?' He looked up at her, irritation hardening his face.

'*Privately.*'

The cramped porch forced the pair to stand closer than was comfortable for either. Not so long ago they would have hugged, but it had been a long time since there'd been any chance of that. She still remembered when, at bedtime, he would call out to her to come and tell him the story of Sedna, the little girl whose grandfather tossed her from his boat then cut off her clinging fingers. 'The fingers became seals and walruses,' she would say, 'and Sedna sat at the bottom of the ocean directing the animals to give themselves to the hunters or to stay hidden in the depths, depending on whether Inuit people made her happy or not.'

'Do I make Sedna happy?' he would ask.

'Sure you do,' she'd say and he'd close his eyes and be asleep in moments.

Now, given his mood, Edie thought it best to get directly to the point.

'I figure the glasshouse was your idea,' she said. 'But why the hell did you have to drag Joe into it?'

Willa had been a pothead for as long as she could remember, she didn't know how long exactly because by the time she'd been sober enough to notice, he had already moved on to heroin. Eventually he'd given that up and gone back to marijuana. Progress of a sort.

He shook his head and let out a venomous snort.

'You're priceless.'

Taking a step back she held up her hands, palms towards him. 'I'm sorry,' she said. 'That came out bad. Can we do this civilized? I just mean, how was Joe involved? Was he smoking?'

It seemed unlikely, she hadn't smelled it on him, but she knew that marijuana made some people depressed, paranoid, and even suicidal.

Willa glanced back towards the living room but Nancy was still in the kitchenette. 'For one tiny second I forgot that everything, *every damned thing*, always has to come back to Joe. Forget it, Edie. I stopped owing you anything a long time ago.'

Edie stood for a moment. Willa was right. She had given up the right to have any claim over him the moment she'd hit the bottle. All those years when he still wanted her to love him as much as she loved Joe and she'd been unable to give him what he wanted. Now he was just content to see her suffer. She'd brought his hatred on herself. It was no less than she deserved.

'Listen,' he said, sounding more conciliatory. 'If I had any idea why my brother killed himself, I'd tell you. But I don't.' A plume of warm air rushed in where he held the door open. 'Joe was complicated. *Ayaynuaq*, Edie, it can't be helped, so just drop it.'

'I would if I could.'

Willa rolled his eyes. 'You wanna know what we did? I'll tell you what we did. We supplied the *qalunaat* at the science station. You wanna know another thing?' He was going to tell her anyway. 'I didn't make nothing from it, Edie, not the whole time. Every damned cent, every loonie went to Joe, his nursing fund.'

Her breath caught in her throat and for a moment she was stuck there, unable to inhale.

'Did you know Joe was gambling?' She wondered if it would give Willa any satisfaction to discover his brother had his own flaws, but saw he was as shocked as she had been. She felt ashamed of herself. 'I think maybe your brother gambled away that money.'

Willa took a step back.

'You're crazy.'

Something occurred to her. 'You weren't . . . he wasn't . . . *using*, was he?'

'Every so often we had a smoke. So what.' He stared at her, searching for meaning, then his face grew as dark as a winter noon. 'Oh, I get it. You think I was trading weed for dope, something I could spike. That's it, isn't it?' He let out an ugly laugh. 'You want to know, was I helping my own brother turn into a junkie?'

'No, Willa,' she said. 'Uh nuh.' The truth was, she didn't know what she thought.

'It ever even occur to you, Joe wanted to use, he had

a whole pharmacy of drugs, more pills than the average junkie could spike in a lifetime, sitting right there at the clinic. All he had to do was to cook 'em up a little and grab the nearest needle.'

She looked at him blankly. It had never crossed her mind that pills could be injected. Willa gave her an exasperated look.

'*Duh.*'

With that he slammed the door and disappeared back inside the house.

She got home and clambered, wretched, into bed, clutching the pillow over her face to block out the world. It was either that, she sensed, or another rendezvous with the bottle and she'd promised herself not to go back there.

Still, the encounter with Willa had hit her like an ice avalanche. How many relationships would she have to ruin before she was prepared to give up? Maybe there was no rationale whatsoever for what had happened to Joe.

Just then, the front door slammed. Sammy burst in.

'Why are you doing this, Edie?' Angry. Again.

She sat up in bed, dazed. Then she laughed at what a fool she'd been to doubt herself. Hunting was the way she made sense of the world. No hunter ever called off a hunt until it was hopeless.

Sammy stood at the foot of the bed. He'd been drinking. 'Leave my son out of it.'

She felt suddenly desperate. 'Which one?' Her voice was harsh. 'The dead one, or the pothead?'

The second the words left her mouth she knew they were incendiary. He took the bait. In an instant, he flared and came at her, a ball of fury. For a moment she thought he was going to hit her; she could see in his face he thought it too. Then he slumped back, slit-eyed with exhaustion.

When he'd collected himself he said:

'The glasshouse thing, Edie, it was my fault.'

'Uh nuh, Joe was gambling, he was in debt.' She wasn't going to let her ex play the martyr. 'He was doing it at the clinic, online, with his credit card,' she said. 'He owed money.' There was no point keeping it from him now.

Sammy looked puzzled.

'Edie, Joe didn't have a credit card.'

He was wrong. She and Joe had filled in the application together. He'd needed the card to buy nursing books from some internet site.

Sammy sat down at the end of the bed, all the anger drained out of him. 'Joe cut up his card. I saw him do it.'

'You mean he maxed it out?' That would explain why he'd come to her for a loan when he needed new parts for his snowbie. This was worse than she'd imagined.

Sammy shook his head. 'No, I did.' His voice faltered. 'I needed a thermal scope on my rifle, I mean, I wanted one. You know, for night hunting. I didn't have any money, and I knew I'd never get credit, so I borrowed Joe's card.'

'You *borrowed* your son's credit card?'

'OK, I took it. And then Lisa persuaded me to buy her a new furnace.'

For the first time in as long as she could recall, Edie was speechless.

'But then the credit-card company contacted Joe and, Jeez, Edie, the whole thing was a mess.'

'So, the glasshouse money . . .'

Sammy nodded miserably. 'Went to pay off the credit card. Which is why Joe cut it up.'

'So his father couldn't steal from him again.'

Sammy snuffled. 'Aw, Edie.'

'I'm tired, Sammy. You can let yourself out.'

*

Lying in bed on her own once more, she tried to figure out the sequence of events. Maybe Joe had set up a gambling account then never used it? But no, that didn't make sense. More likely he had started to use it then, when he saw where it was taking him, he'd given it up. Maybe none of this mattered any more. She'd made a mental note to speak to Robert Patma, but not now. Right now she needed to sleep.

When she woke it was light. But then it was always light now. There was also a man standing in her room. For an instant she thought the *puikaktuq* was back, then the figure resolved into Mike Nungaq.

'You sick, Edie?' He sounded genuinely worried. 'It's late.'

'Uh nuh.'

He held out a mug. 'I made you some tea.'

While she was taking the first sip, he dug around in his pocket and pulled out a padded envelope. 'Your stone came back.' He was watching her expectantly. 'I thought you'd want to know.'

Two mugs of tea and twelve teaspoons of sugar later she was beginning to feel almost human.

Mike handed her the stone.

'Turns out I was right about the meteorite, but, like I said, I'm no expert. There were a couple of things Jack – my friend – pointed out I hadn't noticed. First, this piece of space rock has been on Planet Earth a long, long time.' He pointed to a blackish patch. 'See that there? In fresh meteorites that fusion crust is all over. The dark brown varnish is rusted iron-nickel like I said before, but here, see . . .' He pointed to the outer edge of the rock. '. . . It's smooth, where the outer part vaporized as it fell through the atmosphere.' He pointed to the edge opposite to the first, which was sharper: 'And it's been chipped with a tool, suggesting that it was once part of a larger piece. The tool was non-metallic, probably another piece of meteorite, but you'll see that both edges have the same dark brown varnish, so if it *was* hammered off something bigger, it must have been done a while back. Jack reckons maybe more than a century. He says the oxidation layer is pretty even too.

He paused, glancing over at Edie expectantly. She fixed him with a non-committal sort of smile. Dragging Derek into her fine mess was one thing, but Mike was another: Mike Nungaq actually had something to lose. Disappointment curdled his expression as he realized he wasn't going to get any more out of her, but he took a breath and went on anyway.

'The thing I hadn't noticed, inside here . . .' He pointed to the part that had been drilled out to form a pendant, '. . . are these silvery-white spots, like tiny ice crystals. Jack had a hunch about those, so he scraped some of the rock off and tested it. And he turned out to be right. Iridium. A transition metal, related to platinum but much, much rarer. On earth, iridium is mostly confined to the core, but it's more common in space rocks. Which is why it's found in the craters left by meteors. Astroblemes.'

'Astro what?'

Edie flashed him a look, hoping he would get to the point, whatever it was. She had no idea what Mike was talking about.

'You familiar with the theories about the extinction of dinosaurs?' He finished his tea, gazed into the bottom of the mug and started up again. 'It was the high level of iridium in a part of the Yucatán which gave Luis Alvarez and his team the idea that what did for the dinos sixty-five million years ago was the impact of a giant meteorite.'

Edie coughed politely.

Seeing he hadn't got through to her, Mike took another tack.

'Remember those geologists who came up for the summer a couple of years back, Quebecois, I think?'

Edie cast her mind back and came up blank. 'Geologists are like rocks, Mike, ask me, they all look pretty much alike.'

'I helped this bunch out some. When they finished the project, they sent me a copy of their paper. I remembered something in it so I dug it out. What they found on Craig, Edie, was a small astrobleme. The crater left by a meteor. They just stumbled on it. They were interested in other stuff, see. The thing about the astrobleme only appears in the research as a footnote.

'I did some rooting around. Normally, beneath the 60th, you can trace astroblemes from their magnetic effects. That was how iridium was first discovered. Up here, it's much harder because of the weird magnetic fields.'

Edie registered the point. She was beginning to find what Mike was saying of more interest. The unreliability of compasses north of the 60th parallel was known even to the earliest of the European explorers, but here, well above the 70th, you took out a compass it could be pointing anywhere, depending on the local geomagnetic field.

'So, if there was an astrobleme on Ellesmere, or on Craig Island, it would be more difficult to detect?'

'From magnetic data, yes. Unless you just happened to come across it, like those geologists, the only way to find it, without doing years of complicated geologic research, would be to start from the fragments of meteor that caused it, then work backwards. Even then, it would be a tall order. The meteor usually gets scattered on impact.'

'Mike,' Edie interrupted. 'I'm really not all that bright. You're going to have to help me out here.'

Mike rubbed the stone in his hands.

'What I'm saying, you looked hard enough on Craig you'd find a perfect match to this. Find a few dozen, you could map out the scatter pattern and from that locate your astrobleme. It'd be a helluva job though. I don't have to tell you what it's like out there. Ten months of the year, the whole place is under three metres of ice and snow.'

'But the Quebecois fellows already found it.'

'I'd be willing to bet not many people know that.' Mike slapped his knees and stood up to go. 'Well, I hope that was worth getting you out of your bed for.'

As he reached the door she thought of something and called him back.

'Just out of interest, those geologists, the Quebecois? What were they actually looking for?'

'Salt,' he said. 'Garden variety salt.'

After he'd gone, she went to the bathroom and grabbed a bottle of Tylenol. Her head was thundery with new information. She wondered if it would ever be possible to make sense of it all.

Fixing some tea for herself, she went to the sofa, covered herself in a caribou skin, knocked back a couple of pills and tried to think. All of a sudden, an idea came into her head. It was as a result of something Willa had said. She picked up the Tylenol bottle, shook out a pill and crushed it under her sugar spoon. Then she poured a little hot tea onto the powder. Almost immediately it dissolved, leaving a puddle of liquid on the table. You can inject pills, why hadn't she thought of that?

She visualized the neat pile of foils left stacked in Joe's drawer. Was it likely that someone in Joe's position would have been able to think straight enough to pop one hundred and fifty Vicodin out of their blister packs then stack the packs back in a tidy little pile? It didn't seem so. And it was even less likely that someone could have made him swallow those pills if he hadn't wanted to. But supposing someone had 'cooked 'em up', as Willa called it, and injected Joe as he lay sedated and sleeping? It wasn't beyond the bounds of possibility, was it?

The thought made her sick with horror, but at the same time it made sense. All along Edie had fought against the notion that Joe had taken his own life. It was too easy. Yet until now there had been no way round those irrefutable path lab results. Joe had died of an overdose of Vicodin.

But what if the overdose had been administered by someone other than Joe? What if someone else had stolen into the nursing station and taken the pills then waited for Joe to be alone to inject him? Closing her eyes, she tried to take in the enormity of the idea. Her eyes were still shut tight when the door swung open.

It was her ex.

'Not now, Sammy.'

She wanted to be left alone with her thoughts. 'Edie, I . . .' His voice was whiny, like a beaten dog's.

He was feeling bad about the credit card business and was looking to her for absolution.

'Go away.'

'Aw, Edie,' he said, 'don't be like that. You doing this to punish me?'

'Now let me think,' she said. Her voice sounded harsh and sarcastic.

'Is this because I racked up Joe's card?' The whining evaporated and his voice took on a tone of righteous indignation. 'Or maybe it's those two men I took to Craig?' The idea had only just occurred to him, she could see. 'You're not sore about *that*, Edie? Are you?'

Edie finished her tea. She hadn't given the two duck hunters much thought but remembering them now, she realized just how odd their appearance in Autisaq had been. At the time, she'd been too drunk to make the connection.

Sammy sighed. 'So that *is* it. You want, I'll give you half the fee. Gimme a break here.'

She took a breath and set her mind back, sober as a rock. She wasn't listening to what Sammy was saying to her now because she was too busy trying to recall exactly what he'd said to her on the evening of his return from the trip: how the two hunters had insisted on being taken to Craig and their enthusiasm for the island's geology once they were there. And wasn't there something else about that trip? Of course, she remembered now. The plane with its unfamiliar green livery. Two ideas knitted together in her mind. Hadn't Joe said he'd seen a green plane? He thought he'd imagined it, but what if he hadn't? She felt the palms of her hands begin to prickle.

'Those fellows, you remember their names?' She was aware that her voice sounded inquisitorial, but she couldn't help herself.

Sammy's mouth fell open. He looked at his feet. 'They said they were Russian hunters. What do I know about Russian hunters?'

'Names maybe?'

'You want their *names*? No, Edie, I don't remember their *names*. I remember their money.'

She let out a snort. It was hopeless. *He* was hopeless.

'Sammy, don't take this the wrong way, but I'd really like you to go. Preferably right now.'

He left without a protest, for which she was grateful. Once he was gone, she paced up and down a little. The feeling that she was standing on the edge of something new and unexplored was dizzying. It made her want a drink so badly her chest throbbed with it. *I need to sleep*, she thought. *I need to sleep*.

Without the discipline of the school routine, and with twenty-four-hour light, her body clock had pretty much broken down. She'd begun to lose sense of night and day. She felt light-headed, exhilarated by the possibilities of the truth and at the same time terrified of how close she might be to discovering it. *Maybe I'm losing sense of the world,* she thought. And then, remembering the way the Tylenol had dissolved in the tea, thought, *Or maybe I'm finally beginning to* make *sense of it*.

The next step, she saw now, was to find out who the Russian hunters were and where they'd come from. But not before she'd slept. She lay down and closed her eyes and by the time she rose a few hours later, she had a plan.

Late that night, when Autisaq had gone to bed, Edie crept out into bright sunshine, let Bonehead off his chain, attached him to a leash and made her way to the Town Hall. Leaving the dog tied up outside, she slid Joe's key into the door and, creeping in without taking off her outerwear, she made her way to the mayor's office. Anyone came, she figured Bonehead would give her due warning.

Within seconds, she found a file labelled 'Hunting Permits' and pulled it out. The two men's duck permits were listed by date. R. Raskolnikov and P. Petrovich. No addresses, just mailbox numbers. There was something vaguely familiar about the names. Edie tried to recall where she'd come across them before. In the *Arctic Circular*? Then, in a rush, it came to her. For the only time in her life, she found herself thanking the Canadian government for her ridiculous, southern-curriculum education. Of course she knew. Raskolnikov and Petrovich were characters in *Crime and Punishment*, the murderer and the detective sworn to bring him down. She kicked herself. The clues had been under her nose all along: the pseudonyms, the green plane, the men's keener interest in Craig's geology than in its ornithology. The drink had scrambled her so badly she hadn't been able to put it all together. Joe must have been right. A green plane *had* come over Craig the day Andy Taylor disappeared. And Edie was now pretty sure that she knew who'd been in it.

She allowed herself a triumphant little air punch, then she went back to the files, searching for the flight log, and found it, right where it should be. Sheila Silliq didn't know just what a treasure she really was. On the date in question, a Twin Otter, registration XOY4325, had landed from direction Iqaluit at 10.28 a.m., carrying one pilot and two passengers. Edie committed the details to memory and replaced the flight log.

Out of interest she flipped through the remainder of the files in the cabinet, until she reached a file marked 'SI, personal'. She pulled out the file and found a sheaf of bank statements in Simeonie Inukpuk's name. Following the list of transactions with her finger, she lighted on nothing more interesting than a few sums relating to a womenswear emporium in Ottawa. The mayor often flew in to the capital to attend local government meetings. Either he had a mistress down there or a transvestite habit. Neither of which was of any interest to Edie.

The next page seemed to be from a different account, and listed a number of regular deposits of CA$5,000 each from a numbered account, made in favour of the Autisaq Children's Foundation. Very touching, or it would be, if Edie could conjure a single thing it had ever done for the children of Autisaq.

The door to the mayor's office was locked, so she took out her Leatherman. The locks in the prefabs were all of a kind. In common with most folk in Autisaq, she'd removed most of hers, so she knew exactly how they worked.

Swinging open the pick attachment, she slid it into the keyhole and felt for the lock, which gave way very quickly. She went round to the back of the desk and switched on the computer. While it was booting up, she looked about, not sure what she was hoping to find. The screen glowed then resolved into the screensaver: an image of an iceberg. Computers weren't her thing but she'd had to learn the basics for her teaching. She went into Explorer and clicked on History, running her eye down the list until, unexpectedly, the words Zemmer Energy came into view. Edie took a loud breath. Of course Zemmer wasn't a pizza joint. It was an energy company with something to hide and Felix Wagner, Andy Taylor and now, she realized, Simeonie Inukpuk, were all familiar with it.

She clicked on the URL and immediately a pop-up window appeared requesting a password. She was about to tap in some possible combinations when Bonehead started barking. Racing to the door, she remembered that she hadn't turned off the computer, lunged forward, grabbed the cable and pulled. Then, closing the door quietly behind her, she made her way back along the corridor. Seeing her, Bonehead began whining and coughing, straining against his leash.

From the steps of the Town Hall she saw what it was that had set him off. Immediately in front of her, not five metres away, stood a polar bear, a young male. For a minute or two Edie and the bear watched one another, then the animal turned and trotted away.

Dawn found Edie bumping up and down on rough, ice-ridden breakers in her skiff, on her way to Martie's cabin. If anyone could help her find out more about the green plane, she figured, it would be her aunt.

She found Martie asleep on top of a pile of skins, an empty bottle of Mist beside her. As well as the stench of alcohol there was something else, a smoky, slightly sour aroma. Edie went to the primus to mug up but Martie didn't wake when the kettle started singing.

A handful of cold water thrown in the direction of the sleeping platform had the effect Edie was looking for; pretty soon a face appeared above the skins, squinted across for as long as it took to establish who was fixing tea, then disappeared back under the covers.

'Ah, Little Bear, it's you.' A muffled sound. A hand appeared, rubbing her head. 'What the hell you doing this time of day or night or whatever it is, you crazy creature?'

Edie poured the tea. She'd left in too much of a hurry, hadn't dressed right and felt stupid. The trip had frozen her bones. By the time she was stirring in the sugar, Martie had already noticed her niece's shivers and was holding both arms out and waving her over.

'Don't let yourself get so cold.' She pressed her fingers into Edie's face to gauge her temperature then took hold of her, transferring some of her still sleep-soaked body warmth. Edie sucked on her mug of tea until the lump in her throat went away.

'Martie, I need something.'

Martie said: 'I feel like shit.' She began rubbing at her skin, which was mottled and sprinkled with small lesions.

'You ill?'

Martie followed Edie's gaze. 'Oh, these?' She wafted a hand at a raw patch on her lower arm then slid her arms back under the caribou skin. 'Uh nuh, just allergies.' She put on a smile. 'Now, what do you need?'

Edie drew out the paper on which she'd written details of the plane and read them out. 'You know this plane?'

Martie gazed at the numbers until her double vision cleared, then shook her head. 'Nope, but the registration's out of Greenland, that any help. What you wanna know for?'

'The flight log said the plane came in from the south, from Iqaluit. Any way to know that for sure?'

Martie gave a little hum to indicate she was concentrating. 'What direction was the wind that day?'

Edie reconstructed the scene in her mind, working out where the wind was blowing in from and in which direction the plane landed.

'Either the person who wrote the log doesn't know the difference between the four compass points or someone was lying. That plane is registered in Greenland and came in from Greenland.' A pause while Martie finished her tea. 'Should I be feeling better yet, because I can't help noticing that I don't.'

'Martie, you ever heard of the Autisaq Children's Foundation?'

Martie went back under the covers. 'Is it connected to the Auntie Martie Needs to Sleep Foundation?'

By the time Edie got back home, there seemed no point in going back to bed. She went to the fridge, found a bowl of seal-blood soup, smelled it to check it was fresh, then set it in the microwave to heat. She took a deep breath and held the bowl to her lips. The liquid was thick with granules of congealed, cooked blood. She was conscious of being hungry, though she couldn't feel it in her belly, but the smell made her faintly nauseous. Pinching her nose, she raised her head to open her throat and poured it down. Thoughts flurried about in her mind but the only idea that really settled was the notion that Joe had been murdered. Who'd done it and why remained a puzzle, but she was pretty sure that Welatok's meteorite lay at the heart of it. If Mike Nungaq's theory was right, then the meteorite was a necessary route map to the Craig Island astrobleme. Wagner, Taylor and now it seemed most likely the Russians had all come in search of it.

Why the astrobleme might be of interest, she didn't know, but Wagner had noted some connection with salt, which the Quebecois article seemed to confirm, and both Wagner and Taylor were talking with Zemmer Energy so it made sense to suppose that the crater marked something of interest to them. She couldn't quite figure where the diary pages came in, unless they gave some description of the locale; and whoever was looking for the astrobleme would need the stone to make a match to others in the area and establish the scatter pattern of the impact. So the diary and the stone must be inextricably linked. Together they comprised a map which would allow scientists to bypass years of geological exploration.

What little she knew so far pointed to the possibility that the two Russians were also behind the death of Andy Taylor. It made sense that it was they who'd been in the green plane Joe saw on the day Taylor disappeared. Maybe he'd reneged on some kind of deal, or perhaps it was simpler than that: he was near to finding the astrobleme and they couldn't allow that to happen. If it *was* they who had killed him, they must have done it from the plane. No one could have landed in the blizzard conditions Joe had described. In which case, it was still a puzzle who had butchered and scattered Taylor's remains.

Exactly how all this was connected to Joe's death she didn't yet understand, yet she knew in her bones that it was. She looked about her. The door to Joe's room continued to dominate the space.

She thought about what Sammy had done with Joe's credit card. If she'd still been drinking, she would have reached for a bottle of Mist, then gone round to his house and started a fight.

She remembered her mental note to check with Robert about Joe's gambling. There was a puzzle, right there. The nurse had seemed so sure of his suspicions, but she didn't understand how Joe could have gambled online without a credit card. Maybe she was missing something. Flinging on her summer parka she stepped out into the street.

Robert was in his office, sorting condoms. A pile of musk-ox wrappers lay to his left, the others, seal, walrus and Arctic hare to his right. He signalled for Edie to wait.

'Some dumbass screwed up the musk-ox batch so I'm having to waste my time separating them all out.'

'I can suggest an alternative.'

'You can?' he said.

'You could stop wasting your time and talk to me.'

Robert looked up in surprise, sighed, and put down the condoms.

'Sorry. What can I do for you?'

'You've probably noticed I'm quite stupid.'

Robert nodded to signal he was listening, then checked himself and shook his head.

'What I can't work out is *how* Joe owed money for online gambling.'

He shrugged. 'I guess he just got hooked. People do. Get hooked on things, I mean.' He went back to his condoms. 'Do you mind if I carry on sorting these?'

'No, I mean, I don't know how he owed *anything*. To play online you need a credit card, right?'

Robert shrugged again. 'I guess so.'

She told him what she knew.

Robert stopped his sorting, reached over to the computer and clicked through with the mouse, then swivelled the monitor around to show Edie the password window with the username 'JoeInukpuk' on a splashy portal announcing itself as the Gaming Station.

'This is the site.'

'Put the password in,' she said.

Robert looked taken aback. 'I don't know it.'

'But you knew Joe owed money?'

Robert swivelled the monitor back.

'Yeah, when I first clicked on it the site let me in but when I tried to get back into it later, it was blocked. Some kind of password-protected time lock, I guess. It was weird.' He returned to his sorting. 'You're upset, Edie, we all are. You know – and this is hard to say, I feel really bad I didn't see it coming – looking back I can see Joe had a heap of reasons to want to end his life.'

'He had a heap of reasons to want to hang on to it.'

She heard herself telling Robert about the deaths of Wagner and Taylor, how they were connected. It surprised her to be confiding in him, but there it was. 'I think Joe somehow got wrapped up in it.' She considered carrying on, confessing her theory about injectable pills, but caution intervened and told her that as Edie the woman she was impetuous, impulsive even, but now she needed to be Edie the hunter.

Robert sat back for a moment, thoughts scrolling across his face. Then he got up and taking her hands said very kindly, 'Edie, are you still hallucinating?'

'No,' she lied.

Later, in the shower, she opened her mouth, allowed the water to run in then spat it out again. It was soft, blood-warm and tasted unpleasantly of chlorine. Before they'd always used water pumped directly from the Autisaq lake up beyond the glacier. Now it all had to go through some supposed purification process. Another one of Simeonie's 'modernization' schemes. She turned off the shower and reached for a towel, then decided against it. In the grip of some unfamiliar feeling, she padded out naked into the living room. Outside a pale sun threw sparkles across the sea.

One spring, back when she and Sammy were together, and their drinking was particularly bad, they had taken it upon themselves to go ice fishing up at the Autisaq lake. The lake had been fished out years before, but back when there were still char living there, Elijah Nungaq had returned from a fishing expedition one day claiming to have seen a huge fish, almost as big as a beluga, lurking in the depths of the lake. A hunting party had gone out immediately afterwards but the fish had disappeared. All the same, the creature was spoken about frequently, growing in size and reputation each time, and groups of fishermen and women would periodically go out to the lake to try to catch it.

This is what she and Sammy were doing that day but, of course, within a short while of reaching the lake they were both so drunk they forgot all about the fish, and didn't notice the low clouds and the breeze coming in from the north that signalled a blizzard. The first snow was already beginning to fall when Edie felt a tug on her arm and, starting awake, looked up to see Joe standing above her.

Later, she and Sammy had laughed off the event because they couldn't bear the idea that they owed their lives to a ten-year-old boy.

She was standing in the warm stream of sunlight, playing the memory back in her mind when an idea cut in. Suddenly it seemed very clear what she needed to do next. She dried herself off, dressed and went round to Sammy's house. He was in his usual position on the sofa, watching a rerun of *The Wire*. She noticed that the Bible was face out on the shelf.

'I'm going to Greenland,' she said.

'You're going *where*? Why?'

'Those two Russians, the duck hunters, they came in from Greenland on a Greenlandic plane. I think they might know why Joe died.' She considered telling Sammy about the astroblemes and about Zemmer Energy then decided against it. There were some people who couldn't take too much reality. Her ex-husband was one of them.

Sammy shook his head and tutted disapprovingly.

'Only one person knows why my son died,' he said. 'You want to find out, you have to ask Joe's spirit.'

'You think I haven't?'

'Then maybe he doesn't want us to know.'

'No, Sammy, I think you're wrong. I think he wants us to find out for ourselves.'

12

'Nuuk in *Greenland*?'

Edie gave a thumbs-up to the Inuk man at the airport information counter to let him know she'd got through, then she turned her attention back to Derek Palliser.

'Did those lemmings tunnel through your brain?' she asked.

'What the *hell* are you doing in Nuuk?' He seemed genuinely dumbfounded. 'Edie, do I need to worry?'

'About me?' She snorted. 'Of course not.'

'Why didn't you mention this before?'

'Because I knew you'd interfere,' she said.

The Inuk man began making hang-up gestures.

'But we had a deal,' Derek said.

'Didn't someone tell you yet? People break deals all the time.'

He sighed. 'At some point I'm going to have to get involved.' She heard a rustle of papers. 'You know how it is, nothing stays secret for long around here.'

'You'd be surprised.'

Another silence. 'I guess you're not going to tell me what that means.'

'Uh nuh. Not yet anyway.'

She'd decided not to mention her new theory until she had something more to go on. Her plan was to find the plane and through that the two Russian hunters who came looking for rocks on Craig.

'Anything happens, there's a letter.'

She described where he could find the key to her old booze cupboard, empty now but for an envelope containing the pages she'd found in the ice cave plus four more written in her own scruffy hand.

'Promise me you'll find out what happened to Joe.'

'Edie, we've been through this. You know what happened.'

'I mean, *why*. I want that to be a promise, Derek, not a deal.'

There was a pause, but this time it felt full and potent, like the silence between lovers.

'I promise,' he said, finally; then, in a lighter tone, 'How's Nuuk?'

All she'd seen of the town so far, aside from the airport terminal, was on the approach from the air.

'Awful,' she said. 'Too many roads, not nearly enough ice.'

The man at the info booth began signalling to her again. Derek was still laughing when she cut him off.

'Sorry, we're not supposed to make international calls,' the man at the info booth said.

He had a disc-shaped face with a mouth that looked as though it had got stuck in a permanent turndown. When she'd first spoken to him in Inuktitut, he hadn't understood her. They were speaking in English now, but even then she found it hard to pick her way through his accent. It had unsettled her to discover that not all Inuit spoke the same version of the language.

'I haven't finished,' she said.

The man looked up. His eyes narrowed then he swivelled round, following a sudden commotion. Four uniformed men rushed by, making for the terminal door. The Inuk watched them go.

'Trouble?'

'Protestors.'

'Oh.' The idea seemed strange. Anyone had anything to protest about in Autisaq, they walked into the Town Hall and spoke directly to the mayor.

'Some politician is flying in from Denmark this afternoon to open a new sports centre. Not everyone likes foreigners, I guess.'

He turned back to his desk, distracted now.

'About that something else?' she said. 'A charter plane.'

The man leaned back and shook his head. 'I don't have anything to do with that side.' He seemed relieved that he wasn't going to be able to help her. 'I'm just terminal operations.'

The sound of jeering issued from outside. The man made busy. Edie pulled out the piece of paper on which she'd scribbled the registration of the green plane and pushed it across the desk towards him.

'All I want to know, the name of the charter company operating this plane?'

The Inuk glanced at it, then looked up at Edie, wary.

'You one of them, a protestor?'

A wry smile came over Edie's face. 'Only on my home turf.' Remembering the Inuk pilot, she added, 'I'm thinking of chartering a plane, and a friend told me that the fella who flies this . . .' nodding at the piece of paper, '. . . is one of us.'

He picked up the paper and inspected it, before giving her a pinched look, as though he didn't quite believe her but had decided not to care.

'Looks like Johannes Moller's outfit.' He plugged something into his screen and flipped his finger down a list. 'Yup. He's a Dane but he's got an Inuk pilot works for him, Hans, I think it is.'

'You don't know where I'd find him?'

The Inuk shrugged. 'You could try Bar Rat in town. Lot of bush pilots hang out there.'

By Autisaq standards, Nuuk seemed like a vast urban sprawl. Until now, Edie had never been anywhere larger than Iqaluit. Was there an address?

The info guy shrugged again. He'd been co-operative enough. 'Like I said . . .' he began.

'. . . you're just terminal operations.'

While they'd been talking, another batch of uniformed police had arrived and taken up stations by the entrance to keep the protestors out. Edie brushed by them and out onto the pavement. It occurred to her then that she should have asked the Inuk for the name of a cheap guesthouse, but when she turned to go back inside, a uniformed arm barred her way.

'Only passengers with valid tickets,' the policeman said in English.

Edie tried arguing but the man wouldn't budge.

She crossed over the road alongside the terminal near to where protestors were penned in behind a series of crash barriers. A few were waving placards on which Edie could only make out the Greenlandic words for 'Greenland' and 'Greenlanders'. Native people by and large. They didn't look terribly threatening.

A sign on the other side of the barriers advertised buses to the town centre. There was nothing for it but to make her way through the crowd. A policeman opened the barrier to give her access. She moved through, using her elbows to force open a corridor, and finally came out on the other side near the bus stop. Who'd have thought that human crowds could be noisier than gulls and smellier than a seal colony?

She was trying to fathom out a printed timetable

attached to the stop, when a young Greenlandic woman in a pink fleece leaned towards her and said something in the native language.

'I'm a foreigner,' explained Edie.

The young woman laughed and immediately said in English, 'Not foreign, Inuk.' She introduced herself as Qila Rasmussen. She worked at the airport cleaning and was coming off an early shift. 'First time in Kangerlussuaq?' she asked, using the country's Greenlandic name.

Edie nodded. A bus drew close and was caught momentarily in the crowd. Edie, who knew nothing about Greenlandic politics, said, 'Why do they care so much?'

For an instant, her new friend looked taken aback and she thought she might have offended her.

'We're sick of foreigners interfering in our country.' The young woman lowered her voice. 'I'd be there with them but I have four kids to think about and I need my job.'

The bus pulled up, and Qila stood aside to let Edie get on. She spoke to the bus driver in Danish and helped Edie pick out the correct money for a ticket. They walked down the aisle, Edie selected a seat and Qila tucked in beside her and the bus moved off, shaking and roaring. The only vehicle Edie had ever encountered of similar size was the Autisaq sewage truck, but this bus was louder and rattled along at enough speed to be alarming. She looked out of the window and bit her lip.

They passed by mountains, less craggy than those on Ellesmere but, despite the heat, still snow-coated, bisected by a metal line on which hung what looked like drying racks.

'Do you like skiing?'

Edie turned her head away from the window and gave Qila a blank look.

'The ski lift.' Qila pointed at the metal line.

'We don't have all that much snow where I'm from.' She felt safe enough with this woman. 'It's more rock and ice.' Then she thought of Joe, skiing his way back from Craig Island, half delirious.

They passed beside a long, low building the shape of a door wedge and above it on a mountain slope, a cross.

'You a believer?' Qila asked, suddenly.

Edie looked out of the window to the cross then away across the willow. 'I believe in all sorts of things.'

'We're Christians here,' Qila said quietly. 'Except for a few *qalunaat* who don't believe in anything.'

The road busied between two crags, then fell gradually towards the town. They passed a sign reading 'H. J. Rinks-vej' which looked like the name of the road. In Autisaq, everyone called the streets Street One and Street Two, but no one could agree on which was which.

Buildings began to appear, spread out across low rocks. They trundled on up and soon they could see the whole of Nuuk. Though she knew it was small by southern standards, to Edie's eyes, the town seemed impossibly crowded.

They passed a boxy white building set into the rock and surrounded by carpets of Arctic willow.

Qila said: 'The Hans Egede church. Some people think he was kind of a hero. Have you heard of him?'

Edie shook her head.

'A missionary. He came looking for Viking settlements and got us instead.' She laughed a bitter laugh. 'Still, he was a good man, took the time to learn our language, translated the Bible.'

The bus driver hooted at someone outside, who returned the greeting with a wave.

Qila said: '"Our father, who is in heaven, give us this day our daily harbour seal." That was Egede. We're just about to pass his house.'

They were on the coastal road now, a street so busy with buildings and people that it made Edie's head spin. A way down, the bus slowed to a halt and the doors opened with an alarming hiss. Qila stood up.

'Time to get out.'

They shuffled down the aisle and stepped onto the pavement beside a long, low A frame building painted reddish brown. Edie put her bag down and looked about. The air bore the familiar Arctic smells of dogs and drying fish.

Edie turned to Qila and awkwardly held out a hand to say goodbye.

'Where are you staying?' Qila said.

They were standing before a series of vast glass-and-concrete cliffs set back from the shore.

'Here, the Norblok apartments. We're in Blok 7 . . . The kids are out on the land with their father. There's plenty of room.'

The blank entranceway, steel-fronted elevator, the dreary, concrete stairs and thin, stained corridors were so alien it was hard to imagine any human life, let alone Inuit, who were used to their freedom, being able to survive in so strange a place. As Edie trudged up the steps behind her hostess (the elevator didn't seem to be working), she wondered if Qila ever asked her god why she and her children were forced to live like seagulls perched on cliffs.

They reached the fourth floor and turned left down a corridor smelling deliciously of boiled seal, past five identical doors, each shouldered by two tiny windows through which vague shapes buckled and swung. At the sixth door, Qila stopped.

'This is us.'

The apartment was larger than the tiny windows suggested. The walls were painted in bright colours and with the early afternoon light streaming in the place gave off a cheerful air. The view outside was of the sea with a patch of headland to the north just visible. Edie moved to the window and looked down. Below her were streets and, on either side, apartment blocks exactly like this one.

A slightly older woman wandered into the room from somewhere at the back, bearing a striking resemblance to Qila. She spoke at first in Greenlandic, then, after Qila said something, broke into English, introducing herself as Qila's older sister, Suusaat.

'*Qalunaat* call me Susie.'

She moved across the living room to the kitchenette and put the kettle on. Looking back over her shoulder she flashed a smile. 'But you can call me Suusaat.'

They sat sipping sweet coffee – another novelty for Edie, who generally drank tea – and eating delicate little nuggets of fried blubber.

'Come to see family?' Suusaat asked politely.

'Not exactly,' Edie said. She'd mapped out a story at the aiport in Iqaluit, where she'd changed planes. 'More like to do right by family.'

Suusaat passed round the snack. 'Oh?' She sounded intrigued.

Qila interjected: 'Edie's from . . .' She laughed. 'I don't know where.'

'Umingmak Nuna, Ellesmere.'

'You have relatives up at Qaanaaq?' A wary note had crept into Suusaat's voice.

The Nares Strait between Qaanaaq and Ellesmere was barely thirty kilometres wide and frozen solid for nine months of the year. Until relatively recently families regularly crossed over from Qaanaaq to hunt musk oxen at Hazen. Travel between the two places was now discouraged. In the navigation season the Canadian Coastguard patrolled the area and the Ellesmere police were required to report any Greenlander found on Ellesmere to the RCMP in Ottawa. Many Ellesmere Islanders were at least distantly related to the Qaanaaq Inuit.

'My great-great-great-grandfather was from Etah, near Qaanaaq,' she said, in answer to the question.

The two women flashed each other a look of alarm. Suusaat hissed something at her sister, which Edie did not understand. Qila put her hand on her sister's arm to reassure her.

'Qila's job is terribly important to us, as a family,' Suusaat said, her tone insistent. 'Particularly now I've lost mine. We can't really afford any more trouble.'

Edie was no clearer. 'I'm not at all clever,' she said. 'In fact, probably the opposite.'

Qila said: 'Suusaat was on the classifieds desk of the Greenlandic newspaper, *Kangiryuarmiut*.'

Suusaat took up the tale. 'I feed the odd story to the editorial department. At least, I used to. A week ago I came across some information about the new sports centre. Confidential information. It doesn't matter how. I guess you've heard about the sports centre opening?'

Edie thought back to her conversation with the Inuk at the info desk and nodded.

'My source discovered that it was Fyodor Belovsky, a Russian oil billionaire, who'd put up the money. Belovsky never invests in any country unless he intends to interfere in its politics. Worse, he wanted his donation to be anonymous. I passed the story on to editorial but they wouldn't touch it, so I ran it as a classified. Some people read it and decided to stage a protest. I didn't really think so many people would care. Anyway, I lost my job.'

'When you mentioned having relatives near Qaanaaq we thought you might be involved in the demonstration,' Qila added. 'Because of the dig up near there?'

Edie felt bewildered. Her thoughts had been only to find the owner of the green plane and track down the two men who had flown into Autisaq posing as hunters; men who, she was convinced, had flown over Craig in the same plane the day Andy Taylor disappeared. But the mention of a Russian – and of oil – had ignited her curiosity. Maybe there was no connection between this Russian and the ones who had washed up in Autisaq, but it seemed important to find out.

'Look, I'm not out to cause you any trouble . . .'

'In that case, let's not talk about it,' Qila said decisively.

Picking up Edie's bag, she motioned for her to follow, then pointed to a bedroom door.

'My sons, Tomas and Ortu, share this room. Pardon the mess.' She threw open the door and announced that supper would be in thirty minutes.

Inside, the room was the same tangle of plastic toy trucks and seal bones as Joe and Willa's, the same fug of dust, sweat and accumulated farts. She unpacked her things and sat on the bed. The weight of the last few months pressed down and her eyes began to drift.

She rose later to the sound of knocking. Supper was on the table. It was unexpectedly dark for summer and a low, greenish light was pouring in from outside. She went to the window and looked down, expecting to see a lamppost, then soon realized the light was coming from the sky itself, the colour of emeralds, greener than anything Edie had ever seen on Ellesmere, and miasmic, like the residue of something long since passed. She watched it move, billowing and swaying like a flag, though there was almost no wind. Living so far to the north of the auroral oval, she had hardly ever seen the Northern Lights and never in this formation. The spectacle seemed to transfer its energy to her and she felt suddenly brave and full of purpose.

It was later than she thought. Qila had knocked on her door a while before and, getting no response, delayed the meal. Supper was a stew of halibut and potatoes. The sisters made small talk but it was no good trying to pretend. Eventually, over coffee, Edie told them about Joe, about how he had seen a green plane just before he had died and that she had come to Greenland to trace it.

'Johannes Moller,' Qila said, then clocking Edie's expression of surprise she continued, 'I work at the airport, remember. If there's something dirty going on, Moller usually has a hand in it.' She seemed to hesitate for a moment.

'Joe wasn't my blood, Qila,' Edie said, 'but I swear, he was the same to me as Tomas and Ortu are to you.'

The two sisters sat in silence for a while, then Qila shot a look at Suusaat, who nodded.

'A couple of months ago, two Russian anthropologists got permission to study some of the remains of the old Thule whalebone houses up near Etah. Moller took them up there. Some fishermen saw them disturbing old graves.' Qila bit her lip. 'The authorities don't seem to want to do anything about it. We think there's a connection with Belovsky. Our source said the Russians were wearing Beloil caps.'

The pieces were beginning to fit together. It was possible that these two Russians weren't the same as those who had pitched up in Autisaq demanding to be taken to Craig, but they could at least be working for the same man. The thought that Zemmer and Beloil might be after the same thing set Edie's heart knocking inside its box. 'You think Belovsky bought off the authorities with a sports centre?'

'Of course,' Qila said. 'It's an election year.'

Suusaat took up the story. 'Which is why I got fired for blowing the whistle. The editor of *Kangiryuarmiut* is in bed with the ruling party.'

'Why Belovsky might be in the business of desecrating

Inuit graves, we don't know,' Qila continued. 'Given his business interests, you'd think it had something to do with oil, but the industry here is really tightly regulated. It's unlikely that the government would grant a company with the reputation of Beloil an exploration licence. Besides, all the current interest is in offshore drilling. No land-based exploration has ever really got anywhere in Greenland. Whatever Belovsky wants up there, it's not oil.'

Edie's throat felt tight. A plan was beginning to come together in her mind.

'Would you show me the way to Bar Rat?'

The two sisters frowned. Eventually Qila said:

'If that's really what you want, OK. Moller usually goes late.'

They washed up the dishes, then Edie and Qila went out into the ash-hued night. The aurora had vanished and the grid of lights emanating from the Norblok apartments illuminated the women's path. Qila stopped before a dingy two-storey building, which appeared to be in darkness.

'It's here,' pointing to a door at the top of a small set of stairs. 'But you have to ring on the bell.' She put a hand on Edie's shoulder. 'I saw you at the airport talking to Pedr. I was just coming off shift. We collect our payslips from the office next door.'

'Is that why you approached me at the bus stop?'

Qila shrugged. 'If you'd been *qalunaat* I probably wouldn't have, but you're Inuk and you seemed *pivinik*.' She took a step back. 'Like you wanted to be useful.' She gave a small smile. 'I knew you were after something. Be careful.'

Edie returned the smile.

'Say Julia sent you. We'll expect you back later.' And with that she turned and started to pick her way back up the track.

Edie called after her. 'Who's Julia?'

The reply came back mixed with laughter. 'My Danish name.'

Not long after Edie's knock, a large, bearded *qalunaat* came to the door. He made a point of looking the tiny figure standing on the other side up and down, then said something in Danish. Edie introduced herself and repeated Julia's name.

'I'm looking for Johannes Moller.'

'Not a Greenlander, eh?' the man replied, switching seamlessly into English.

'No.'

The *qalunaat*'s smile melted into his beard, though whether he was sneering or simply amused Edie couldn't tell.

'We can always use new ones.'

He ushered her through a corridor then out of a door at the back into another, much smaller building.

'Now I see why it's called Bar Rat,' Edie said.

The *qalunaat* let out a belly laugh. '*Rat* is Danish.' He pumped his fist up and down. 'It means joystick, sweetheart.'

He opened the door and waved her in. 'Enjoy.'

Edie had seen enough TV cop shows to know she was in some kind of sex club. A few men, mostly *qalunaat*, were sitting around tables surrounded by half-clad, mostly native, women. Some were playing cards, others drinking and talking. The air was thick and acrid with cigarette smoke and Edie could detect, somewhere beneath it, the tang of marijuana.

The bearded *qalunaat* led her over to a table in the corner where a huge, red-faced blond man in his late fifties was playing chess with a smaller, younger Inuk.

'Julia sent this one. She's foreign.'

Moller looked up. Moller's chess partner looked up. The Inuk said:

'They're usually better looking. And younger.'

Edie swallowed the knot gathering in her throat. 'Go find yourself a fuck, Little Man, I need fifteen minutes with your friend.'

The Inuk man let out a contemptuous snort.

'Sweetheart, it looks like you need one more than me.'

It wasn't often that Edie resorted to brute force, but sometimes there was just no alternative. This was one of those times. Swiping the Inuk man's queen from the board and grabbing his hair, she thrust the chess piece firmly up his nose. He gave a sharp cry and winced. A bubble of blood oozed out then grew into a thin trickle.

'With you, I can see a fuck isn't likely to take more than a few seconds,' she said. 'So for the remaining fourteen minutes, you and your whore will just have to make polite conversation.'

The man stood, bowed over his nose, and shuffled away.

Moller gave her an admiring look.

She introduced herself as Maggie Kiglatuk, using her mother's name.

'I'm going to need a plane.'

'Where to?' Moller wiped his hand across his mouth. He looked oddly perky all of a sudden. Edie got the sense that he needed the business.

'Qaanaaq.'

His face fell. He made a dismissive gesture with his hand. 'Air Greenland fly up once a week. You can buy a ticket at the airport.'

'No, I need a charter.'

She knew enough about the scheduled flights to realize that she didn't have the money for a one-way ticket, let alone a return. Besides, she didn't want to appear on any passenger lists. Her plans had just got more complicated. She wanted to check on the Russians up in the north, hoping they were the same two who had flown into Autisaq on Moller's plane, perhaps even the same two who had flown over Craig the day Andy Taylor disappeared. 'There'd be eight of us, and we'd need picking up on Ellesmere.' She was about to say Autisaq, then stopped herself. It was better that she kept as much of her true identity to herself as possible. 'At Kuujuaq. Could you do that?'

Moller considered a moment. 'Don't you people usually travel over the ice?'

She'd anticipated this.

'It'll be mostly elders, going to see relatives. The ice across Smith Sound is really rough. Besides, the government is paying.'

Moller suddenly looked extremely interested.

'We don't usually fly over to Canada north of Baffin because the katabatic winds can be tricky. It wouldn't be cheap, you understand, but we've done it before. My associate, Hans, he's Inuk, like you, he can fly a midge through a tornado.'

'Well, if you've done it before . . .' This was going better than she'd anticipated.

'We've taken scientists, you know, those kind of folk.' He craned about, searching for someone, then pointed to a man sitting at the bar. 'You want to meet Hans, I'll call him over.'

Edie squinted through the cigarette smoke until she recognized the pilot who had brought the two Russian men into Autisaq several weeks back. The odds on the Russians in Qanaaq being the same men who had gone hunting with Sammy had just shortened considerably.

'Not now,' she said. She was pretty sure he hadn't seen her in Autisaq, but she didn't want to take any chances at this moment. 'I'd need to check out your credentials first.'

Moller opened his pack of cigarettes and offered them to Edie before taking one himself.

'Sit down, Maggie, be friendly.'

Edie sat.

'Licences, permissions, we got those.'

'I was thinking more by way of a trial run. Next time you're going up to Qaanaaq, I could come along, check it out.'

Moller looked sceptical.

'Our elders are very precious to us.'

Moller nodded, took another drag from his cigarette and stubbed it out on the table.

'What the hell,' he said, finally. 'Be outside Egede's church at five.' He checked his watch. 'Seven hours from now. We're doing a cargo drop, you can tag along. If the weather is as good as the forecast says we'll be in Qaanaaq tomorrow afternoon.'

Back out in the street, Edie found a phone kiosk, went in and rang Derek Palliser's number, surprised at how glad she was to hear his voice. It was a short conversation. She told him she was going up to Qaanaaq, he asked her why and she said she couldn't say. He didn't like it but she wasn't ready to tell him what she suspected until she was more certain. Pride, most likely.

Signing off, she retraced the route back to Blok 7. The bell in Hans Egede's church was ringing ten as she opened the door of Qila's apartment. Inside, all was quiet except for the soft, muffled sound of breathing coming from one of the bedrooms. A single lamp dimly illuminated the living room and kitchenette. There was hot coffee in the machine and a note beside it with instructions written in misspelled English for sorting out the hot water. In her bedroom she found a newspaper clipping, with a note from Suusaat scrawled on the bottom.

Third standing from the left is Belovsky.

The picture was one of those stiff line-ups you often saw in the papers. Here it consisted of *qalunaat* men, a couple of dozen by the looks of it, aged mostly in their forties and fifties, grouped in two rows, the front one seated and the others standing behind them.

Beneath the picture was a caption written in what she took to be Danish, with the exception of the English words 'Arctic Hunters' Club' picked out in italics. She counted three in from the left, and saw a tall, square-built man with the neck of a walrus and the eyes of an orca. As a rule, you could divide the *qalunaat* men (and it was almost always men, though a few brought their wives to go duck hunting whilst they were chasing bear) who came up to the Arctic to hunt into two types: the lean, nostalgic kind and the raging superego. The print quality of the picture was poor, but Edie could tell that Belovsky was one of the latter.

She tiptoed to her room and tried to get some sleep before heading back out to meet Moller. She kept waking, disturbed by the feeling of being so close to some piece of the puzzle that lay just beyond reach. The third or fourth time, she checked her watch, and decided to rise. The sisters were still sleeping. She'd forgotten to turn off the coffee and now helped herself to what little remained. It was as bitter as walrus bile, though it had the desired effect of jolting her awake.

She picked up the photo and was about to slip it into her pack when her eye was drawn to a familiar face. Seated at the extreme right of the picture was a small, balding, slack-jawed man who looked as though he'd made an art form of the business dinner. She zoomed in, squinting for a better look. This fellow sported a brushy moustache, but in every other respect the match was exact. The man she was eyeballing was Felix Wagner.

A harder look only confirmed her suspicions. She knew that Taylor was connected to the Russians via the green plane and that Taylor and Wagner had some connection through Zemmer Energy. The photo proved there was also a link between Wagner and Belovsky. Was it possible the two Russians up in the north were associated with Wagner in some way? Who was Wagner working for, Beloil or Zemmer? And which of these were involved in Wagner's death?

Creeping around so as not to wake her new friends, Edie threw her toothbrush and underwear back into her backpack, picked up the photo, slid it into her pack as well, and went out on the street. The temperature differential between day and night was much more noticeable here in Nuuk, so much further to the south than Autisaq, and Edie quickly grew chilled in the deep grey pre-dawn mist, but she was too anxious about meeting Moller to go back and reorganize her clothes. During one of her many wakeful periods last night, she'd found herself worrying about what she would do when she got to Qaanaaq.

Now, waiting for Moller to arrive, she was anxious that he had tricked her. She decided if Moller hadn't showed up by five fifteen she would start making her way to the airport and would remain there until she found him. Her instincts told her to be very careful. She was heading into danger, but the hunter in her told her she was also closing in.

At almost exactly five, she heard the sound of an engine and a battered-looking jeep appeared. As it neared she could just see Moller's white face illuminated in the gloom. The vehicle slowed then came to a stop beside her, Moller threw the door open and she clambered inside. The Inuk pilot, Hans, sat in the back seat. He showed no signs of recognizing her.

'Hey.' She threw him a sympathetic look and got no response.

The airport was deserted, save for a nightwatchman

who nodded at Moller and let them through. The jeep bumped across the service area and halted before a tatty-looking office building. Inside was a row of lockers. Moller drew out a key, opened one of the lockers, took out a file and stashed it away in his bag.

She helped them load up some boxes and an hour or so later the green Twin Otter took off with Moller at the controls. Climbing rapidly above low summer clouds, they headed west with the wind, then at twelve hundred metres Moller turned the little plane and they began to edge north along the coast. Once they had left Nuuk behind, Moller pulled down the sun screener, drew out the file he'd removed from his locker, and began making entries into it. Beside him, Hans stared out of the window, lost in thought.

Down below, the beginnings of the nautical dawn cracked the horizon. How odd, Edie thought, to have lived your whole life in the south, below the Circle, never to have seen the midnight sun nor lived through the velvety blackness of a polar winter day. You had to feel sorry for southerners, even the Inuit ones. Especially the Inuit ones.

The wind blew up and they found themselves bumping and shaking through a thick band of cloud obscuring the coastline below. The little plane jagged from side to side, plunged, then ballooned upwards once more. Though jumps and falls were no more alarming to Edie than a ride in the skiff across a summer swell, the movement brought on nausea and to distract herself she passed the time replaying scenes from *The Gold Rush* in her mind.

Before long, in the gaps between the clouds, the great blue crescent of Disko Bay appeared, closed in at its northern rim by Umanak Fiord and to the east by the ice at the mouth of the Kangia glacier. Beyond Kangia the ice field at Sermeq Kujalleq spread out as far as the eye could see.

'Take a good look,' Moller shouted from the front. 'And

wave it goodbye. Another twenty years . . .' He drew a hand across his throat.

A little further along they passed a handful of finger fiords, smaller and thinner than those on Ellesmere, and speckled with stands of stunted spruce.

A while later, a ringing in the ears and an empty feeling in the belly alerted Edie to the plane's descent and she realized she must have been asleep; her eyelashes were heavy with tiny flakes of crust, like new ice. Suddenly they were among high, wispy clouds and below them stretched a black basalt coastline. To the east the dark rock gave way to striped gneiss. The sea lay below them, funnelled here and there into fiords and open-mouthed bays. There were no more trees.

As they headed further north the sea grew increasingly flecked with chunks of floating ice. About midday, they passed over the scattered buildings of Thule Airbase just south of Qaanaaq. From here, the coast of Ellesmere was clearly visible across the grey-blue expanse of Smith Sound. A small, sharp wave of panic travelled up Edie's spine. What she was doing was reckless and ill-thought-out. It was clear to her now that Wagner, Taylor, maybe even Joe, seemed to be bit players in some larger game.

Below her, she saw innumerable fragments of something or other caught up in a kind of current, whirling around a central axis.

'Garbage gyre,' shouted Hans, picking up on her interest. 'Cruise-ship junk, most likely.'

The thing looked more like the pictures of galaxies Edie had seen in school textbooks. Or a black hole.

They gradually lost altitude until, at Qaanaaq, the plane passed low over the source of the gyre, a giant hull of a ship in a deep-water harbour. On the quayside knots of camera-wielding *qalunaat* milled about.

'Like he said, garbage,' observed Moller drily.

13

Edie and Hans stood at the entrance to the storage facility building while Moller fiddled with the padlock on the door.

'The boss says you've got family here,' Hans said. 'I was born in Siorapaluk, less than a sleep away.' He was speaking in a kind of Inuktitut that Edie found easier to understand than the native dialect in Nuuk. He said it was Inuktun, the dialect of the polar region.

'What took you down south?'

'I guess I sold out,' Hans said. 'And now I work for this jerk.' He gave her a penetrating stare. 'You're not really here to hire a plane, are you?'

Edie hadn't anticipated this. She began to fumble for an answer, but he said, 'Don't sweat. It's not like I'm going to tell anyone.'

Moller prised off the padlock and threw open the door to reveal a gloomy single room stacked with boxes behind which he had set up a tiny and rudimentary living area with two sleeping bags, an electric heater and a primus stove. While Moller went inside, Hans went to the ATV and started hauling boxes. Edie followed him.

'How did you know?' she hissed.

'On the plane,' he said. 'I could smell your fear.'

Moller reappeared. 'Without wishing to disturb your cosy native get-together, Hans and I have work to do.'

Hans flipped a thumb at his boss, and said in Inuktun, 'He can't understand and it drives him crazy.'

Moller, to Edie: 'Any case, don't you have family to go to?'

She darted a glance at Hans but he gave no sign that he was about to give her away.

'They're out at summer camp,' she lied, then, trying to sound casual: 'I'm gonna hang out in town till they come for me.'

Moller gestured towards the interior of the unit. 'You want to make yourself useful before you go, put some coffee on.'

The two men returned to the plane. Edie stepped into the shed and took in the interior. Immediately inside the door was a series of hooks on which hung ropes, waterproofs and a harpoon. Below them was a shelf holding a couple of discarded primus stoves and a box of ammo. On the floor resting on a tarp, between an assortment of rusty cans, was an ancient-looking .22, barrel-up and covered with dust. Moller's bag was lying on the table next to a camp bed.

Quickly, she opened it and slid out the file of flight manifests she'd seen on the plane. She flipped through to April, running her fingers down the lists of clients and their bills of lading. Her fingers chased forward through the pages. Then she saw it. 'April 22, Qaanaaq–Craig Ø, R. Raskolnikov, P. Petrovich.' The word '*kontant*' followed, along with a figure in US dollars. She recognized the two names from the records in Autisaq as the same fake ones used by the two duck hunters who went to Craig with Sammy. It seemed overwhelmingly likely now that the two men digging up graves were the same as those who had passed over Craig the day Andy Taylor disappeared.

The sound of boots came from outside. Scrambling to replace the file back inside the bag, Edie managed to wheel round just as Moller appeared through the door.

'That coffee ready?'

'Make your own coffee. I just remembered my cousin said she might come in early. I have to go.' She was already wondering how to get herself out to the dig site. 'I'll catch the scheduled flight back next week. I'll be in touch about the charter.'

An airport worker gave her a ride into town. Qaanaaq itself was the usual Greenlandic configuration of jauntily painted wooden A frames fixed to the rock substrate. There was a serviceable-looking harbour and what appeared to be a store and a church. Edie was struck only by the number of *qalunaat* decked out, for the most part, in new and expensive cold weather gear roaming the streets like hungry bears and among them, Inuit.

She walked along with her backpack slung across her shoulder, unnoticed in all the busyness, and after a short while came to the local post office and telecoms centre which served as an information point for tourists and scientists. Conscious that she would pass as neither, she pushed open the door and walked in.

An Inuk man looked up from his desk and greeted her with a quizzical smile, which she met with a relaxed one of her own.

'I'm working in the ship's laundry,' she began in Inuktitut. 'But I do a little bit of guiding on the side, earn some extra cash.'

'Right,' the man replied in Inuktun, smiling more broadly now. He introduced himself as Erinaq. 'From across the water, aren't you?'

She could see he was already on her side.

'Originally.' Trying to put on her best winning look. 'I need a boat, a bit of fishing equipment.'

His face fell. 'Nothing doing. Every single craft that's

not already out is full with tourists. You won't get a boat in Qaanaaq, or not till the *Arctic Princess* sails in a couple of days.'

She saw him looking at her hands. There was a moment of tension.

He said: 'Look, I may work at a desk, but I'm still Inuk.' He pointed to her hands. 'I know rifle callouses when I see them. Unless you've found a way to shoot laundry clean, I'd bet any money you're a hunter without a permit.'

Edie shrugged: 'And if I am?'

Erinaq's face split into a smile. 'Good luck to you. Ask me, permits are for *qalunaat*.'

She went down to the quayside where the *Arctic Princess* was tied up and considered her options. The most sensible one was to make some excuse to return to Nuuk with Moller, and wait till the Russians came back through the city, which, she supposed, they must at some point. She discounted it in a second. Too full of uncertainties. Besides, she was in the mood for confrontation. If Joe had been murdered, she rationalized, and Beloil had something to do with it, it would be easier to confront the Russians here, where they were off guard and, she supposed, unsupported. If she was lucky they would assume she was out fishing or hunting and ignore her. If she wasn't, and they were paranoid, they might suppose she had come to try to stop them digging up graves. Either way, so long as she held her cover, they'd be unlikely to feel threatened by her, a lone woman.

She'd need a boat and a gun. The gun was no problem. She'd already staked out the .22 rifle in Moller's shed. The boat was going to be harder.

As she sat thinking, a *qalunaat* man approached.

'You coming to the crew party tonight?'

'I'm not invited.'

As she spoke, an idea suddenly came to mind. She

glanced up at the ship and counted the lifeboat stations. There were four, each containing a Zodiac inflatable. 'But I'd like to come,' she added.

'Good.' He winked at her. 'From nine. Just tell the guards that Nils sent you.'

She winked back.

From the quayside she went directly to the store and bought a few strips of maktaq, and a half-kilo of caribou jerky. At the information office there had been a small café. There she ordered hot sweet tea and some kind of stewed meat. No one seemed to take much notice of her.

At six the café closed and she left. The moon was in its up phase, and the tide would be coming in. She had already worked out the timing. The walk to Moller's shed would take her an hour, maybe a little more if the going proved rougher than it had seemed on the ATV. The walk back down the quay would take quite a bit longer, because she would be laden. Once she'd got on board the ship and released the Zodiac, she'd need to find somewhere close by where she could hide until the early hours when everyone would either be sleeping or too drunk to notice her leaving the harbour.

She reached the airport in good time, walking slowly to avoid breaking into a sweat, and coming up crouched and low onto the ridge beside the landing strip where she was least likely to be spotted. Reaching into her bag she took out her hare-fur mufflers and tied them over her kamiks. Up here the wind hummed and the haul ropes on the wind sock clanked against the retaining pole. There was sufficient ambient noise to cover her, she thought, but the strip was gravelled and would crunch underfoot and she didn't want to take any chances.

On the far side of the strip she turned and began to

pick her way slowly downwind towards Moller's unit. You never knew if there might be dogs. She made the final approach as she would stalking an animal, step by step, knees bent, breath quiet and shallow, torso perfectly still. Creeping around the back she squatted down out of the wind, pressed her ear to the wall against which the sleeping bags were strewn inside, and waited.

Edie slid round to the unit door and began very gradually to edge it open. Inside, all was dark. When the snoring continued, she slid in. The rifle and harpoon were where she was expecting them, on the wall beside the entrance. She reached out for the rifle first, feeling for the carry-strap and edging it away from the tarp. Slowly and with infinite care she lifted it and placed it over her shoulder. The box of ammo was next. Sliding her right thumb along the shelf she stopped at a small, crescent-shaped knot in the wood. With her thumb in the knot she marked out two widths with her left hand. Then, with her right she reached up and clasped the card box cover, feeling for the tell-tale fraying along the left edge. Lifting the box with both hands she swung it slowly through the air and into the side pocket of her pack. A close fit, it made a rustling noise against the nylon as it slid in.

Instantly, she froze, peering into the darkness, listening for the sounds of sleeping at the back of the unit. The snoring continued, tapering now into a soft hiss like that of a surprised harp seal. Relaxing, she reached into the dark once more. All she needed now was a length of rope, a net and a harpoon. The net was easy; she slung it across her pack and secured it with an elastic band. The harpoon was more challenging, the point getting stuck momentarily in the wooden shelf above it. Edie reached down, and, working very slowly, cut a groove in the floorboards with her hunting knife. The pole immediately relaxed and she slid it gently from its moorings. Until she could fashion a strap from the rope, she would have to carry it in her hand.

Last, she reached for the coil of rope itself, using her hands once more to measure fifteen widths to the right of the place where the harpoon had been. At the back, a body shifted in sleep. She waited for whoever it was to settle, steadied her heartbeat and focused once more. Slowly, she reached out for the rope, intending first to get its measure, knowing that she would have to lift the entire coil up and then out from the rusty nail on which it was hanging. With her free hand, she measured its heft. The coil was of old-fashioned hemp, not polyester as she'd supposed, and heavier as a consequence. Edie pushed the rifle further onto her back so that there was no danger of it falling forward, then she leaned in and with a hand on the coil very slowly heaved it upwards. There was a sudden twang and something metallic landed on the floor. Edie looked up and to the back of the shed and thought she saw something glitter. She focused on the spot, willing her eyes to find their night sight more quickly. Gradually, two small sparkles resolved themselves. Someone was looking at her.

There was a pause, an unbearable moment of tension and she found herself squinting into a thin light. Her right hand automatically left the rope and reached up to shield her eyes and in the shade of her palm she saw the pilot, Hans. Then the light clicked off and she was left for a moment standing in the sea of rusty brown and orange behind her eyes. She reached around her shoulder for the rifle then, realizing it was too late to load it and too dark to see, she grabbed the harpoon. The eyes continued to stare, but they did not move. Finally she heard a whisper, in Inuktun: '*Aivuk!*' Go!

She slung the coil of rope over her shoulder and backed rapidly towards the door. Once she was out she turned and ran, swinging her legs in a skiing motion, skimming across the hummocky muskeg, just as her mother had shown her many, many years before. The chase scenes she knew so well from the movies flipped unbidden through her mind and her breath pooled out into the chill air. When she reached the other side of the landing strip she stopped and looked back but there was no one following.

At the edge of the plateau, she gathered herself, took off her mufflers and quickly repacked her bag. Over the other side of the landing strip, Moller's shed lay obscured. Around her, the tundra glowed silver blue. She turned to face her destination. Though it was not dark, the lights of the *Arctic Princess* blazed in the harbour. Already Nuuk seemed like a world away. She took a deep breath and began her descent towards the sea.

It was well past midnight before she reached the quayside and stood before the ship. The gangplank was down and the vessel rose and fell softly on the swell. From inside there came the sound of music but there was no one on deck. It was cold, and the air smelled of ice. The harbour was empty.

Edie looked about to check she wasn't being watched and stepped onto the gangplank. The ship was older and scruffier than she'd imagined, the paint peeling, a light crusting of rust across the joints and rivets. The music was much louder than it had seemed on shore.

She slipped onto the main deck and took her bearings. There was no sign of any guard. It seemed they were all below, making the most of their passenger-free evening. Every so often female laughter broke through the beat and a tangy alcohol haze rose upwards on the breeze. If all went well, she'd have the Zodiac in the water in a matter of minutes. Feeling cheered by this thought, Edie began a slow slide around the darkened cabin rooms towards the aft deck.

She had reached the captain's cabin, when, with no warning, the deck door suddenly swung open and a man's face appeared. In the backlight from the corridor, she could see leathery skin fading out to silhouette. For a moment he seemed not to see her, then his gaze fell full on her face. He smiled the wavy smile of a drunk and stepped out onto the deck. Edie shrugged her right shoulder so the rifle and harpoon were hidden behind her back.

The man stared at her for a moment then said something in Danish.

Edie shrugged, hoping he would consider the gesture sufficient answer and return below deck.

'You're local?' he said, this time in English.

Edie nodded. 'Danish very bad. I clean.'

'Oh,' the man said. He tapped his nose with his finger. 'We are making a very big mess tonight.' He laughed at his own joke. 'Plenty for you to do.'

And with that he retreated back inside the ship and closed the deck door. She saw his shadow passing into the passenger cabin area, and then disappear.

Edie breathed out the thrumming in her chest. Then she slid onto the stern deck, avoiding the neat coils of rope and chain. Making her way around the railings she reached the Zodiac on the port side. The inflatable was in no better shape than its mother ship, but someone had at least bothered to pull a tarp over the outboard. Both oars were sitting inside, along with several coils of rope, a lifebelt and two large jerry cans marked 'gasoline' and 'water'. The holding ropes led up to a winch and the boat itself was enclosed in a kind of cradle. At the base of the winch itself was a large metal flap covering the controls. She gave the lowering button a small, experimental push. An alarmingly loud clanking sound started up. For a moment Edie froze, waiting for a nearby door to fling open and a security detail to come bounding out. Snatching up her bag, the rifle and harpoon she threw them under the tarp. That way if anyone did come she could feign innocence, say she was using the deck as a high lookout from which to spot seal moving in the water.

Quickly attaching ropes to the grab handles on each side, she passed them around both deck cleats to attach each to the winch with a hitch knot. She took out a piece of maktaq from her bag and used it to grease the winch and its handle. Then slowly, carefully, she began to turn the winch, easing in the lengths of rope. The winch responded to the greasing, the only sound coming from it a faint clicking as the rope torqued around the barrel.

She returned to the Zodiac and, using her hunting knife, carefully cut the cradle and the restraining ropes, waiting for the little boat to steady before beginning the slow process of letting out the winch ropes. At the other end of the ship, loud, off-key attempts at 'I Will Survive' drifted from the state room. When the ropes finally went slack, Edie pulled the winch lever into the locked position then set about tying Moller's rifle, the harpoon and her pack with bowlines onto a single rope so they could be lowered into the Zodiac afloat on the black water. Now there was no turning back. She took a deep breath to calm herself, grabbed at the rope and began to rappel down the ship's side.

Soon she was reaching out for the Zodiac, taking hold of the grab handles and pulling herself in. Cutting the keeper ropes, she pushed off from the *Princess* and began to row steadily out into open water. The sea loomed vast and inky, joined seamlessly at the horizon to the sky. The oars constantly hit bergy bits and scraped jarringly against growlers. Rowing close to the shore she followed the coastline until, looking back, all she could see of Qaanaaq was a faint bloom of light pollution far away. It was only then she allowed herself to turn towards the shore.

She slept in the boat on the beach and woke to the matt, chalky light of the summer day. She boiled water and melted a piece of jerky into it. The coast here was completely unknown to her, but the story of Welatok's journey had been passed down so meticulously across the generations that it felt oddly familiar. She intended to stop off at Siorapaluk, the last and most northerly settlement, pick up some food and get directions for the safest passage into Etah and the dig site.

The outboard started and the Zodie began bumping across the swell in a favourable wind so that by the time the sun was fully over the horizon, the settlement was already in view as a sprinkling of dots sitting below cliffs so jammed with dovekies and murres that they writhed like maggoty meat. As she approached, the smell of guano was almost overpowering. Before long, she guessed, the birds would be heading back south.

She pulled into the little bay then chuntered slowly up to a long jetty and tied up while two young boys and a girl of six or seven watched with a mixture of excitement and fear.

'Are you from the government?' one of the boys asked.

Edie pointed out across the water. 'No, from over there.'

The children looked at one another as though they'd never heard of such a thing. Eventually, the little girl said: '*Illiyardjuk*, an abandoned child?'

'*Immaluk*.' A long time ago.

'What are you now?' the girl asked, more boldly this time.

Edie thought about it. Finally she said, '*Saunerk*.' A bone.

Ever since Joe died, she had felt like the framework of some unfinished soul. The children laughed and led her to the store, diving about, shouting '*saunerk*, *saunerk*'.

Inside, the cashier, a thick-set Inuk with a bloodless-looking face, followed her around the aisles, keeping a few paces behind, pretending to be assessing the stock. She in turn pretended not to notice him, casually picking out another box of ammunition, some rope, a flensing knife, and another plastic jerry can for water, then adding to this a large tin of syrup, a few pieces of cinder toffee and some tea bags.

'Going hunting?' he said, ringing up her things.

'You could say that.'

The man began packing her purchases into a plastic bag. He looked up and met her eye. The look was not friendly.

He handed her the change from her shopping, pressing the coins into the palm of her hand so hard they left little rings.

The children were standing outside the store, wearing hopeful expressions. She pulled the toffee from her bag and watched them reach out for it, whooping and racing away.

She carried the shopping back to the Zodiac without running into anyone else. Apart from the children, the settlement seemed dead. From the numbers of seabirds and the sheltered coves she could tell that it would be good hunting here. The locals were probably out, stocking up their meat caches in time for the dark period.

The thought brought on a wave of homesickness. This time last year she would have been out seal hunting with Joe. Now instead she was hunting for the truth and that was like hunting a fish in murky water with nothing but your hands. You could never see the whole of it, only little flashes here and there, and when you reached out, it slid from your grasp.

The turf and sod huts of Etah, long since abandoned, lay at the base of a small fiord surrounded by mountainous crags whose multiple erosions provided the nesting ledges and coves for dovekies. Like those further south at Siorapaluk, the birds were preparing to return to sea, but for now their presence created a tremendous noise and stink. Anyone on land would not hear the noise of the engine over the great chorus of bird chatter. To be on the safe side, Edie cut the engine anyway, and carried on with the oars.

At the far end of the fiord, a launch bobbed at anchor, its keeper tied several times around a boulder on the beach. Of the two Russians there was no sign. She found a small concavity in the cliffs with a long, concealed strip of pebbled beach, hauled the Zodie beyond the tide line and tied up to a nearby rock with a buntline hitch. She meant to find the men and then, what?

What would she do with them then? Kill them? If they had killed Joe, she would pull the trigger without a second thought. But in her heart she already knew it wouldn't be like that. She suspected that whatever she had stumbled upon was bigger than Taylor and Wagner, bigger even than Joe. Most likely the Russians were minor players, grunts in some huge and complex enterprise that would eventually render the Arctic the same as everywhere else, a landscape held to ransom by human need.

She imagined corralling the men into the launch at gunpoint, taking them the fifty kilometres across open water to Ellesmere. Then what? They'd still be hundreds of kilometres from the nearest settlement. Perhaps she could leave them there, tied up, and head down to Autisaq to fetch help. But abandoning them like that would make them hopelessly vulnerable to wolves and bear.

She thought once more of Joe. She was pretty sure now that he'd witnessed Andy Taylor's death and someone had murdered him to keep him quiet. What she couldn't work out was how they had managed it. A plane landing or even an unfamiliar snowmobile arriving in the settlement would have been spotted and reported.

Felix Wagner came to mind, then the zig-zag footprint with the ice bear at its heart. Everything pointed to the possibility that the Russians, or at least their handlers at Beloil, had an accomplice in Autisaq. Which meant that whoever had killed Joe was someone he knew. The thought winded her. How could anyone who knew the man believe that Joe would have taken his life? The betrayal made her nauseous.

The light was fading now and the sky was too cloudy for the sun to break through. A sudden feeling of exhaustion swept over her and it struck Edie that she had not slept a whole night since Joe died. For now, she needed to rest. Finding the men would be easy, she was sure of that. In all this vast space there was nowhere to hide from eyes who knew what to look for. They would have left traces, prints in the muskeg, disturbances of the willow and old fire circles.

Creeping back across the shale, Edie clambered into the Zodie. Tonight she would sleep inside the boat with the tarp pulled over the top.

She woke with the strong sense that someone was holding something to her head. Then she registered the gun. The man on the other end was the skinny Russian who had landed in Autisaq a few months before, claiming to want to hunt duck. She'd seen him strolling along the road towards the store. It was a relief, in a way, to know her search was over. This was the encounter she had been hoping for, albeit not in quite the manner she'd imagined. Her hunch had been right.

'Sleep well, Maggie Kiglatuk?'

It was so obvious, she kicked herself. Hans had had second thoughts and betrayed her to Moller who had taken the precaution of phoning his clients. In her mind she hastily reassembled what little information she'd given the two pilots. Had she provided them with any reason at all to connect her to their activities on Craig? No, she was sure not. Immediately, she felt a lot calmer. They would presume she was one of the protestors against the grave digging, someone with family in the area who was keen to protect a burial site. So long as they didn't connect her to Autisaq or to Craig itself, she wouldn't be enough of a threat for them to want to see her dead.

The man motioned her out of the boat. Behind him stood the blond, who had strange iceberg eyes, his hands on the Zodiac's outboard motor. She saw him pull out the fuel hose from the tank. He fired up the engine cord and the machine sputtered, roared for a short while then fell dead.

'What a pity,' the blond said. 'It broke.'

'Luckily, we have come to the rescue,' the skinny one chipped in.

He gestured at Edie with his rifle. It was not a make she recognized. Russian, she guessed. She nodded in the direction of her backpack. The skinny guy smiled and shook his head.

'Good sense of humour,' he said, picking up her rifle and harpoon. He unzipped the bag, peered inside and threw it back in the Zodiac.

They scrambled along the shale then up a steep slope, Edie sandwiched between the two men, until they were standing on top of the cliffs, the dovekies clattering beneath them. The sun had begun its circle low above the horizon and the air was so clear they could see the purple shadows of Ellesmere Island to the west. Tramping on, Edie conscious always of the rifle aimed at the back of her head, they passed below them on a wide stretch of shale beach the remnants of the great whalebone huts built by the Thule, who had travelled east across the ice from Canada more than a thousand years before. Edie stopped momentarily to catch her breath, but the blond hurried her on with a hiss. It began to spit, the rain spiny with ice blown in from the northwest.

Ahead of her, Skinny turned and shouted something in Russian to the blond with the rifle making up the rear. He replied and they quickened the pace. They were passing alongside a gravelly plateau, scattered with vast slabs of grey rock on which cotton grasses fluttered. Up ahead, a makeshift path gave onto a slope leading back down towards the sea, and they turned off and began their descent along the cliffs.

Below them, on a stretch of shale at the bottom of the fiord, was a sprinkling of old sod huts, marking the now abandoned Polar Inuit settlement of Etah, once the most northerly habitation on the planet. It struck Edie more forcefully than ever that this was not human terrain, but a land governed by other, more ancient, rules. She watched Skinny striding along fifty metres ahead. Her earlier plans now seemed ludicrously over-simplified. Even were she to extricate herself from his particular situation, it would be far too dangerous, too logistically complex to try to round up the men and take them back to Ellesmere. Besides, she still didn't have the evidence she needed. Better to stay put and try to work out exactly what the two men were doing. So long as they continued to think of her as just a protestor, she had some cover. From Skinny's confident manner, the unnecessary speed, she could see that he thought he had the land licked; but from their hastiness alone Edie knew that neither Russian truly understood the north. When the time came, Edie Kiglatuk meant to make the most of their ignorance.

The two men had set up camp beside the huts, using those that still offered some measure of protection from the wind and rain to house their equipment. From the size and depth of the fire circle, and the number of garbage bags lying inside one of the turf huts out of the way of bears, Edie guessed the men had been at camp for about a month.

Skinny directed Edie towards a hut nearest to the two sleeping tents and the two men followed her inside. The tinny aroma of damp hit her but the interior of the hut felt warm and free of draughts. The men had laid a tarp down and on it placed two fold-up chairs. It was to one of these that the blond now directed her while Skinny fetched a coil of rope from a kit bag in the corner and began to secure her hands and feet to the chair. The situation was slightly absurd, she thought, like something from a silent comedy, and if it weren't for the fact that it was taking all her energy not to be afraid she would have laughed.

The blond put down the rifle and began heating some coffee on one ring of a portable gas burner. On the other he placed a frying pan and into it a large dollop of fat from a tin.

'So, one of those natives who hates white men, huh?' His English was better than Skinny's but it was his friend who was the leader.

'Not *all* white men,' she said. 'But you definitely.' Knowing they had no idea of her real intention made her feel more secure.

The blond let out a thin laugh. He'd poured some batter into the frying pan and it now gave off a thick, slightly sour wheaty smell.

'Hungry? Too bad.' He poured some coffee into a plastic mug and brought it to her lips. She took a little and immediately spat it out.

'Without sugar it's disgusting.'

The blond shrugged. 'Moller said you were a handful.' He looked her up and down. 'A very *small* handful.'

Skinny burst in and gabbled something in Russian. From then on, the blond ignored her.

Not long afterwards, the two men headed out. Edie watched them go, waited a long, long time, then with tremendous effort, she rose and, taking the chair with her, shuffled on her knees to the entrance of the hut and looked about. There was the usual cluster of expedition paraphernalia stacked up neatly against the walls of another turf house: ropes, a couple of books, climbing gear, wet suits, several primus stoves and back-up gas canisters, an ice pick for chipping out sweet water-ice and a camera on a tripod. She wriggled and tried to work her hands loose, feeling for the knot, but from the position of the ropes she surmised that Skinny was some kind of mariner, because he had tied her with a perfect buntline hitch. There was no way of getting out of that one.

Rocking back and forward in the chair, taking tiny steps, Edie wormed her way towards the piles of equipment, hoping to find, if not a knife, then some kind of edge with which she might cut the rope. There was nothing, but as she manoeuvred the chair back to its original position, the back leg caught on one of the two books in the pile, sending it flying to the ground. Anxious not to give away what she had been doing, Edie turned the chair and by jigging up and down managed to flip the book over. As she did so, she noticed a book mark. Using her toe, she flicked the pages forward. The book was some kind of nineteenth-century printed diary, with entries divided up by date. Every so often she came across a lithograph, mostly of stereotypical Arctic scenes familiar to her from similar books in the Autisaq school library: strangely drawn bears and ragged, implausibly beached icebergs. A curio. She was about to push it back, when the page flipped and she found herself staring at the face of Joe Inukpuk. The image was so exact an impression of Joe that it was as though Edie had been thrust forward in time and was looking at her stepson twenty years from now. There he was, older and more weathered, but her stepson all the same. Yet his outfit was too old-fashioned to have come from anything but the past.

Beside the Inuk man stood a *qalunaat*. The two men were passing a knife between them. In the background were the cliffs and ice-crimped moraine of Northwestern Greenland and when Edie squinted at the picture it became clear that the two men were standing on exactly the same beach as the one the two Russian men had escorted her from only a few hours before. Beneath them was a caption, in Danish, of which Edie managed to make out two words: 'Karlovsky' and 'Welatok'. Her confusion fell away. The man she was looking at wasn't Joe at all but her great-great-great-grandfather, an ancestor she and Joe shared. Welatok must have met this man, Karlovsky, in Greenland, and either guided or traded with him. Could it be *Welatok*'s grave the Russians were looking for?

Edie shuffled her way to the front of the hut, pushed open the door with her head, and looked about. There, on the horizon, was a faint human presence. In front of her, at a distance of about ten metres, was a camera mounted on a tripod. She had an idea. Dropping to her knees she began very slowly to shuffle across the shale towards the camera. It was an exquisitely painful journey. Each time she put her knee down, the stones bit in through the layers of leather and cloth, spiking the skin. The most direct route left her too exposed – she assumed the men would have binoculars – so she was forced to wind her way around the remains of two of the turf huts for cover. As she lowered one knee and then the other, the points of shale in her skin drove in a little deeper so that by the time she reached the tripod her trousers were soft with blood and the skin on her knees burned like frostbite.

From this position it was impossible to shift backwards

in order to resume sitting on the chair so there was nothing for it but to take her weight on her knees once more to lift herself up to the camera. It was only by stretching as far as she could that she could raise herself high enough. In this position the shale bit savagely into her knees and the sharp edge of the chair sank into the skin of her back. She took a deep breath and thought, *this isn't Edie, this is Kigga and Kigga can do these things*.

Straining, she managed to put her eye to the viewer. Her heart sank. The lens was directed at just the wrong angle. She would have to find a way to pivot the camera thirty degrees to the right. Plus the zoom wasn't on. She took an agonizing step back on her knees and craned her neck. From that angle she could just see a button that looked as though it might be the zoom. Another couple of inches and she would be able to press it down with her chin. Approaching the camera once more Edie took a deep breath in, pressed down on her knees and reached up with the whole of her trunk. At last she felt the cool of the plastic case on her chin and, moving along gently until she felt the slight raise of the button, was about to open her jaw and press down when a piece of shale suddenly gave way under her left knee, sending her off balance. Unable to use her hands to save herself, she toppled sideways, the left side of her jawbone crunching onto the stones. She felt the bone dislocate from its socket and, moments later, a searing pain. When she looked up she saw the camera skewed at an improbable angle where she had dislodged it as she went down.

For a moment she wanted to give up. But only for a moment.

The first thing was to ignore the pain. She had a method for this, something her father had taught her. She sat with her eyes closed and replayed the scene in *Safety Last!*, with

Harold Lloyd eighteen storeys up hanging on to the hands of the giant clock, until the pain lay somewhere beneath the laughter and she could at least think clearly again. But it wouldn't be for long; pretty soon, the pain would take over once more. She needed to manoeuvre her jawbone back into its socket. By moving her foot as though she were about to tread on her toes, she was able to lift the knee on the dislocated side a little closer to her head. She took a huge breath, leaned over and pressed the dislocated jaw into the knee. The pain was so excruciating she thought she might black out, but soon she felt the pop of the jaw re-engaging and what had been unbearable became simply agonizing. Her face would swell around the dislocation, but she'd at least be able to use her mouth.

What she needed now, Edie thought, was some kind of stick she could hold between her teeth to prod the camera zoom. But where to find such a thing? The nearest tree lay two thousand kilometres to the south. She looked around. Edging herself across the shale she made her way past the fire circle towards the stack of equipment. Then something told her to take a knee-step back. There, among the charred remains of heather and the tiny nubs of willow twigs, she spotted a ballpoint pen that must have fallen from one of the men's pockets. The end had caught the flames, the plastic whorled into a mess of carbon and burned ink. She kneeled over it, bent across and with a tremendous effort of will craned her neck and plunged her face into the pile of ashes. She pulled back up onto her knees, and slowly, slowly, with the pen between her teeth, made her way across the shale to the tripod.

Positioning the camera with her head, she prodded the on switch then the zoom. There were a series of *inukshuk* on the bluff above the plateau and, below them, burial cairns. The Russians were busy removing the stones from the cairns. She backed off and, using the pen, let off a shot. The motor whirred in and shot off a few more frames.

Sweaty and weak, she now needed to get back to the hut before the men returned. There, taking advantage of the softness of the pressed mud floor, she was able to spear the front legs of the chair and, rocking back and forth, propel herself back upright into a sitting position. Her jaw pulsed and jammed, as though someone was using it for ball practice, but at least it was warm inside the hut and her sweat would not freeze before it had a chance to evaporate.

It began to get dark in the hut and though it was still light outside, Edie could already feel the drop in temperature signalling the approach of what would pass for twilight. Her knees ached and her jaw was swelling fast and for the first time she became conscious of a tremendous thirst. There was no sign of the men. She wondered if they might have just left her there to die.

A long time later, she heard voices then the sound of boots on the shale. The blond came in first.

'Oh, it's you,' he said, as though he'd forgotten her.

She peeled her tongue from the roof of her mouth, which left both with the feeling of having been stripped. 'I'm thirsty.'

The blond came over and untied her hands. He passed her a beaker of water and as he did so noticed the swelling of her jaw and the blood on her knees. He shot her a look, expecting an explanation, but she avoided his gaze.

'We get what we want, then we let you go,' he said, anticipating what was going through her mind. He was lying and he wasn't very good at it. Another reason to focus on him, Edie thought. His humanity made him vulnerable.

Skinny came in then. He saw Edie's face and looked impressed.

'She try and escape?' he said, passing the blond his rifle. 'Next time, use this.'

While the blond retied her wrists, Skinny swung the bag that was over his shoulder onto the ground and removed from it a handful of small rocks. The two men pulled out some equipment and began measuring, chatting away in Russian for a while. Edie tried to focus on the conversation, listening for familiar words, sounds. From time to time one of the men raised a rock to his mouth and licked it. One by one they threw the rocks outside.

Skinny started to fix the evening meal. The smells of cooking began to chase out the odour of damp. When the food was ready, Skinny poured out the contents of the pan into two bowls and handed one to the blond. The blond took a spoonful then pushed his plate away. An exchange of what sounded like insults followed, and then the blond turned to Edie and said in English:

'My friend thinks he is Auguste Escoffier.'

Edie shrugged.

'You try,' the blond said. He moved towards her and lifted the spoon to her mouth. 'Food is terrible, no?' he persisted, determined to recruit her to his cause.

Edie moved the food around her mouth. Her head was swimming in pain and her jaw prevented her from chewing but she wanted to seem obliging. Eventually, she swallowed. 'A little more salt, perhaps.'

The blond laughed. Another exchange of insults followed then Skinny made a sudden lunge for the frying pan, threw it across the hut and stormed out.

'Now my friend thinks he is artist,' said the blond, wearily.

Not long afterwards, Skinny swept back in toting a plastic carton. Snatching up the bowl, he tipped the carton over the remains of the blond's meal.

'*Soll*,' he said to Edie. 'You eat now.'

Edie bit back the pain in her jaw and put on what passed for a smile. *Soll*. The word had come up again and again when the two men had been licking the rocks. They were looking for a salty stone.

'I've just lost my appetite,' she said.

Later, the blond loosened her ties so she could wash and see to her bodily functions. He was setting about retying her wrists when a clattering came from outside. The sound of Skinny shouting sent the blond scuttling out to investigate. For a moment chaos seemed to break out and there was wild shouting followed by gunshots. A while later, the blond appeared at the entrance to the hut. He seemed exhilarated and out of breath.

'Bear.' He walked around to the back of the chair and resumed tying Edie's hands. 'He ran away.' Then, chuckling to himself, 'Don't get any ideas. For you, it won't work.'

A long while later, she heard noises of the two men settling in for the night, then quiet. Edie's jaw was a walrus in rut, puffed and roaring. Thoughts tumbled incoherently through her mind only to return to a single source: the ridiculous optimism of her plan. Sometime in the night, the *puikaktuq* appeared, momentarily, standing in the doorway. A throb started up in her right eye, followed by a ringing in the ears. It could be the result of the injury to her jaw, but she didn't think so. She held her breath, waiting for the ancestors to begin to speak to her, but nothing came. Then the *puikaktuq* faded and she was left alone. A terrible bleakness crept over her, a fear that she was going to die out here and that what she knew would die with her and no one would ever find out that Joe Inukpuk did not kill himself but had been murdered.

At that thought, fear turned immediately to anger, which gave her a new courage. She felt for the knot around her wrists with her fingers, tracing the contours of the rope once, twice and a third time to be sure, then she smiled to herself. The rope was hemp. Hemp had elasticity, she could work it. Better still, the blond had tied a square knot. So long as she could find a way to ease the tension, it would give. She pressed her wrists together experimentally. Slowly, she began to twist them away from each other, pressing the flesh until it burned to give her more room to manoeuvre, thinking about her escape.

There was no other way back to the boats except by retracing the path along the cliffs and she would be visible all the way. Then there was the matter of the outboard on the Zodie. The men hadn't thought to remove the oars but she could never out-row them if they chose to come after her in the launch. As for the larger vessel, she'd need the ignition key to start the engine, unless she found a way to pull-start it. That might be possible, but she'd only ever hot-wired the kind of small outboards which came attached to skiffs and Zodies.

She laid her hands flat against one another as though she were praying and pressed, repeating the action until she felt the sides of the square knot loosen. Within minutes she'd prised it open and was untying her feet. There was a flood of pain as the circulation returned.

The wind was coming in from the east now, whipping across the tundra and making it sing. The moon was rising, part obscured by cloud but she was confident that she could remember the way back to the boats. The camera tripod was standing just inside the doorway. For an instant she thought about stealing a gun and shooting the men as they slept, but what if she woke them first?

She flipped the memory card from the camera and dropped it in her pocket, then hurried back along the path.

By the time she reached the beach some of the cloud cover had gone and the moonlight was reflecting off the sea, producing a dank silver light. She made her way to the Zodiac and pushed off the beach.

Soon she was rowing in a strong, helpful current towards the launch. She tied up, pushed the oars, her backpack, jerry cans of sweet water and the cans of pemmican she'd bought in Siorapaluk onto the deck of the launch and hauled herself up.

The outboard was a Johnson 150hp, an unfamiliar model. A large, fit man might pull-start something that big, but she would have to take off the keyswitch and hope the wires were labelled. For that she would need a screwdriver.

She looked about the deck for some tools then remembering her hunting knife in the backpack she found the blade in the pocket where she'd left it. Her jaw pulsed and thrummed. Quickly, she rummaged through her things, looking for something to bandage around her jaw to stabilize it.

It was then she remembered her wallet. She'd definitely had it with her, but it didn't seem to be in the backpack. She was sure the Russians hadn't touched the bag, so then, where was it? A memory bubbled to the surface. Of course! She'd taken it from her pack when she paid for her food at Siorapaluk then put it back in the pocket of her parka. It must have fallen out at the Russians' camp. She had all her money in it, but she didn't need that now. Tucked into a side pocket was a photo of Joe and with a jolt she realized that the other pocket held her guiding licence, on which was neatly written her name and address.

The sun would rise again soon and the Russians would

wake and find her gone. If they found the wallet they would immediately make the connection to Autisaq. She had no doubt then that they would come after her.

She moved quickly to the outboard and pulled the starter cable, but she wasn't strong enough to get up enough speed on the cable to get the engine firing. Moving back to the wheel column, she pulled out the rope that had been wound around her ankles, and began to tie a length from the wheel to a cleat at the edge of the seating bay, so that when the engine started, the launch would steer true while she made her way from the outboard. On the wheel column she could see that someone had hung a key on a little hook. She picked it up and inspected it, moving once more to the stern. The key slotted straight into the starter. Whoever owned the boat had kept the spare on hand.

She moved over to the anchor winch and hauled it up, checked the tow line to the Zodie then stepped along the deck to the Johnson. Freed from its anchor, the launch began to drift and pitch. Above the wind and the slap of the water, she could hear the flutter of her pulse. Edie looked out to sea. The Canadian border lay fifteen kilometres into the gloom. Beyond that, at the same distance, lay Ellesmere Island and between herself and it, the most dangerous waterway on the planet.

14

The launch moved slowly past the shore-fast ice into the band of water just off the coast where there was only fragmented year-long ice. For a while it hit a particularly strong band of current and seemed to be going nowhere. The pain in Edie's jaw was excruciating now. Not for the first time since she had arrived in Greenland, she was afraid.

At Siorapaluk she turned the launch to the west. The wind was steady but low and coming from the northeast, and the current pulled against the little boat and dragged at the Zodie behind. It was tempting to go with it, but Edie knew that it would be a mistake to turn south until she was nearing the ice foot on the eastern coast of Ellesmere.

Further out into the channel, the launch began to encounter larger floes and the leads between them became smaller and more transient. The little boat slapped against the water, grinding its way every so often across a thin patch of soupy ice, each judder and shake rattling her bruised and swollen jaw. The coast of Greenland was nothing more than a dark stain in the sky now, and Ellesmere not yet visible through the low cirrus cloud and frost smoke. A voice told her that Inuit did not move away from the sight of land, that she was taking a crazy risk, but she knew that to turn back to Greenland would bring a world of trouble on her head. She had stolen a gun and a boat. Worse, if the Russians had found her wallet and connected their trip to Autisaq to her arrival in Etah she had no doubt that they would track her down.

There was no radio on the launch and from its age and condition Edie guessed it belonged to a local hunter. The Russians almost certainly didn't want the attention a fancier boat might have prompted. She doubted that the launch had ever been expected to make this crossing. Already it had begun to moan and a faint grinding sound issued from the engine.

It had been a warm summer, the ice pack in the North Water was much more fragmented than usual and as the current passed through the narrowest strait at Smith Sound there was a stretch of chaotic swell where the moving floes were at their most active. If she misjudged her moment, the launch could be crushed in seconds.

In all her thirty-three years, Edie Kiglatuk had never heard of an Inuk making the crossing alone by boat. Even in navigation season, hulls and engines were always in danger of icing over. If the engine seized, she'd have to lift it from the water and find something to chip at the ice. If the hull iced, in all likelihood the pressure would crack the bulkhead and the launch would go down. Then she would be dependent on the Zodie.

There was no choice but to try to come in close to Alexandra. South of the Prince of Wales Icefield she was much more likely to run into icebergs and at this time of year the freshwater ice was at its most unstable. A large berg had only to turn over or to shatter and she would find herself in a swell ten metres high.

At Alexandra she would have to use the current to drift south, close to the Ellesmere shore, and save her fuel supplies for the journey into Jones Sound. She had to pray that the weather would stay clement or that she would run into a walrus-hunting party off the Ellesmere coast.

Whichever way you looked at it, the trip was daunting.

Further into the channel the swell stiffened, waving foamy flags as it rose and fell. The air grew as cold as winter, a bone-dry cold, which meant that, for the time being at least, there would be no blizzard.

Looking out across the sea Edie saw a cluster of empty plastic bottles rafting about on the swell, remnants of the garbage gyre dumped by the *Arctic Princess*. For a while she followed the drift of trash, noting the turns of the currents, until finally her eyes reached the horizon and she spotted in the sky above it a soft darkening, signalling land. It came to her in a fierce flash of longing then that Ellesmere was somewhere just beyond her vision, and in that moment nothing was real to her except home and how to reach it.

Whether it was a change in the vibration of the water below the launch or something in the air she could not say, but Edie's hunter's instincts detected a vessel approaching long before anything came into view. Best case, it was nothing, a trawler, maybe, or a scientific vessel. Worst case, the Russians. Cranking up the engine as much as she dared given the ice conditions, she set the launch due west and locked the wheel.

By the time the vessel came into plain sight it was already close: an icebreaker looming out of the mist like some giant, malevolent whale. The ship's horn blasted a warning. She thought about increasing the throttle, but conditions were treacherous. If she hit a floe at speed the launch would peel open like a tin can. In seconds, she'd find herself head down in the freezing water without so much as a lifejacket.

In the end, she decided there was no point in trying to run away. It was hopeless. She was like a harp seal in the presence of a hungry bear. All she could do was kill the engine and pray.

Soon after, the ship slowed and for a few minutes an odd, thick silence filled the space between its massive hull and the launch. Her eye was drawn to movement on deck. She squinted, struggling to get a better look. They were lowering a Zodie into the water.

The livery of the Canadian Coastguard came slowly through the low mist. Her heart lifted. At least she'd made it as far as Canada without the Russians catching up with her. The high-pitched pulse of the winch stopped and was replaced by the sound of an outboard. The yellow outline of the satellite vessel emerged from the mist.

As the craft drew close, the moving shadows devolved into the shapes of six men. The helmsman cut his engine and for a moment the vessel drifted on the current. Edie stood motionless on deck. One of the men waved his arms. Another man was standing beside him now: he appeared to be looking at her through a pair of binoculars. The first man stretched behind him and brought out a megaphone but the sound that reached her was that of a fox barking. She raised her hands to show them she was not armed.

'Are you alone?'

She nodded.

The man with the binoculars moved closer to his fellow, who leaned into his megaphone again.

'This is the Canadian Coastguard. We are authorized to board your vessel. If you resist, we will take measures to prevent you leaving the scene.'

They drew alongside and a man threw a rope on deck and motioned for her to secure it for boarding. The two men and two armed guards jumped on deck. One of the armed men wound the sheet around a cleat then caught a second rope and tied the two vessels together.

The unarmed man who had spoken through the megaphone started to talk. Edie knew the words but they didn't seem to get through to her. She noticed that the man's eyes were two different colours, one hazel, and the other green.

'Do you speak English? *Nakinngaqpin*?' Where do you come from?

'Autisaq.'

One of the armed men did a quick tour of the launch, came back shaking his head.

'Alone?' The man with the odd eyes gave Edie a quizzical look and held up one finger. '*Ui*, husband?'

She replied in Inuktitut: '*Uiggatuk*, no husband.' The man leaned back on his hips, shot her a puzzled look and repeated what she'd just said, unable to get his head around it.

Edie sighed. 'Look, sailor-man,' she said in English. 'I'm divorced, OK? It's not unknown. Now, what do you want?'

One of the armed men sneezed away a snigger.

The man introduced himself as Lieutenant Fisher. 'This launch yours?'

'It is now,' she said.

The two unarmed men looked at each other. Fisher seemed unconvinced.

'I got it from a Greenlander,' she said. This much at least was true.

'Mind if I see your papers, ma'am?' Fisher over-enunciated the words, as though talking to a baby. He'd noticed her jaw and was wondering whether to say anything about it.

Edie said: 'You own a vehicle, mister?' Fisher shrugged and averted his eyes. 'If a bunch of men with semi-automatic weapons turned up on *your* doorstep asking you where you got your vehicle, what *you* gonna say?'

Fisher took a large breath and cringed as the freezing air filled his lungs. Clueless, Edie thought.

'That Zodie yours too?'

'How d'you think I got over to Qaanaaq?' She wondered if she could ask for a ride, without arousing anyone's suspicions. A tow would be good. Save time, gas, give her some protection till she got into home waters.

Fisher peered at the name painted on Zodie's side. '*Arctic Princess*?'

'That's me,' she said.

Fisher clocked that he'd got a case on his hands and swallowed hard. 'ID?'

Edie gestured towards her pack and Fisher motioned for his friend to collect it, giving her passport the once over.

'You need to let customs know you bought the boat,' Fisher said, searching for the appropriate tone of authority.

He began to wave the armed men back onto the satellite vessel.

'Before you go,' she said, 'any chance of a tow and a Tylenol?'

She waited while Fisher spoke into a radio mike. A moment later he reappeared.

'Ma'am, we're going to have to ask you to step on board.'

An hour later Edie found herself sitting on a plastic chair bolted to the wheelhouse deck, dressed in an oversized tracksuit borrowed from ship's supplies, her hands drawn tight with plastic cuffs, doing her best to avoid answering Captain Paul Jonson's questions. Some painkillers they'd given her had reduced her discomfort but made her feel spacey.

'What happened here?' Jonson was saying. 'In my experience, you people don't steal.'

'It was more like borrowing,' she said, playing dumb.

You people. If she was lucky, this Jonson fellow would treat her like a child, rap her on the wrists and let her go. Confiscate the launch maybe, but then he'd have to take her home. Worst case: a trip back to Greenland and straight into the waiting arms of the Russians. One thing Edie knew, if she was going to be any good to Joe, she needed to stay out of jail.

A flash of pain bit through the analgesic; she lifted her hands to stroke the painful spot.

'I'll have the medic look at that,' Jonson said, then, gesturing at the burn marks left by the Russians' rope around her wrists, signalled for the guard to remove the cuffs. 'And those. I guess we were a little hard on you, eh?'

She made a point of rubbing the sore part of her wrists and grimacing, wanting Jonson to feel her pain. He was OK, she thought, rough-looking on the surface, filthy nails and a scraggly beard like a moulting musk ox, but there was a nub of civilization somewhere further in.

'Honest truth, Miss Kiglatuk, I don't give a bear's ass about the Zodie. Cruise ships have no place up here, you ask me. But when there's a complaint, you know, there are procedures.'

She'd explained her presence in Greenland as a desire to visit her great-great-great-grandfather's grave. The way she'd woven the story, she'd heard the rumours that a couple of Russian guys might be digging up her ancestor's body. An Inuk couldn't let anyone do that. The shame, the misfortune it would bring, no *qalunaat* could fully comprehend the horror of it. So she'd taken it upon herself to fly to Qaanaaq to try to stop them, she said. Someone – she didn't volunteer Moller's name – had offered her a free ride back to Nuuk in their plane, then reneged, leaving her with no money and no other choice than to try to get home on her own. She'd sensed then Jonson had some sympathy for her, and made a note to play on it.

'If all this happened in Canada, we'd have been able to smooth it over,' he said. 'We can get you back to Autisaq, but I'm afraid you'll be under lock and key while you're with us and the authorities will be waiting for you on shore.' He shot her a sympathetic look. 'It's the best I can do.'

After the sod hut, the holding cell on board the Canadian Coastguard icebreaker *Stefansson* seemed pretty fancy. There were clean sheets on the bed, a flush toilet and a sink with hot and cold water. The ship's medic made a brief appearance, inspected Edie's jaw and wrists and gave her some strong painkillers.

At six the guard brought a plate heaped with barbecue ribs and some sweet thing, none of which she could eat. Not long after, he returned to take away the tray and to ask her if there was anything else she needed and when she requested a pen and paper he reappeared with a reporter's notebook and a pencil, apologizing. For some reason he didn't really understand, he said, detainees weren't allowed pens.

She had planned to spend the remainder of the evening trying to piece together all the information she'd gathered about the Russians, but the painkillers made her first woozy then brought on an exhaustion so deep there was nothing she could do but give in to it. But the sleep didn't last for long, and was replaced by flashbacks and morbid thoughts. She woke with a head full of questions. What was Felix Wagner's connection with Belovsky? Could he have been working for Zemmer and Beloil without either of them knowing at first? Did the Russians find out? What were the salty stones the Russians were looking for among the graves at Qaanaaq? Were there other meteorites, other astroblemes? And if the astrobleme signalled the presence of gas or oil, could it be that salt was the third marker, the roadsign, along with the diaries and the stone? Joe had got in the middle of all this, somehow. Perhaps he was only witness to Andy Taylor's murder, or maybe there was some greater involvement. Edie didn't yet know. Of one thing she was sure, though. Everything came back to a single overriding question: if someone *had* killed Joc Inukpuk – and she felt in her bones that someone had – then who was it? If she could find out why her stepson was killed, she was sure the answer would lead her to the killer.

A shrieking sound put an end to her thoughts. Somewhere beneath her, the ship's engines thumped and churned and a dreadful squealing and thudding issued from somewhere at the ship's fore. They were pushing through the floe. Edie went to the door and peered through the peep portal. A thin light shone down the corridor, illuminating the empty space. She turned back towards the cell.

I need to be home, she thought. I need to talk to Derek Palliser and Mike Nungaq.

When, some while later, the guard reappeared with a breakfast of eggs, toast and coffee, she asked how long it would be before they were in Autisaq waters and got a shrug in response. He wasn't sure how close to Autisaq they were going. The patrol was already late – they still had to make a scheduled stop at the science station before heading south – and the captain was keen not to delay the hand-over so had arranged for the authorities to rendezvous with the ship in mid-channel. Which authorities, the guard didn't know and he didn't care. He hadn't seen his kid for two months and he didn't appreciate having to stop to pick up people who should know better than to steal launches.

He came back for her not long after. He was sorry, but the rules specified that Edie would have to be cuffed during the transfer. Personally, the guard said, he thought that was crazy, but then she couldn't really say she hadn't brought it on herself. Edie held out her wrists and went along with it.

At the wheelhouse, the cuffs came off and a couple of men she hadn't seen before took another statement from her and asked her to sign some forms. At the end of the process, the guard re-attached the cuffs and led her out onto the deck.

Another man Edie hadn't seen before emerged from the wheelhouse and came over to where they were standing. He spoke softly to the guard for a moment or two then the guard turned to Edie and took her firmly by the arm. 'We're going back,' the guard said. She felt his hand tighten its grip on her arm as he swung her away from the rail.

A feeling of foreboding cast a shadow in her mind. Weren't they just going to make a routine transfer? What had happened to make them change their minds? She thought of resisting, even jumping overboard, but she knew she couldn't survive in the water long enough to make it to shore and, besides, they'd surely send a launch out to pick her up or, worse still, pick her off as she struggled in the water. Edie closed her eyes. To lose sight of Autisaq was unbearable when they were so near. She felt her throat swell and the breath fluttering in her chest like a trapped moth.

The guard opened the door to the wheelhouse and guided her inside. Captain Jonson was standing with his back to her and, hearing the door, turned briefly.

'Have a seat. No point in keeping you out in the cold,' he said, returning to his business.

I belong in the cold, she thought, but didn't say.

They waited. From time to time men came in delivering information. Jonson barked instructions back. At one point he radioed someone with an update. Console lights blinked on and off. Edie's nerves grated. She sensed she was still being processed. The feeling of being in a stranger's hands so close to home made her profoundly anxious.

Then Jonson unexpectedly announced that the Mounties were on their way. The word alone sent panic blading through her body. The Royal Canadian Mounted Police had a fearsome reputation on Ellesmere. It was they, after all, who had tried to corral her grandma Anna and others into Alexandra Fiord and, when that proved impossible, dumped them on a beach on the Lindstrom Peninsula and left them there to die. She tried to keep the panic down and think. The nearest RCMP post was a thousand kilometres away. Why would the RCMP get involved? Was this because the case crossed national boundaries? Her spirits sank. If it was true, she was screwed.

Jonson turned again. His face bore a look of impatience. He wanted her out of his jurisdiction as soon as possible. Just then the door opened, a man entered and saluted. Jonson wheeled about and acknowledged the greeting. Two men in a different uniform followed behind. With a thump of relief, Edie recognized the first as Constable Stevie Killik. Behind him, bringing up the rear, was Derek Palliser.

Derek caught Edie's eye and winked. In that moment, Edie could have jumped up and kissed him.

Back home Derek insisted she get her jaw looked at by Robert Patma at the nursing station and took her there, in case she was tempted not to bother.

'How'd you do this?' Robert probed the jawline gently with a thumb and finger. Edie shot Derek a warning glance.

'Fell off the snowbie.'

Robert handed her some anti-inflammatories and a few strong painkillers.

'Lucky you didn't have a really serious accident,' he said. 'Drinking and driving.'

'She's got the obligatory lecture coming right up,' Derek said.

The moment they were alone in the police office with the door shut, Derek shrugged off his professionally cheery air.

'What the hell were you thinking?'

'I guess I wasn't.'

'If Jonson wasn't such a maverick, you could easily have ended up in an RCMP jail.'

Edie did her best to look humbled. She wanted to tell him what she'd uncovered in the fews days she'd spent in Greenland, but he hadn't yet finished scolding her. 'We got enough on our plates, Edie, what with the election, and now the old man going missing.'

Edie said: 'I forgot about the election.'

Derek took a long draw on his cigarette and flipped his eyes skywards. *Lucky you.*

Edie backtracked. 'Koperkuj?' Somehow, she already knew.

'Didn't show up to collect his welfare. Seems like he hasn't been at home for a while and no one seems to have seen him.' Derek's eyes narrowed. 'How did you know I meant Saomik Koperkuj?'

'Women's instincts.'

'Edie, I just dragged your sorry ass out from under a whole heap of shit, but I can just as easily put you right back in it.'

For a moment they looked at one another, an exhausted woman and a washed-out man. Then he said, 'I have to go organize the search.'

From the police office, Edie went directly to the store and was relieved to see only Mike at the cashier's desk. She bought an envelope and a stamp for Greenland.

'I heard about your ride from the coastguard, Edie,' Mike

said. He tapped his face to indicate he'd noticed her injury. 'I hope you know what you're doing.'

'As much as I ever do,' she said.

Mike gave her a worried smile.

She put the memory card from the Russians' camera in the envelope and addressed it to Qila at Blok 7. Maybe she could do something with it, send it to a foreign newspaper that might run the story.

At that moment Minnie Inukpuk came in and began weaving her way towards the booze display. Etok emerged from behind the post office counter carrying copies of the latest edition of the *Artic Circular* and hurried after her, Mike following close behind. Edie knew what this meant: Minnie had started stealing, Etok was about to give her a rough time over it and, in his usual peacenik fashion, Mike was going to see if he could prevent a flare-up. The sound of voices ensued, and moments later Minnie burst out from behind the aisles and made for the door, keenly pursued by Etok, scattering newspapers as she ran. While Etok watched Minnie disappear down the street, Edie bent to pick up the mess. Restacking the newspapers, her eye was drawn to a picture of a black seabird on the front page. Beneath it was printed the word Zemmer. She slid a copy into her pocket, returned the remainder in a pile to Etok, and made her way home in double time.

The house was just as she'd left it, unpleasantly warm and a little lonely. She pulled out the *Circular* and unfolded it. Almost the whole of the front was taken up with news of a huge fire at one of Zemmer's drill platforms in the Sea of Okhotsk, off the east coast of Russia. It had happened two days ago and the seabird was only the latest casualty. Forty-three rig workers had been killed in the initial blast and another twenty-seven were unaccounted for. A vast slick had already begun to form around the platform and experts were predicting that it could spread to an area the size of Delaware. A spokesman from Zemmer insisted that the security systems on the rig itself had been breached and a piece of pumping equipment tampered with. A Russian-made detonator had been found at the site but the spokesman refused to speculate who might have been responsible. At the bottom of the page there was a link to the editorial comment page:

The start of a new oil terrorism?

The commentary went on to speculate that the explosion was the work of Chechen separatists.

Edie put the paper down. Was it too much to imagine that this was Beloil's way of killing two birds with one stone, of drawing attention away from whatever they were doing in the Arctic and at the same time taking out the competition, in the certain knowledge that the spotlight would not fall on the corporation itself? What was the saying: war is the continuation of politics by other means. What if here war was the continuation of *business* by other means?

She unpacked the few things she'd managed to retrieve from the Zodie, made some tea and stuck a bowl of frozen seal stew in the microwave to cook. While it was heating, she took a shower and oiled and replaited her hair. The old man popped into her mind and she pushed him back out. Everything in its own time.

The outside door swung open. Her heart lurched. She leapt up and sprang towards the utility room where she stored her rifles. Moments later, Sammy burst through the door to the snow porch, his face split in a broad smile.

'What a great smell.'

He was just the person she wanted to see.

'Dinner,' Edie said, 'for one. Don't tell me you and Nancy

split already.' She motioned him to sit. 'You scared me,' she said. This had to be the first time in her life she had been spooked by an arrival.

'*Scared* you?' Sammy seemed shocked. He took her hand and patted it in a brotherly fashion. 'Whatever you're up to, I get that you have to do it, but Edie, look at yourself.' He reached out and gently stroked her cheek. The swelling was beginning to go down, but the whole of her jaw was livid with bruising. In spite of her efforts with her hair, Edie knew she didn't look her best.

'Don't put yourself in harm's way. Joe wouldn't have wanted that and I don't either.'

She took this in. How she wished she could confide in Sammy, good old Sammy, but this was her responsibility now and she didn't want to drag him into it.

'You want some stew? I can put some more in the microwave.'

He shook his head. 'Nancy's heating pizza.'

'Oh,' she said, swallowing her disappointment. For a moment, they both sat and absorbed what needed to be absorbed.

'I guess I should be getting back,' he said.

At the door to the snow porch he turned. 'I fed your dogs while you were away,' he said. 'Bonehead, the others, like you said.'

'Thanks, Sammy.' He still had the capacity to touch her.

'When I went around the back I noticed you got a bit of ice heave. Nothing serious, but you might get someone to check out the piling at the back of the house.'

She thanked him again. For an instant their eyes met and she felt an intense pressure, then he turned and went back through the door.

That night, for the first time ever, she slept with the doors locked.

15

As Edie made her way to the Northern Store to call the Rasmussen sisters, it snowed for the first time since the spring and though the last remnants of the sun melted the sprinklings along the shoreline as they fell, a dusting remained up on the cliffs as a reminder of what was to come. At the store Etok was in the office and Mike was occupied with the arrival of a new delivery from the supply plane. Edie waited till no one was looking and picked up the phone. Since losing her job, and then her wallet, the only money she could lay claim to was the few dollars Sammy had lent her.

'*Ai?*'

'Qila?

'Hey, Edie!' Qila laughed. 'We sent your Russian friends' pictures to *Sermitsiaq*, the Greenlandic language newspaper, and they printed the story. Can you believe it, the police actually did something! They're being deported back to Russia next week.'

Edie felt herself smile. This was good news. Her instincts told her that Beloil wouldn't stop until Belovsky had got what he wanted, but this at least bought everyone some time.

'Did they say anything about why they were up there?'

'Who, the police?'

Edie corrected her: 'The Russians.'

'Same as before. That they were only interested in

digging around the foundations of sod huts. They said they didn't know they had disturbed graves. But the pictures were clear.'

'I'm glad they're gone,' she said. If they'd found the wallet, the Russians would know that Maggie Kiglatuk was not who she said she was.

'Did you check those diaries I mentioned in my note?'

Qila said: 'Yeah. I found a copy in the library. You were right about Karlovsky. He did meet with Welatok.' She let out a short, ironic laugh. 'That *qalunaat* wrote a *lot*, too much. He was, what do you say, a wind sack.'

'A windbag.'

'Yes, a puffed-up old windbag. But he knew your great-great-great-grandfather. They met in Etah. For a while Welatok guided him, but then he decided not to do it any more.'

'Did Karlovsky say why Welatok changed his mind?'

'You know how it is, Edie. One minute he complains the natives are hard to read, the next that we're simple-minded as seals. Karlovsky says Welatok had some kind of stone. The *qalunaat* had never seen anything like it before.' She paused. 'Is this helpful?'

'Yes, yes,' Edie said, sounding encouraging. Hadn't Mike Nungaq said that the fragment in her possession was chipped from something larger?

'OK, then, there's more.'

'I'm all ears.'

'Ears? What?'

'Listening, Qila, I'm listening.'

'Oh. Well, now, this stone. Karlovsky wanted it, but Welatok wouldn't trade it with him. He offered Welatok two rifles, but Welatok didn't hand it over. He said some other *qalunaat* had betrayed him and he wouldn't trade with them any more.'

'Fairfax.' Edie steadied herself. The story was finally coming together.

Qila said: 'Who?'

'It doesn't matter.'

'So Welatok decides he won't guide Karlovsky any more and leaves camp. Karlovsky tries to follow Welatok into the interior, but there is no game and his dogs begin to starve, so he has to turn back. This is what he says anyway.'

'You don't believe it?'

'No. I think Karlovsky caught up with Welatok, killed him and took all his things, including the stone.'

'How do you figure that?' The version passed down in the family was that Welatok had died out on the land of starvation, or cold, or both.

Qila sounded a little put out. 'I haven't just invented this story, if that's what you mean. I have evidence.'

Suddenly Edie could see why the *puikaktuq* seemed to be Joe and yet not Joe. The vision that had come to her was the spirit of Joe and Welatok, two murdered souls calling to her from the other world.

'Karlovsky talks about shooting some of the weaker dogs and feeding them to the others on the journey back from the interior, but he went out with a twelve-dog team, so he must have got more dogs from somewhere, or there would not have been enough to return to Etah.'

'You think he took Welatok's dogs.'

'Not just dogs, the stone, everything. The diary ends not long after Karlovsky tried to buy the stone from Welatok but the introduction says Karlovsky got lost in a storm shortly after his return and his body was never found. It says that some Inuit fellas turned up with Karlovsky's notebook and sold it to the rescue party who came looking for him. But I don't think that's how it happened.'

'Why not?'

'It was June. No storms up in Etah in June. I think Inuit found out what Karlovsky had done to Welatok and killed him.'

Edie listened and thought hard. Robbery, low theft, was almost never a motivation for murder in Inuit culture as it was in the west, but revenge, yes. Inuit were big on revenge.

'So the Russians weren't looking for Welatok's grave?'

'No, they were looking for Karlovsky's.'

'Then why didn't they just say that?'

'Because they would have drawn more attention to themselves,' Qila said.

Edie thought about this and realized she was right. Felix Wagner, Andy Taylor and the two Russian men all wanted the same thing, but the Russians had been smarter about it. Andy Taylor might have thought it was the perfect cover bringing Bill Fairfax up to the Arctic, but with all the fuss there would have been in the western press, it was an act of suicide. Once the Russians got wind of it, Taylor didn't stand a chance. Disinterring a few natives might make the Russians unpopular in Greenland, but, as a news story, it wouldn't travel.

What was still puzzling was why the Russians had had to resort to such measures in the first place. If they had shot Taylor and dismembered his body, why hadn't they found the stone around his neck?

Edie was ending the call as Mike appeared from the back of the store.

'Asking first would have been nice.' He sounded a little put out.

'I'm sorry, you were busy. I'll reimburse you, but it might have to wait.'

Mike threw her a disapproving look.

'Mike, I owe you.'

'You got that right,' he said.

Back home, Edie made herself an extra-sweet brew and tried to think back over the months to Wagner's death. Everything she'd discovered so far suggested that the two Russians, Skinny and the blond one, were passengers on the green plane Joe had spotted. They knew Andy Taylor had the stone and the diary. How they knew, she wasn't sure. Perhaps Taylor had been playing the same game as his boss, Wagner, courting both sides. In the process of hunting Taylor had the Russians spotted Joe? Perhaps they'd tried to kill him too, but had lost him in the snow. Conscious that they'd been seen, they could have contacted their mole in Autisaq. That person had gone to the nursing station and, finding it empty, taken enough Vicodin to kill a man, and a hypodermic, sought Joe out and made sure he would never wake up again.

Frustrated in their attempts to retrieve the stone with the minimum fuss, she imagined that the Russians were forced to start looking elsewhere. From Karlovsky's diaries they'd deduced that Welatok had another stone and worked out that Karlovsky had taken it. All they had to do was to locate Karlovsky's grave among the many scattered in the tundra around the old settlement of Etah and hope that the stone had been buried with him.

As for the local agent, the executioner, everything pointed to Simeonie Inukpuk: his reluctance to investigate the deaths, the regular payments to some bogus children's foundation, the sudden burst of spending on consultants and fancy election posters and the web history suggesting that he at least knew about Zemmer. But how was she going to prove it? And even if she did, who would listen?

*

She fried some char, stuck *The Gold Rush* on the DVD player and sat down with her supper. She'd just started eating when sudden, unexplained sounds of someone moving about in the snow porch stopped her. Suddenly all she could hear was her own quickened breathing. She was reaching for the door of the utility room, where she'd left her rifle, when a voice called out, 'Edie?' and the inner door to the snow porch swung open.

Auntie Martie. For a moment the two women stood and stared at one another, then Martie began to laugh.

'Shit, you look like you just saw a ghost!'

Swinging over, she gave her favourite niece a long, hard hug.

'How you doing, Little Bear?'

Edie smiled. 'Sometimes I'm OK.' She motioned for her aunt to sit and brought her over a brew and some fried char.

Martie looked at the tea. 'On the wagon again?'

Edie nodded. 'A coupla months.'

Martie patted her on the knee. 'Good for you.' She picked at her food and gave her a thumbs-up.

'You heard about the old man?' she said. 'He was a crazy old walrus, but I was kinda fond of him. I guess you know that back in the day Koperkuj and me, well . . .' She put the fish plate down on the floor by the sofa. She looked terrible, Edie thought, not eating either. Not like Martie. The woman usually had a big appetite.

'I don't guess you got a glass of Mist?'

Edie shook her head.

'A beer then?'

'Uh nuh.'

'Thing is, about the old man. You know he had some . . .' She hesitated, searching for the right words. 'What I'm saying, he had some goings on.'

If there was a story, Edie wanted to hear it.

'That glasshouse business?' Martie began.

'He was in *that*?' This was the first Edie had heard. Another thing Willa had cut her out of.

Martie: 'It got hauled away. The boss at the science station, he got it torn down. But the old man, see, he wanted to start afresh, set it up somewhere else. Said he had a diamond he could sell, get the capital together.'

'Oh.' Somehow this changed everything. 'You think that's why he went missing?'

Martie was trying to get to something, but she hadn't got there yet. 'Why are you coming to me with this now?' Edie said.

Marie shrugged. 'I guess I only just remembered.'

Edie sensed it was her turn to truth-tell. 'The diamond, Auntie Martie, I traded it with the old man.'

'You did? Where d'you get something like that?'

'I don't think it's real, leastwise I don't know. He had a trinket, a stone, I wanted it.'

'A stone?' Martie seemed puzzled. 'You traded a diamond for a stone?'

Edie opened her mouth then realized that she'd never be able to explain it all. She was already half way to the snow porch by the time Martie said, 'Hey, where are you running off to?'

'Wait for me here, Martie?'

'You tell me where you're going!'

'To Willa.'

Martie shrugged. As Edie walked down the street she could hear her aunt muttering, 'Crazy emeffing Little Bear.'

Edie found Minnie in her usual place on the sofa, surrounded by bottles. She hollered, 'Get out, bitch.'

'Top o' the morning to you too.' Edie sailed past her and headed towards Willa's room.

Minnie tried to rise, then she gave up the struggle and flapped her fists disconsolately instead.

To Edie's relief, her stepson was sitting on his bed, playing video games. She stood at the doorway.

'Fuck off, Edie.'

Edie felt a sharp pain dig her heart. She swallowed back the desire to reach across and hold him.

'What was the old man doing in your little glasshouse project?'

For a second he looked up, thinking to deny it.

'I don't know why he's disappeared, that what you think?' He went back to the game. His voice was strangely calm. 'In any case, they want me, they can come and get me.'

'If who want you, Willa? What the hell?'

Edie took a deep breath to calm herself. Could it only have been a few months ago that Autisaq was as calm as a lake? Now it was as stormy as a northwest wind.

Willa shrugged. 'The guys in Kuujuaq, Toolik and Silliq.'

She wasn't surprised by the names. Toolik and Silliq had a reputation, even as far away as Autisaq. 'Any case,' Willa continued, 'why are you so concerned about me all of a sudden?'

She held her hands up in a gesture half borne of frustration, half of surrender.

'I thought the glasshouse was over.'

'It was, it is.' Willa sighed. 'What can I tell you?'

'The truth would be good.' Edie tugged on her tails. 'That is, if it's not too much trouble.'

Willa raised his eyes to heaven but he went on talking. 'The old man did a bit of gardening for a percentage of the crop. Saved us from going out there all the time, drawing attention. Toolik and Silliq moved his product on. I don't know, maybe they got sore when it all came to a stop, thought Koperkuj had cheated them out of a profit. Ask me, the old man's gone AWOL. Now, can I have some *peace*?'

She stood silent for a moment, trying to think of a way to reach him.

He turned back to his Xbox. 'That means fuck off, Edie.'

She backed away and found herself on the street heading towards the police office. Someone needed to tell Derek Palliser to check out Toolik and Silliq when he got back to Kuujuaq. He'd stayed in Autisaq to direct the search for Koperkuj. It was only fair on the old man and, besides, a warning needed to be sent to the two men not to go after Willa. She didn't want to wake up one morning to find that something had happened to him too.

Derek Palliser was on the sat phone. When he was done with the call, he made a note on a map and turned to her with a wary look.

'Derek, I've got a lead on the old man. You need to arrest Willa Inukpuk.'

Derek shook his head in astonishment. 'Hell, Edie, I do believe you've finally cracked.'

She passed on the information Willa had given her.

'So you see, I need him out of harm's way.'

Derek Palliser raised his eyes to heaven and reached into the drawer for his gun and cuffs.

'Sometimes, Edie, I wonder what terrible things I did to you in the last life, I really do.'

'You think Toolik and Silliq could have hurt the old man?'

'You'd asked me that a month or two ago, I'd have said no way. Now, I don't know. Something dark is blowing through this island, damn me if I know what.'

Edie opened the snow porch into her own house and heard a whistling sound. A hunting knife landed with a *thunk* in the door frame beside her head.

'I gave that knife to Koperkuj myself when we were doing what we were doing. Recognize it anywhere.' Martie walked over and retrieved the knife, then, inspecting it, added: 'There's a fault in the first and second serrations. Mike let me have it for fifty bucks. The old man was a cut-price fuck, even in his glory days.' She frowned. 'What you doing with it?'

Edie made a gesture of surrender. 'I dropped by his cabin, just a social call, some time past. The old walrus met me with his .22. Thought I might have to defend myself.'

'You took his knife?'

'Don't sweat it, Auntie Martie, he'll get it back.'

'Oh.' Losing interest. 'You see Palliser?'

'Yeah.' A sudden thought struck Edie with the force of a whirling wind. 'Martie, can you wait here?'

Martie rolled her eyes. 'Right, I ain't got nothing else to do.'

Edie went out to the meat store, plucked the tin of Andy Taylor's bones from the shelf and poured them out onto the living-room table, rooting around until she found a piece of femur that bore knife marks and held it to Koperkuj's blade. The match was exact.

'Here's a thing.'

Martie chuckled. 'The old walrus always hated *qalunaat*,' she said. Her face grew serious once more. 'You don't think . . .?'

'Uh nuh. Andy Taylor was shot in the head. But it explains why there were no snowplane tracks.' Also why the Russians had come back for their 'eider hunting', though Edie decided to keep that fact to herself.

Martie shrugged and lifted her palms in the air: 'I have no idea what you're talking about.'

Edie said: 'A thermal scope.'

'No clearer.'

'Andy Taylor could have been shot from the air with a thermal scope.' That way the target didn't have to be visible to the eye. The scope could lock on to body warmth. But the poor visibility meant the hunters couldn't land. After the Russians shot Taylor, the old man must have found his body and cut him up.

'What's that got to do with the price of fish?' Martie said. She was genuinely bewildered.

Edie shrugged. She didn't know. Not yet.

Not long afterwards, Derek Palliser came round to report that Willa was safely locked up in the police cell. He was flying back to Kuujuaq to question Toolik and Silliq, leaving Stevie in charge of the internee. Once Pol had dropped him at Kuujuaq, he'd carry on with the S&R for Koperkuj.

As he was about to leave Edie asked him to wait two minutes while she heated something in the microwave. When it was done, she got out a thermos and poured in the contents of the jug.

'For Willa. It's his favourite. Blood soup.'

The following morning she got up early and made bannock bread and hot tea for breakfast, remembering, as she loaded syrup on her bread, that today was the day of Simeonie Inukpuk's talk on the future of Autisaq. For as long as she could recall, Simeonie had been talking about converting the tiny settlement into some kind of High Arctic commercial hub, a rival to Resolute, which currently pulled in all the polar expedition business. Most people in Autisaq, the majority of Autisaqmiut, considered his ideas to be a pig flight, but more recently, Edie noticed, something had shifted. Autisaqmiut were beginning to accept that the Arctic had a limited lifespan. When the ice melted and the waters rose, they wanted to be sure of their place on the liferaft.

Plus people were beginning to look around for someone to steer it, and a number, among them the man himself, had decided that Simeonie Inukpuk might be Autisaq's best hope. Only yesterday John Tisdale had been round to let Edie know that Simeonie would see Edie's attendance at the event as a 'positive sign', hinting that he might even consider giving her back a few hours at the school.

It went without saying she had no intention whatsoever of going. Instead, she spent the early hours cleaning and loading her rifles and hiding them in secret places around the house. The Russians might be out of the picture for now, but that didn't mean their trigger man was. She took the stone from her bedside table, emptied out the sugar tin, put the stone at the bottom and buried it in sugar.

Mid-morning, she pulled on her outerwear and slunk out into the deserted streets. Making her way up to the store she found Mike Nungaq hunched over the entranceway. He had the glove of his right hand in his mouth and was working the key of the door with his ungloved hand.

'How was the talk?' she said.

He shrugged. 'I've heard it all before.' He stood up and cracked open the door. 'We're not all like you, Edie.' There was a hint of irritation in his voice.

He began stomping the new-fall snow off his boots and smiled a little to remind her that he was still her friend.

'I've got to open up,' he said. 'Will you be at home later?'

'I did think I might go to the opera, but if you're coming round . . .'

Mike registered the joke but let it slide over him. 'I've got something you might find interesting.'

'Sure,' she said. 'Can you bring a large bottle of pancake syrup? I'm all out. Pay you when I see you.'

He elbowed her. 'Old Mikey's not sweet enough these days, huh?'

*

Needing space to think she took a hunting rifle, went down to the shoreline, jumped into her kayak and headed west towards Jakeman Fiord. The snow geese, jaegers and dovekies had already disappeared south. The few summer weeks of sun and flowers and new life were gone, but, she realized now, she had barely noticed their progress.

As she was pulling the kayak back up onto the beach at Autisaq, she saw Mike Nungaq coming down to meet her. They went up to the house together. He put her groceries down inside the snow porch and continued to hover by the door.

'My rockhound friend,' he began. 'The one who identified your meteorite?' He delved into his pack, brought out a small wad of printed papers and held it out to her. 'He sent me this. Thought you might like to take a look.'

Edie took the paper from him, began scanning it.

'Good luck, Edie.'

She watched him leave, almost running down the path to get away from her. Was it really so difficult to be her friend these days?

The paper turned out to be an excerpted article from the *Geologist*, entitled 'Iridium enrichment in astrobleme-type formations', written by several professors or researchers from some of the more prestigious American universities. She began the first sentence, got to the second and felt hopelessly lost.

A few brews later she was beginning to understand the abstract, though she'd not had the courage yet to delve into the main body of the article, let alone to look at any of the bewildering array of graphs and tables associated with it. The gist of the piece, she thought, was that iridium-rich meteorites embedded in a sodium chloride substrate were known to act as a kind of vast geologic plug, preventing the escape of gas reserves beneath. Remove the plug and the gas was there, just waiting to be tapped.

What she hoped the article confirmed was that her hunch had been right all along. The stone Beloil and Zemmer had both pursued across the Arctic bore traces of salt. All anyone who had it needed to do was locate the exact spot from where Welatok had taken it and they would find gas reserves lying somewhere below the surface. She imagined the whole of Craig Island sitting on one great tank of gas. How much would that be worth? Three men's lives? Dozens? Hundreds even? And what else would have to go? A way of living? The Arctic itself, maybe?

Pulling down the sugar tin from the shelf, she dug about for the stone, sitting with it for a while, moving the weight around between her hands, exploring every little indentation with her fingers until the pads of her fingertips were sore. This was why Felix Wagner seemed so indifferent to hunting, why he and Andy Taylor were so hopeless at it. Wagner had a pretty good idea of where Welatok had first found the meteorite and was trying to locate the spot without raising too much interest from others in the same game. He'd covered all bases by playing Zemmer and Belovsky off against each other. And it had got him killed.

Edie went over to the door to the room that would always be Joe's, afraid of what she might see there, but needing to see it all the same. She pushed the door; it gave a little, and then jammed. Determined, she pushed harder, first with a hand, then, when that didn't work, by leaning into it, but the wood seemed stuck just outside the frame. Then she remembered Sammy mentioning ice heave. It must have lifted the floorboards. She'd need to take the door off and shave it a little. Of course, it would be easier just to leave it. She didn't need the room and she couldn't afford any repairs right now. All the same, even though she hadn't been in the room since May, to abandon it like that felt intolerable, an insult to the one who had once inhabited it.

She fetched her strongest hunting knife, the one she used to butcher walrus. It took a while; the hinges had never been oiled and they were gummed up with paint and, where the paint had peeled, rusted, but Edie was assisted in her task by the ease with which the wood gave way. It was the first time she could ever remember being glad for the cheap temporariness of the fittings. Once she'd got the hinges off, it was a small matter to heave the door away from its frame and lay it roughly up against the wall.

She flipped on the light switch in the room, went in and was met by a surreal sight. In places the floorboards had been forced upwards until they formed taut little slopes and hillocks. In other places, they seemed to have sunk into the supporting beams beneath them, or perhaps it was that the supporting beams had risen up to meet them. The ice had heaved up the supporting stilts and they in turn had pushed the beams up towards the floorboards. Clots of yellow foam insulator had been forced up through the cracks in the boards, giving the floor a diseased look, as though it had been attacked by some virulent fungus. It must have been this movement, she thought, which had caused the creaks and rattles she had for many months attributed to the *puikaktuq*. She'd been too drunk or too hungover to put the pieces together.

Aside from the floor, which, admittedly, was pretty bad, the room wasn't far off how Joe had left it; his nursing textbooks still sat on the shelves, his stethoscope was there, too, along with the nurse's electronic thermometer Edie had bought him for Christmas. The bedclothes had long since been stripped and burned, but the mattress and the frame remained. She hadn't touched it since Joe's death but now she went and sat down on it. In all the tumult of wood against ice, the frame had shuffled forward and wobbled on the uneven floor. For the first time, Edie was looking around the walls of his room from his perspective. It was from here that Joe saw the world.

Standing up, she began to push the bed into the corner, but the front leg nearest the corner jarred against some warping of the wood. Getting down on her knees she peered under the bed at the stuck leg, meaning to lift it over the warp in the boards. She was about to heave the bed frame when she felt something crackle under her little finger, a wrapper, perhaps from a packet of cookies or a candy bar. She pulled at it, but it seemed to be stuck in the crack between the floorboards and would not move.

Edie withdrew her arm and cursed her lack of domestic care. She dragged the bed away from the corner. As she'd thought, there was a piece of transparent cellophane, some kind of wrapper, sticking up from the wood. It must have fallen through the crack when the boards moved. She bent to pull it up, but it was as immovable as before. There was nothing for it, Edie thought, but to work the wrapper from its hiding place. Moving closer, she saw that, just in the spot where the wrapper protruded, the wood had warped into a mound about the size of a tea cup. The wrapper must have fallen through before the ice heave, then been pushed back out again. Edie leaned across and pinched the corner between her thumb and finger and pulled. She thought to get her knife and simply cut it off, but something stopped her. In any case, it was giving way now, the corner growing larger bit by bit until she could see it was a piece of plastic film, Saran Wrap perhaps, folded several times into a neat square with the remains of something inside. Out of simple curiosity she held it closer to her face. Inside there were smears of what looked like chocolate and, in among them, a few deep brown flakes. Holding the wrapper up to the window, she could now see several strands of blue-black hair: hair so unmistakeably Joe's that she dropped the film momentarily. Then, picking it up again, she put it in her pocket, and moved the bed back into its usual place. Taking stock of the room, it seemed to her that the walls themselves had distorted, as though she was looking at them through a fairground mirror.

An idea was forming in her mind, a huge, unstoppable idea, growing less fragile minute by minute, like a great ice field at the moment just before it sets hard. Someone else might have called it a hunch but to Edie this was no work of her own, but a notion that had been planted in her head by whatever was with her, what had come to her in Joe's room.

She stumbled into the store room and took out her telescopic rifle lens, the same one she'd used to read the diaries. Part of her wished Derek Palliser was around, but she also knew that she needed to do this alone. Trembling, she switched on her desk lamp and held the film close to the light, but her grip was so uneven that getting a focus on the contents proved impossible.

Growing impatient with herself, she stood up after a short while, went to the DVD player and switched it on. In a few moments, she felt calmed. Taking a bulldog clip from the desk drawer, she attached the film to the light and used two hands to steady the lens. The brown flakes resolved in the scope into a series of papery fragments, not brown close up, but a kind of mottled purple, and criss-crossed with a series of fine lines into tiny and uneven geometric shapes.

Human skin, she thought, but of an odd, unusual colour, not simply skin that had long since been discarded or rubbed off, more like skin left out on the tundra. She moved the scope over the square. Human head hairs, blue-black and dead straight, and towards the middle of the wrap two of another kind, shorter and with white follicles at the ends, too short to be pubic, too thin to be from the eyebrow. More like nostril hair.

Fumbling about in the cupboard under the sink, Edie drew out a pair of vinyl washing-up gloves and pulled them over her hands. She knew that at some later date, a defence lawyer standing in some southern court might say she had tampered with the evidence after what she was about to do, but it seemed to her that she was on the brink of something irreversible, some irrefutable proof written in hair and skin, and that in the light of this, the inflated to-ing and fro-ing of some abstract system suddenly seemed impossibly distant.

Returning to her desk, she pulled out a piece of paper and laid it across the surface, placing the square of film carefully on top. Then slowly, painstakingly, she began unwrapping it, fold by fold. It struck her how neatly it had been done, with an almost origami-like precision. Nothing Joe did was ever this neat. With the exception of his nursing textbooks, which he'd always set aside and treated as though they were made of some delicate, membranous fabric, the remainder of his few possessions had always been stacked in shaggy piles into which he'd dig tunnels from time to time, like a lemming.

She brought the scope to focus on the purplish brown flakes again. When he came back from Craig, the skin on Joe's nose and two of his fingers had been slightly frostbitten from his journey. Frostbite usually made the skin mottle, then darken, and peel. She prodded the plastic with a gloved finger until she could see a flake clinging to it, then slowly pulled the wrap open a little further, mindful of keeping its contents from spilling, until there was before her on the table a large rectangle, serrated on one side where the plastic had been torn from the roll.

Like the folding, the removal of the sheet had been done with care, she noticed, an almost perfect serration. Whoever had excised it from the roll had been meticulous about it. Nothing about this suggested Joe. She spread the sheet out, and then noticed the hole. It was small, less than the circumference of a cent, and the edges were relatively smooth, as though it had been sucked out. Beside it, only a centimetre or so away, there was an indentation of about the same size and shape, but here the film was still present, though it had been distorted by stretching. Between these two marks, or rather, very slightly below them, was another, larger and more uneven impression in the film and it was here that that the greatest concentration of skin flakes clung to what looked like grease. Inspecting it more closely, Edie could see a band of stretched film lying above the hole, running the length of the hole and its twin indentation. She gazed for a while at the configuration of stretches and tension marks until she was conscious of a dull ache running along her neck and realized that she had twisted her head around forty-five degrees to the horizontal. She straightened up until the ache stopped and slowly turning the plastic a hundred and eighty degrees she saw it, clear as a good spring day. It was unmistakeable. Imprinted onto the plastic film was the impression of a face, with a hole where the left nostril would have been.

She was hit by an odd sound then, somewhere between the cry of a baby and the howl of a wolf, realizing only an instant later that this was her own voice letting loose the months of grief. Here it was, proof incontrovertible: someone had murdered Joe Inukpuk and the murder weapon was clinging to her hand.

16

The moment the warning alarm on the instrument panel started beeping Derek Palliser knew the plane was going down. There was nothing to be done about it because there was no knowing where the damned pilot had got to and Derek didn't know how to fly. From where he was sitting, in the co-pilot's seat, the interior of the plane seemed to disappear off into a deep gloom. The warning bleeps continued and Derek suddenly found himself transported into a darkened room. It took him a moment to realize he'd woken up.

He brushed his hand over his face, reached out to the clock on the bedside table, hit the snooze button and deduced from the flashing LED that the power must have cut sometime in the night. In reaching for his watch he managed to sweep it off the bedside table onto the floor, so he tried pulling open the drapes, then remembered it was dark more often than not, now, in September. Soon, the last sunset of the year would be upon them.

The beeping continued; someone was trying to get through on the radio. Derek got up, turned on the light, pushed on his mukluks and pulled on his down parka, then picked up his watch, read the time and cursed. There was only one person who would radio him at four thirty in the morning.

The temperature differential hit him full in the face. He made a note to himself to turn up the thermostat, then remembered that it was Misha who liked to keep the place overheated, whereas he preferred it cool. Just one of the many ways in which he didn't miss her. Though it was painful to admit, he'd been having his suspicions about the timing of her arrival, only a day or two after his indiscreet conversation with the Russian scientists at the Eureka weather station. The woman had tipped him completely off-orbit. Was it too fanciful to imagine she was some kind of spy? He smiled grimly to himself. *Paranoia*, he thought. *Where did I pick that up from?*

In the comms room he leaned into the mike and greeted Edie Kiglatuk.

'How did you know it was me?'

'Male intuition.' He was still pissed off at her for treating him as though he was some kind of personal assistant, to be drafted in at her convenience. 'Is this about Saomik Koperkuj? I talked to Toolik and Silliq. Nothing doing.' Much though he disliked the dismal duo, he didn't have anything to link them to the old man's disappearance.

'Derek, you need to get back here.' He noted the tension in her voice.

'Edie, I just got home. Stevie's still in Autisaq. Whatever it is, he can handle it.' He was sick of her telling him what to do. She was beginning to sound like a bully.

'I need *you*.'

Wasn't that what most men wanted, to be needed by a woman? Why, then, did it make him feel a sudden desperate desire to be somewhere else? He fumbled about in his pocket for a cigarette then remembered he had his pyjamas on.

He said: 'I guess you already know what a crackpot you are.' Reaching into the desk for one of his many caches of emergency Lucky Strikes, he took one out and lit it. He waited for the nicotine to hit.

'Right.' There was a pause. 'You don't want to help, that's fine. I'll do this on my own.'

Derek said: 'Yes.'

'Yes what?'

'Yes, you've been doing it on your own since the spring, remember? And some time soon I'm going to have to come in on it.' She cut him off with a little wounded sounding 'uh huh' which made him feel bad. 'And yes, *unofficially* I'll help. I'm in Autisaq in a couple of days anyway for the election.' He looked at his watch. 'Tomorrow, I'm there. You can tell me what you've got up your sleeve then. If it still fits up your sleeve, that is, what with the giant tangle of paranoia already there.'

There was some interference on the radio for a moment, then Edie's voice came through mid-sentence, '. . . so it has to be later on today.'

Dammit, the woman could be maddening. She was like some appalling avalanche. He sat back and thought about it. What difference would a day make? He could put his foot down, but then she'd keep at him. He had finished his business in Kuujuaq for the time being and planned to fly over anyway. He guessed a few hours earlier wouldn't make any difference. He could camp down in the detachment office in Autisaq overnight and be ready to supervise the ballot box first thing on Wednesday morning. The more he thought about it the more he realized it might actually work out better that way.

He said: 'What you got?'

'Proof.'

'Proof of what?'

'Murder, homicide, unlawful killing, I don't know what you call it, but I got proof.'

He thought about asking her to elaborate, then decided it was best not to talk about it over the radio.

'OK, Edie, I give in,' he said. 'Weather permitting, I'll be with you by late afternoon.' Official police tone: 'This better be good.'

The flight into Autisaq was, for the Arctic at least, relatively smooth. Derek preferred it when he could not see the ground below, though today there was enough moonlight reflecting off the ice to bring into relief just how little ice there was for a September day and just how many leads criss-crossed the floe.

The plane came in over the mountains, bumping a little across the direction of the wind. As they drew near the strip, Derek could see that the terminal building had been festooned in bunting. In the twenty-four hours he'd been away the place had been transformed into what looked like a celebration of the Great Leader in some totalitarian flea-pit. Simeonie Inukpuk's face grinned from every window and announcement board. Even Elijah Nungaq, who was on shift hauling cargo at the airstrip, was dressed in a Vote Simeonie Inukpuk tee.

'Am I going mad or is he supposed to be the opposition?' Pol said, as they made their way across the landing strip into the terminal building.

Derek said: 'Seems to me, we're all going mad, one way or another.'

The incumbent mayor was waiting for them just outside the terminal, talking to Stevie.

'Heard you were coming in a day early.' Simeonie clapped Derek on the back and waggled a finger. 'Spying, eh?'

The smell of alcohol and barbecuing meat and the sound of loud music drifted from the Town Hall. While Derek went inside the police office, Stevie parked the ATV. Derek's plan was to check on Willa, debrief Stevie on the search for the old man then take himself off to Edie's house. He lit a cigarette. From the snow porch, two scantily clad men were clearly visible, clinched together in a bear hug in the mayor's office in what looked like an Inuit wrestling match. It was one step beyond weird.

'Don't ask me, D,' Stevie said, strolling in. 'I'm just the grunt.'

Willa was asleep on the cell cot and Derek saw no reason to wake him. He returned to the office and instructed Stevie to release him the moment he stirred. To keep him locked up any longer without formally charging him was against regulations. The irony of this sudden shot of punctiliousness tickled Derek. He'd spent the past few months gradually jettisoning the regulations one by one until the police service was so light it almost never touched the ground. Still, there were lines in the sand, even for Derek. He couldn't keep the kid without charging him and he wasn't about to give him a criminal record on some whim of Edie's.

Stevie handed him a steaming mug.

'How'd the S&R go?'

'Black hole.' Stevie had been to Koperkuj's cabin and found his gun and skiff missing. Otherwise, nothing. 'Wouldn't be surprised he's just gone AWOL, D. The type, by all accounts. I guess there's not much to be done but wait. That cabin though, Jesus Jones, what a state.'

'What kind of a state?'

'A mess, crap everywhere.'

'No sign of burglary?'

'Nah, just your basic bachelor stuff.' Stevie thought for a moment, blushed, then offered his boss a repentant look.

'Sorry, D, I didn't mean it like that.'

Derek went through to the bunk room to freshen up, intending to take a few moments' shut-eye before heading down to Edie's, but the instant his head hit the pillow he found himself back in the pilotless plane. Only this time there were no warning lights. He woke with a start and immediately detected the presence of someone in the room.

'Bad dream?' Edie was sitting cross-legged on the floor beside the door. There was a hard glitter in her eyes, which made her very beautiful, and Derek surprised himself with his awkwardness at being disturbed in such intimate circumstances. He'd never thought of himself as shy.

'How long have you been sitting there?'

'Stevie let me in.'

He swung his legs round so he was sitting up on the bed.

'Shall we do this in the office?'

She hesitated.

'I don't know if Stevie should hear this. The thing is, Derek, we're going to have to dig up Joe.'

The idea was so preposterous he assumed she was joking. Even Edie knew you couldn't go around exhuming the dead. He let out a short, bitter laugh.

'You know how insane that sounds, right?' From the fixed expression on her face Derek could see that she was beyond the point of caring about the consequences of her actions.

'Edie . . .' He didn't know how to put this delicately. '. . . you're not, you know, you don't think maybe, the drinking?'

'My son was killed, Derek. Besides, I quit.'

Stepson, he thought, your *stepson*, but judged it best not to say.

She went on, drawing from her pocket what looked like a plastic bag, describing how she'd come across the sheet of Saran Wrap, how she'd unwrapped and inspected it and what she'd found. He listened until she'd finished. It was certainly odd, more than odd, sinister. On the other hand, suicides were notoriously hard for family members to accept. This crazy idea that something had happened to Joe on Craig had become a kind of obsession with her. The thought even occurred to him that she had invented the Saran-Wrap story, planted the hairs in it, made the indentations, the hole through which she claimed Joe might have struggled to take a final breath, in order to get him on her side. In her present state of mind, he wouldn't put it past her.

On the other hand, what if this so-called evidence was what she said it was? She'd been right about Samwillie Brown's murder when everyone else had put his death down to an accident. And there was a great deal they still didn't know about the deaths of Andy Taylor and Felix Wagner and which Simeonie in particular didn't seem to want them to find out. Could he afford not to take her seriously?

'The lab results are pretty undeniable,' he said, lamely. 'The kid had enough Vicodin in his body to fell a walrus.'

'I know what it looks like but the body never went for a full post-mortem. I guess everyone was so sure it was a suicide. Derek, the moment we saw those blister packs neatly stacked up in the drawer next to his bed, I knew something was wrong. I just didn't follow through. I wish I had. He'd already taken a Xanax, he would have been so out of it, anyone could have done anything to him by then.'

She was right. If he'd been following proper procedure he would have insisted on a full autopsy. He'd made desultory inquiries but there was no pathologist available to fly up and like everyone else he'd assumed the evidence was pretty tight and hadn't pushed for any further forensic investigation. There was the added problem that Joe's parents, like many Inuit, were against any kind of interference with the body but, really, he probably should have insisted.

'How'd they get it into him?'

'Easy,' she said. She had it all figured out. 'By injection.

You crush up the pills with water, administer the solution and you've got yourself a suicide.'

'Then why use the plastic?'

'Pills are unreliable. People throw up, they lapse into comas, they don't die outright. I don't know. Maybe whoever did this really wanted to be sure Joe wound up dead.'

'But why? All we have on him is a bit of petty dope-dealing and a few gambling debts.'

Edie shook her head. 'Not the gambling debts. We were wrong about that one. To get an online account you need a credit card, and Joe didn't have one. We were wrong about a lot of things.'

'The question remains.'

Edie took a deep breath. 'Here's my thinking. Some of it I know for sure, other stuff I'm having to guess at.'

Derek thought immediately of the Brown case.

'I know what you're thinking,' she said. 'But just because I'm paranoid doesn't mean I'm wrong.'

He couldn't help but laugh. The woman had an answer to everything.

'Felix Wagner was trying to pin down the exact location of a gas reserve,' she went on, 'maybe a huge one. He got Bill Fairfax to sell him a fragment of meteorite, which Sir James Fairfax had traded with my great-great-great-grandfather, Welatok, along with three pages from the explorer's diary describing where Welatok had originally found the stone. Fairfax was in some kind of financial trouble, he needed the money and I guess he didn't know the significance of the meteor. It was a particularly rare kind, one with a high concentration of iridium, characteristic of rocks that act as a kind of plug in an astrobleme, a meteorite crater. You take out the meteor and whoosh, up comes the gas.'

He took a good look at her and felt bad for ever thinking of her as an avalanche. She was a sunburst, a great ray of light.

'Normally, you can locate astroblemes very precisely from the magnetic field created by the fragments of meteorite all around it,' she went on. 'Only up here . . .'

'. . . the magnetic field gets screwy,' Derek interjected. 'And the geology of the region is barely mapped.'

'Exactly. So all Wagner had to go on was the stone itself, the diary pages and the probability of finding salt near the entrance to the gas plug.'

'Salt?'

'Halite, they call it. Rock salt. It's like the grease in the plug, far as I can make out, kinda keeps it airtight.'

'How does all this tie up with Andy Taylor? Or with Joe for that matter?'

'Wagner was involved in something called the Arctic Hunters' Club. Taylor told me his boss was into all that old explorer stuff. Wagner knew Bill Fairfax through the club. What I'm guessing, when Fairfax got himself into some kind of financial trouble, Wagner stepped in and offered to buy the stone and the part of the diary he was interested in, leaving Fairfax free to sell the rest at auction. Despite all that club stuff, Wagner wasn't an experienced Arctic hand, so he needed someone to accompany him. Taylor had been in Alaska a while and I guess Wagner was impressed by him, though I'm still trying to work out how, given what an asshole he was.'

'Go on,' Derek said.

'The way I think it happened, Wagner spread himself too thin. He got into bed with two competing energy conglomerates: Zemmer, an energy corporation out of Houston, Texas . . .'

Derek interrupted. 'The ones involved in that oil spill off the coast of Russia?'

Edie ignored the question.

'And an outfit called Beloil, owned by an oligarch called

Belovsky, who Wagner met through the Arctic Hunters' Club.'

Two apparently separate pieces of information snapped together in Derek's head.

'You think Beloil could have sprung Zemmer's pump?' He was thinking about the Russians he'd met in Eureka, how they'd seemed particularly interested in him.

'Those Russian guys, the ones in Greenland. What did they look like?'

Edie's description didn't fit what he could remember of the two men at Eureka, but that wasn't to say they weren't working for the same outfit. His thoughts moved to Misha. Was it too far-fetched to imagine she'd been drafted in to distract him, after all?

'Great way to take out the competition.'

'But why would Zemmer try to pin it on Chechen Islamists?'

'Maybe that way, they get the US Government pouring troops into oil-rich regions so they can suck the oil out of them. Mention the words Islamist, someone in Washington DC adds another few noughts onto the defence budget and no one complains. In any case, either Zemmer or the Russian guy found out they were being misled and wanted Wagner taken out and they got some local guy to do it.'

'You work that out how?'

'Anyone from outside, we would have heard the plane, we would have seen something. The footprint I saw at the site of the shooting? You'd have to know the land, at least a little. I guess, I've just got a feeling . . .'

'. . . a *feeling*?' Derek drew back, sensing Edie was about to go off on one of her flights of fancy.

'Yeah, Derek, a *feeling*. You know, those things people have which govern their actions? Love, hate, greed, ambition, that kind of thing.'

Right now, Derek had *feelings* of his own. He was beginning to *feel* that they had just descended into the realm of supposition. *Feelings* had to be backed up by *evidence*, or they were no good to anyone.

'You're saying you have a *feeling* there's a killer in Autisaq.'

'What I'm saying, someone's in on this.'

He lit up a Lucky Strike. 'You said way back that Taylor took the stone and the diary from Wagner?'

'I saw him do it, Derek, I just didn't realize at the time. When I arrived after Wagner was shot, Taylor was fumbling about in his boss's parka. I just kind of assumed he was loosening it, trying to make Wagner more comfortable. Then later, I found the diary pages hidden in some ice next to Taylor's snowbie. I don't know why he hid them. Maybe he heard the plane and got spooked.'

'You saying someone more powerful wanted that stone and the diary, so Taylor had to go?' Derek said.

'I'm sure of it. Joe told me he saw a green plane that day. I traced it to a fellow called Johannes Moller in Greenland. The day Andy Taylor disappeared, Moller hired it out to two Russians, the same guys who came over on a duck-hunting trip a while later and insisted on going to Craig. They have links to Beloil.'

'You think the Russians shot Taylor?' Derek followed the smoke from his cigarette, momentarily lost in thought. Then he remembered. 'The air was like porridge that day.'

Edie was a couple of steps ahead. 'Moller has an Inuk pilot, Hans. He'll fly through anything and the Russians could easily have used a thermal scope. But not even Hans could land, so they couldn't get the stone.'

'Which is why they had to come back,' said Derek.

'Right.'

He could feel the energy coming off her.

'I think both Joe and Koperkuj heard the shot,' Edie continued. 'While Joe strapped on his skis and went for help, the old man found Taylor's body, took the stone from around his neck and cut up the body. I found the knife he used. The cut marks are exact.'

'Why would he do that?' The idea seemed unlikely.

Edie shrugged. 'The old man never liked *qalunaat* much. I dunno, maybe he was covering up the fact he'd taken the stone.'

Derek was conscious that he had begun picking at the fingernail of his left index finger, a tic he associated with a feeling of not being entirely in control. Already, he had made up his mind to check out the facts on his own. If any of this was to come to court, he'd need to build a case from the evidence. So far, he hadn't seen much of that. Just some cut-up bones, the knife supposedly used to cut them, the witness of a difficult woman and a piece of Saran Wrap that could have come from anywhere and, until there was clarification from the lab, might well contain almost anything.

'The two Russians, the Beloil guys, turned their attentions to a second stone, or rather, part of the original one, which they knew was up in Northwest Greenland.'

'There are two?'

'I had the one Koperkuj found checked out. It was chipped from a larger piece. Most likely Welatok divided it. Maybe he knew he'd get more for it that way, maybe he just wanted a piece that was the right size to hang round his neck. Who knows? In any case, at least one other fragment made its way to Etah.'

'How?'

'Welatok took it.' An impatient tone had crept into Edie's voice, as though what she was saying was so supremely obvious that only dumbasses like himself needed it spelled out. 'He showed it to this Russian explorer, a man called

Karlovsky, up there in Greenland. Karlovsky wanted it but at the last minute Welatok wouldn't sell. I think Fairfax had tricked him and he got spooked and thought Karlovsky would do the same thing. But the Russian went one better: he killed Welatok.' She flapped her hand. 'In any case, all you need to know is that the Beloil fellows were trying to find the second stone.'

'And did they?'

Edie shrugged. 'I don't know. I had to leave before the finale.' She bit her lip. 'I doubt it, though. They were still up there when Qila sent my pictures to the newspaper.'

'OK,' said Derek, 'so now I have no idea what you're talking about.'

'That bit doesn't matter,' she said.

A thought crossed Derek's mind. 'Did Koperkuj know how important the stone is?'

Edie shook her head.

'Anyone know Koperkuj had the stone? Or that you've got it now?'

'Apart from you and Mike Nungaq? Uh nuh.' This news was a relief at least. 'Well . . .' Edie went on: 'I left my wallet at the camp in Etah. If they found it, my alibi for being there would have blown.'

Derek lit another cigarette. He had the feeling he was going to be needing the rest of the pack.

'What did they need the meteorite for in the first place?'

Edie gave an impatient little snort. 'To confirm that it was the kind associated with gas reserves, then as a template for others they might come across in the area. When a meteor falls to earth, it kind of explodes on impact. By finding the fragments, you can build up a scatter pattern that leads you to the epicentre of the impact crater.'

'The impact crater being . . .'

'. . . the astrobleme.'

'Which marks the location of the gas. Somewhere on Craig.'

'Right.'

'How convenient,' he said. The story was beginning to make sense to him.

Edie looked puzzled. Derek tried not to show his pleasure at having finally stumped her.

'Craig Island is one of the few High Arctic islands that's not a designated National Park. Historical quirk. Anywhere else, to get an exploration licence you're going to run into years of legal wrangling. So far as the law is concerned, Craig is wide open.'

They both sat back in silence, each digesting what the other had said.

Finally Derek piped up: 'How would the Russians have known Taylor was on Craig?' He regretted the question as soon as he'd asked it. The answer was obvious. 'I get it,' he said. 'Either there's the local tipster or Taylor was playing them too.'

'Right.' There was a glitter in Edie's eyes still, a kind of shimmering sense of mission, as though she had an animal in her sights and was perfectly poised to bring it down. 'Which is where Simeonie Inukpuk comes in.'

Derek gave an involuntary little snort.

'C'mon. All this election stuff: the posters, the pins, the marketing whatevertheyares. Don't you think it's all just a little weird? I've seen the mayor's bank statements. Simeonie's got money going into some trumped-up foundation. Regular payments.'

'It's called a wage, Edie. Remember a wage? It was what you used to have before you started interfering in all this.' The moment the words came out of his mouth, he regretted them. 'Sorry, I'm just tired.'

'Apology accepted.'

'It's just – the mayor, I can't see it.'

She suddenly looked exhausted. 'You know, I really don't care any more. I just want to know who killed my boy.' She bit her lip hard.

Derek leaned in and took her hand. How small it was. He felt almost overwhelmed by her then, this tiny woman with her limitless loyalty to a ghost.

'I wouldn't ask you if I didn't need help.' Her expression grew suddenly wild, and she reached over and grasped his face and shook it. 'Have you forgotten who we are? *Inuttigut*. We are Inuit. We live in a place littered with bones, with spirits, with reminders of the past. Nothing dies here and nothing rots: not bones, not plastic, not memories. *Especially* not memories. We live surrounded by our stories. It's one of our gifts. Unlike most of the rest of the world, we can't escape our stories, Derek.' She took his hand. 'We need to know how Joe's ends. That's why we have to dig him up.'

Derek sat back, momentarily silent. He knew that what he was about to say could land him in all kinds of trouble, but he also knew that didn't matter any more.

'People will be sleeping off their hangovers tonight, and from the look of the sky, there'll be moonlight.'

'You mean you'll come?'

He nodded.

Edie smiled, reached over and gave him an Inuk kiss.

'Another thing.'

He felt his heart sink a little but motioned her to continue.

'I want Willa in on this one.'

17

In the hours before they set off, Edie fed the dogs from her seal-meat cache and packed her rucksack with jerky, two thermos flasks of hot sweet tea, a primus stove, her ivory snowknife, a torch and a hunting knife, then filled a waterproof pack with her tent, the Remington, a back-up flashlight and battery pack, ice pick, harpoon, rope, portable generator, caribou sleeping bag, fishing light, spare set of sealskin outerwear, spare gas and ammunition. That done, she made herself a passable stew with a good helping of blubber, and settled down in front of *Safety Last!* to compose herself for the journey.

Aside from her own desire to uncover the truth, there were good reasons for the urgency. Every day now the temperature was falling fast, with a thick hoarfrost creeping over everything, and there was a sharp gusting wind blowing frost smoke into the air. Any moment now the ice would collide into frazil and anyone wanting to travel on it would have to wait until it had thickened over and solidified. Once winter really set in, the earth would ice up and the rocks over Joe Inukpuk's body would freeze together and refuse to yield up his bones. They would have to wait until the spring to dig him out and by then it might be too late.

The movie had long since finished when she woke to the sound of Derek opening the door. Some memory of a dream about the *puikaktuq* still lingered in her mind and a current of anxiety pulsed in her right eye.

'D'you bring Willa?'

'I sent him ahead to check over the launch,' Derek said, indicating that he'd wait for her outside.

She got up, shook herself down and went out to the snow porch to pull on her sealskins, mitts and kamiks. Derek was standing by the steps, his breath pooling in the darkening air.

By the time they reached the boat Willa was on deck, tying down the gear. For a moment he caught her eye, then he looked away.

They started out slowly, picking their way through the skeins of ice lying in the water by the shore. When they were out into clearer water, Derek handed the wheel to Willa, who picked up speed and turned the launch due south. The tiny lights of Autisaq were a good way behind them now.

The wind picked up and was blowing in steadily from the west-north-west, its low whistle obscuring the sound of the engine. The launch began to pitch less now they were out in open water. Edie stood close to Willa, waiting for his resistance to her to soften. She reached out her hand and placed it in the crook of his elbow. He took his eyes off the route momentarily.

'I'm sorry,' she said.

They approached Craig in the moments just before dawn. A smear of sun peeked blood-red over the horizon to the south, then bloomed over the water, bleaching as it rose and strewing new, pale yellow light across the high cloud. When it became apparent that they had veered slightly off course, Willa righted the launch, proceeding along the coastline south towards Ulli. Dropping anchor just short of the shore, they waded into the water and lined up in chain formation, passing their kit from one to the other, until it sat in a pile on the beach. There they rested briefly, brewing up hot tea and refilling the thermoses.

Warmer now, they gathered their things, leaving the sat phone, primus, a lightweight, portable gurney and a few other bits and pieces behind on the beach. While Derek and Willa heaved shovels, lights, tents and rifles onto their backs, Edie picked up the thermos, Derek's video camera, a crowbar and her Remington, and the threesome began to make their way along the shingle.

The path to Joe's grave lay at the other end of the beach, via a moraine meander up onto the cliff and along the bluff. Filled with the sense of what lay ahead, no one spoke. The cairn was covered with hoarfrost now, but already the morning sun was beginning to heat the rocks beneath and the delicate frost filigree was shining wet.

They kneeled in the ice and Willa said a prayer. Then, while Derek mounted the camera on its tripod, Edie and Willa unfolded the lights, set the generator running and readied the tent. The plan was to remove the rocks over the cairn until the pelts covering the body appeared. Then they would erect the tent over the site to protect the corpse from the elements and work with lights inside the tent. The camera would be witness to the whole event. Derek had already insisted that what went on inside the tent would be men's work. Edie had no inclination to argue.

Once the equipment was ready, Derek switched on the camera and they began, slowly, so as not to break sweat or disturb the position of the body. They removed the stones from the cairn, one by one, starting with the smaller ones at the top of the pile. As the rocks grew larger they worked as a team, Derek levering with a crowbar while Edie and Willa manipulated each rock in turn onto a piece of tarp then rolled or dragged it to the side, stacking it into an orderly pile with the rest. They worked steadily and in silence and as they levered and rolled and heaved, the pile of boulders and rocks covering the body of Joe Inukpuk grew smaller and smaller and the pile beside the grave larger, until, gradually, the caribou skins covering the body became visible. They cleared the area and erected Edie's tent around the site, and the two men disappeared inside and began the grisly work of clearing the last of the stones, and heaving the body of Joe Inukpuk from the ground.

For a while Edie busied herself rearranging the rocks on the tarp, but when that became too much, she sat back on the pile she'd made and waited. From inside the tent she could hear Derek murmuring instructions. The wind came up, rushing along the tundra and tumbling with a slicing whistle from the cliff. A gust caught at the tent flap, and for a split second she could see the two men bent over the caribou-skin shroud. Over one side of the skin, stiff and petrified, she saw an arm and a hand, shrunken, brown, the skin scaly as a hoof. Then Derek reached over to zip the flap and she turned away. Some strong force rose up in her and she began to whisper, *isumagijunnaipaa*, *isumagijunnaipaa*, forgive me, for all the times she had failed the boy who had treated her as a mother.

A long time later – she had no idea how much time – she heard Derek's voice calling her. He came up to where she was squatting, leaned down and enveloped her in his arms. He was smiling and the warmth of his breath spread across her face. He'd seen it, a tiny shining fragment of plastic trapped almost in the bridge of Joe's nose. They would have to take the body back to Autisaq for examination by a pathologist for confirmation, but this was what they were looking for and each part of the procedure had been captured on camera, so there would be no chance for any lawyer to claim that the evidence had been tampered with.

They had wrapped the body back up in its caribou shroud. Willa was still at his brother's side, saying his prayers. Derek would go down to the beach, call the pathologist in Iqaluit on the sat phone and bring back the gurney. They'd carry Joe wrapped in his burial pelts. He suggested Edie stay with the body. When Willa was done, he'd be in need of her. The experience had hit him hard.

Edie watched his wolf-fur hat disappear over the moraine. For a while she could hear the soft squeal of his boots on the stones, then there was only the wind. Standing beside the tent, she thought about what she had said to Derek, about Joe's story needing an ending, and realized she'd been wrong. Joe was Inuit and Inuit lives were like sundogs or Arctic rainbows, they ran not in lines but in circles. Even now, as they exhumed his body, Joe's spirit was in the sky, a star waiting to be reborn. It was she, with her *qalunaat* blood, who demanded resolution. It was she who could only find her way to a singular truth.

The cloud had come down now and the wind had stilled a little. Willa appeared from the tent, his rifle in hand, alert, and with the intense muscular concentration of the hunter in the path of his prey. He checked his ammunition and flipped off the safety. There was an eager look in his eye.

It had been a very warm summer and the birds had remained to raise second broods. These must be the juveniles from that final hatching. Edie had never seen them stay so late. As the flock rose and fell, swooping across a gust, banking into the weak thermals, she was struck by how much it behaved as a single entity, a vast, fluid, kinetic essence.

The sound was almost deafening now, a great raucous clamour, rising up then bouncing back onto the water. As the flock approached, from what now appeared to be a great duck cloud, snow seemed to be falling. Willa had seen it and dropped his rifle to his side. Cottony wisps of feathers caught in the wind and whipped towards them.

Soon the shadow of the birds was directly over them and the air so thick with their moult that Edie could hardly see Willa for the storm of feathers swirling about and piling like snow at their feet. And all of a sudden the air was dark in their shadow, the clanking of the birds so loud and the smell of guano so overwhelming that they could do nothing but stand in awe, dumbfounded by the spectacle. Only when the last of the stragglers had passed did Willa bend down, scooping up an armful of the feathers and flinging them into the air. Then Edie joined him and soon they were laughing and playing like children in snow, so lost in the game that it took Edie a second or two before she fully registered the sharp crack of a discharged bullet, followed shortly by another, then a third from a different direction. Her body jerked upright so quickly that for an instant she imagined she had been hit.

Checking her rifle was loaded and the infra-red scope was working, she motioned Willa to stay down and remain where he was, then, grabbing her pack and crouching low, she edged her way along the moraine towards the beach. Reaching the cliff line, she dropped to the muskeg and scanned about the tuff and tundra. Below her, on the beach, she could see the pile of supplies outlined against the shale, but there was no sign of Derek or of whoever had fired the shot. Edie began to pull herself forward on her elbows along the cliff line towards the path leading down to the beach. Reaching it, she lifted herself into a low squat and began making her way along the moraine, weaving between the larger boulders. Half way down, where the path disappeared behind an outcrop of rock, she risked stopping to look about.

The outcrop terminated in a ledge over the beach itself

and, dropping to her belly once more, Edie edged herself across until her head and shoulders were clear of the rock altogether. From here she could look down to the foot of the cliff where it joined the beach shale. Derek Palliser was pressed close to the rockface, scanning the low hills to the northeast of the beach, his rifle grasped in both hands, one leg, clearly injured, sticking out stiffly to one side. An image sprang to her mind, of Felix Wagner's body bleeding out in the snow, and she realized how much she needed Derek to live.

Gathering herself, she reached out for a large handful of feathers and flung them out over the ledge onto the shale. Derek registered the cascade, and looked up. His body relaxed a little. Pointing to the injured leg, she gestured a question mark. He shook his head to say he couldn't move it but indicated he was OK. She pointed to her rifle and raised her hands but he shook his head violently, not wanting her to go after the shooter. Again she indicated the rifle and made as if to start up and he conceded, gesturing across the shale and using his hands to indicate that the shooter had clambered up into the fold of low cliffs on the other side of the beach.

The first two shots had issued from the other side of the shale, the last was Derek's reply. The shooter had taken off into the low rocks and hummocky tundra to the northeast, in the opposite direction from Joe's grave. Most likely, given the pattern of the shots, the shooter was alone, but in this situation, the safest course of action was to assume nothing.

Weighing up her options she decided finally to descend to the beach, making her way along to its far end, then clamber up into the low cliffs using a small finger cliff as cover. If the man was wounded, there would be a blood trail to pick up. She might be able to tell something about the gravity of the injury from the trail. That would give her some clues as to how long he was likely to be able to keep moving before he went down.

Creeping along the moraine path, keeping low to the ground, she inched her way down onto the shale until she was standing in the lee of the cliff. It seemed that, wherever he was, the shooter either couldn't see her or that something – physical injury or strategy – had stopped him from taking a shot at her. She stopped then and listened for sounds, but the wind was keeping up its steady, camouflaging whistle. She moved forward along the beach's edge, her footsteps softened through the piles of eider moult. Towards the northeastern edge, where the beach gave way to a low rising bluff, she caught sight of a series of red beads, livid against the snowy ground cover. Mouthing a few words to honour the spirits of the birds for their intervention, Edie then bent to inspect the trail. From the pattern of trampled feathers she could see that the man's right arm was bleeding heavily. She guessed that the bullet had severed an artery. He wouldn't be able to keep walking for long. The movement would pump blood from the injury and weaken him further. He would most likely try to hide out somewhere until he felt it was safe to break cover. She wouldn't have to follow this ribbon across the feathers far, she thought, until she found his hiding place.

She made her way to an outcrop of low, flat rock only a few metres from the edge of the bluff, but hidden from view, her rifle grasped in both hands, approaching it at an angle, with her right leg swinging out to the side so that she would make contact with the rock with her foot before she could trip over it and injure herself. At the rock's edge, she squatted down and scanned the trail. She didn't want to have to shoot the man, but if he threatened her, she was fully prepared to do so.

Once she had convinced herself she was in no imminent

danger, she followed the trail leading northeast. There were fewer feathers here, and the blood splatter became more erratic. The injured man had been trying to run, but the footfalls were too short. He was growing weak, she thought, and possibly confused.

Taking a breath to calm herself, she picked up a piece of shale and, flinging it in the hope of attracting fire, ducked back behind the rock and waited for a response. Nothing. The man either hadn't seen her or was in no position to engage. Shuffling forward with her rifle held to her face, she skirted around the rock then out from behind it into the open towards the trail.

The shooter was still bleeding badly and leaving bloody crush marks in the willow from his footfalls. The prints were large, she noted, made not with kamiks but most likely with commercially manufactured snow boots; and he was leaning to the left, no doubt to compensate for the weakness in his right arm. Judging from the degree to which the blood had already coagulated, he had left the scene immediately after the shots rang out. A professional hunter, someone for whom the kill was absolutely the centre of his focus, would have tried to get another shot at his target, she thought. Whoever this guy was, he was an amateurish kind of assassin.

As she advanced, the blood became more plentiful and fresher too, the rusty spots of the earlier trail replaced by a thick red rope. Not far on, the trail ran into a long esker which she and Joe had always called *uvingiajuq akivingaq*, because it looked like a huge bull walrus. Instead of going over the top, which was the quickest way, the trail stopped. Here, there were crush marks and more blood where the shooter had hesitated.

It was quite possible, she thought, that the shooter was no more than a few metres from her on the other side.

Protected from view by the gravel slope Edie followed the trail with great caution, as it hugged the contours of the gravel pile, then disappeared. She was about to round the shorter, easterly edge of the ridge when she thought twice and halted.

Retracing her steps, she reached the spot where the shooter had stopped and began the slow crawl upwards. Here on the northern incline snow had been swept in and clung, easing her progress. The sky was deep grey in foggy cloud. The wind had stopped gusting and a thin rain had begun. She moved gingerly, careful not to lose either her purchase on the shale or her breath. There would be less wind noise on the other side and she was anxious not to alert the wounded man to her presence. At the crest she lay still, well out of sight, her parka hood pulled across to obscure her face. She looked into the sky and silently called on the spirits, then, bit by bit, she inched forward until the top of her head protruded from the edge of the esker and waited, making slow fists with her fingers and toes to stave off the cold. She was vulnerable in this position, not simply from the shooter, if he was there, but from the wind that whipped the crest, pushing gravel down the slope.

The thin rain made it impossible to see what lay below. She waited. After a long while she heard a crunching sound and, looking down through the fog, saw a faint light flash on and off. The man was there and it seemed he was looking at his wristwatch. She considered shooting at the position of the light, but decided it was too risky. But the man had just given her some valuable information. If it was a watch, then the shooter could only be *qalunaat*. No Inuk would take a wristwatch hunting. She sat back and allowed herself to absorb this. It was good. If the shooter was *qalunaat* he would have an Achilles heel. Up here, they all did.

Very carefully, she advanced along the ridge, checking

the shale on the southern incline. It was looser there and devoid of plant life. One sharp kick in the right place and she might be able to cause it to avalanche downwards. Most likely, the avalanche wouldn't kill him – the stones were small and not very sharp – but it would certainly stop him from going anywhere. She thought about what could go wrong, the gravel not moving, or worse, sending her tumbling down with it, and quickly decided it was worth the risk.

Raising both feet she swung them with all her strength into the shale. At first nothing much happened; a few fist-sized pieces of rock began to shift, then the whole incline became fluid, shifting and sliding until a critical mass was reached and the stones began to clatter down the esker onto the man below, raising a great cloud of dust. Edie heard a sharp cry, then nothing. The fog made it impossible to see what lay below.

For what seemed like an age, she waited, allowing the shale to settle, then she began, with patient care, to clamber down until she could just make out a man's form. It looked as though he had taken a defensive position on his knees, with one hand curled over his head and the other on his rifle. The avalanche had knocked the weapon from his hand and it now lay a few feet from his outstretched right arm. He was buried up to his shoulders in shale.

She called out but he did not answer. Slowly, step by step, her feet set parallel to the ground, and with her rifle at the ready, Edie edged her way towards him. Still the man did not move. Reaching the ground, she went with caution towards the rifle, and with her weapon still trained on the man in front of her, she squatted down and removed the clip, putting it in the pocket of her parka. Slinging the rifle over her shoulder, she moved towards the shooter, pinned in his pile of shale. The realization hit her that he might have died. Blood seeped from the pile.

Piece by piece, she began frantically pulling off the rocks, flinging them out onto the muskeg. Before long, the man's parka appeared under the rubble. She reached out and touched him, but he made no attempt to free himself. His face remained obscured by a balaclava, and he was still too weighed down with shale for Edie to be able to drag him clear. Quickly, she began to scoop at the sides of his burial cairn, tossing handfuls of shale out into the darkness.

Finally, when the body was clear enough to move, she bent down and rolled him over. He was a big man, tall and muscular, his body type and clothing identifying him immediately as *qalunaat*. Derek's bullet had hit him in the wrist, severing the radial artery and partially amputating the hand. Red crystals had formed across the surface of his parka. Running her hands under his outerwear, she checked him for weapons and found none. In any case, he was unlikely to be a threat to her now. In the period since he'd checked his watch, he'd lost consciousness – perhaps as a result of the shale fall. His pulse was very weak. She knew she wouldn't be able to lift him on her own, but she could fetch Willa and together they might well be able to pile him onto the gurney they'd brought to take down Joe's remains. Pulling off her scarf she made a crude tourniquet and pulled it tight around the forearm above the partially amputated wrist. Then, gingerly, she removed the balaclava.

Edie slumped back. The man was Robert Patma. For a moment she thought she'd made a mistake, then it occurred to her that perhaps *Patma* was mistaken and the whole episode had been one terrible error, a genuine accident in which Robert had shot at what he thought was game, then panicked when he realized it wasn't; but even as she thought this, her heart told her that it wasn't true. She felt winded, confused, thoughts careening recklessly round in her mind. Grabbing her pigtails she tugged hard to bring herself to her senses, then, slinging Patma's rifle around her shoulder and rounding the esker, she made her way as fast as she could back to the beach, calling out that everything was OK. There Willa was by Derek's side, pressing the wound on the injured leg to staunch the bleeding. There was an anxious pall on his face. Fonder of the policeman than he'd let on, Edie thought.

'Did you get him?' Derek asked. When she did not answer, he said, 'It's not as bad as it looks. I don't need putting down.' He smiled thinly. 'Not yet, anyway.'

Edie said, 'Willa and I will have to lift him out to the launch on the gurney. He's alive but only just.'

'Well?' Derek said, his mouth bunched in pain.

'Well what?'

'Well, who the hell just tried to kill me?'

Edie felt breathless, the after-effects of the adrenaline kicking in.

'It looks like Robert Patma.'

'The nurse?' Derek was as floored by the news as she had been when she first peeled away the shooter's balaclava.

For a moment they looked at one another, thinking the same thought.

'He alone?'

'I hope so.' There had been no other footprints.

'We'd better get him to some help,' Derek said.

Willa took a breath. 'Are you *crazy*?'

For a second Derek didn't answer, as though he was considering the possibility, then in a resigned voice he said, 'I guess I'm just police.'

Edie and Willa approached the esker cautiously, on foot.

Robert Patma was lying where Edie had left him, trapped in shale. Willa moved towards him slowly and lifted his head, which fell back. Edie took the pulse on the unsevered wrist. Robert Patma was just about still alive.

'Let's start digging,' Edie said.

It took a couple of hours to extract Robert Patma from his rocky prison, then they lifted him onto the gurney and slowly manoeuvred him into the launch, cuffing his one good hand to the guard rail. Then they went back for Joe.

They stacked the corpse between the two wounded men. Willa took the wheel while Edie found some Vicodin in the first-aid kit. Robert Patma remained unconscious. She called Stevie on the detachment sat phone and told him what to expect.

'Patma, the nurse guy? What the hell?'

'Your guess,' Edie said.

Stevie undertook to call in medics in Iqaluit. They could probably be in Autisaq within a few hours. He offered to patch in a call so Derek could speak to them directly, but Derek didn't think much of the idea. It was just a muscle wound, he said, painful but not life-threatening. The bleeding had stopped and once the Vicodin kicked in, he'd be fine. Edie protested, but for a man whose right leg was out of action, Derek was pretty good at digging in his heels.

By the time they got back it was already dark. Stevie was waiting for them at the quay with Sammy Inukpuk and Mike and Elijah Nungaq. The men carried Robert Patma and Joe Inukpuk, Edie followed behind with Derek on an ATV and Willa went off to brief Simeonie on the day's events.

While Stevie returned to the police office to check on the likely arrival time of the medics' plane, Edie cleaned and bandaged Derek's wound.

Robert Patma had been put in one of the medical rooms. The door had been locked from the outside and Sammy sat beside it with a loaded rifle.

'Didn't see that one coming,' Sammy said.

Stevie reported that the medics had been weathered out and wouldn't be arriving till tomorrow morning. They'd left detailed instructions on how to deal with the two patients and someone would call every hour to check on their progress. Meanwhile, Robert Patma was to be kept guarded.

They moved back into the waiting area.

'We should check Patma's apartment,' Edie said.

'I've told Stevie to apply for a warrant.' Derek winced. The painkiller was wearing off. 'We're doing this the official way, Edie. My way. Patma dies, I don't want to find myself at the end of a lawsuit.'

Edie scanned the medics' instructions, then reached out and patted his arm. 'I'll get you some more Vicodin.'

In the matter of Robert Patma's apartment, she had her own ideas.

The key to the safety deposit box was in Robert Patma's office desk. She opened it up and took out the pharmacy key. Running her eyes over the rows of medicines, she came across a box of Vicodin sitting high up in a corner. By jumping and grabbing she managed to wrest a pack off the shelf, but in doing so knocked a box beside it off. Luckily, it didn't break.

There was a small set of steps sitting in the far corner, so she pulled these over and clambered on. She was about to slot the box back into place when something right at the back of the shelf caught her eye. There was nothing remarkable about the package except that the writing was in Russian. She pulled it out and opened it up. Inside were leaves of foils, each holding a dozen tablets.

She gave Derek the Vicodin without mentioning her find.

'Wanna rest up the night at my place?'

Derek looked unsure, unhappy about imposing.

'It's my bed or that freezing bunk in the office, listening to Stevie snoring. Or you can lie nice and cosy next to the fella who tried to kill you.'

'When you put it like that,' Derek said. He looked embarrassed. 'But Edie . . .' Their eyes met. Edie mustered a smile.

'I said you could sleep in my bed, Police. That's S.L.E.E.P.'

She helped him limp home, then fixed some soup for the two of them. Within moments of his head touching the pillow, Derek Palliser was sleeping deeply. She waited a while, until she was sure he would not wake, then slunk back out into the night.

The door to the nursing station was on the latch, as she'd left it. Sammy was sitting outside Robert Patma's room, rifle in his lap, fast asleep. She went back to the safety-deposit box, found the key to the morgue and let herself in. For a long time she just sat with Joe, running over their happy times together in her mind.

Then she said: 'I miss you, Joe,' left the room, went back to the safety-deposit box and fished around among the keys. She tried each in turn, but none fitted Patma's apartment's lock so she reached into her pocket and drew out her Leatherman.

Inside the apartment, the blinds were drawn. She flipped on a lamp on the table by the sofa.

The first thing that struck her was how incredibly neat the place was. The living room was laid out symmetrically, with matching side tables and identical lamps. The open-plan kitchen looked completely unused. Fine white crockery was stacked in soldier-like rows on shelves in the glazed cabinets and pristine steel utensils hung from hooks on the walls. All the usual cheerful mess of cooking – scarred pans, greasy oil bottles, and novelty drying cloths – had either been hidden away or did not exist.

The living room had the same show-home look. The two black leather sofas were eerily immaculate, as though they had never been sat upon, and were flanked by black occasional tables, on each of which stood identical cream-coloured lamps. A series of black-and-white chrome-framed prints of Arctic scenes lined up along the back wall, presenting the sanitized, picture-perfect, people-free Arctic fantasy beloved of southern photographers and artists. In the corner was a telescope, set to look out across Jones Sound.

Two further rooms with a bathroom sandwiched between them lay beyond the living room down a corridor. One served as a bedroom; Robert Patma had converted the second into a study. Both far corners of the room were occupied by matching wooden filing cabinets. On the desk in the office there was an envelope postmarked Tallahassee, Florida with a date of a week ago. Inside was a handwritten letter addressed to 'Dear Bobby' and signed 'Mom and Dad', along with a photograph of two elderly people arm-in-arm beside a swimming pool. She turned the photo over. Someone had pencilled the words 'Jerry and June Patma' with the date on the back.

Hadn't Robert told her his mother had died? There was some muddle over it, she recalled, a bit of embarrassment when she'd got confused about which parent he'd lost. Now it looked as though he'd made the whole thing up.

She tried the filing cabinets. They were both locked, but the locks gave way surprisingly easily to the file attachment on Edie's Leatherman. In the first cabinet, Edie found nothing of interest, but the second Patma reserved for his financial dealings. These files were marked on the covers only by a long string of numbers. Edie picked out a file at random and sat at the desk to read it. Inside there were a couple of certificates marking completion in some aspect of nursing training, the odd bill for household goods and services, and a few bank letters. The file appeared to follow no particular order or system, which was odd given how picky Patma seemed in other aspects of his life. Edie picked another file, but it was the same story, an odd assortment of bills, financial statements and guarantees for electrical products.

Then it occurred to her that this wasn't random at all. To an outsider, the files seemed disorganized and undifferentiated but Robert Patma knew exactly what document was where. The codes on the files enabled Patma to retrieve them at any time, but they made it extremely difficult for any outsider to locate any one particular paper trail.

She flipped through the files and pulled out a couple of bank statements detailing half a dozen money transfers into Patma's account. The transfers were for relatively large amounts but there seemed to be no pattern or consistency to them, except that they were all from the same source, a name in Russian script. She checked through the files and found two more recent statements, but the payments appeared to have stopped. Folding three or four of these transfer notices into her waistband, she returned the files to the cabinet and left the room.

Next she turned her attentions to the medicine cabinet in the bathroom, which was filled with the usual assortment of Tylenol, shaving foam and ear buds. Next she tried the bedroom, but there was nothing in the bedside tables, or under the bed. None of the half-dozen pairs of outdoor boots lined up in the shoe rack in the wardrobe bore the same polar-bear tread as the one she had found after Felix Wagner's shooting.

Drifting back into the study, convinced, still, that she

had missed something, she yanked out one of the drawers of the second filing cabinet. The force of the pull shifted the cabinet slightly on its castors and as it rolled forward, one of the floorboards moved beneath it. As she pulled the cabinet out a little more, she could see that the board had definitely been loosened. She reached down and with one finger of her right hand pulled it open, a little at first then more swiftly as her finger curled underneath. What lay there sent a terrible pain racing up her spine. She tried to take it in. Her head reeled and for a moment she thought she would pass out.

Stacked in neat rows, ten by ten, were dozens of empty pharmaceutical blister packs, aligned crosswise, one foil lying one way, the torn covering over the plastic capsules so neatly pressed back into place you would almost think it untouched, the next foil, its capsules also neatly covered, stacked on top of it in the other direction.

It was not the usual way a person might stack used and discarded blister packs but Edie had seen precisely this arrangement before. There was no doubt about it. The person who had stacked these foils was the same person who had arranged the Vicodin packs in the drawer of Joe Inukpuk's bedside cabinet.

Robert Patma.

She turned the foils over in her hand. The lettering matched the Russian script on the box in the pharmacy. She found a piece of paper in Patma's printer, and noted it down. Then she replaced the blister packs, and put back the loose floorboard.

From the office she went directly into the kitchen, flinging open the drawers and cupboards, until, eventually, she found what she was looking for. On a shelf so high up she had to stand on the worktop to reach it was a catering-size roll of Saran Wrap. She pulled it down, knocking over a salt grinder. Leaving the grinder where it was, she turned the wrap over in her hand. The label seal was missing and some of the plastic had been torn from the sheet using the neat little row of metal teeth. The cut edge was almost perfectly even, with hardly any broken serrations or stretch marks, the work of an exceptionally neat person. Edie already knew where she would find its match.

Sammy was still sleeping in his chair outside the medical room. So long as she was careful, she wouldn't wake him.

Working as quietly as a hunter stalking its prey, Edie pulled the box of Russian pills from the shelf in the pharmacy cupboard and took out fifteen foils, then she crept past Sammy and tiptoed to the door. She twisted the lock until it clicked open and slipped inside.

18

Edie watched Robert Patma breathing, with the hypodermic on the table beside him. Her mind zoned in and out, the thoughts like lichens stuck in willow thicket; dense, livid stains competing for air. She scrolled through the events of the past months, thought about Wagner and Taylor, about Derek and the *puikaktuq*. Mostly she thought about Joe.

In the few minutes since she had found the Saran Wrap in Robert Patma's kitchen, it was as though she'd been in-habited by some other, unfamiliar, self. It was this other person who had taken the box of Hydal from the shelves, who had sneaked past the sleeping Sammy into Robert Patma's room, then crushed the tablets, one by one, into a tiny avalanche of white powder and drowned it in saline. This alternate self was sitting with her now, watching Robert Patma breathing, while the real Edie conjured up happier times with Joe.

A head appeared around the door, startling her out of her thoughts. It was Sammy.

'Edie, what are you doing in here?' He was blinking away sleep.

'I don't know,' she said. It came to her then, in a rush, like meltwater breaking over a dam. *She was contemplating murder*.

'You coming out now?' He hadn't noticed the Hydal.

'Give me a moment.'

Sammy raised his eyebrows just enough to let her know he considered her behaviour strange. 'A minute, then,' he said.

The instant he disappeared round the door, she picked up the hypodermic and, rushing to the medical waste-only bin, threw it in. Then she piled the blister packs in after it and, grabbing a pack of lint dressing, tore open the wrapper and threw it on top to disguise the contents.

The patient lay beside her, sleeping peacefully. A wave of nausea passed through her body. She retied the tourniquet she'd put around his wounded arm, then, for the last time, she turned her back on Robert Patma and tiptoed out.

Sammy was sitting in his guard's chair, an anxious expression on his face.

'Sammy, don't mention this to anyone, eh?' She put a hand on his shoulder, then slipped away.

Back home, she made herself a cup of tea and lay down on the sofa, dazzled by a magic lantern of thoughts. She tried deep breathing to relax, but after a few minutes sat up, too wired to settle. There was a DVD lying on the table. Without looking at it, she slotted it into the machine. The screen flickered for a moment then the familiar face of Harold Lloyd appeared. Only then did Edie feel the tears come.

Martie found her on the sofa a few hours later.

'Robert Patma, eh, who knew?' Her aunt shook her head in disbelief. Her voice lowered into a conspiratorial rasp. 'There's a dark spirit living in Autisaq,' Martie said. 'I seen him, Edie, a dark, dark spirit.'

'I thought you don't believe in bad spirits, Auntie Martie,' Edie said, yawning. 'Only bad people.'

'I don't know, Little Bear,' Martie said. 'I don't know.'

They continued the conversation over a breakfast of tea

and bannock bread with syrup. Martie shook her head sadly as Edie told her all that had happened. When she'd finished her bread and syrup she stood to leave.

'Don't get dragged into this any further, Little Bear,' she said. 'It might be bigger than you think.'

'It's too late, Auntie,' Edie said.

She was in the shower when the air ambulance announced its arrival with a loud overhead whine. By the time she dressed, the medics would be arriving at the nursing station. She hoped they'd find Robert Patma alive. She knew now she didn't want him to die. She was convinced in her own mind that Robert Patma had killed Joe Inukpuk on the orders of the Russians, who were supplying his addiction. Maybe he'd started out as a paid informant. What if the gambling debts he attributed to Joe were actually his own? Maybe it was no more than that for a while, but everything changed when he got hooked on painkillers. At first, she imagined, he'd supplied himself from the pharmacy and when he could no longer keep his habit fed that way, the Russians stepped in to provide him with what he needed. Maybe he was connected to Zemmer, too, though there was nothing to suggest it. The Russians extracted a price from him and that price was Joe.

For what seemed like an age she allowed the warm water to cascade over her body. Then she scrubbed herself once more and oiled her hair. By the time she got out of the shower, Derek had left. There was a note in the kitchen by the kettle, saying that he and Stevie had gone to get Derek's injured leg sorted out.

It was only when she was returning from the hospital with Derek several hours later that she sensed someone had been inside the house. There were subtle differences in the position of certain objects. She could see immediately, for example, that her pile of DVDs had been picked up and put back at an ever so slightly different angle and a few of the books on her shelf had been taken out and slid back in. It was the same in the bedroom and kitchen, tiny hints that cupboards had been opened, fingers slid into nooks, boxes searched, corners inspected.

It wouldn't serve anyone right now, she thought, to mention this to Derek or to Stevie. Most likely it was nothing. Willa had been in, perhaps, or Minnie, hoping to find some booze. She thought of Koperkuj, still missing. The timing troubled her.

She waited until Stevie was gone and Derek was asleep to check for the stone at the bottom of the sugar barrel. It was still there. She put the barrel back in its place, licked her fingers clean and chastised herself for being paranoid.

The man who had killed her beloved Joe in exchange for a few pills was being moved into the air ambulance right now. A police pathologist was examining Joe's body at the morgue, looking for needle marks. In another hour or two, the evidence that Robert Patma had murdered Joe Inukpuk and the murderer himself would be on its way to Iqaluit and she would never have to see Robert Patma again. As she'd sat beside him last night, listening to his breathing, and contemplating putting a stop to it, the idea had come to her that he was nothing, an addict, but then Sammy had come into the room and she'd thought of herself, of her ex and of Willa. *At some point in our lives, hadn't all of us been the same?* Whatever Robert Patma had done, he wasn't so different from the people she loved and she could no more put an end to his life than she could kill Sammy or Willa.

And yet, knowing now, as she did, that Patma had been behind Joe Inukpuk's death didn't solve the mystery entirely. His absence from the community during that first blizzard, when Felix Wagner was shot, had been real enough, even if he had fabricated the reason for it. Robert Patma could not have killed Felix Wagner because he wasn't in the vicinity when it happened. So if Patma hadn't, who had? There wasn't much to go on: a footprint, committed to memory. She thought again about the stone and the trouble it had caused. Whoever had killed Wagner wanted it and there was no reason to suppose he or she wasn't still out there. Her uneasiness extended back to the feeling that the house had been broken into, then back further still to Martie's warning that whatever she had got herself into *may be bigger than you think*. Did Martie know something about Koperkuj's disappearance she wasn't telling?

Edie checked that Derek's breathing was coming soft and regular through the darkness of her bedroom, then she pulled on her parka and hat, pushed her feet into her shit-kickers and went outside. She headed for the little coffee shop at the back of the Northern Store where Martie was often to be found when she was in town, but she wasn't in there today. As she was making her way to the front of the store, Mike popped up from behind the Doritos stand.

'Edie, thank God. I always had that nurse down as a good kid. What happened? I heard he was a drug addict.'

'News sure travels.' Edie smiled with the shutters down. She knew Mike well enough to recognize when he was fishing for more gossip and she really didn't want to get into anything now.

'Nicky, the air-ambulance nurse, came in here for some coffee. She said Dr Urquhart told her Patma got his drugs from Russia. What's that all about?'

Edie had no wish to add her voice to the gossip mill. 'Listen, Mike,' she said. 'I'm kind of in a hurry. You seen Martie?'

Mike looked momentarily taken aback at the abrupt change of subject.

'She was here earlier, but I guess she left already.'

Edie thanked him. From the store, she went back home, packed a few things, left a note to say where she was going, and headed out. In a day or two it would be possible to travel on the sea ice but there still wasn't quite enough snow for the snowmobile, so for now she would have to use Derek's ATV. In three weeks' time the dark period would close in on them completely. If there was a black spirit somewhere around Autisaq, she would need to find it while there was still light to see it by.

She pulled the ATV onto the rocky tuff beside Martie's cabin and stood before it for a moment, calling her aunt's name. For a while she listened at the door but no sound came from inside. She tried the handle; the door was open but instead of going in, she went around the back, to a small cluster of outbuildings: a shed that served both as a store for equipment and for drying sealskins, an abandoned dog kennel and an open-sided port where Martie kept her vehicles. The ATV was not in its usual place.

A couple of summers ago a construction team had built a rough gravel path from Autisaq all the way to Martie's cabin in the hope that it would help her get to the landing strip without losing her flight slot, since she was so often late, but the path had broken up in the first frost and all but the kilometre or so section nearest the cabin was now impassable. Martie often took her ATV out to where the path ended and hiked from there up into the low hills to hunt hare and to pick the tiny cloudberries that appeared on the southern slopes after a good summer. Since it was cloudberry season, she was probably there now.

Edie took off her outerwear inside the cabin and made herself a brew, thinking to wait for her aunt to return.

Sitting at Martie's broken-down old table, she reached over and absent-mindedly picked up an old spoon lying there to stir the sugar in her tea, thinking about what she would say to her aunt when she came back. The act of stirring raised all sorts of questions in her mind, and she began to wonder why she'd come, whether the events of the last few days had made her a bit oversensitive, if not paranoid. She pulled out the spoon, noticed that the back was covered in some kind of soot, and tossed it to the other side of the table. Hygiene was never Martie's strong suit.

As she drank her tea, the feeling grew that she would have done better to have remained in Autisaq and found out who had been responsible for searching her house. She felt bad, too, leaving Joe's body to be opened up without her being there. It was almost as though she'd abandoned him again. And then there was the policeman. It dawned on her that she was worrying about Derek more than was strictly necessary but there it was. He was just one more reason to be back at Autisaq.

She grabbed her parka and her pack. As she was about to shut the door, her eye was drawn to a hook fixed to the frame. On the hook was a padlock key. It aroused her curiosity partly because she'd never seen it before and partly because she'd never in all her life known Martie to lock anything. None of the outbuildings were locked as she recalled, and since Auntie Martie didn't even bother to lock her plane, it seemed odd that she would think to attach a padlock to anything else she owned. On an impulse, she removed the key.

She looked about the mess of cans, animal skins and fishing and hunting equipment strewn around the cabin for some kind of padlock, then she went back outside and checked the doors to the outbuildings. Martie's snowbie was in the port, with its key dangling from the ignition. Edie put her head around the door to the shed. Inside was the usual clutter of cans of creosote, antifreeze and oil, along with a few harpoons, baffles, lures, *ulus* and other pieces of outdoor equipment. In one corner there was stacked a pile of sealskins, but no padlock and nothing to which a padlock might be attached. She closed the door to the shed again and told herself she had no right to meddle in her aunt's business. She should put the key back on the hook before Martie came home or she'd be obliged to explain herself.

As she walked around the side of the shed, resolving not to pursue the matter any further, she noticed that the dog kennel had been moved recently, disturbing the imprint of lichens that had grown around its previous position. She went closer. From the scrape pattern on the rock it looked as though the kennel had been swung around a number of times. She pushed it experimentally, and noticed as she did so a hatch in the shed wall, corresponding to the space behind the pile of skins inside. It was here, neatly inserted so that it lay flush with the wall, that Edie found the padlock. Inserting the key, she flipped the lock off in one move of the wrist. The hatch door gave way to reveal a small metal box, like a safe. There was nothing inside. As she shut the door a sour smell hit her that was familiar from somewhere, though she couldn't put her finger on it. She locked it back up. For the second time that day she felt shabby, contaminated. Martie was her kin and she had no business messing with her stuff. She pushed the kennel back against the side of the shed, replaced the key on the hook inside the cabin door and left.

It wasn't until she was out in Jones Sound that she remembered the odd burn marks on the old spoon she'd used to stir her tea. And it wasn't until she remembered the spoon that she recalled she'd left her tea mug lying on Martie's table.

Derek was sitting on the sofa as she walked into her house. He was in a considerable state of agitation. In his hand was the clipped picture of the members of the Arctic Hunters' Club that Qila Rasmussen had given her back in August.

'Why didn't you show me this before?' There was a pained look on his face and he was biting back his anger.

'I don't know,' she said, bewildered. 'I mean, I told you, about Felix Wagner and the Belovsky fellow.'

'We have to leave,' he said. He launched the picture at her. 'Now.'

'Leave?' She felt confused. 'Why?' She'd never heard him sounding this crazed; his voice had become almost hysterical. She wondered whether it was the effect of the drugs he was taking. 'Listen, Derek, I really, *really* don't know what you're talking about,' she said. 'And in any case, you can't go anywhere with that leg.'

Holding the photo out to her, he said: 'Which of these men have you seen before?'

She looked carefully and pointed to Felix Wagner, then to Belovsky.

'No one else?' Derek invited her to look again. Her eyes scanned the rows but there were no other familiar faces. She shook her head.

Derek pointed to a tall, distinguished man with a beard and a large, aquiline nose, standing at the back. 'You don't know him?'

'Uh nuh.'

He took in a breath and gave a little bark of comprehension.

'That explains a lot,' he said, his voice less aggressive now. 'I guess I assumed you would have come across him.'

'Why?'

'Edie, the man in the photo is Professor Jim DeSouza.'

It took a moment for her to register the name. Of course, DeSouza ran the space science station on Devon Island.

'You think he knows what happened to Wagner?'

'It would seem something of a coincidence if he didn't, don't you think? Fairfax, Wagner, Belovsky, all in this mess, and DeSouza just an innocent outsider? Last couple of times I saw him he seemed real edgy. Any case, I think we should pay him an unexpected visit.'

Edie gestured at the policeman's injured leg. 'I'll go.'

Derek gave a bitter laugh. 'Oh no, you don't get to write me off that easily, Edie Kiglatuk.' He fixed her with a look that made her pulse thud.

While he'd been waiting for her, he'd formulated a plan. They would need to confront DeSouza when he was least expecting it, before he had time to construct some rationale for himself. If he had nothing to do with Wagner's death, he'd have nothing to hide. Flying was no-go. They'd have to get advance permission to land at the science station and it would be impossible to fly in without everybody knowing about it. The approach would have to be by sea. Jones Sound was only very newly frozen and still unreliable, the ice thin and sappy in places, and turbulent, as slabs of new ice churned in the currents. The more even weight distribution of dogsleds made them safer on such ice but snowmobiling would be faster, and they were in a hurry.

Derek had it all worked out. On the north Devon coast, not far from the station campus, but out of sight of it, to the east of Cape Vera, there was a thin finger fiord, protected from the prevailing easterly winds by a small island at its foot, where the ice usually stabilized early. They would pull up there, where their lights couldn't be seen, and camp out the night. Just before dawn, they would make their way overland to the station. If they were lucky, they would surprise DeSouza at his breakfast.

Edie said: 'When do we start?'

Derek got to his feet. 'How about now?'

It was a rough crossing. The snowbies bounced from the curdling ice like punchballs swinging from a fist, and they had to stop over and over again to make their way around open leads. Beyond the multi-year ice foot, the wind picked up and for a while their ears were filled with the alarming sound of newly forming ice heaving up from the pressure of the swell beneath. Derek had refused any painkillers for his leg, saying he needed his wits about him, but Edie could see that he was all washed out and relying on his Lucky Strikes to get him through. For all that, though, they made it past Craig Island just as twilight fell. A thin red sun hovered across the horizon like a bloodied eye for a moment, then was replaced by a glaucous moon.

They continued in a southwesterly direction towards Devon, zig-zagging across loose-forming pan into Bear Bay. After another three hours, Sukause Island appeared in the moonlight. The fiord lay just ahead. The wind died and the air began to curdle with frost smoke.

They decided to set up camp, eat something and catch some rest. Anyone who saw their lights or heard their snowbies would assume they were a hunting party.

Without speaking, they transferred the equipment from the snowbies to the beach. Not long afterwards, they had the tent up and were sitting inside, eating caribou jerky and drinking hot tea. Outside, it grew misty. Derek ate very little and said less, though from the way he was sitting, injured leg held out stiffly, a taut expression on his face, Edie could tell he was in a good deal of pain. The doctor, Urquhart, had given him some Vicodin and Xanax to help relax the injured muscle and she suggested he take them both. He could sleep, while she watched for a change in the weather. If visibility improved, she promised she'd wake him. The look of gratitude and relief on his face told its own story.

For a while she listened to his breathing, allowing herself to be reassured by its soft regularity, then she went out and took a short stroll along the shingle. The twilight had long since passed, and the sky had deepened to a fierce, uncompromising black. Though the mist had cleared somewhat, the remnants of frost smoke still hung in the air. She would let Derek sleep a bit longer. A few hours wouldn't make a difference one way or the other. It was the middle of the night. So long as he didn't get wind of their arrival, DeSouza wouldn't be going anywhere.

She let herself back into the tent. Derek slept on. The wind crept up and began whooping along the cliff overhead before tumbling onto the shingle. Then there was another sound on shingle, something heavier and rhythmic and not propelled by the wind. It came again, the same, unmistakeable rattle of something living moving, a fox perhaps. On second thoughts, the footfall was too heavy for fox, too heavy even for wolf or caribou. Instinctively, she tensed, her breath held fast in her throat, listening for animal sounds while the crackling of the shale came closer, then slowly began to retreat towards the cliffs.

Most likely it was musk ox or bear but, remembering the missing Koperkuj, Edie decided to investigate. Reaching for her hare-fur mufflers, she tied them around her kamiks then, grabbing her rifle and ammo belt, screwed on the night sight, brushed aside the canvas, zipped up the tent flap behind her and set off alone.

19

The rifles's night sight illuminated the deep, dead dark of the shingle and picked up some indentations in the shale mass, leading off up towards the slopes at the west. It wasn't as easy to see as Edie had anticipated. Everything around seemed in motion. The footprints were diffuse and the wind was already blowing them away, but they looked as though they'd come from two legs, not four.

They'd not told anyone except Stevie where they were going, so whoever was out there, it couldn't be DeSouza. Stevie wouldn't have told a soul. A hunter most like, perhaps even Koperkuj himself, though it seemed unlikely.

She took a breath, put all thoughts and words out of her mind. From now on, she would rely only on the evidence of her senses: the sound of the wind, the indentations in the shale and the bitter tang of crushed caribou moss as she trod through the light snow. Moving softly, almost soundlessly, psyching herself for an encounter, she followed the line of footprints as they stretched into the darkness. She made her way across the beach, alert, her heart pounding, until she reached the slickrock below the cliffs. There she stopped, crouching low, waiting. More cautious now she was sure the source of the prints was human. Pretty soon she heard a low groan and moved forward, silently, with her knees bent, using the night sight to see her way through, her trigger finger at the ready.

At a stepped ledge where the rock fell away, she lowered herself so that she was sitting with her feet dangling onto the surface below. Tapping with her toes, feeling for a step, she eased herself onto the rock. The groaning grew louder. Unmistakeably human, it seemed to be coming from around the side of a large boulder. Staying low, she called out, but got no response. The wind brought a scent to her nostrils, a smell so familiar it felt like a friend. Blood.

Moving forward, slowly, leading with her rifle, she called, '*Kinauvit*?' Who are you? Nothing. At the boulder she rested for a moment, picked up a stone, threw it to attract fire then, when there was no response, mustered her courage, raised her rifle, readied the sights and leapt round the rock.

Through the night sight she could see a bundle lying at an odd angle: a human being, either dead or unconscious. She reached out and pushed the barrel of her Remington against the body. Nothing. Flipping on her headlamp she saw what she immediately thought was the victim of a bear attack. Though the body seemed untouched, the face was mashed, a dense slub of flayed skin and clotted blood, the features all but erased. Slinging her rifle around her shoulder, she reached down and placed two fingers on the carotid. There was a pulse. As she removed her hand, her fingers made contact with metal. A familiar gold chain glinted in her headlamp. It was Old Man Koperkuj and he was still alive. Just.

She took his shoulders and turned him over then took off her fur hat and laid it under his head. As she did so, his arms flopped across his body and she saw that he had been tortured: his hands were meat stumps from which the fingernails had been ripped out.

He lay completely still now, the bloody hocks of hands bunched against his face. Everything in her Inuk soul went out to him. To violate an elder this way was as obscene as violating a child.

She stroked his head. 'It's OK.'

Koperkuj was in no state to move. It couldn't have been his footfall she'd heard in the shale. Immediately, she clicked her headlamp off and was reaching for her rifle when the dazzle of a powerful lamp blinded her. It took a moment for the red sparks behind her eyelids to clear, but when they did she could see standing before her the craggy outline and aquiline nose of the man in Qila's photo. Professor Jim DeSouza. He was pointing a rifle directly at her.

Her instincts told her she was dealing with someone very sick. 'This man is an elder,' she said.

'That's not my fault.' DeSouza moved closer, kicked her rifle away and picked it up. His voice grew quiet and conspiratorial.

'You know what I want, if you hadn't taken it from him, this wouldn't have happened.' He must have sensed her revulsion because he drew back a little. 'He was more protective of you than I'd imagined he would be. It took a lot for me to get it out of him.' He nudged at the old man's hands with his boot.

'He doesn't like *qalunaat*,' Edie said.

'I don't blame him.' DeSouza's face was as contorted and brittle as the branches of an ancient, wind-whipped willow. 'People should stick with their own kind. We'd all be much happier that way.'

'I can tell you where the stone is,' she said.

'Yes,' he said. 'I know.'

'Please,' she said. 'We have to get the old man some help.' The word 'please' sounded odd coming from her mouth. It was not an Inuit word. But then the professor was not Inuk.

DeSouza clicked his tongue against his teeth.

'Forget him, he's gone.' He had lost weight since the photo was taken, and his face looked drawn. 'For a moment there I thought you might be interesting, intelligent even, but now I see you're just as dumb as all the others.'

'The others?'

'Natives,' he said. She felt the contempt leaking from him. The moment to reach him was lost.

He picked up her rifle and with one hand cracked it open and took out the clip. Then he flipped his chin, indicating the space behind her. As she turned he pushed the barrel of the rifle into her left hair braid and raised it. The gesture was intimate, violating, as he had intended it to be. 'You go first.'

They scrambled down onto the beach. The first intimations of nautical dawn, a browning of the night around the southern horizon, had picked out the contours of the tent. There was no light on inside and none came on when they approached. Derek Palliser was still asleep.

Edie felt DeSouza's rifle nudge her pigtail.

'Wake Palliser.'

She called but there was no answer.

'He's hurt. He took a Xanax, some painkillers.'

DeSouza's face clouded over. He nudged Edie in the back with his rifle then passed over some rope.

'Tie him up and do it properly. You try to get away, I'll do to him what I did to the old man. Then I'll come for you. Open the tent flaps so I can see you.'

'We're further ahead than you think,' she said, binding Derek's wrists. 'We know exactly where the stone was found. We can take you to the source.'

Behind her, Edie could feel DeSouza's body tense.

'We're all the same to you, aren't we?' he said. *'Qalunaat.'* He coughed up the word as though it was some kind of infection. 'Just after the money. That was Wagner, Fairfax too. Small men with petty dreams. I couldn't be less interested in that.'

For a moment Derek seemed to rouse himself, then he fell back into a stupor. Edie shut up and kept tying her square knot.

'You think I've taken leave of my senses, don't you?' he said. He began to inspect her rope work, pulling on the knots a couple of times. 'Maybe I have.'

They moved back onto the beach, leaving Derek trussed up in the tent. DeSouza made Edie kneel on the shale and had her put her hands on her head, execution style, while he stood close by, rifle in hand, scanning the sky. The stones bit into her knees. She considered the possibility of flinging a handful of them in his face, but she sensed that by the time her hands even reached the stones, he'd have killed her. They waited.

So long as she hadn't yet given DeSouza the stone, he would keep her safe. After that, he'd take her out onto the tundra somewhere and get rid of her. Apart from Derek, who would go out of their way to discover what had happened to her? Mike? Stevie? Martie? Neither Mike nor Stevie would stand up to Simeonie. As for her aunt, she didn't know any longer.

The thin cuticle of the sun had circled a few degrees further round the horizon, too weak to haul itself into the sky. A terrible bleakness came over her. She struggled against it, but it was like the great dark period, omniscient, ineluctable. This won't do at all, she said to herself. Edie might be feeble, but Kigga doesn't give in. She looked to the horizon once more. The sun was rusting, falling away into the darkness, but not quite gone yet.

Not quite gone.

The only chance she saw now was to draw him in, to make him imagine she was sympathetic to his cause. She waited a while until she felt his body relax and the stink of his adrenaline softened, then she pitched in.

'I know places where there might be other stones,' she said. 'Meteorites.'

DeSouza didn't reply. She tried again.

'If I knew what you were looking for, exactly, maybe I could help you? I know the land.'

A snort. 'How could you possibly know what I might be looking for?' He moved around so she could see his face. 'How could you even begin to understand?'

She nodded, submissive. 'I know I'm stupid.' He looked at her. 'I have my uses, though. If we run out of food, I can bring down a caribou at a kilometre.'

DeSouza laughed. 'We're not going to run out of food,' he said, then, flipping at her pigtails with his rifle: 'What are your other uses?'

Edie closed her eyes and swallowed. 'You're right. I'm useless, what's worse, a female. But I'm wondering, given I'm no use to anyone, can I put my arms down now?'

DeSouza let out an impatient little sigh, but he did not protest. He looked drained, she thought, almost spent.

'The scientists here,' he said, gesturing northeast, beyond the cliffs, towards the science station campus, 'they do good work, you know, mechanical stuff, mostly, developing vehicles and sample collectors.' He wasn't really talking to her but, rather, she realized, to himself, to the other, saner part of himself.

He fell silent. She understood then. He was fatally lonely. All her life, she'd watched the Arctic destroy men like DeSouza. They came up north with their fantasies of self-reliance and rugged individualism only to discover they weren't so rugged after all. Soon enough, most of them found that they needed people. And those who didn't lost their minds. Right now, DeSouza was at a crossroads, she thought. He could go either way.

He stared at the sky for some while, then he turned his head to look at her. After a long time he said:

'You know what makes meteorites special? Apart from the gas?' He tried to muster some righteous anger but what came out sounded weary.

Edie felt a deep, warm relief. He wanted to connect.

'I suppose you'd say meteors came from the spirit world, some baloney like that.'

Edie grimaced. 'No,' she said. '*Spirits* come from the spirit world. Meteors come from outer space.'

'ALH 84001, you know about that?' he said. She had proved herself sufficiently that he wanted to pull rank on her. This was good.

She shook her head.

'No, of course you don't,' he said, pleased.

'You could tell me,' she said. 'Just to pass the time. Or, if you don't feel like it, I've got some stories.'

'Christ, no,' he said. 'Goose-men, walrus spirits, I've had a bellyful of that shit. Smile, interact with the natives, kiss my ass.'

'Then educate me,' she said.

He looked at her quizzically. She answered him with a weak smile. She'd offered him an outlet for his loneliness and he'd taken it.

'ALH 84001 is the fancy name for a meteorite found in Antarctica. Ten years ago, a guy called David McKay, working at the Johnson Space Center in Houston, claimed it contained fossilized life.'

A thin, cold snow was beginning to fall. DeSouza got up. They were obviously waiting for someone, or something.

'Ah shit,' he said.

Edie craned her neck in the direction of the tent. 'It's warm in there.'

He motioned her to go ahead. At the entrance to the

tent he told her to stop and lift the flap far enough back so he could see in. He went in backwards, took out Derek Palliser's rifle, cracked it open and threw it into the snow. While he was occupied, Edie peered into the gloaming, trying to think of some way she might trick DeSouza out of his weapon. Her eye fell on the footprints he had made in the new snow. The pattern was familiar, the same zig-zag with the brand stamp and the ice-bear logo she'd seen up on the bluff just after Felix Wagner was shot.

The professor emerged from the tent carrying a reel of fishing twine. Pushing Edie inside with his rifle butt, he motioned her to sit then bound her ankles and wrists. Then he sat back and lit one of Derek's Lucky Strikes. Silence fell, interrupted only by the sound of the policeman's light snores. It seemed as though DeSouza had decided not to say any more. She'd have to tread carefully. She knew for sure now that he was a killer. He had shot Felix Wagner. She wanted him to know that she knew, that someone else was keeping his secret. Waiting until he'd nearly finished his smoke, she ventured:

'Is that how you and Felix Wagner met? You both worked at the Space Center?'

DeSouza shrugged. 'The guy was a jerk. A zero.' His face contorted into a snarl. They'd met as freshmen at the University of Washington's Arctic Club, he explained. Later, after Wagner had made a lot of money in real estate, he used his connection to DeSouza to join the Arctic Hunters' Club.

'Felix was a hustler, not a real hunter. Once he was in the club, he cultivated Fairfax for his contacts and Belovsky for his money. You should have seen him, oiling up to those guys. Bear hunting in the Caucasus, shooting pheasants in some English castle. It was grotesque.'

'That was when he found out about the stone and the diary, right?' Edie watched DeSouza's face for signs of irritation but saw none. He seemed to have forgotten that she was his captive.

'I guess that selling the same information to Zemmer and to Belovsky and thinking neither of them would find out wasn't exactly a smart move,' she said.

DeSouza looked at her with an expression of grudging admiration. He was back in the game.

'Not so stupid as you say, eh?' he said, with some regret. 'Better for you if you had been.'

'Wagner was stupid and look what happened to him,' she said. 'Andy Taylor too.'

DeSouza's snarl returned. 'Wagner always had these hangers-on and they were always bozos.' He took a breath to calm himself. 'I didn't have anything to do with the Taylor business. Didn't have to. The Russians got there first.' DeSouza laughed.

Edie took her cue and went in closer. 'Tell me about ALH 84001.'

He looked at her, weighing up whether or not she was worth the effort of engagement, then softened. The loneliness again.

'Last year,' he said, 'McKay went back to the stone and analysed it using . . .' He hesitated, shot Edie a wary look and drew back. 'Never mind.'

Edie brought to mind the report Mike Nungaq had given her, and scanned through all the technical terms she could remember.

'Electron microscopy?'

DeSouza cracked a tiny smile. Her reward was for him to continue. Right now, what he needed, even more than he thought he needed the stone, was someone who understood his obsessions.

'All the work so far has been focused on magnetite. All the official work, that is.'

'Official work, walrus ass,' she said, dismissively.

'I'm getting to like your style,' he replied, more relaxed now.

'It's just a lack of brains,' she said. He was so easy.

'You know what nanobes are?'

She shook her head. This time she really didn't.

'Tiny, fossilized extraterrestrial forms, a billionth of a metre in diameter. They've been found in magnetite and halite here on earth and in ALH 84001. Some say they're a form of life but it's never been proved.'

She could feel the energy coming from him again.

'I think I can prove that they *are* life and what's more, that they lived on Mars.'

She held her breath. There was a plane coming. She could feel the rumble before the noise became audible. DeSouza hadn't detected it yet.

'Do you know what that means? Men win Nobels for less.'

So that was it. The realization was all the more terrible for its mundanity. Like so many brilliant men and women driven solely by their ambition, DeSouza had traded in his humanity somewhere along the way.

'But to do that you need the stone,' she said, a little too loud, eager to distract him while she tried to determine the direction of the engine sound.

He tipped his head slightly to the side. 'And research time.'

'Which costs money,' she said.

The engine was audible now. DeSouza had heard it. He motioned Edie to stand up then, taking out his hunting knife and cutting the fishing line around her ankles, he said:

'Come meet an old friend.'

It was snowing and a low cloud had fallen across the sea. The sound of the plane grew louder. As they stood on the shale listening to the swell of the engine, the air began to vibrate. Instinctively, Edie checked the direction and strength of the wind. *Tarramiliivuq*; it was turning to the north. A terrible dawning began to edge its way across her mind.

Johannes Moller. That fat old walrus fart was in this deeper than she'd realized.

A spot appeared among the clouds, blooming then resolving into the familiar shape of a Twin Otter. But the plane coming towards them wasn't Moller's.

It was Auntie Martie's.

A surge of hope shot into Edie's throat. She wanted to whoop. Martie had seen them.

'She's your aunt, isn't she?' DeSouza shook his head. 'And you people always say family comes first.'

She looked at him, anxious now and unsure of his meaning.

The plane was descending rapidly and heading directly for the shoreline. Edie waited for Martie to swoop up and bank around in preparation for a landing on the water parallel to the shore, but the Otter advanced towards the land, dropping until it seemed as though it was skimming the waves. DeSouza began to look alarmed.

'What the fuck?'

The Otter kept on coming. It was no more than a hundred metres from them now, flying so low they could feel the air around them being sucked towards the wings, so close that Edie could almost see the expression on her aunt's face. As it grew nearer, DeSouza cracked. She heard him cry then make a sudden dive for the shale, covering his head with his hands, his rifle lying unprotected beside him. The plane roared overhead then swooped upwards. In an instant Edie was making a beeline for the rifle, struggling against the ties on her wrists. The plane rose and banked.

Before she could reach it, DeSouza jumped up and grabbed the weapon, swinging it wildly. Before he could gather himself, the plane had turned and was coming in for another pass.

Edie watched it approach. As the Otter swung in low once more she stumbled backwards, making for the tent. Momentarily distracted by the sound of her feet on the shale, DeSouza lurched about and raised his rifle. The bullet passed her with a whistle and ricocheted off the rock behind. The plane was nearly on DeSouza now. She saw him drop and again cover his head with his arms. Racing for the tent, she scoped about for Derek's rifle, thinking she might just have time to grab it, dive into the tent, cut the fishing line around her wrists and reload before DeSouza got to her. By now the plane had completed its swoop. She could hear the engine screeching into an ascent. Behind her, DeSouza would be lifting himself off the ground. Her head was fizzing and she felt every muscle stiffen. Glancing back, she saw him raise his rifle and instinctively hit the shale.

The plane was banking over the sea ice, preparing for another pass. DeSouza was heading her way now, shouting and screaming obscenities, his rifle pointed at her head. She felt her breath catch in her throat. Suddenly, DeSouza stopped, settled the rifle into his shoulder and leaned into the sight. There was a loud crack and for an instant everything seemed to stop. She felt a spray of blood across her face and she froze, uncomprehending. DeSouza fell forward.

He was kneeling in the shale, his face buried in it as though he had been caught drinking at a stream. An unearthly gurgling sound was coming from his chest. A pool of blood began to spread out from his mouth. Edie stood up and turned to see Derek Palliser, lowering his rifle and cracking a smile.

'Square knots.' Derek limped towards her. 'Edie, you think of everything.'

As the plane moved out into the open water and was coming round for a landing she told Derek what had happened, filling in the details as they went to fetch Saomik Koperkuj, carrying him back to the beach in a tarp. He was so light, so frail, it was a wonder he was still alive, but he was. Sick, with a shallow, racing pulse, but alive.

Martie was waiting for them. There was no time then for explanations. They loaded the old man onto Edie's snowmobile trailer and from there onto the seaplane.

By the time they went back for DeSouza he was already dead.

'You go with the old man,' Derek said. 'I'll call the science station, get someone to come pick up the director.'

She and Derek looked at each other. Something passed between them.

A short while into the flight, Koperkuj seemed to regain consciousness and began to groan. Edie reached for the first-aid kit tied to the back of the bulkhead and pulled it down. The plane gave a little lurch over a cloud and dislodged a box packaged in shrink wrap lying behind it. Pushing it to one side, Edie took out a foil of Vicodin tabs from the first-aid kit, crushed a couple up, pulled aside the old man's trousers and, donning a pair of vinyl gloves, inserted the powder into the old man's rectum. Pretty soon, the groaning stopped.

She pulled off the gloves and threw them aside, picked up the box and noticed the distinct vinegary, vegetable smell, the same smell she'd noticed in Martie's cabin. Her aunt was preoccupied with something on the instrument panel. Drawing out her knife, Edie made a small cut in the shrink wrap around the box then through the card, opened it up and inserted her thumb and finger. A white powder clung to her thumb. She raised it to her mouth and took a little on her tongue. The bitterness made her shiver.

She thought about her aunt's incessant scratching and the burn marks on the spoon in her cabin. She remembered now, too, how delicately her house had been searched, with a knowledge of the places she might put things, care taken to put every object back in its exact place. So that's who DeSouza had meant by an 'old friend', when he had ironized about Inuit putting family first. It was Martie he'd been waiting for, Martie who had warned DeSouza they were on their way.

The realization hit Edie like a rogue wave, turning her mind in so many directions she had to take hold of her breathing to collect herself. Then, when she was calm, she very quietly reached for her weapon. She approached the cockpit. Martie felt the gun barrel against the back of her neck and let out the screech of a cub abandoned by its mother.

'Edie, no.'

At the cry, Edie pressed the barrel in harder. Her skin prickled with adrenaline.

'The only reason I'm not killing you right now is that someone has to fly. But you pull *any* tricks, and I mean any tricks, I'll send us all down.'

She took a moment or two, gazing out of the window down to the grey, hypnotic water of Jones Sound. When she felt calm once more, she said, 'How long till we land?'

'Twenty minutes.' Martie's voice sounded as though it had jammed inside her head.

'Then that's how long you've got to explain yourself.'

It had started out as some extra cash on the side. The dope – methamphetamine – came up on the Arctic Patrol ship labelled 'scientific instruments' and was collected by DeSouza personally. The ship's captain, Jonson, was in on it.

Martie was the bag woman. Every so often she would land at the science station strip, pick up a box and drop it in Iqaluit.

Martie paused in her explanation.

'DeSouza told me the dope-running was funding important research.'

'You know he shot Felix Wagner, right?'

Martie nodded reluctantly.

She'd found out long after the event. DeSouza had followed the hunting party, waiting for the moment Wagner was alone and he could disable him and take the stone. He fired off the shot, but then Andy Taylor appeared. DeSouza hadn't meant to kill Wagner, but he wasn't too sorry that he had. He claimed Wagner knew how much he needed that stone, he owed him. But instead Wagner had sold out.

'Shit, Edie, he said what he was doing would change the world. When everything got used up here, he said, people would go and live up in the stars with the spirits. I don't know zip about science. I know about flying planes. So I thought, what harm can this do? It wasn't like the dope was coming into Autisaq.'

'But then you started using.'

'I don't know how it happened.' Another agonized bark. 'I guess I just started tooting every now and then to keep up my concentration, you know, for the flying. Then the old man found me at it, so he joined in. No one even noticed the consignments were short. But DeSouza came by the cabin one day when me and Koperkuj were sampling the wares. That's when I realized he was using too.'

'And that's when he found out about the stone.'

'Uh huh.'

'Koperkuj wouldn't give it to him?'

'You know how the old man was . . .' She hesitated. '. . . is. He wouldn't sell his own turd to a *qalunaat*. Next time DeSouza came round, he told him he'd lost it. DeSouza didn't believe him, but the old man wouldn't budge. That was why he let you have it, so that DeSouza wouldn't steal it.'

She glanced back at the old man.

'He gonna be OK?'

Edie shrugged.

'You gotta understand, Edie, in the early days, DeSouza was all right. Things changed once he'd got sight of that stone. And then the meth. I dunno, he just went dark.'

'A dark spirit.'

Martie nodded.

'And then Koperkuj went missing . . .' Edie continued.

'All honesty? I didn't know what had happened. Far as I knew, DeSouza believed the old man had lost the stone. Neither Koperkuj nor DeSouza realized I knew you had it, so I figured I was safe. But then DeSouza let slip he'd seen the old man just before he disappeared so I figured what he was up to with him. The stuff I told you about Koperkuj dealing weed? I knew you'd tell Palliser and I assumed he'd make the connection with the space station and go check out DeSouza.'

'And you thought you'd take the stone from my house and give it to him, he'd release Koperkuj and everything would be just fine.'

'Something like that. Shit, it sounds crazy, Little Bear, but everything got so fucked up. When I couldn't find the stone and I saw the photo on your couch I was worried and then later when I came round and you'd gone, I panicked. I figured you'd worked it out.'

'And you called DeSouza.'

Martie was wordless for a moment, her voice drowned in the tide of her feelings. Autisaq appeared ahead of them now, tiny and frail before the great, ferocious sweep of Ellesmere.

'I hate what I did, but I tried to make it right in the end.'

Edie put down the rifle, closed her eyes and took a deep breath. 'Just land us, Martie, then get the hell out of my sight.'

20

The new nurse, Diandra Smitty, met Edie by the tea urn in the waiting room of the Autisaq nursing station. Diandra was a large, blowsy woman, the 'polar opposite' of Robert Patma, as she often liked to say, and the only black white person most of the citizens of Autisaq had ever come across. In the three and a half months she'd been in the role, Diandra had listened to the elders chewing over old wisdom and old cures. Bit by bit she had begun to incorporate traditional practices into the healing on offer at the nursing station, and this had won her a place in Autisaq's affections. The tea urn, too, had been Diandra's idea.

'Hey, Edie,' Diandra said. 'Visiting with the old man?'

Edie picked up her tea and began ladling in the sugar. Diandra always observed how much sugar Edie put in, but she never said anything. Edie liked her all the more for that.

'How's the new volunteer?' Edie said. For the past two months Willa Inukpuk had been putting hours in at the station, helping Diandra with the administration.

'He's doing great,' Diandra said. 'Funny, but some people just *are* natural-born healers. Willa, he's one of them. Just didn't know for a long time, is all.'

Just then Willa appeared from one of the consulting rooms, saw Edie and threw her a fragile little smile. As the winter progressed, relations between the young man and his ex-stepmother had thawed somewhat. The time Willa had spent working with Diandra had transformed him. Edie had never seen her stepson so purposeful, so comfortable in his skin.

Diandra disappeared back into her office and Edie headed for Saomik Koperkuj's room. In the early days, when it was still touch and go, they'd wanted to air-ambulance him out to a proper hospital in Iqaluit, but he'd point-blank refused to go, said if he couldn't stay on Umingmak Nuna he might as well be dead. His experience hadn't mellowed the old man; he was as ill-tempered and snippy as ever but, luckily for them both, Edie never expected him to be any other way.

Her twice-weekly visits had become woven into the fabric of both their lives. They each knew the score. Her role was to act out that visiting him was a burden, while he pretended to find her an interfering pain in the ass. They both had a whale of a time. Koperkuj knew much more about the old ways than Edie had realized and he'd been keen to pass his knowledge on. Over the weeks, she'd learned how to blow footballs from walrus bladders and cure snowblindness in dogs by running a flea over a hair in their eyes. He'd taught her how to approach a ptarmigan so that it thought you were a seal, and shown her a fail-safe way to jig for sculpin. She couldn't recall a time when she had grown more, both as a hunter and as an Inuk. But, of course, she never said that to the old man.

Just as she reached it, the door to Koperkuj's room swung open and Martie stepped out. Edie knew from Willa that her aunt came regularly into the clinic to visit Koperkuj and get help with her addiction, but the remainder of the time Martie took pains to stay out at her cabin and Edie had managed to avoid running into her. The two women hadn't spoken since the flight back from Craig.

'Hey, Edie.' Martie's voice was soft with regret.

Edie couldn't bring herself to ask after Martie's health so she said the next-best thing.

'How's the old man today?'

'He's cool.' Martie gave a fruity little chuckle. For a moment her eyes shone with their old energy. 'He says he wants to make an honest woman of me. Imagine, after all these years.'

'You gonna say yes?'

'Are you crazy?'

Edie smiled. They passed one another. It was an awkward moment, brimming with unsaid things. Edie took the door and watched her aunt make her way down the corridor towards the waiting area. Just before she reached it, Martie hesitated and looked back.

'Hey, Little Bear, Willa tell you I'm clean?'

Edie nodded. Martie just stood there for a while. She was smiling but her voice sounded choked.

'Can't keep a thing secret in this place.'

'Sure hope not,' Edie said. Then she took a breath and walked through the door into the old man's room.

Saomik Koperkuj was sitting up in bed watching a DVD. During the weeks and months of his convalescence, Edie had gradually introduced him to the greats of silent comedy and now they had a kind of routine going where Koperkuj would tell a story or two about the old days then they'd watch a silent short together. Koperkuj was particularly fond of Buster Keaton, said the comedian reminded him of himself as a youngster. He'd nicknamed the man Kituq, thought it made him sound Inuk. Liked it better that way.

'You run into Martie?' he asked.

'Yeah.' She took the old man's nailless hand and squeezed it gently. Koperkuj stared at the screen in front of him and grunted. Then he squeezed Edie back.

'I can't stay long this time, I have to get to the airstrip.' She wanted to catch Derek Palliser before he got wrapped up in official police business. 'I don't know if there'll be time for a story.'

He sat up in bed, his face still a mess of scars he called his war wounds. He didn't seem to care too much about them.

'Saomik, mind if I ask you something?'

He'd never spoken about what he'd done with Andy Taylor's body, only that he'd been out hunting when he heard a shot and finding Taylor lying dead, removed the stone from around his neck.

'You gonna ask the question whether I mind or not.'

'Why did you cut up Andy Taylor's body?'

Koperkuj's lips tightened into a scowl. He'd said all he wanted to say about that time.

'Man was dead,' he mumbled. 'And the dogs was hungry.' He glanced at Edie and when he saw she wasn't shocked, a look of relief came over his face. 'There, I said it once, don't intend to say it again.' He folded his arms, as though to emphasize the point. 'Now tell me, how's that Pauloosie boy?'

Not long after DeSouza's death, Edie and Derek had confronted Simeonie Inukpuk over the monies going into the Autisaq Children's Foundation. The newly elected mayor didn't even try to deny he'd been accepting bribes from the oil companies to be pro-resource development. He'd embezzled government funds too. A deal was struck and shortly afterwards the Autisaq Children's Foundation appointed Mike Nungaq as its executive officer. The Autisaq Children's Rockhounding and Camping Club had its first expedition not long after. It was followed by a computer club and there was talk of raising money for an indoor swimming pool. Edie was reinstated to her teaching job at the school. A few times, she'd taken the whole class down into Saomik Koperkuj's hospital room for some lessons in traditional

Inuit knowledge. The kids loved the old man, and in his gruff way Koperkuj returned their enthusiasm. His particular favourite was Pauloosie Allakarialak. Reminded him of himself at the same age, he said. Under the old man's tutelage, the bewildered, wounded boy of a year ago had completely disappeared. This new Pauloosie had started writing Inuktitut song lyrics. Now he was talking about becoming Autisaq's first Inuit rapper.

'He's good,' Edie said.

'Tell him to come by sometime,' the old man said. 'I prefer his company to yours.'

'That's a relief,' Edie said. 'Been looking for any excuse not to have to come.'

'I never asked you to.'

'I only do it to get the Rev Whathisname off my back about not going to church.'

'Won't do you no good,' Koperkuj said. 'You're going straight to hell anyway.'

She left the old man with some homemade blood soup and scooted up to the airstrip. A group of people in business suits and parkas were hanging around the terminal, trying to squeeze various pieces of native handicraft into their luggage before the flight out arrived. Simeonie was standing in their midst, attempting to marshal the proceedings. He acknowledged her with a nod. They weren't exactly friendly with one another but, since the confrontation, he'd been surprisingly polite, fearful, she supposed, that she might cxpose him in public.

Derek Palliser was talking to Pol Tilluq up by the luggage scales. He spotted her, waved an arm in the direction of the suits and mouthed the word 'consultants'. Edie shrugged and mouthed back, *Ayunqnak*, it can't be helped.

Since the events of more than four months ago, she'd

barely seen the police sergeant. He'd spent some time convalescing in Iqaluit, then been flown down to Ottawa to receive a commendation from the government. After that, he had returned to Iqaluit for a while to work with the prosecution lawyer for Robert Patma's trial, which was scheduled for the summer. The *Ottawa Citizen* had printed his picture on page seven and the *Arctic Circular* had carried a long article about his lemming research and named him Northern Communities Policeman of the Year. Misha called not long afterwards. He'd been wrong to suspect she had anything to do with Beloil, he said, but he didn't invite her back to Kuujuaq.

Edie elbowed her way through the crowd towards him. He flashed her a smile and got a stupid grin in return.

'Hey, Police. Spare a moment later?' she said. 'I got a favour to ask.'

He gave her a look of mock despair.

'I'm just crazy about you, too, Sergeant Palliser,' she said.

The remainder of the day, she taught class, ate a hot supper of caribou tongue at home and packed her trailer. Around five she called in at the police office. Derek was clearing the last of the papers on his desk.

'You ready?'

'As ready as I'll ever be, not knowing where we're going or what we're doing.'

She winked at him.

'Trust me,' she said.

He laughed. 'Right.'

They took the snowmobiles out over the pressure ridge near to the shore and onto the ice sheet of Jones Sound. It was biting cold now, fifty below with wind chill, but the ice was the best travelling they'd had all winter: still, firm and settled, and the moon was high and bright, the stars littering the sky like so many snowflakes. Three and a half hours they journeyed south. Eventually, with the outline of Craig Island looming from the dark ahead, Edie stopped beside a large berg, whose northwest side had collected great banks of snowdrift, compacted in the wind. She swung from the vehicle and went over to check.

She shouted over to Derek: 'Three-layer snow.'

The policeman brought his vehicle in closer and switched off the engine. 'You planning on making a snowhouse?'

'What else do you do with three-layer snow?'

Edie fetched her walrus-ivory snowknife and began sawing out blocks.

'You know what night this is?' she said.

He thought about it for a moment and shook his head, stumped.

It was the last night of the Great Dark Period, a night most High Arctic Inuit spent all winter looking forward to, the end to four months of twenty-four-hour darkness. Just before midday tomorrow, the sun would rise for the first time, if only momentarily. It would be the first they had seen of it in more than a hundred days.

They found a good spot for a house, far enough from the berg not to be in danger of shattering but near enough to be protected a little from the prevailing winds, and loaded the blocks of snow she'd cut out onto the trailer. The snow-house took them three hours to build. When it was up, Edie crawled inside, tamped the floor, laid caribou skins, put up lamps and cut a window glazed, in lieu of seal gut, with a piece of plastic. They drank hot tea and rested for a while, sitting on the skins, Derek smoking, neither of them saying much.

Edie went out onto the ice, taking her walrus knife with her, and beckoned for Derek to follow. Cutting a hole in the ice, she squatted down beside it. For a while she was silent, running the events of the past months over in her head. Then she reached for the thread of seal leather around her neck, untied it and handed it to him. He took it and laid it on the palm of his hand. It was the first time he'd seen the stone.

'Doesn't look much, does it?' was all he said.

She said: 'I want you to throw it into the sea.'

He reached over the hole in the ice, lifted the necklace above it and dropped the stone. They heard a tiny splash, then nothing. It began to snow, thick discs of infinite, microscopic complexity, tumbling down from high, patchy cloud.

'I'm tired,' she said suddenly.

He nodded. 'Let's get some sleep.'

They returned to the snowhouse and slept for a long while. When they woke, Edie brewed hot tea from berg ice and heated the seal stew she'd brought.

That week, the *Arctic Circular* had reported that the oil spill in the Okhotsk Sea had proved worse than Zemmer had predicted. The oil company's shares were on the floor and environmental groups were calling for the company directors to be prosecuted for breach of their fiduciary duties to the people affected by the spill. Zemmer had scaled down its exploration operations. The corporation wasn't likely to be back in the Arctic again for some time. Beloil, too, had taken a heap of bad press after someone posted footage of two of its employees robbing graves on YouTube. Its chairman, Belovsky, had publicly promised to get to the bottom of the incident. In the meantime, Beloil was laying low.

'I guess there'll be other oil outfits up here,' she said, spooning up the stew. 'Bringing bigger machines, more money.'

Derek agreed that in the long run, they were unstoppable.

'And in the short run?'

'I've been thinking about that.'

The policeman outlined his plan. At the time of the National Parks Act, back in the 1920s, when most of the rest of Ellesmere and its outlying islands had been designated as National Park, Craig had been left out. It was an anomaly which made the island very vulnerable. But Derek had been thinking, if he could persuade the National Parks board that there were special reasons for redesignating Craig then, at least for the foreseeable future, they might issue a pending order over the island. If that happened, no one – not the Town Hall or the Nunavut legislature or even the federal government would be able to issue resource exploration licences for the island – until the redesignation issue had been sorted. Even with evidence of the existence of a gas field on Craig, no one could buy their way into a drilling operation there.

'So I'm thinking, the summer Wildlife and Parks expeditions make audits of Ellesmere's rare and endangered animal populations,' Derek went on. 'But when it comes to more common wildlife, they rely on my reports.'

She laughed. 'Not lemmings!'

He grinned back. 'Lemmings, yes, on which, if you remember, Edie, I'm something of an expert.'

'I do believe I had forgotten,' she said, cutting him a wink.

There were two species of lemming, he said, the common collared, *Dicrostonyx torquatus,* and the North American brown, *Lemmus trimuscronatus*.

'There are all kind of sub-species and variants, but for our purposes, let's just say there are two.'

'And what are our purposes?'

Derek held up his hand.

'I'm coming to that. Up here *D. torquatus* is very common, but *L. trimuscronatus* is rare everywhere, so rare in fact that it's on the IUCN list of threatened species.' Derek smiled. 'To this point in time, there has never been a sighting of *L. trimuscronatus* north of Baffin Island.'

Edie considered this fact for a moment. She raised her palms as if to say, 'And?'

'As Wildlife Officer for Ellesmere Island, I'd obviously be duty bound to report to the Canadian Wildlife and Parks Service any sightings of *L. trimuscronatus* on Craig Island, even if they were unconfirmed.'

All of a sudden, Edie could see where this was going.

He held up his palm to indicate that he wasn't finished.

'There would have to be demographic, environmental and habitation studies. And what with the research period confined to a couple of months in the summer, who knows how long they might take?'

A laugh escaped Edie's lips.

'You're almost as cunning as those oil men,' she said, admiringly.

'Even a lemming brain has its uses,' he said.

They beamed at one another, then she stood up and reached out a hand.

'Come on, Police,' she said. 'Let's go outside and wait for the sunrise.'

Acknowledgements

I was greatly assisted in the early development of this book by a grant from the Arts Council England. Thanks also to Simon Booker and Dr Tai Bridgeman, who read a number of drafts and had many useful suggestions to make. I am grateful to my agent, Peter Robinson, to Stephen Edwards, Margaret Halton, Kim Witherspoon and the staff of Rogers, Coleridge and White and of Inkwell Management. Very many thanks are also due to Maria Rejt, Sophie Orme and the team at Mantle and to Kathryn Court, Alexis Washam and the team at Penguin USA. Any errors are mine alone.

A note on Inuktitut and on places in the book

Many of the places in this book including Ellesmere and Devon Island, part of the Queen Elizabeth group in the Canadian High Arctic, and Qaanaaq and Etah in Northwest Greenland, are real. Others, such as Autisaq, Kuujuaq and Craig Island, are inventions. There is a real weather station at Eureka on Ellesmere Island and a scientific research station on Devon Island, but any resemblance between these real-life facilities and/or their personnel to the fictional ones described in this book is entirely coincidental.

Inuktitut is a highly sophisticated, polysynthetic Eskimo-Aleut language spoken by Inuit across the Arctic region. It is broken up into a number of regional dialects which form a linguistic chain. Each dialect is mutually intelligible to neighbours but not those far away, so an Inuk from Greenland may not be able to communicate easily with another from, say, Alaska. Some dialects are written in the Roman alphabet, others in a syllabic alphabet created by missionaries in the late 1800s.

Inuktitut consists of morphemes, the smallest units of meaning, which, in relation to one another, build into compound words. These compound words may be the equivalent of a whole sentence in Indo-European languages, e.g.

pariliarumaniralauqsimanngittunga, which means 'I never said I wanted to go to Paris.' Additional morphemes can be used to change the nature of the root morpheme, so *qinmiq* means dog, *qinmiqtuqtuq* going by dog team.

Inuktitut both supports and reflects the Inuit world-view. It is highly relational and tends to deal in the concrete rather than the abstract, shying away from generic nouns. In their traditional hunting culture, it was less useful to Inuit to know there were fish in a river as to know exactly what species of fish and in which part of the river they were to be found. Place names, too, tend to be specific and functional. Inuit call Ellesmere Island Umingmak Nuna or Musk-Ox Land to signal to themselves and to future generations that the island is a place where musk ox can be found and hunted. Even today, when new words have to be conjured, these have a concrete, descriptive quality. The word for computer, *qarasaujaq*, means 'something that works like a brain.' It is, however, a myth that the Inuit have hundreds of words for snow. In fact they have about the same number of 'root' words for snow as Indo-European languages but the nature of Inuktitut means that to describe what we might call 'frosty, sparkling snow,' Inuit can use a single polysynthetic word, *patuqun*.

Spoken Inuktitut makes a soft, rippling sound, like water running over pebbles in a brook. It is unusual for Inuit to raise their voices and it's considered rude to ask direct questions. Edie Kiglatuk is an exception to this, which may partly explain why she is such an outsider in her own world.

Sadly, some Inuktitut dialects are now in grave danger of disappearing. Where possible, I have tried to use the North Baffin or *Qikiqtaalukuannangani* versions of Inuktitut words in this book, but it is more than possible that some inconsistencies may have crept in, for which I can only apologize.

M. J. McGrath's second novel is available from Penguin.

Read on for the first two chapters of . . .

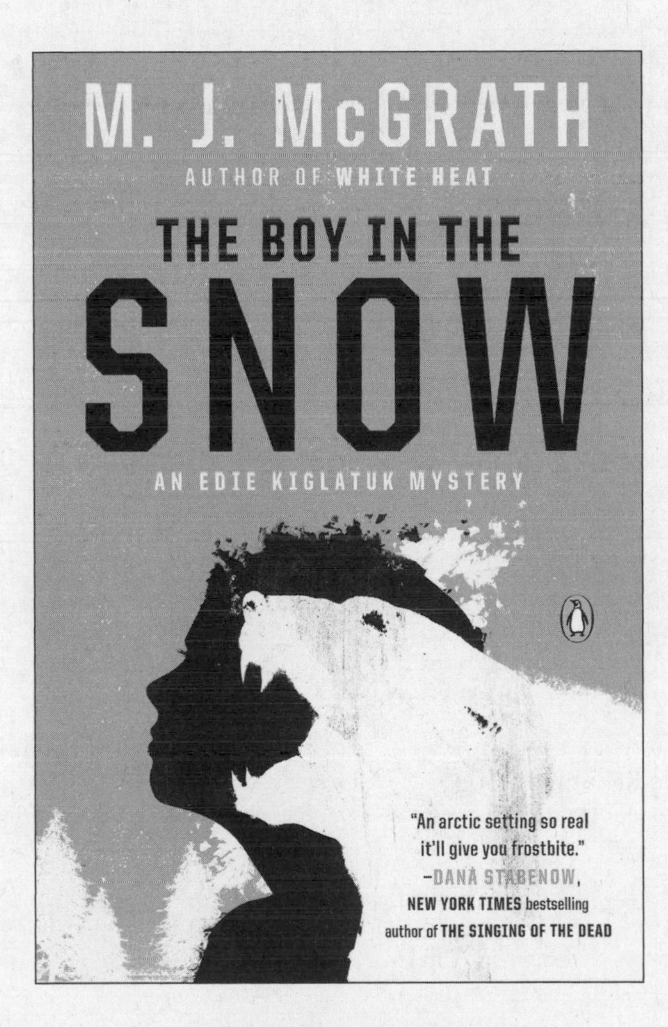

ISBN 978-0-312414-6

1

Edie Kiglatuk had no way of knowing how long the bear had been looking at her. His eyes, brown and beady, were like dark stars in a summer sky, set in clouds of fur. He raised his nose and snuffled, scenting her out, his huge body framed by the snow-laden spruce of the Alaska forest.

She had spent enough of her life around polar bears to be sure that, despite its colour, the animal standing before her wasn't one. Ice bears had longer heads, sharper snouts and smaller ears. This creature was different, snub-snouted and raggedy, the size of a black bear. Only not black. And, with its brown eyes, no albino either.

On the long flight over from her home in Autisaq in High Arctic Canada, Edie had passed the time reading guides to Alaskan flora and fauna and it now occurred to her that the animal was a spirit bear. *Qalunaat,* white folk, called them Kermode bears but the native people, the Gitga'at, knew them as *mooksgm'ol,* and never hunted them. They said the bears were outsider animals, creatures with the power to pass messages across the invisible portals between the living and the dead.

Something in her felt compelled to get closer. Swinging from her snowmobile she landed with a dull thud in the snow. Alarmed, the animal gave a short bark and rose on his hind legs. He was about six feet tall but his stance wasn't so much aggressive as . . . *As what?*

Edie had been around bears all her life, but there was something about this one she couldn't read.

For a moment the animal continued to face her, his nostrils flaring, small eyes brown and shiny as rain-soaked rock, then he dropped back down and slowly began to tromp away among the trees, turning his head from time to time to make sure she was not following.

Or maybe to make sure she was.

The animal reached a patch of sunlight between two spruce, stopped and turned around. Then he stood, making little coughing sounds, his breath fogging the air.

Waiting.

She moved towards him, slowly at first, then with more confidence. For a few moments he stood fast, then he turned and began to lumber further into the forest. She continued forward, sure now that the bear was leading her somewhere, that he had sought her out.

Glancing at her watch, she saw it was just past 9 a.m. In two hours from now Sammy Inukpuk would be pulling into the official start of the Iditarod dogsled race at Willow, expecting to see his ex-wife among the backup crews. It was her job to make sure he had all the supplies he needed and to offer moral support at the start of what were bound to be two of the most challenging weeks of Sammy's life as he raced sixteen dogs 1150 miles through some of the toughest terrain on the planet. From then on, she'd remain in Anchorage, organizing supplies and being on hand to receive any dogs that might get injured en route, while her old friend and ally, Derek Palliser, provided logistics support and managed communications up at the race finish in the northwestern town of Nome.

Edie walked on, the bear maybe fifty feet ahead, through stands of white spruce then out into clumps of quaking aspen, wading through deep snow, her heart thudding in her throat. It seemed as though they had been travelling a long time when, all of a sudden, the bear stopped and swivelled about. He was a long distance away now, his body visible through the trees like a patch of mist in the dark. He watched her heading closer for a while, then raised his head and smelled the air, turned and cantered away.

Edie looked about. For the first time in her adult life, she realized that she was lost. Glancing back at her footprints, she could already see that the bear had led her round in circles, jumbling the prints into a series of long switchbacks. Now she found herself in a dank world full of shifting shadows and strange, whispering sounds, like something from a childhood dream, with absolutely no sense of where to turn next. She felt her throat tighten and her palms begin to sweat.

She took in a deep, calming breath and stood listening, absorbing the sounds of the forest and trying to take some meaning from them. Where Edie came from, up on Ellesmere Island, just shy of the North Pole, there weren't any trees, only raw, rocky tundra. On a clear day you could see the earth's curve. The unfamiliarity of the landscape was just one more thing about Alaska she hadn't really thought about when she'd agreed to step in to help Sammy after his one surviving son, Willa, broke his arm. Now the wind picked up and began snaking along the forest floor, bothering the snow into little fountains of flakes. The trunks of the spruces all around her creaked very softly and a drift of accumulated powder snow swept from the branches and tumbled to earth. If she'd been in Alaska any longer than two days she might already know where the prevailing winds blew from, but even of that she was ignorant. She looked up but could not see the sun through the canopy. No chance of knowing which direction she was going in.

Far away, a few ravens chattered, a nearby twig snapped, and there was the rustle of something low to the ground, a fox perhaps.

It had been crazy irresponsible to come out here without so much as a rifle, the kind of thing she'd had a habit of doing when she'd been drinking. The kind of habit she hoped she had kicked.

A thin rumble came to her, more a vibration than a sound, then it deepened and grew louder until it resolved into the deep whine of an engine and she felt a hollowing sense of relief. The vehicle drew closer and before too long a snowmobile came into sight. She grinned and waved and waited but when the vehicle carried on without even slowing, she ran into its path, shouting and waving her hands, bewildered. The driver opened his visor and a pair of eyes almost lost in a furze of salt and pepper facial hair looked out. A female passenger in silver fox mitts sat impassively behind him. Under their down parkas, they both appeared to be wearing long, billowing tunics and matching trousers. The couple had obviously been doing the week's grocery shopping. There were bags hanging off the snowmobile's every surface.

'Hey, didn't you see me waving?' She felt irritated. Did people have no manners down here? 'I'm lost. I need to get back to the Hatcher Pass.'

The man shrugged. 'You're on Old Believer land,' he said simply.

She wanted to say that right now she didn't care if she was on Kiss-My-Ass land, but held back. 'I need directions to my vehicle.'

The man looked momentarily surprised, but then he flipped his head in the direction he and his companion had just come from. 'If you can't make out your own tracks, then follow ours,' he said. 'Was that your snowmachine down there on the track?'

Snowmachines. That's what they called them down here in the south, in Alaska. Where Edie was from, you saw a snowmobile with no one on it, you didn't just ride by, you stopped to make sure no one was in trouble.

'You always this helpful?'

The man sucked his teeth disapprovingly. 'The concerns of the worldly are no concerns of ours,' he said, then glancing back at the woman sitting behind him he seemed to relent a little. 'We don't appreciate outsiders trespassing on our land is all. If I were you, I wouldn't be fixing to come up this way again any time soon.'

With that, he let go of the brake, flipped his visor and swung on the throttle. The snowmobile began sliding forward and Edie watched the two travellers disappear into the gloom of the forest, then she turned and followed the man's instructions, keeping their snowmobile tracks in view to her left. A while later a gap in the trees signalled the position of the road back into town and in the distance she caught a glimpse of her vehicle.

Relieved, she began to walk towards it. Where the tracks finally gave out onto the packed snow of the path, not far from the snowmobile, she spotted a bright yellow object lying at the base of a spruce, protected from the snowfall by the tree's branches, slightly to one side of the pass itself. The thought occurred to her that something had been thrown from the couple's snowmobile. Straying from the track a little, she wandered over to take a look.

Closer up she was surprised to see that the yellow object was a tiny wood-plank house of the sort you might make for a small dog, about a yard long and half as wide, with a sloping roof and solid sides. The front was decorated with ornate shapes, and there was a door, fastened shut with a crude wooden lever.

Edie looked around. A very thin layer of snow had collected on the roof, but there was none banked up against the sides, suggesting that the house had been there since the last snowfall, but most likely not much longer. There were no animal or human tracks either around or leading up to it. The little house sat as though it had always been there in the snow, as though it belonged to some other reality and there were tiny fairies living inside.

All thoughts of getting back for the Iditarod had gone from her head. She called out, having no sense of who or what might answer, but there was only silence. Reaching the house, she crouched down and with her right hand turned the lever on the little door. She could see something inside, though it was too dark to see what. Her first thought was to draw out whatever it was, but something stopped her. The spirit bear came to mind, the power of its quiet, ghostly pallor. She was struck suddenly by the realization that it was the bear who had led her here, that the spirits had sent their messenger to draw her to this very place.

She went back to the snowmobile, took her flashlight out of the pannier, trudged back to the house and opened the door once more. The light revealed a package, wrapped in a very elaborately embroidered red cloth. Edie reached out carefully and touched it. The cloth itself was crisp without being frozen hard. Since it was probably –25, even in the relative shelter of the forest, it was unlikely to have lain there for very long, she thought. She opened the door wide, reached in and pulled at the object. It was unattached and came away quite easily. The cloth was exquisite, satin she guessed, and embroidered all over with a pattern of flowers and tendrils. In places there were ribbon ties. Whatever was inside was very hard, something long frozen. She stood up with the package in her hand, moved over to the snowmobile, and rested it on the saddle so she could take a better look. Tucked in under the ornate fabric, she saw now, was a square of white linen-like cloth. She pinched it between her finger and thumb. Almost instantly, the cloth came away and as it did so, it seemed to dislodge the ties around the parcel, exposing what lay inside.

In an instant, her breath left her and a burning, tightening sensation shot up her spine. She blinked, trying to make the terrible thing go away, but when she opened her eyes it was still there. She felt herself lurch away. Her legs no longer held her and she reached out and grabbed the nearest tree. She felt faint, then wanted to throw up, but did neither. Clasping her arms around her chest, she closed her eyes and squeezed hard until the pain calmed her. When her breath returned, irregular, gasping, she eased herself back towards the horror she had released from its tiny yellow house.

There, lying on the saddle of the snowmobile, was the body of a baby boy, a month or maybe two in age, lying on his belly, dead and hard frozen. The boy's arms were raised, the hands balled into tiny fists, the legs angled down from the body as if in repose, his skin glittering with ice crystals. The skin on one shoulder was puckered with what looked like an ice burn but there was nothing to suggest how he had died, or when.

Reaching out with the utmost caution, she clasped the body at the shoulders with her mittened hands and slowly turned the boy over. His face was veiled with ice, the eyes were closed and he wore an expression of softness and calm. He looked so waxen, so distant from life, that, for the tiniest instant, Edie convinced herself he was a doll even as she knew that she was looking at a corpse.

Onto the delicate new skin of the boy's body someone had smeared grease and what looked like charcoal, or maybe ashes, in an elaborate, inverted cross.

2

Anchorage Mayor Chuck Hillingberg helped his wife Marsha out of the official vehicle at the Iditarod HQ near Willow, just outside of Wasilla, and beamed for the waiting cameras. His colleague at Wasilla City Hall, J. G. Dillard, the only mayor in Alaska to sport a comb-over, came striding over, hand outstretched, pulling his mouse of a wife behind him, eager to join in the picture-taking. Chuck had no interest in the man – unlike Chuck, who had thrown his hat into the ring for the upcoming race for Alaska governor, Mayor Dillard wasn't going anywhere – but today was all about playing nice.

'We're sure glad to see you both up here,' Dillard said. 'Thought all that time in the big city, maybe you both forgot your Wasilla roots.' It was said with bonhomie, one mayor to another, but there was an edge to it. On the drive up (Chuck had wanted to take the mayoral 'copter but Marsha had dissuaded him on the grounds that it would look too fancy, and in this, as in so many other things, she'd been right), he'd decided to make this section of his day all about loyalty. He'd not been on the ground for five minutes and Dillard was already questioning his hometown identity. It pissed him off.

'Never forget home, JG,' Chuck said, pumping the hand offered to him. That much was true, at least. Chuck never had forgotten home, which, for him, was Jersey City, New Jersey, a place he'd left at the age of four and still felt an almost painful nostalgia towards. As for Wasilla, he loathed the place with an unholy passion. People went on about the spectacular setting of the town, bounded by verdant valleys to the south, the Chugach Mountains to the east, the Talkeetnas to the north. They rattled away about its clear water, its homey Christian values and community spirit. People like J. G. Dillard. All Chuck could recall of his years in Wasilla were the godawful winters he'd spent cooped up in his tiny bedroom in the family cabin on the Willow side of the town, not ten minutes' drive from where they were now, listening to his hippy dropout parents taking out their disappointments on each other, and longing to be somewhere, anywhere, but the self-proclaimed Duct Tape Capital of America.

From the bank of cameras, Dillard led them to an OB truck parked just shy of the race starting line. Already knots of people had gathered on either side, stamping off the cold and chattering excitedly about who they were tipping to win the race. Chuck's director of communications, Andy Foulsham, had reminded him over breakfast that he and Marsha were scheduled to do a joint interview on KTMS, the local TV station. At the door to the truck Chuck stopped and waved Marsha in before him. Over the long years of their marriage, he thought, they'd really got the public affection thing off to a fine art. It made his heart sing to think how good they'd got. Who would believe that they hadn't actually kissed and meant it since they were college students together at U of Alaska? In the world of municipal and state politics they were a roaring success, their marriage often referred to as one of the most stable partnerships around—and in a way it was. All kinds of things held marriages together. Among them, secrets.

He'd already got the most challenging part of the day over, giving a speech at the soft start of the Iditarod race down in Anchorage early that morning, timed to make the breakfast news shows. Unlike the official start, this earlier, soft start in Anchorage was all about family. Parents got to take their kids to pat the dogs and ride with the competitors' sleds for a while. His speech then had been all about Alaska's rugged community spirit, how the Iditarod, a race whose proud origins in an epic emergency medical run to get supplies of diphtheria vaccine to the remote settlement of Nome, epitomized Alaskan grit and generosity. The speech had gone well, he'd been able to harness the positive energy of the morning whilst subtly allying himself with the courage and tenacity of those original sledders. The message he hoped he'd left in Anchorage was that a vote for Chuck Hillingberg in the upcoming gubernatorial race was a vote for the spirit of the Iditarod.

As the Hillingbergs clambered onto the truck, Chuck decided to let Marsha do most of the talking. He listened to his wife charming the interviewer with a few of the downhome huntin' and shootin' stories of her youth. In fact, she'd not been hunting very much, certainly not as much as Chuck, who'd spent a great deal of his adolescene taking out his rage on everything from muskrat to moose, but Marsha always made a great job of playing up her rugged, homestead raising and, since she was an only child and both her adoptive parents were dead, there was no one left to contradict her. Unlike him, she didn't have to fake her enthusiasm for the state. She'd always said to him that there weren't many places in America where you could do more or less as you pleased and get away with it. Living in the frontier state really was like the tourist brochures suggested, 'Beyond Your Dreams, Within Your Reach'. The trick, Marsha always said, was to ensure that nothing was beyond your dreams.

He had first noticed her as a bright, determined sixteen-year-old during her campaign for Prom President at Wasilla High. She was beautiful then, he thought, her long, chestnut hair thick and glossy, the slim waist unspoiled by age, but it wasn't her looks which attracted him so much as the streak of ruthlessness he detected in her smile. The story of her adoption moved him because he could see how absolutely determined she was to fit in, to change the circumstances of her birth: to become an Alaskan. From that first meeting at the Prom President stump, he knew she was going places and she wasn't going to let anyone stop her.

They'd split up briefly when he'd got the intern job at the Washington offices of Steven Horowitz, the Republican junior senator from South Carolina, but she'd taken him back when he returned, broken, carrying the burden of his own hickness. He and Marsha had got married later that year. It wasn't a marriage of convenience so much as a confluence of mutual interest.

For the last year, this interest had been focused on the gubernatorial contest. Up to a few weeks ago, the incumbent, Tom Shippon, had been looking pretty invincible. The Shippons were Alaska royalty, a genuine 'sourdough' family, Alaskans before Alaska officially became a state in 1958. Tom's father, Scoot, had been closely involved in Alaska politics since before then. The Shippons had fingers in every pie from the salmon fishery through timber to oil and gas exploration. About the only enterprise they weren't directly involved in was tourism and leisure. Pussy business, Tom Shippon called it, though only ever in private.

Chuck had neither the advantages of incumbency nor the kind of pedigree which automatically got you where you wanted to go in state politics. It was hard for a boy from New Jersey to go against that and hope to win. Other outsiders had tried but few had succeeded and they'd usually been blocked from taking up top positions. He looked too much like a *cheechako*, a greenhorn. In the early stages of the campaign, there were those who had even accused him of abandoning Alaska by going Outside to Washington, which, given that it was twenty years ago, was just ridiculous. But Alaskans did persist in thinking of themselves as separate and apart. You were either for them or against them, which was why the episode in Washington was seen by some blowhards as an act of treachery even now.

Over the past year, he'd had to work twice as hard to convince them that he was Alaskan at heart, which was all the more difficult given that it wasn't true. As councilman, then Mayor of Anchorage, it wasn't all that difficult for his opponents to set him up as a big city man, remote from the concerns of real Alaskans. Which was where Marsha had come in. Her genuine enthusiasm for the state had helped make him look like more of an all-state kind of a guy. The image uplift had assisted him in tangible ways, not least of which was in campaign funding. He was aware that no amount of schmoozing or reassuring patter about the depth of his devotion to the forty-ninth state would encourage the wealthy sourdoughs of Alaska to put their hands in their pockets for his gubernatorial campaign to the degree to which they had done almost automatically for Shippon, but he'd been able to raise enough to at least present a challenge. Until last week his campaign team would have said, even on the most optimistic forecasts, that the chances of him ousting Shippon were pretty low, but that was before the unemployment figures came out and the polls showed Shippon's popularity starting to go south. Somewhere in all those stats was an opportunity, the biggest opportunity of Chuck Hillingberg's life. But the campaign needed money to be able to push it through, which was why, after he'd fired the Iditarod starting gun, he was heading directly to a $10,000-a-plate luncheon back at the Sheraton in downtown Anchorage. He'd already given his fundraising speech dozens of times. The message was the one business people and entrepreneurs always wanted to hear. Alaska needed to rein back state spending and find new and innovative ways for private enterprise to grow and develop. But now there was a new energy to it, fuelled by the belief that he just might win. Over breakfast, Marsha, his communications director Andy Foulsham and himself had decided that his lunchtime speech needed to reflect the campaign's new confidence. He was intending to say that the Alaska state motto, North to the Future, meant North to a future only Chuck Hillingberg, as governor, could deliver.

He climbed down the steps of the OB unit back out into the cold sun of the Alaskan March morning. In the fifteen minutes that he and Marsha had been in the mobile studio, the crowd had swelled considerably and he was pleased to see a bank of TV cameras in the press enclosure. Walking from the unit along the barricade, he was flattered to observe friendly and familiar faces pressing forward to say hi or shake his hand, until he remembered that Andy had fixed it that way. Well, never mind. The TV crews didn't know the difference.

The fact that the race soft-started in Anchorage gave Chuck one of his few advantages over Tom Shippon and he meant to make the most of it. As mayor of the city, it was easy for him to take ownership of the race, even when it moved to its official start in Wasilla, and there was nothing that Shippon, stuck in the governor's residence way down in Juneau, could do about it. The race was huge statewise, but it also had considerable national and international reach. The Iditarod may not be the only dog race on the planet, but it was the one with the richest provenance and in many people's eyes the only one that really counted. Folk who had no interest at all in dog races had heard of the Great Race of Mercy, the heroic five-and-a-half-day trek during the fierce winter of 1925, when 20 mushers and 150 dogs rushed to bring diphtheria antitoxin

675 miles across the Alaskan ice to the remote gold-rush town of Nome and thereby prevent an epidemic. And even if people didn't know the details of the event, many had seen Balto, the lead dog in the final relay team, immortalized in bronze in New York's Central Park. Since the first race commemorating the Great Race of Mercy in 1973, the Iditarod had grown enormously in terms of the number of competitors and, more significantly for Chuck, in terms of its profile. Back in the twenties, live news of the epic journey was broadcast on the new medium of radio. Now, TV crews flew in from all over world and, with the twenty-four-hour news cycle, they had plenty of time to fill. Within minutes of the start of the race, clips would be all over the Internet and he, Chuck, hoped to figure in at least some of them. Wasn't Andy always telling him that maintaining a healthy Internet profile was as critical to electoral success in the twenty-first century as cross-country stump tours had been for politicians in the nineteenth and twentieth, a cheap and dynamic platform from which the Hillingberg campaign could spin blogs and tweets non-stop from now until election day. Take command of the blogosphere and the twittersphere and you were already halfway there. Wasn't that how Obama had done it?

Mayor Dillard led them over to inspect the dog teams and to talk to a couple of the big hitters: Steve Nicols, the favorite and last year's winner, and the challenger, Duncan Wright. While Chuck busied himself with the two frontrunners, Dillard's mousy wife took Marsha to connect with one or two of the stragglers whom Andy Foulsham had previously identified as having some kind of news potential, one a widow whose husband had been killed in a rig accident up on the North Slope oilfield, another a native man who'd come all the way from High Arctic Canada and was running the race in tribute to his dead son.

That done, Chuck and Marsha made their way up to the podium

by the starting line. The crowd was roaring now, eyes fixed on the line-up of dogs and sleds and the heroic sledders who were about to set off on their epic, two-week, 1150-mile journey through mountain ranges and ice fields, through the rocky scree of the Farewell Burn, along the great ice ribbon of the Yukon River and through the shifting pan of Norton Sound to the finish at Nome, knowing that of the ninety-seven teams in the race, somewhere between twenty and forty would be forced to drop out.

Dillard climbed the steps onto the podium and began the introductions. Someone flipped on the rousing music and on a signal from Andy Foulsham, Chuck and Marsha followed Dillard up the steps hand in hand, Chuck grinning and nodding in acknowledgement, Marsha smiling mutely by his side. As the dog handlers began bringing out the teams, Chuck moved to the microphone and said his piece, then he raised the starting gun and fired into the air. A tremendous chorus of shouts from the mushers and howls from the dogs came up from the track, followed by the whoosh of sled runners on compacted snow. As the sleds flashed by, the dogs straining at their harnesses and picking up speed as they spun further into the distance, the crowd went crazy.

Chuck stood back and was so absorbed in the furore he didn't notice the tiny, good-looking native woman in a sealskin parka pushing her way through the crowd, frantically waving her arms and shouting, until she was almost on him.